FICTION   Stirling, Jessica.
STIRLING
           The strawberry
           season.

WITHDRAWN

		DATE	

THE STRAWBERRY SEASON

THE STRAWBERRY SEASON

Jessica Stirling

St. Martin's Press ✹ New York

www.stmartins.com

ISBN 0-312-26654-5

First published in Great Britain by Hodder and Stoughton, a division of Hodder Headline

First U.S. Edition: December 2000

10 9 8 7 6 5 4 3 2 1

CONTENTS

CHAPTER ONE

The North Quarter

It was close to nightfall and the sun, veiled by fast-moving cloud, was already sliding towards the horizon when Fay Ludlow came over the crest of Olaf's Hill and first looked down on Pennypol. She was so relieved to have arrived at her destination that she felt like weeping. She was not much given to weeping, though, for marriage had taught her that there was no profit in self-pity. If her husband had been with her she would have pursed her lips and dug her fingernails into her palms rather than give him the satisfaction of seeing tears in her eyes. Her husband was not with her, however. He was four hundred miles away in Derbyshire and now that she had finally arrived on the wild west coast of this remote Scottish island she felt sure that she had put herself beyond his reach.

Everything about Scotland was new and unexpected. Until yesterday she had never seen the sea, had never travelled on a railway train, except once when old Mr Musson had been smitten with pleurisy and she had been sent to Buxton to help Josh market the fruit. Buxton was not much more than twenty miles from Fream but it had seemed a long way to her then. She remembered how she had clutched her pennies tight in her handkerchief and had imagined that every man in the market-place was a thief. She had come a far piece from Fream now, though, and the wind from the sea seemed fresher than the breezes that raked the dreary uplands of Derbyshire had ever been.

She knelt by the rocks that marked the end of the ridge and looked down on the derelict farmhouse. A high drystone wall snaked away into a fold of the moor, a stream spilled ferny patterns across the sand and a little stone jetty was tethered to one corner of the bay. An upturned boat no bigger than a broom seed lay close by.

The sheep that skulked among the tussocks were not the rotund white-faced Exmoors that made up Sir Johnny Yeates's flock or the soft French Merinos that Colonel Liversedge nursed on Fream's home pastures but tough little Blackface hill ewes. The cattle that browsed above the tide line were dark and scrawny compared with the sleek dairy cows of Fream and Cloudshill. And as she glanced up a raucous accumulation of seabirds wheeled over the ridge and vanished downwind as if to announce her arrival to the folk of the north quarter. Pennypol, Pennymain, Crove and Fetternish: only the names were familiar. In reality she knew little or nothing about this big, awkward island or the people who lived here.

In the lounge of the *Grenadier* crossing from Oban, for instance, an old woman had addressed her in a language that Fay had never heard before.

'I'm sorry,' Fay had said politely, 'I don't understand.'

'So you will not be having the Gaelic, will you not now?' the old woman had asked in a slow, sing-song voice. 'Och well, is that not a pity. Where is it you will be going without the Gaelic to help you?'

It had popped out before Fay could help herself. 'To Fetternish.'

'To Fetternish, is it? Well now, you will be doing fine without the Gaelic there, I'm thinking. Is it the big house you are bound for?'

'Yes,' Fay had answered. 'Do you know it?'

'Aye, everyone knows Fetternish House. Are you another of Biddy Baverstock's relatives come looking for work? Is there no work in England that you have to be coming all the way to Mull in search of it?'

'I've heard that Mull is a peaceful place, and very grand.'

'Grand enough, I suppose.' The old woman's smile had held more than a hint of malice. 'If it is peace you are after, however, you will not be finding much of that in Biddy Baverstock's house.'

Nervous at being interrogated, even by a stranger, Fay had retreated from the passenger lounge to watch the mainland dwindle behind the steamer's wash and to study the map she had purchased in the early light of morning in the railway station in Glasgow. The map had been her lifeline. It had finally set in perspective the landscapes through which she travelled and had focused her aim on the one place in the world where she might find not just allies but friends.

She knelt on the high ground above Pennypol Bay with the map tucked into a pocket of the big canvas sack that she had stolen from the hook behind the door of the cottage on Cloudshill Edge. It was the one thing, apart from a little money, she had taken from him to which she could not fairly lay claim.

It still smelled of sheep smear and black powder and the scales of the trout her husband had caught on the stretch of the Fream where Cloudshill servants were not supposed to fish, but everything would stink of him, no doubt, until the salty winds of Mull washed the bad memories away.

She was unaware that she was crying. She was really overjoyed to be crouched on the barren hillside above the turf-roofed cottage with the waves sweeping the beach and islets, and headlands reaching out to the horizon as far as her eye could see. The fact that her sanctuary was spare and empty did not matter. All that mattered was that she had shaken her husband off at last and that he would never think to look for her here.

Picking up the lambing sack she wiped her eyes on her sleeve and headed, limping, downhill towards the derelict farm.

*   *   *

It was a day like any other except that no two days were ever quite the same for those who lived on Mull's north quarter. From the terraces of Fetternish House impressionable strangers could look out upon the ocean's shades and shifting hues and decide what the weather would be like for the rest of the day. If they happened to be right they would consider themselves wise in country matters and believe, quite wrongly, that all it took to be an islander was a knowledge of winds and weather and tides.

What went unremarked by those who visited Fetternish just for a week or two, however, were the subtle changes that took place in the earth itself, the small miracles and disasters that occurred under the rocks or between the roots across the whole harsh organism of moor and hillside and shore. They did not see the crumbling basaltic shelves off the tide-line's edge or the rotting carcasses of ancient oaks that Robert Quigley hauled out of the peat bogs, or the rabbit hordes that destroyed the sweet green pastures, or the voles that gnawed away the roots of new tree-plantings, down and down into the kingdom of the tick and the husk worm, the louse, the maggot and the mite.

By God, though, you could drop a Mull man down on the outermost tip of Caliach Point and he would be back home in half an hour and telling you how the mackerel were running and which ewe had a cough or which cow would calve before morning, for if there was one thing that islanders did understand it was how to listen to and interpret the arcane utterances of nature.

It came as no surprise to George Barrett when his third son, Billy, lifted himself from the heather beside the ailing ewe and said, 'I smell something.'

Barrett — everyone called him Barrett — wafted away the cloud of black flies that hung about his head and sniffed the dank morning air. Beneath his big hands the upturned ewe wriggled and kicked. He held her almost effortlessly, and thought: It's a sure sign of ageing when the boy can smell something that I cannot.

'What is it, son?' he said.

'Smoke.'

Barrett studied the sky, sniffed and spat. He could smell nothing out of the ordinary, only the ewe's wet fleece and the stench of suppuration from her rotting hoof. At the ripe old age of thirty-eight were his senses already deserting him? Perhaps he had married too early. Muriel, his bride, had been betrothed to Donald Campbell, one of Vassie's brood from Pennypol, but Donald had drowned in a storm off Arkle and she had settled for Barrett instead. As far as he could tell she had not so far regretted it. She had presented him with ten healthy children in eighteen years and not one thrown before its time or lost to sickness afterwards. But now the bottom had fallen out of the wool market, employment was drying up and it seemed as if the golden years were over for master and servant alike. Billy's older brothers had already gone to work in Glasgow and Billy would be next to leave.

Barrett sniffed the air again.

'Get on with you, son,' he said. 'You cannot be smelling anything from a half-mile away, not even with this wind to help you.'

'I can, Dad. I can. It is the stink from an old hearth.'

'What old hearth? There are no old hearths here.'

'There is at Pennypol. That must be where it is coming from.'

Weary of being pinned down, the ewe kicked frantically, broke a bit of wind and uttered a loud *baaa-aaah* to remind her keepers that her patience was by no means infinite.

Barrett sighed and set about paring the under-run horn on the sheep's forefoot with his clasp knife. He worked quickly but carefully, for a cut on the sensitive underlying matrix would cripple the ewe completely. He held the beast with his knee and reached out behind him. Billy put an uncorked whisky bottle into his hand. The bottle contained a solution of formalin and copper sulphate mixed to a recipe passed on to Barrett by his father who had been a shepherd on Fetternish long before Austin Baverstock's widow had inherited the estate. Stooping over the sheep, he sprinkled a generous amount of the solution into the cup of the hoof and squeezed. The ewe bleated plaintively.

'So there is smoke coming from Pennypol, is there?' Barrett said. 'Well, perhaps you would care to turn your nose that way again and tell me who has been lighting a fire in the hearth since nobody ever stops there long.'

'Why do they not, Dad?'

'Because it is a place of bad omen.'

'The woman cannot know that then.'

'Woman? What woman?'

Innocently, Billy said, 'The woman who is cooking her breakfast in a black pot on the fire in the old hearth.'

Barrett had already guessed what was going on but he was reluctant to spoil the lad's fun. 'Even in my heyday,' he said, 'I could not pick up the scent of a female from much more than a quarter of a mile. Can you be telling me what this lady is having for her breakfast, you and that long nose of yours?'

'Porridge.' Billy grinned. 'Mind you, that is by way of being a guess since I did not see her fill the pot with oatmeal, only with water.'

'So you saw her, did you? And what were you doing at Pennypol?'

'Looking for the old ewe which, by the by, I did not find.'

'No, because she was never lost in the first place,' said Barrett. 'Is some woman putting up at Pennypol right enough?'

'Aye,' the boy answered. 'A woman I have never seen before.'

'Old or young?'

'Older than I am — but not by much.'

'Did you speak to her?'

'No, I noticed her from the hill when she was drawing water. I know she had a fire going because there was a deal of smoke, so much smoke I thought she had set the roof alight.'

'A thunderbolt could not be setting that mouldy old roof

6

alight,' Barrett said. 'Even so, I think we should be reporting the matter to Mr Quigley.'

'She might just be a tinker passing through.'

'It is too early in the year for tinkers.'

'Perhaps times are hard for tinkers too,' Billy said.

'Times are hard for a lot of people but tinkers are not among them,' Barrett said. 'We had better be reporting the matter.'

'I could go over and see what the woman is doing now, if you like.'

'Oh, so she's pretty, is she?' Barrett said.

Billy blushed. 'Dad!'

Barrett laughed and got to his feet. He hefted up the ewe and turned her.

As he did so a collie rose like a wisp of black and white smoke from the bracken, long pink tongue hanging out, yellow eyes fierce and attentive.

'Are you for penning her, Dad? The ewe, I mean.'

'No. We will be taking a look at her again this afternoon to see if her hoof has improved. Put her down on the flat by the gate for the time being.'

'Am I not to go over to Pennypol then?'

'To gawk at this beautiful female?' Barrett said. 'No, I will go myself.'

The boy frowned and shook his head, the joke forgotten.

'She is not beautiful. I think . . .' Billy hesitated, 'I think perhaps she has been damaged.'

'Damaged? What in God's name do you mean by "damaged"?'

Billy could not bring himself to explain. He shook his head. 'Go and see for yourself, Dad,' he said, then with a little whistle to alert the dog, gathered in the limping ewe and strolled her gently towards the gate.

Innis Tarrant had spent longer than usual at prayers that morning. Some mornings she would kneel before the Blessed

Mary only for a minute or two, others she would linger to offer thanks for all the blessings that had been bestowed upon her. Last thing at night, however, her prayers were more concentrated and she would kneel beneath the silver crucifix that Gillies had given her and pray for her sister Biddy, for her daughter Rachel in Glasgow, for her daughter Rebecca who was flighty and stubborn and too full of modern ideas, and, of course, for Gillies Brown, the friend of her heart these many, many years.

Now and then she might also put in a word for her husband and son, that they might find happiness wherever they happened to be. And that morning, with the March wind blustering about the stone-built cottage, she had offered a prayer for her mother's soul and the soul of her father, both long departed, for in spite of Father O'Donnell's assurances to the contrary, she had a suspicion that neither Vassie nor Ronan Campbell would be entirely at peace in the mansions of the Lord.

Safely removed from the pernicious influence of crucifixes and painted statues Becky Tarrant slapped the frying pan with beef dripping and clattered it down upon the stove to indicate disapproval of Mam's devotions, which to her way of thinking were almost as pagan as Auntie Aileen's communion with the elves and fairies. Rebecca was small-built, not striking like her Aunt Biddy but with more than a share of her grandmother's sallow, hot-eyed character. She was a tireless worker, attacked all her tasks with determination and even routine chores like feeding hens, lighting fires and cooking breakfast were performed at top speed.

'Are you not done with your chanting yet, Mam?' Becky yelled.

She was due at the big house at eight o'clock and Maggie Naismith, the housekeeper, would not tolerate tardiness. It was now a little after seven.

The kitchen was steeped in grey daylight but the coals in the hearth and flickers of flame within the iron cooking stove gave some cheer. Becky had been bustling about for the best part of an hour. Hens had been fed and eggs gathered. The dog — a lively spaniel pup which, much to Becky's consternation, refused to be regimented — had had a plate of oat mush and mutton scraps thrust under his nose, and the last item on Becky's agenda was to make sure that her mother consumed an adequate supply of nourishment before she, Becky, left for the half-mile hike to Fetternish House. At one time half a dozen servants had staffed the house but the Baverstock-Quigley fortunes had slumped badly in recent years and Becky was well aware that Aunt Biddy and Quig were sailing close to the wind these days. Becky's sister and cousins had gone to the mainland to complete their education; if she had complained loudly enough no doubt funds would have materialised from somewhere to send her to college too. Becky, however, had chosen to remain on Mull to look after her mother.

'I am serving your porridge now, Mam.' She clacked the ladle on the rim of the pot. 'I am putting the eggs into the pan, so you had better be saying goodbye to Our Lady if you want your breakfast piping hot.'

Unperturbed by her daughter's hectoring, Innis emerged from the back bedroom. Becky was so like her grandmother that Innis occasionally wondered if the old woman's spirit had found refuge in the girl. Becky even looked a little like Vassie but without the harsh lines that hardship and a vicious marriage had imprinted upon her, Innis's, mother.

'Do you want to make me late?' Becky snapped. 'Do you want me to be told off by Maggie Naismith for the third time this month?' She ladled porridge into a bowl and placed the bowl on the table which, because the morning was chilly, she had dragged closer to the fire. 'Now, will you please tidy yourself and sit down.'

To humour her daughter Innis peeped into the mirror that hung on the bedroom door and pretended to primp her hair which she had worn short for a number of years in a style quite tidy enough for a country woman.

'I don't know what it is about saying prayers that makes you so untidy,' Becky went on. 'Two eggs?'

'One will do me fine, thank you.'

Becky broke a fresh egg and slid it expertly into the pan.

'You don't eat enough to keep a bird alive, if you ask me.'

'Well, Becky,' Innis said, 'that is just how it is with old people.'

'Are you being sarcastic?'

'Take it how you will, dearest.'

Becky glanced round. 'Hoh! I do not know why I put up with you.'

'I am never too sure myself,' said Innis.

Becky cracked a third egg, deposited the shell into a wooden bucket in which food scraps were kept, then, after wiping her hands on her apron, pulled out a chair and seated herself at the table. In a matter of seconds her porridge bowl was empty. She returned to the stove and had just lifted the fish slice to bathe the egg with fat when a noise outside made her turn towards the door.

'What's that?' she said.

'It will just be the dog, I expect,' said Innis. 'Did you let him out?'

'Of course I let him out.' Becky removed the egg from the pan, put it on a plate and laid the plate on the lid of the stove. 'If it is Kilty he's kicking up a fair old fuss. One of Barrett's ewes must be in the garden again.'

Innis shook her head. 'The ewes are all in the south-west pasture at this time of the year.' The spaniel's frantic yapping roused vague anxiety, remnant of the fear that had troubled her for years. 'Go and see who it is.'

Becky pulled open the door and admitted a swirl of wind followed immediately by the yapping spaniel. Innis stared at the shape in the doorway and sighed inwardly when she recognised George Barrett.

'That animal is too far frisky for his own good,' Barrett said.

'It is high time you let me teach him a thing or two about obedience.'

'Is that why you've come bothering us at the crack of dawn,' Becky said, 'to tell us our dog needs training?'

'What is it, George?' Innis said. 'What brings you here so early?'

'There is someone camping at Pennypol. Billy spotted them.'

'Tinkers, it'll just be the tinkers,' said Becky.

'It is not the tinkers,' Barrett said.

'Who is it then?' said Innis.

'A girl.'

The wind skated into the kitchen and flirted with the thin piece of carpet in front of the hearth and Innis was filled with an unusual foreboding, for, Catholic or not, she had never quite managed to shake off her belief in second sight and for weeks now Aileen had been mumbling and muttering about strangers coming up out of the hill. It was just part of Aileen's weirdness, however, and no one had paid much attention to the woman's rantings.

'What — what sort of a girl?' Innis said.

'A cripple by the looks of her,' Barrett answered.

'Cripple or not,' said Becky, 'you should have shoved her off.'

'It is not my place to shove her off,' Barrett said.

'Don't tell me you're too timid to chase away trespassers,' Becky said. 'What's she doing on Pennypol, anyway? There's nothing there to interest anyone.'

'By the look of it,' Barrett said, 'she's settling in.'

'Settling in? Without paying rent?' Becky declared. 'Well, Aunt Biddy will soon put a stop to that, won't she, Mam?'

'Yes, dear,' Innis answered warily, 'I expect she probably will.'

Two pairs of cotton drawers, stockings, two plain blouses, a patched flannel petticoat and three woollen vests had been stuffed into the lambing sack together with an old skirt and work shirt. She had travelled in her Sunday best but had jettisoned the fancy hat she had bought at the vicarage fête in favour of a stout straw bonnet. And she had left her good shoes behind; the boots that Josh had relined after her accident were much easier to walk in. Her certificates were folded into the Bible that Mrs Musson had given her on her tenth birthday, not the exact day on which she had been born but the anniversary of the day on which her mother had died and she, still an infant, had been taken into the care of the estate. She had never known who her father was: some travelling man she supposed.

The Mussons had no children of their own. They had cared for her well enough and were strict but not cruel. They had even allowed her to attend the day school at Cloudshill until she was strong enough to wheel a barrow and ply a Dutch hoe and could be put to work in the gardens to pay for her keep. She had slept in a cot in the loft of the Mussons' cottage, which was better than the cubby-hole in the potting-shed that poor Josh had had to put up with when he was fetched from the poorhouse at Medlington. She thought of Josh as she unpacked the little pouches of seed that he had given her before she'd left Fream. They were tokens, good luck charms, of little practical value to a real market gardener. But he had told her that they would spoil for want of air and though she reckoned most seeds were hardier than Josh gave them credit for, nevertheless she placed the pouches on a sagging shelf on the rear wall of the cottage to let them breathe.

She had brought one pot, one that her husband would never miss, and a canister of tea and sugar; which was just as well, for there was nothing in the cottage, not one cracked cup or empty bottle in which she could have carried water from the stream, let alone a kettle in which to boil it up. By any standards the farmhouse at Pennypol was a dismal place. The walls were smeared with bird droppings, the floor crusted with cattle dung, and the hearth was nothing but a primitive circle of stones under a gaping hole in the roof.

She had set a fire of straw and driftwood and coaxed a match flame into the kindling until at last smoke began to coil up through the roof hole. She had gone out into the fine, sifting rain then and followed the path to the stream. She had filled the pot with icy brown water and carried it carefully back to the cottage and set it on the fire to boil which, eventually, it did. Then she had seated herself on the ground with her back against the wall and stretched out her aching leg and cupped the pot in both hands for warmth, and drank tea and ate the remains of the corn loaf she had brought from home and, looking up, had seen the sky through the roof hole and a glimmer of stars among the clouds, the very same stars that looked down on Fream and the limestone ledges above Cloudshill.

She had known then for sure that she had done the right thing in running away from Gavin Tarrant, not to save herself from punishment but to protect the foetus within her, the little swelling seed-thing which, if her reckoning was right, was already three months old.

It had been almost three years since Innis had last visited Pennypol. The cottage in which she had been born and raised held no pleasant memories. In fact, her childhood had been so scarred by their father's drunken brutality that she was surprised that Biddy, Aileen and she had survived at all.

She came by the long route round the back of Olaf's Hill. Although she was fit and healthy – Becky would have added 'for her age' – Innis was no longer quite as spry as she had once been and preferred well-worn paths to heather tracks and steep shortcuts. Passing the skirts of the moor, she saw the islets and the bay and the old cottage all slot into view one by one, just as they had always done. Weeds had taken over her mother's vegetable plots, however, and the patchy little fields where oats and barley had once flourished had been consumed by the insidious growths which if left unchecked would eventually drown not just Pennypol but Pennymain and Fetternish too in a vast sea of bracken.

The wall was still intact, though. The sturdy drystone dike that her sisters, her mother and she had built to keep the Baverstocks' sheep off the Pennypol grazings was a monument of such art, craft and pointless determination that half a lifetime of equinoctial gales had damaged it hardly at all. The girl crouched in the shadow of the wall. She crabbed along with her chin tucked into her chest and advanced with a dipping motion of the left shoulder and a twist of the right hip that threw her forward only eight or ten inches at a time.

She looked so ugly and defenceless that Innis understood now why Barrett had pleaded urgent business with the flock and had vanished over the ridge at something approaching a gallop. Becky would not have been so gracious. Becky was furious at the very idea of a stranger invading the property and at this moment, Innis reckoned, would be pouring out the news to Biddy and Quig and urging them to take stern action.

When Innis reached the end of the wall, the girl looked up and waved. And Innis realised that she was not deformed at all but had bent over to dig in the thin topsoil and that the crabbing motion indicated nothing more than a slight limp.

'What are you doing?' Innis called out.

'Putting in a few seeds,' the girl replied. 'Lupins. I think there are some African marigolds too but I doubt if they will like the cold ground.'

'Why are you planting flowers here?'

The girl held up a canvas bag no bigger than a tobacco pouch.

'Josh, my friend, put some seeds in my luggage. I don't know why, because he's convinced that flowers won't grow this far to the north. Are you Mrs Baverstock?'

'There is no Mrs Baverstock,' Innis said.

'Oh, no!' She was slight of build and had towy fair hair, just a shade darker than Aileen's. One eye was closed by a puffy swelling that caused her to squint. 'Oh, dear me! Is Mrs Baverstock dead?'

'Of course she is not dead,' Innis said. 'Mrs Baverstock has married again and become Mrs Quigley, although some folk still do call her Baverstock.'

'Doesn't Mr Quigley mind?'

It was just the daft, difficult sort of question that Becky might have asked.

'It is immaterial whether Mr Quigley minds or not,' Innis said. 'Besides, it is none of your business. Why are you scattering flower seeds when you will not be here to see them bloom?'

The girl tucked the spade under her arm. It was a blackened heart-shaped peat-cutter with a broken shaft that Innis dimly remembered having used herself far back in the past. The iron blade was still intact though and the girl had managed to excavate a shallow groove two or three inches deep with it. Innis knew little about flower culture. The border at Pennymain was a riot of colour from mid-May to late September but that had been Michael's doing and since he had left home she contented herself with just keeping it in order season by season.

The girl shrugged. 'Even if I'm not here to see them they will make a fine surprise for someone. I'm not so sure about the African marigolds.' She stuck the blade of the peat-cutter into the ground and looking directly at Innis, said, 'If you're not Mrs Baverstock – I mean Mrs Quigley – then who are you?'

'I am Mrs Tarrant,' Innis informed her. 'Bridget Baverstock's sister.'

'Ah!' the girl said. 'I thought it might be you.'

'Never mind who I am,' Innis said. 'I want to know who you are and what you are doing on our property?'

'My name's Tarrant too, although I think I'd prefer to be known as Fay Ludlow, if you've no objection.'

Innis drew her shawl tightly about her shoulders. 'Why should I object? And why do you say that your name is Tarrant?'

Tarrant was *her* name, her daughters' name, the family name, the name she had adopted before the altar in the chapel at Glenarray on the day she'd married Michael all those years ago. She had no trouble with names as a rule, no difficulty in keeping track of the Campbells, Baverstocks and Quigleys who were no longer here. She could rhyme off the names of her brother Neil's children, for instance, and tell you what subjects her nephew Donnie taught in the Glasgow High School and how many children he and his wife Tricia had and what their names were, though this was less surprising, for Donnie and Tricia visited Fetternish every summer. She could even tell you — a feat that amazed her sister — what had become of a few of those 'cousins' whom neither she nor Biddy could quite claim as kin since their grandfather, old Evander McIver, had been more scrupulous about keeping up the stud book for Foss bulls than recording his own late-season matings.

She did not know what had become of her husband and son, however, and her first thought was that the girl with the towy hair and damaged eye might be Michael's most recent conquest or even his bastard child and that he had sent her here to pave the way for his return.

'Did you not say that your name is Tarrant?' Innis asked.

'I'll be calling myself Ludlow, though, now I'm here.'

'Yes, yes, you may call yourself what you please,' Innis said impatiently, 'but who *are* you and how do you know who I am?'

'He told me about you.'

'He?'

Innis waited for an answer, her heart flapping in her chest.

'My husband.'

'Michael?'

'No,' the girl said. 'Gavin.'

'My Gavin, do you mean?'

'Yes, Mrs Tarrant.' The girl nodded. 'Gavin, your son.'

*   *   *

16

'Oh, dear me, no!' Biddy said testily. 'You must not take us for simpletons, Miss Ludlow. If you think you can waltz in here claiming to be my nephew's wife without one scrap of evidence to prove it then you are very much mistaken.'

'Biddy . . .' Robert Quigley murmured.

'I will handle this matter, Robert, if you please,' Biddy said.

Quig gave the little bow that he had perfected over the years to indicate not so much submission as acknowledgement that the lady of the house was entitled to first say in all things. Later he would take her to one side, have a few quiet words with her and depend on her good sense to ensure that right decisions were reached; compromise not capitulation had always been a key feature in their relationship.

Age had laid few marks on Robert Quigley. His hair had thinned somewhat and he had developed a certain strictness about the mouth that had not been evident when he had served as Evander McIver's factotum on Foss, but he was still lean and nimble and if he worried about Biddy and the children and the demise of trade he gave no outward sign of it. Biddy, on the other hand, had changed considerably since her second marriage. She was still striking enough to turn heads in Princes Street on those rare occasions when business summoned her to Edinburgh, but motherhood and maturity had mellowed her conceit and she pretended that she no longer cared what men thought of her. She had grown plump but not portly. Constrained by a bit of boning in formal gowns and day-dresses her figure was set off by a cascade of auburn curls which, with just an occasional application of henna, kept her looking younger than a woman tottering on the verge of fifty.

Sheaves of letters written to and received from lawyers had added an element of continual qualification to Biddy's conversation. 'The first question that springs to mind,' she went on, 'is why you have chosen to come to Mull to escape Gavin. After all this is – or was – his home. We are – or were – his family. Do you suppose that we will take you in just because you claim to be his wife?'

JESSICA STIRLING

She stood by the window of the drawing-room with her thumbs tucked into the waistband of her skirt and scrutinised the girl with all the severity of an advocate pleading a capital case. Biddy was backed by old Willy Naismith, gaunt and shrivelled but alarmingly alert, who from a chair near the fireplace weighed up the situation with all the astuteness for which he had once been renowned.

If the girl was intimidated by the grand, shabby drawing-room with its views of the sea, she gave no sign of it. The moment Biddy paused for breath, she said, 'If you're asking if I'm legal married to Gavin Tarrant then see, here's my wedding band.' She fished in a pocket of her skirt and brought out a cheap enamelled ring which she displayed on the palm of her hand.

'All I see there,' said Biddy, 'is a trinket that could have been purchased at any fairground in the country. A ring is proof of nothing.'

'Unless,' Willy Naismith put in, 'it carries an inscription.'

The girl turned, frowning. 'An inscription?'

'Aye, lass,' Willy said. 'Writing on the back, linking your name with his.'

'No, sir, there is no writing on the back. Gavin wouldn't pay for writing.'

'Where did you buy it?' Biddy said.

'I didn't buy it. Gavin bought it.'

'Where did he buy it then?'

'In Buxton.'

'Is that where you were married?'

'It was.'

'In church?'

'Before the registrar in the town hall.'

'Did Gavin have to marry you?'

'No, he . . .' Fay hesitated.

Biddy folded her arms across her bosom. 'What? What reason did he have for marrying you that you haven't told us about?'

18

'He said he loved me,' Fay answered. 'But he didn't love me. He wanted me for other things.'

'What other things?' said Biddy.

'Sir Johnny – Sir John Yeates – wouldn't make Gavin up to flockmaster or tithe him the cottage on Cloudshill unless he got married. Gavin wanted the post bad and picked me for a wife just because I was handy.'

The swollen eye had begun to water. She wiped it with her sleeve, shaking her head impatiently as if she had been let down by the bruised ducts and broken flesh. She had not been offered a chair and stood crookedly, rocking a little on one heel, dabbing at her eye with her sleeve.

Innis looked away: Quig too.

Willy said, 'How long was it before he started beating you?'

She sighed, not surprised at being found out so soon. 'That night.'

'Your wedding night?' said Biddy. 'He struck you on your wedding night?'

Fay hesitated, then said, 'You see why I had to get away.'

'When did the marriage take place?' Quig said. 'How long ago?'

'Two years back last harvest.'

Biddy glanced at Innis who continued to stare out of the window. There was no sound in the drawing-room except the squeak of the girl's heel on the flooring. What, Biddy wondered, was her sister feeling at this moment, what sort of guilt had this pathetic creature roused in her? Did Innis feel responsible for what her son had done and what her son had become? Or was Gavin Tarrant simply the inheritor of all that was bad in the blood of the Campbells? Biddy longed to cry out, 'Go away. Go away, girl, and leave us in peace,' but Gavin was not her son and it was not up to her to reject his runaway wife.

Willy leaned forward, fists bunched on the curve of his walking-stick. He smiled at the girl, showing worn brown teeth. 'Tell me, lass, where were you born?'

'In Fream, on Sir John Yeates's estate.'

'Where are your parents?'

'My mother died when I was small.'

'And your father?'

'I never knew who he was, sir. A travelling man, I think.'

'You've no need call me "sir", ' Willy said. 'I'm nothing special in this household. Fact is, I started out in much the same way as you, as an orphan. Were you put out to a family on the estate?'

'I was, sir,' Fay said.

'Were they kind to you?'

'Kind enough. They let me go to school.'

'Good,' Willy said. 'That's good. What then? Work in the kitchens?'

'In the gardens.'

Willy nodded. 'After your marriage to Gavin Tarrant you did not work in the gardens any more, though, did you?'

'No, I was took to live with him in a cottage on the Edge.'

'What's the Edge?' said Biddy.

'On the Peak, where the sheep are.'

'There would be no gardens for you to look after on the Edge,' Willy said.

'No, sir, none worth the name.'

'Did you miss the gardens?'

'I did,' Fay admitted. 'It was bleak on the uplands. I saw nobody except the shepherds' wives, and not much of them. Gavin did not enjoy company.'

'Is that why you ran away?' Biddy asked.

Fay shook her head. 'I ran away because he treated me bad.'

'What does your husband look like?' Willy said. 'Tall and fair, is he?'

'Oh, no! He is short in height but broad in chest and shoulders. His hair is black and he wears it in a little pigtail.'

'Do you think that Gavin resembles his father?' Willy asked.

'I do not know, sir. I never met his father,' Fay answered.

'Perhaps he's dead. Gavin's father, I mean?'

'No, he isn't dead, sir. There were letters from him, though not many,' Fay said. 'Gavin wouldn't let me read them. He kept them hidden in the box where he kept all his papers.'

'Are you sure,' Innis said, 'that these letters were from Michael – from Gavin's father and not, say, from a friend?'

'Gavin has no friends.'

'And you,' Willy said, 'have you no friends?'

'I had friends, sir,' Fay said. 'I had friends when I lived in the gardens. Josh was my friend.'

'Ah!' Biddy said. 'Ah-hah! Now the truth comes out. Was Josh your lover?'

'Oh no. I never had no lover,' Fay said. 'Josh was just – just a friend.'

Innis said, 'Is Josh the person who gave you the seeds?'

'Yes.'

'Are we to take it that Josh knows you've come to Mull?' said Biddy.

'I told Josh of my intentions, yes,' Fay said. 'He even put new leather on my boots, for he said there would be nothing but rocky roads in Scotland.'

'Who else knows you're here?' said Innis.

'I told nobody except Josh. I didn't even tell Mr Musson. I decided what had to be done and when Gavin went off to the gathering of the ewes I packed my bag and walked to the railway station and bought a ticket.'

'With your husband's money,' Biddy said.

'I had some money saved, money of my own,' said Fay. 'Seven shillings, that's all I took from Gavin. Seven shillings from his box.'

'Is that the truth?' said Biddy.

'Yes, Mrs Bav – Mrs Quigley, that's the truth.'

'Willy,' Biddy said, 'what do you make of it?'

'Well, it's a credible tale. She wouldn't be the first young woman to be tricked into a bad marriage.'

'I wasn't tricked into marrying Gavin, sir. I went willing.'

'Be that as it may, you've deserted your husband and Mrs Quigley is entitled to enquire why you're seeking refuge here,' Willy said. 'In fact I'm a wee bit curious myself as to why you picked Fetternish of all places.'

'Mull's the last place Gavin will think to look for me,' Fay said. 'He will never come here to look for me. Never.'

'Why is that?' Willy asked.

'I don't know, sir. Something happened here, I think,' Fay said. 'Something he never talked about. He told me a little about the island and the cottage where he was born and how green and lovely it all was. He told me that he and his father had tried to purchase a piece of ground to farm for themselves but were denied it.'

'What did he say about me?' Biddy asked. 'About us?'

'Little enough,' Fay answered. 'When he was fuddled with drink he would let things slip, though, and I remembered him mentioning your names.'

'Drinking!' Biddy exclaimed. 'That's it! God, he's Dada all over the back.' She flung up a hand in despair. 'Are we *never* going to get rid of that old devil? Is it not enough that we had to suffer him when he was alive and now that he's dead we're going to have to go through it all again with his grandson?'

'Calm yourself, Biddy,' Quig advised.

'Calm myself? How can I be calm when we're discussing Gavin Tarrant who, need I remind you, tried to murder you when he was not much more than a child and for all we know might be planning to come back to finish the job?' She turned to Fay. 'Aye, you did not know *that*, did you, girl? That's why your husband left Mull and why he dare not return. He shot this man here, Robert Quigley. Pointed a shotgun straight at him and pulled the trigger. That's why we don't want Gavin here – no, nor his wife.'

'I take it, Biddy,' Willy said, 'that you don't doubt the girl?'

'No, I don't doubt her,' Biddy said. 'I just don't want her in my house.'

'I will take her,' said Innis. 'I will look after her.'

'Conscience?' Biddy snapped. 'Dear God, Innis, conscience will be the death of you. What if she's left a trail for Gavin to follow? What if he turns up here to murder us all in our beds?'

'You forget, dear,' Quig said, 'that I wasn't Gavin's prime target.'

'I haven't forgotten *anything*,' Biddy declared. 'I remember that day as if it were yesterday.'

Time, age, illness and the distractions of holding together a failing estate had not eliminated the memories of that desperate period in her life, for the Campbell inheritance was as chequered as the whole sad history of the island itself.

'I am not going to turn her away, Biddy,' Innis said.

'You're still hoping that he'll come back, aren't you? Sixteen years, sixteen years and you still can't give him up,' Biddy said. 'Are you hoping he'll finally answer all those letters you posted off into oblivion or that he'll come trailing after Gavin, if Gavin does come trailing after his wife? Is that why you want to have her in your house? So that Gavin will have to come to you to get her back?'

'Gavin will not set foot on Mull,' Fay said. 'He hates you, all of you.'

'Why would he hate us?' Biddy shook her head. 'What harm did we ever do him?'

'What we didn't do was drown him at birth,' said Willy. 'I'm thinking that was maybe our first mistake.'

'It seems that you are not welcome here, Fay,' Innis said. 'You may stay with me at Pennymain until you find work and a place of your own.'

'There is no place for her on Mull,' Biddy said, 'and no work for anyone.'

'Aye, but there is ground,' said Fay promptly.

'If you mean land then yes, there's land,' Biddy said. 'But it's *my* land and I'll not be giving away one acre of it, not to you or anyone else that Gavin Tarrant might send to wheedle on his behalf.'

'Gavin didn't send me,' Fay said. 'I only want a bit of ground for a garden. I'll even break and dress it from the sod if needs be. I thought perhaps there might be plots going a-begging down by the old cottage.'

'Nothing will grow on Pennypol.' Biddy hesitated. 'However, if you insist on remaining here my husband will find some work to keep you occupied. But I warn you, we can't afford to offer you regular employment.'

'Temporary work will suit me fine,' Fay said. 'Thank you, Mrs Baverstock.'

'Quigley,' Biddy said. 'My name is Quigley. And from now on, young lady, your name is Ludlow. You will be known as Fay Ludlow, no relative of mine. Do I make myself clear?'

'As a bell, Mrs Quigley,' Fay said and with a grateful little bob of the head allowed Innis to lead her from the drawing-room.

CHAPTER TWO

Bread of Angels

Long before Gillies Brown had ever set foot on Mull there had
been schools all over the island, an assortment of parochial
establishments that operated on principles that were, to say the
least, rather less than educationally sound. At one time there had
even been an Academy of Industry for young females housed in
Tobermory jail, which was no reflection on the honesty of local
girls but rather on the total absence of a criminal class to provide
said jail with the proper sort of inmate or, in fact, any inmates at
all. Since then parliamentary acts, revisions of acts, amendments
to revisions of acts – the applied wisdom of industrious
committee men to whom education mattered more than breath
– had increased state regulation and introduced a raft of rules
that had robbed Gillies and his daughter Janetta of much of their
individual authority.

Each weekday, for instance, the older lads and lassies were
whisked off in a horse-drawn omnibus to school in Tobermory
where, out of sight of parents and prying neighbours, they
learned to smoke tobacco, nip whisky and flirt with each other
more or less like their brethren in the big cities: not, it must be
said, that Tobermory was a den of vice or that the masters were
lax in their duties or, indeed, that Tobermory was so very far
removed from the sleepy little village of Crove where Mr Gillies
Brown, his daughter Janetta and two ministers of the Gospel

guarded the moral and spiritual welfare of the young. None the less, education was on the march if not the rampage, and the eighteen schools that remained on Mull when the twentieth century opened the doors of opportunity were subject to inspection and rules of allocation like schools all over Scotland, and the Browns, father and daughter, were obliged to comply with the laws of the land or to leave the profession to which they had dedicated the best years of their lives.

One benefit of state intervention was that the parish of Crove had received a generous grant of government money with which to erect a new school building to replace the low, two-roomed cottage that had served three generations of little scholars before it had been all but swept away in the great Crove flood of 1899.

The new school was constructed of imported brick, not local stone. It was angular and upright and rather stern, similar, some said, to Miss Brown herself. The spacious, well-lighted classrooms were topped by the headmaster's apartments which comprised a sitting-room, two bedrooms and a spartan kitchen within which Gillies Brown and his spinster daughter Janetta were obliged to take up residence, thus abandoning the cottages at An Fhearann Cáirdeil that they had rented from Biddy and that had been their home for many happy years.

There were advantages to living in a new house above the school, of course. The building had running water and an indoor lavatory and master and mistress no longer had to face a three-mile hike to and from work every day. The main disadvantage – which Netta felt less keenly than her father – was that Gillies Brown and his dear, close friend Innis Tarrant got to see less of each other. And at last the villagers gave up gossiping about the schoolmaster and the abandoned wife of Pennymain, for it was generally agreed that his prissy daughter Janetta would not permit her father to get away with anything that smacked of hanky-panky.

The Browns' transfer from An Fhearann Cáirdeil scotched the last flicker of scandal. By 1908, when the first of the strangers turned up in Crove, not a head turned or an eyelid blinked when Innis popped into the Browns' house above the school or when Gillies borrowed the Reverend Ewing's little pony-trap to clatter out to Pennymain.

Gillies had been married before, to a Glasgow girl, Clara, and had slaved in the classrooms of that indefensible city. When poor Clara had died, however, Gillies had dragged his young family north to take up a teaching post in Crove and soon thereafter had fallen in love with Innis Tarrant, wife of the Fetternish flockmaster, and she with him. Guilt and excitement had followed in about equal measure as the friendship had blossomed and found strength but now Gillies had reached an age when the future no longer seemed limitless and Innis's company was no longer enough to keep anxiety at bay. Three of his four children and one of Innis's daughters had gone off to the mainland, the school's population was thinning and he feared that before too long there would be no pupils left to teach and that the new school would be forced to close. Sometimes, particularly in the dreary depths of winter, he would glance back at what he had missed and wonder if he had sacrificed just a little too much for Innis's sake. But then spring would come round again and he would waken in the mornings and turn over in bed and listen to the gulls crying and would think how fine a thing it would be to have Innis all to himself, not here in the schoolhouse but at Pennymain or in the ancient farmstead at An Fhearann Cáirdeil with just the sounds of the sea beating on the grey rocks and the sighing of the wind in the grasses.

'Daddy, are you awake?'

'What?'

'I asked if you were awake?'

'I am. Yes, I am.'

'Do you want this tea?'

He struggled reluctantly into consciousness and, out of habit, rubbed his hands over his scalp to restore blood to the few sensible cells that remained.

'Tea?'

'In a cup,' Janetta said, 'on a saucer.'

'You spoil me, Netta.'

'Do you want it or do you not?'

He peered up at her rigid black skirt and starched white blouse. Her only adornment was a silver-plated pocket watch clipped to a buttonhole. She was thin, much thinner than her mother had been even in the final days of her illness, but it was vitality not disease that prevented the flesh from settling on Netta's bones. She had thick fair hair pinned up in an unflattering 'cottage-loaf' style cribbed from a reproduction of a painting entitled *Spartan Women* which, for some reason, she had found appealing.

She peered down at him as if he were a grubby schoolboy. 'Answer me.'

One of the problems of old age – well, not quite old age – was that you could no longer hop enthusiastically from sleep to wakefulness. Gillies tugged at the collar of his night-shirt to hide the mat of white hair that covered his chest and held out both hands for the teacup. He sipped obediently.

'Lovely, thank you,' he said.

She continued to watch him, frowning. 'Have you heard?'

'Heard what?'

'She's taken someone to live with her.'

'Pardon?'

'Your friend, she's taken in a lodger.'

'My . . . Oh, Innis, you mean?' He sat up in the narrow bed. 'When you say Innis has "taken someone in", do you seek to imply that she has deliberately deceived someone for her own gain or do you wish me to understand that she—'

'For heaven's sake, stop playing the fool,' Janetta said. 'Innis has taken in a girl, a young woman, a young *English* woman, I believe, to lodge at Pennymain.'

'Has she?' Gillies swallowed a mouthful of tea. He steered the cup on to the saucer, groped on the bedside cabinet for his spectacles and fitted them over his nose. Netta swam swiftly into focus.

'Did she not tell you?'

'I saw her last Wednesday and she said nothing to me about expecting a visitor,' Gillies said. 'Who told you?'

'Miss Fergusson.'

'Who told her?'

'Muriel Barrett.'

'What other salient facts did Barrett's wife impart?'

'None,' his daughter said. 'That is the point.'

'The point? Oh-hoh, yes, I see,' Gillies said. 'You want *me* to find out what's going on at Fetternish.'

'If you will.'

'If I can.'

'Of course you can,' Janetta said. 'Innis Tarrant has no secrets from you.'

'Well, a few, perhaps just a few,' Gillies Brown said. 'What day is it?'

'Saturday.'

'Saturday.' He nodded. 'I'm expected at Pennymain for lunch anyway, so satisfying your curiosity should not be too difficult.'

'I'm not curious personally,' Janetta Brown said. 'I'm not much of one for prying, as well you know, but I do feel a certain obligation to find out what I can.'

'An obligation to whom?' Normally he would have eased himself into the day by teasing his spinster daughter about her circle of female friends, all of whom were inordinately fond of poking their noses into other people's business, but Netta's news had made him uncharacteristically impatient. 'Never mind.' He gripped a handful of sheets and blankets. 'I do believe I'll be getting up now.'

'For what?' said Janetta.

'To have my breakfast.'

'And then?'

'I think I'll trot over to Pennymain somewhat earlier than planned.'

'*De bonne volonté?*' Janetta said.

'Willingly?' said Gillies. 'Why, child, of course – willingly.'

'Why, Daddy, you're just as nosy as the rest of us,' Janetta said.

'Yes, dear,' said Gillies with a sigh. 'I confess that in this instance I am.'

According to Mr Musson it was possible to work some land in any sort of weather and that soil mattered more than climate when it came to selecting vegetables for a profitable crop. In fact Mr Musson had dinned the rudiments of gardening wisdom into her so thoroughly that Fay hardly needed to employ thought at all but could almost rely on instinct to help her reach decisions.

On the bleak uplands high above Cloudshill the lapwings would be diving hither and thither in search of nesting sites, ravens would be mating and hawks plunging down to feed on young rats or the first flush of spring rabbits. In the orchards around Fream the stench of fresh manure would hang over the hedges and Josh would be out with the strawberry pots and old Mr Musson with the grafting-wax to propagate the plum trees. Here on Mull, however, she had no pattern to follow when it came to cultivation, only the screaming of seagulls over brown bracken and grey rock and in the gully behind Pennymain a gush of water from a broken pipe and a tangle of briar, bramble and blackthorn so dense that she did not dare venture down there at all.

Even so the brisk bright breeze and blinks of sunshine brought a lift to your heart whether you were cutting raspberry canes in Derbyshire or scratching in the wrinkled earth of an island on the edge of the Atlantic, and Fay felt decidedly cheerful and optimistic about the future. Becky, her sister-in-law, seemed unaware that this was a day when you just had to be out and about, making ready for the growing season. On that bright, blustery March morning, however, Fay did not much care what

Becky Tarrant thought of her; she continued to potter about in Innis's garden in spite of the fact that she knew that she was being observed and probably criticised.

'What is she doing now, for heaven's sake,' Becky groused, 'scratching away at the grass like a blessed chicken?'

'I think,' Innis answered, 'she is testing the soil.'

Becky peered from the kitchen window. 'Haven't you told her that a few puny wee bags of seed won't turn Fetternish into the Garden of Eden?'

'I am sure that she knows that already.'

Becky turned from the window. 'I should have been consulted, you know. Why didn't you consult me before you invited a total stranger into our house? It's my home too, you know.'

'I thought you believed in charity.'

'I believe that a community should look after the poor and needy, which,' Becky said, 'is quite a different thing from taking in every mongrel who happens to turn up on your doorstep and hand you a hard-luck story. She's a sponger, Mother, and if there's one thing I cannot abide—'

'The one thing that I cannot abide,' Innis interrupted, 'is inconsistency. One minute you are down on Fay for working and the next you are condemning her for being a sponger.'

'Scraping holes among our rose bushes isn't my idea of work.'

'Your father planted those rose bushes – and the vegetables too.'

'So you keep telling me.'

'If it had not been for his efforts, times we would have had nothing to eat.'

'Now who's being inconsistent?' Becky said. 'If we're so hard up, Mother, why have you saddled us with another mouth to feed?'

'I did not say that we are hard up now.'

'Yes you did.'

'We are better off than most folk,' Innis said. 'Besides, the girl is a stranger and in need of help. Kindness is the bread of angels, remember.'

'I'll bet Dada didn't tell you that?'

'No, he didn't,' Innis admitted.

'It would be some cranky old priest like Father Gunnion.'

'Father O'Donnell as a matter of fact.'

Becky leaned on the draining board and greased the frying pan.

Eggs were set out in a bowl, eggs that the girl had helped gather. Fay Ludlow had been up and about long before she, Becky, had thumped her bare feet to the floor. Such willingness irked Becky. It seemed altogether too ingratiating. She did not like the girl, did not like the look of her, all grubby and scratched, with a kink in her nose and a half-lame leg. She had been utterly flabbergasted when her mother had come down from the drawing-room in the big house with the trespasser clinging to her arm and had introduced her as enthusiastically as if she were a prodigal returned. Indeed, Becky's first thought had been that the girl *was* blood kin, one of the illegitimates that Great-Grandfather McIver had sired before he'd popped off and Foss had been abandoned and Quig and Mairi, his mother, had come over to Fetternish to manage the cattle and, soon after, to marry into the family.

She remembered these events only dimly and her great-grandfather not at all. What she had heard of Evander McIver, though, did not make him sound endearing. To her way of thinking he sounded like a selfish and unscrupulous opportunist without an ethical bone in his body, not a legend from a lost age of individualism. Becky had no desire to see the graves of her great-grandparents on the sea-lashed islet beyond the last outpost of civilisation. But if this girl, this Fay Ludlow, with her stunted accent and mysterious bruises really did stem from the lower branches of the family tree why, Becky wondered, was her mother so reluctant to admit it?

'Very well, Mother,' she said. 'Enough nonsense. Why won't you tell me who Fay Ludlow really is and what she's doing here?'

Innis lingered in the doorway of the bedroom.

Becky could make out the flickering candle before the Virgin and wondered gloomily what the offering signified since Lent and Easter were weeks away and there was no special saint's day to celebrate at this time of the year.

'She is just a poor girl in need of help.'

'Nonsense!' Becky exclaimed. 'Tell me the truth. Is Fay Ludlow my half-sister? Has Dada been sowing his wild oats?'

'How could she be your half-sister?' Innis said. 'She's too old.'

'What age is she? Seventeen?'

'Eighteen, I believe. Too old, you see. Your father was still here with us when Fay was born.'

'Where are her parents?'

'She is an orphan.'

'Oh, dear me!' said Becky. 'She really is piling it on.' She tested the temperature of the stove top with a quick pat of her hand. 'I find it hard to believe that you would be taken in by a story so patently made up. If Fay isn't Dada's daughter then, is she his sweetheart?'

'Becky! No, she has never met your father.'

'Is that what she told you?'

'Yes.'

'Why?'

'Why?' said Innis.

'If Fay Ludlow's a casual visitor why would you ask her about Dada?'

'She came here,' Innis said, cautiously, 'because . . .'

'Go on.'

'Because she heard that we might be looking for a gardener.'

'A gardener? *Are* we looking for a gardener?'

'Willy thinks there is too much good ground going to waste on Fetternish, ground that might be earning money for the estate.'

'I suppose you'll be telling me next that word of Willy Naismith's bright idea filtered all the way down to – where is it? – Derbyshire, and that our Miss Ludlow promptly sat up and

declared, "Oh, yes, that is for me. I will pack my bag and head for
Scotland straight away"? Mother, you are telling me a pack of
lies. I assume there's something about Fay Ludlow you don't
want me to know. Will you at least tell me how long she's going
to be with us?'

'She has only just arrived.'

'When does she plan to move on?'

'I do not know where she would be moving on to,' Innis said.

'So we're stuck with her?'

'So it would seem,' said Innis.

She was relieved to see Gillies striding down the hill, for she was
in sore need of a shoulder to lean on. She had expected him
about lunch-time but the fact that he had arrived early pleased
her; no one else could provide her with the kind of advice and
support that she needed at this time, not even Quig.

Quig had taken over management of Fetternish after Hector
Thrale, the previous factor, had died. He looked after Pennymain with the same thoroughness as he looked after the other
tenanted properties and had always been a tower of strength. For
years he had taken care of Aileen and her son Donnie and after
Foss had been abandoned to the seals and the gulls marriage to
Biddy had seemed like a just reward for his loyalty. Innis
respected and trusted him but the unguarded affection that
Quig and she had shared when they were young had gone, and
for the best part of twenty years it was Gillies Brown who had
been her mainstay.

It was about half past ten o'clock when Gillies appeared.
Taking advantage of the weather Innis was hanging out sheets
and blankets. Becky had flounced off to the big house immediately after breakfast and Fay, with Innis's permission, had set
off for Pennypol. She watched him come through the gate and
cross the corner of the drying green. She smiled and offered her
cheek for a kiss.

'You are by way of being early, are you not?' she said.

'I am,' Gillies said. 'It's such a grand morning that I couldn't bring myself to stay indoors a moment longer.'

'Is that the only reason?'

'Well, Netta did mention something about a visitor.' He glanced towards the cottage. 'Is she here?'

'She is not a visitor,' Innis said. 'She will be staying with us for a time.'

'What does Becky have to say about that?'

'Trust you to be getting straight to the point,' Innis said. 'Becky does not know who the girl is. If she did she would be even less pleased.'

'According to word passed down from Barrett the girl is a cripple,' Gillies said. 'Is that why you are looking after her?'

'No.' Innis paused. 'I am looking after her because she is Gavin's wife.'

'Gavin's wife!' Gillies said nothing for a moment then added, 'Come to you for protection, I take it? Is Gavin in hot pursuit?'

'She says that he is not.'

'What about your Michael?'

'She says that she has never met Michael.'

'Do you believe her?'

'Yes, I believe her,' Innis said. 'Even so, I'm frightened. Years without a word from either of them, twelve years at least – and now this. Last I heard they were living in the Borders and working sheep on the Ettrick Pen.'

'You've never put them out of your mind, though, have you?'

'No, not completely,' Innis admitted. 'He is my son, after all.'

'Why did she leave him?'

'He beat her.'

'Is that what she told you?'

'Yes.'

'I wouldn't take everything this girl tells you at face value,' Gillies said. 'She might be as much at fault as Gavin. Where is he right now?'

'Shepherding in Derbyshire.'

'Well, that's far enough away, thank God. Did the girl travel all the way from Derbyshire just to find you?'

'She has no one else to turn to.'

'Hmm,' said Gillies.

'You sound sceptical.'

'Aren't you?'

'I like her,' Innis said.

'You hardly know her,' Gillies said. 'And you must not feel responsible for what's happened. If she's had a troubled marriage then that's her fault, or Gavin's, not yours. How many other people know who she really is?'

'Biddy, Quig and Willy, that's all.'

'Not Becky?'

'No, not Becky.'

'Sooner or later you'll have to tell Becky the truth.'

'If I do it will be all over the island before long and all the rumours about Gavin and what he did will start up again, and all the talk about us.'

Gillies put an arm about her. 'Where is the girl now?'

'She has gone over to Pennypol.'

'What for?'

'To look at the plots. She's a gardener.'

'Is she? How odd!' Gillies said. 'Well, why don't we walk over there and let me take a look at her.'

'Size her up, do you mean?'

'Something along those lines,' said Gillies.

She had no fear of the truculent ewes that had wandered over the brow of the hill to inspect her, nor of the shaggy brown cattle that loped, bellowing, up from the shore. Bullocks, she knew, were more curious than aggressive and she stood her ground in the wreckage of the onion patch and let them charge up to her and dither and prance, snorting, behind the rusty fence until she threw up her arms and shouted, '*Shoo*,' and sent them stampeding back to the sands.

The boy, though, was just suddenly there. For a moment she thought it might be Gavin slyly observing her as he had observed her from the lee of the potting-shed or the greenhouses. The boy was nothing like Gavin, however. He was slim and spindly in the way that young boys are before they shoot up.

She had spent an hour measuring the ground, pacing it out at eight long strides to the rood, and marking it with small stones: 'squaring the plot' Mr Musson called it. When she had finished her rough calculations she rested on the grass at the top of the rows and stared at the sweep of land dipping away from her, down to the lip of the beach and out into the sea.

As soon as she spotted the boy, she scrambled to her feet and waved. 'I saw you yesterday,' she called out. 'Oh, you thought I didn't see you up there on the hill but I saw you, yes, I did.' She moved towards him. 'Tell me your name?'

'Billy, miss.'

'Billy Miss?'

'Billy Barrett, miss.'

'Don't go calling me "miss". My name is Fay. I think it would be quite proper for you to call me Fay.' He was twelve, perhaps thirteen years old, solemn but not sullen. 'Don't you want to know what I'm doing?'

'I know what you are doing, miss.'

He pressed an arm behind him and flattened his palm against the gable, as if at some point he might need a push for a flying start.

It was not the fact that she was a stranger that bothered him, Fay reckoned, but the fact that she was a girl. She remembered how she'd felt when Josh had first been brought to Fream, how attracted to him she had been because he was older than she was. She remembered the queer sensations that meeting Josh had roused in her, an inexplicable feeling of urgency, of needing to grow up quickly.

'What am I doing then?' she asked.

'You are measuring Vassie's patch.'

'That,' Fay brushed the bridge of Billy's nose with her forefinger, 'is exactly it.' Billy's cheeks turned dusky pink under his weather tan. She went on, 'Do you know what I'm measuring it for?'

He let out his breath, and said, 'I know what it was that Vassie grew.'

'And what did Vassie grow? Tell me.'

'Potatoes, leeks, cabbages and onions.'

'Do you remember old Mrs Campbell?'

'She was dead before I was born.'

'How then do you know what she grew here?'

'Mr Quigley tended the plot for a while, then my dada kept it going until the cattle got on to it and Quig said it was not worth the cost of proper fencing.'

'Are you the shepherd's son?'

'I am.'

'Are you going to be a shepherd too?'

'No.'

'No?'

'There will be no call for shepherds by the time I am grown up.'

'Are you not grown up now?' Fay said.

'I will be going away to the school in Oban when I am fourteen.'

'How long will you be schooled at Oban?'

'For one year,' the boy answered, 'then I will be going away to Glasgow.'

'Is that where they go, all the young men?' Fay said. 'To Glasgow?'

'The most of them.'

'And the girls, what about the girls?'

'Those who are for service, it is Edinburgh for them.'

'Does no one of your age stay on the island?'

'Only those who do not have money to leave, or those who are willing to settle for the fishing,' Billy said, 'or those whose mothers are afraid of what will become of them over on the mainland.'

'Are you not afraid of what will become of you over on the mainland?'

'No, miss, I am not afraid of anything.'

Fay sighed. 'I wish I were more like you, Billy.'

She was tempted to stroke his nose again as if he were a charm that might bring her luck, but she did not wish to embarrass him. He was so different from her husband that he seemed to belong to another species entirely. She found it impossible to believe that Gavin had once stood on this spot and gazed out at the sea as Billy Barrett did now; and she could not imagine Gavin, even at thirteen or fourteen, conversing with a woman as if she were his equal.

'Are you going to be staying here?' Billy asked.

'I hope so.'

'It is not much of a place to be living in.'

'No,' Fay agreed, 'though I have seen worse.'

'Is it worse where you come from?'

'Different,' Fay said. 'Where I come from is far from the sea.'

'Are you a planter?'

'A planter?'

'A horticulturalist.'

Fay was surprised that Billy even knew the word. 'No,' she said. 'I'm a gardener, plain and simple.'

'Will you be working for Mrs Quigley?'

'If she will take me on.'

'My dada says that Mrs Quigley is on her uppers and that if wool prices do not rise soon she will be forced to sell Fetternish and we will all be out of work.'

'How can Mrs Quigley be short of money when she lives in that fine house?'

'I do not know,' Billy said, 'but my dada says she is.'

'Doesn't she have children? I thought she had children?'

'Two of them, a boy and a girl.'

'Where are they?'

'At school.'

'At school in Oban?'

'Huh!' Billy said. 'No. Miss Brown taught them when they were small but then they went off to school in Edinburgh, even Christina, the girl.'

'That must be costing Mrs Quigley a pretty penny.'

'Aye' – Billy nodded gravely – 'it must.'

'I really thought Mrs Quigley was rich?'

'Everybody thinks she is rich,' Billy said. 'Is that why you came to Fetternish, miss, because you heard she was rich?'

'Oh no,' Fay said. 'I came because I heard that the boys on Mull were handsome – and it seems that they are.'

The compliment seemed to skim past him. He leaned against the wall, resting on his hands. 'Is it a husband you are looking for, miss?'

'No, Billy, I'm not looking for a husband.'

'There are few men here. My sisters complain about it, though they are too small to be looking out for husbands yet.' He hesitated. 'Was it a man that did that to your eye?' She had almost forgotten about her eye. Perhaps her bruises and her limp were the reasons why Billy Barrett felt at ease with her. 'I am sorry, miss. I should not have been asking such a question of a lady.'

'Do you think that's what I am, Billy, a lady?'

'Aye, all girls are ladies when they reach a certain age.'

'Who told you that?'

'My father.'

Fay smiled and, stepping back, pointed to the stone markers. 'I'm going to grow strawberries here,' she told him. 'When they're ripe I'll let you eat as many as you can carry in your hat.'

'Strawberries will not grow in this climate.'

'I'll make them grow,' Fay promised. 'You'll see. I'll build a special little wall to gather in the sun. I'll feed them with good manure to start them off right and I'll sprinkle them regular to keep them free from yellow-edge.' She glanced round, grinning. 'Alpine,' she said. 'Small-fruited Alpine. Belle de Mews or Brilliants or Crestas, or all the lot of them. And do you know what, Billy? With any luck we'll have strawberries for Christmas. How would you like that?'

'I would like that fine, miss,' Billy said.

'Fresh strawberries,' Fay said. 'Do you like fresh strawberries, Billy?'

'I am not sure if I do or not,' Billy said. 'I have never tasted one.'

'Oh, that's sad,' Fay said, 'never to have tasted a strawberry.'

Looking up, she caught sight of Innis Tarrant and a tall middle-aged man coming down the track towards her. Billy saw them too.

'I had better be making myself scarce,' he said.

'Oh! Why?'

'That's Mr Brown, the schoolmaster.'

'I see,' Fay said. 'Well, I doubt if he's hunting for you on a Saturday.'

'He will have come to look you over,' Billy said.

'I hope he likes what he sees,' said Fay.

'He would be daft if he did not,' said Billy and slipped away round the gable before she could thank him for the compliment.

CHAPTER THREE

Scandal and Concern

In Harrogate or Bath the influential ladies of the town would probably have met in a tea-shop to discuss the appearance of a female stranger in their midst and to put her, socially speaking, in her place. Crove, however, had no tea-shop and its influential ladies – the schoolteacher, the Quigleys' housekeeper and the minister's wife – had no choice but to assemble on the narrow pavement outside Miss Fergusson's cramped little shop.

Miss Fergusson had been tottering about behind the counter of the general store for ever, it seemed. She was one of several monuments to the changeless quality of village life, along with the parish church, the other church, the Free, the McKinnon Arms, and the Wingard Community Hall which had lately been reroofed in a black Ballachulish slate that seemed more appropriate to covens and conventicles than dances, concerts and ceilidhs. Hens continued to strut about the doorsteps, roosters to chant reveille from the dung-heap behind the livery stable and the pervasive aroma of peat smoke still hung over the white-washed row of cottages that flanked each side of the main street. The new brick schoolhouse was tucked away behind the cottages, screened by a great emerald-green spruce tree that seemed to have grown inordinately tall in the past few years, which was more than could be said for poor Miss Fergusson who had withered almost to nothing.

Service in the shop had never been swift. Lately it had become so tardy that some villagers preferred to ride the horse-bus into Tobermory than wait for a basket to be filled and a bill added up in Crove's only store. To most folk, however, Miss Fergusson's remained a place where you could while away a pleasant hour or two exchanging news and views, or if you were the lady Frances Hollander, Mairi Ewing or plain Janetta Brown, in piloting the local bonnets and shawls through the perilous shoals of gentility.

By rights Biddy should have been part of the charmed circle, for at one stage in her career she had been privileged to hob-nob with the aristocracy. 'Privileged' was not a word Biddy would have chosen to describe her experiences with Lord Fennimore's shooting set, though, and, disillusioned with the upper crust, she had long since abandoned her social aspirations. She was friends with the minister's wife. Mairi Ewing was, of course, her mother-in-law. It was she who had persuaded Quig to quit Foss for Fetternish and had thereafter set her cap at and duly married the Reverend Tom Ewing. Biddy had never quite forgiven Mairi for stealing away her confidant. In the past few years she had even come to resent the lingering influence that the woman still had over Quig and had deliberately reduced social contacts between the manse and the big house.

She was also friends with the schoolmaster's daughter but had no time for Frances Hollander who had taken possession of The Ards when the Clarks had finally sold up and whose claim to be 'a lady' was, Biddy suspected, little more than an affectation.

Frances Hollander drove into Crove every Saturday afternoon in a well-upholstered four-wheeled vehicle that she insisted on referring to as an American buggy, though everyone knew it was just a fancy version of a pony-trap. Frances seldom travelled with a servant and no male hands were employed at The Ards, not even a farm manager. Rumour had it that Quig might soon take on some of the little estate's managerial duties — for a fee, of course. It would be no skin off Quig's nose to do so, for The Ards lay close to Fetternish and Barrett was already tending the handful of sheep that remained from the Clarks' flock, mainly burned-out rams and cast ewes that Mrs Hollander could not bear to have shot and lugged off to the knackers at five shillings the carcass.

Frances Hollander might have been more readily accepted in the village if she hadn't insisted on dolling herself up in tailored suits, hobble skirts and huge cartwheel hats that on blustery afternoons required not so much management as taming. The pony, one of Angus Bell's less recalcitrant beasts, was used to working without a guiding hand. He brought the buggy to·the roping-rail at the top of the steps on his own initiative and waited while Frances stepped down: stepping down was not that easy on tiny, highly polished boots with four-inch heels. She hovered in the region of thirty-three or -four but she was so pert and delicate that susceptible males often mistook her for twenty-two or -three. Her eyes were elongated by expert applications of mascara, her hair was blacker than Ballachulish slate, and she spoke with a husky, hesitant lisp that many people, women as well as men, found irresistible.

'Mairi,' she crooned. 'Mairi, my dear, how are *you* this fine spring day?'

As a rule the minister's wife bowed to no one but her husband but even she dipped a curtsy to 'Lady' Frances Hollander. She still had some respect for style if not for titles. There had been a time when she had thought that her son, Quig, was moving up in the world by marrying Biddy Baverstock. Now, though, she was not so sure; her daughter-in-law's treatment of her son sometimes seemed so offhand as to be almost cruel and whatever charm Biddy had once possessed had dwindled long ago.

Many years occupancy of the manse had diminished Mairi's flamboyance but she still managed to sport large silver earrings and a hat so peppered with feathers and cloth flowers that most ministers, let alone their wives, would have condemned it as idolatrous.

'I am very well, thank you, Frances,' she replied and then,

wasting no time on small talk, added, 'I take it you have heard that we have a visitor?'

'Why yes, I did hear something of the sort.' Frances extended a hand to Maggie Naismith who took the hand in both of hers as if she intended to kiss it. 'I was *rather* hoping that Margaret here might be able to provide us with a *little* more information.'

Maggie said, 'Well, I have heard that she is planning to stay.'

'At Fetternish, do you mean, with Bridget?' Frances said.

'At Pennymain, with Innis.'

'Why would she wish to stay with Innis?' Mairi asked.

'It is a mystery to me,' said Maggie.

'A mystery,' Frances Hollander said. 'Oh, I do so love a mystery.'

Frances herself was something of a mystery, a fact of which the ladies present were very well aware. There was quite enough room in their lives for more than one mystery, however, and if one happened to run into another so much the better.

With a little wriggle of the shoulders, Frances turned to Janetta. 'And you, my dearest, have you heard anything that we should know about?'

'Not I,' Janetta said, ungrammatically. 'However, my father has gone over to Pennymain for his dinner – I mean, of course, his lunch – and I'll be very surprised if Innis doesn't take him into her confidence.'

'Of course, she will. I'm sure she will,' said Frances. 'And *you* will be taken into *his* confidence, will you not? And you will tell *us*.'

'I will prise it out of him, never fear,' Janetta promised.

Frances's laughter, like her voice, was breathless and lisping. She reached for Janetta's arm and hugged it to her breast, a gesture that offended no one except Netta herself, for Netta found it difficult to accept that anyone would dare exhibit so much affection on a public highway. As the oldest child she had been obliged to help her father raise the little ones after her mother's death. Perhaps the need for discipline had increased her natural reserve. Whatever the reason, she seldom showed tenderness or allowed her iron will to be tarnished by kisses and cuddles, yet when Frances Hollander touched her Netta did not pull away.

'What purchases do you have to make today, Frances?' Mairi enquired.

'Not many,' Frances answered. 'I took the buggy into To-bermory on Wednesday and brought home our week's supplies. All I need, I think, is a quart of paraffin oil.'

'Miss Fergusson is out of paraffin,' Maggie said. 'The whole-saler in Oban won't send her any more until she pays her bill.'

'I'm surprised she is able to pay any of her bills,' said Frances. 'If she moved a little faster she might make a little more money, don't you think?'

'She is old and not interested in making money,' said Mairi. 'I expect when we are old we'll have no more sense than poor Miss Fergusson.'

'I hope I never reach the stage where I can't pay *my* bills,' said Frances.

'I agree.' Janetta was acutely conscious of the fact that Frances was still holding on to her arm. She glanced nervously at the Saturday afternoon traffic. Several small boys were slinking about plotting how to be up to no good. There were women with toddlers clinging to their skirts, and men loitering aimlessly outside the McKinnon Arms.

'Tom has a new barrel of lamp oil in the cellar,' Mairi said. 'He will be only too pleased to measure you out a quart, Frances.'

'Why, that would be most generous,' Frances said. 'Do you not find that the poor quality of the oil that one buys from Miss Fergusson makes the wicks brittle?'

For several minutes Crove's arbiters of taste discussed the properties of paraffin with a seriousness that would have amused their male companions to whom the cleaning and filling of lamps was a matter of routine. Only when that subject had been thoroughly explored did Frances ask, 'Have *you* seen the girl yet, Margaret?'

'I caught a glimpse yesterday,' Maggie said. 'Odd-looking person, not quite a woman and not quite a girl. Did you know that she has a broken face?'

'Broken?'

'I would say that she had been punched.'

'Punched, indeed? By whom?'

'Her husband, perhaps?'

'Who is her husband?' Frances asked.

'That's the mystery,' said Janetta.

A thought strayed into Mairi Ewing's mind, a thought that did not bear too close an examination. Of all Frances Hollander's acolytes she was the oldest and least impressionable. She remembered Michael Tarrant vividly: a handsome, sour-faced man with angry eyes. There had been ugly rumours about Michael Tarrant's relationship with Biddy Baverstock, a suggestion that Quig might not be the father of Biddy's first child. Quig ignored the rumours, of course; as far as he was concerned Robbie was his son and nobody had better try to tell him differently.

Listening to her friends gossip it occurred to Mairi just how much things had changed in Crove, that the tattered barbarism of the last century had been replaced by gentler sentiments. She rather missed the vigour of the old days, the clamour and striving, the dramas of ambition and desire that had teased the community and kept everyone on their toes. Now we have nothing better to do with ourselves, she thought, than prattle about the price of coal oil and speculate on why Innis Tarrant has taken in a stray.

Mairi had intended to invite the ladies up to the manse for afternoon tea. She had baked a batch of scones and had warned Tom not to sprawl in the parlour with his trousers unbuttoned and his false teeth wrapped in a handkerchief on the carpet beside him. Even a Church of Scotland minister was entitled to take his ease now and then, of course, to dismantle himself, as it were, in the privacy of his own home, but sometimes she wished that her husband had not allowed himself to become quite so soggy in his declining years.

An inexplicable burst of resentment should not prevent her doing what was expected of her, Mairi told herself. She gave a little shake of the head, just enough to make her earrings jangle and had just opened her mouth to issue the invitation when Janetta cried out, 'My God, will you look at that? What does he think he's playing at?' as the Fetternish dogcart came clipping into the main street.

Gillies Brown was driving. By his side was a young woman with fair hair. She was obviously excited at being hurled along at high speed and clung to the schoolmaster's arm and chirped in delight as the dogcart bounced over the lumpy cobbles. On the bench behind the couple Innis Tarrant bobbed up and down in a manner far too energetic for a woman of mature years.

The unusual sight cheered Mairi immediately.

She lifted her hand and waved as the vehicle sped past.

Janetta was less sanguine.

She stepped off the pavement and cried, 'Daddy. You, Daddy, just where do you think you're going?'

Grinning broadly, Gillies plucked off his hat and waved it. 'Tobermory,' he shouted. 'We're off to Tobermory,' just as the dogcart rattled past, heading for the bridge at the main street's end.

The girl rose against the lowering sky as if she were about to take wing and the cart keeled over, tilted up on one wheel. Gillies, Innis and the girl flung themselves instinctively against the tilt and the cart righted itself and went bowling off along the road that led to town.

'I take it,' Frances said, 'that was the woman in question?'

Maggie nodded. 'Aye, that was her, no doubt about it.'

'What on earth is she doing with your father?' Frances asked.

'And why is he driving her into Tobermory?' Maggie added.

Speechless with embarrassment, Janetta could only shake her head, while Mrs Mairi Ewing, ever the diplomat, cautiously suggested that now might be a good time to repair to the manse for tea.

'Humiliated,' Janetta said. 'That's what I was – humiliated.'

'Calm down, dear, calm down.' Gillies hung his hat and scarf on the peg behind the door. 'I was just having a bit of fun for a change.'

'Well, you might have chosen to have your fun elsewhere,' Janetta said, 'instead of flaunting yourself all over Main Street. I presume you've had supper?'

'I scrounged a bite at Pennymain.'

'From that – that girl?'

'Oh come along, Netta,' Gillies said mildly.

He tried to put his arm around her but she would have none of it. She stalked away. She did not flounce: Gillies reckoned that his daughter did not know how to flounce. Sometimes he wished that Netta had inherited a little more of her mother's warmth. He followed her into the living room, frugal and studious, not nearly as cosy as the long low rooms in An Fhearann Cáirdeil had been. He watched her lope into the alcove where an elongated, chest-high cooking stove steamed away day and night, a stove that was fed by economical little spoonfuls of coke and kept the whole house warm.

In the grate in the living-room a peat fire pricked the gloom of the spring twilight and through the uncurtained window Gillies could make out the curve of the ridge beyond the river and the dark bearded shapes of the tree plantations that crept down towards the village from the old Wingard place. A solitary light winked in the vast overcast expanse of moorland that undulated away towards Calgary and he liked to imagine that it shone in Innis Tarrant's window – which of course, it did not – to fancy that he was there instead of here, looking back at his spinster daughter in the schoolhouse, peeping into a life that seemed inert compared to life at Pennymain.

Abandoning the window, he seated himself in a chair at the hearth and resisted the temptation to pick up the iron poker and stir the peat sods in the shallow grate. Netta did not allow him to break up the smouldering sods and it would be a good quarter of an hour yet before she would deem it dark enough to let him light the lamp or even the fat tallow candle on the shelf. Her starched, high-collared blouse was a pale blob in the darkening kitchen. He watched the garment jerk with the tightly coiled gestures that Netta adopted when she was annoyed.

She stalked out of the alcove carrying a teapot and a cup.

One cup? Oh, dear! Gillies thought, I'm really in for it now. He watched her set the teapot on the side of the hearth, balance the cup and saucer on the what-not that served as a table. She seated herself on a ladder-backed chair that had been lugged all the way from their tenement house in Glasgow, the same chair in which her mother had nursed the children. How amazingly close in time that seemed, Gillies thought, yet how astonishingly distant, as if the pliant infant that Netta had once been and the woman who had nursed her had departed together.

She filled her cup with strong brown tea and returned the pot to the hearth.

She clinked the cup on to the saucer.

'Father,' she said, 'what on earth possessed you to behave like that?'

'Nothing possessed me. I took Innis and – and her friend into town.'

'Driving like a madman?'

'Briskly,' he said. 'Briskly, not dangerously.' He hesitated. 'Fay – the girl – isn't used to being driven about and I thought she would enjoy a wee turn of speed.'

'And did she?'

'Hmm, she seemed quite thrilled by it.'

He was no match for Janetta in the interrogation stakes. She could extract from him all manner of things that he would prefer her not to know about.

He paused, then said, 'Look, what do you want to know about her? Let's not beat about the bush, Netta. I saw you with your friends and I know only too well how nosy they are.'

'Nosy?'

'Concerned – how concerned about other people's business.' He held up his hand to forestall her protest. 'There's no scandal attached to Fay Ludlow. She's looking for work, that's all.'

'What sort of work does she do?'

'She's a gardener.'

'There are no gardens on Fetternish.'

'It's a bit more complicated than that. She's an orphan, you see.'

'Oh, yes, of course. How convenient.'

Gillies let out a little sigh and sat back in the creaky armchair. 'Do you want me to tell you about Fay Ludlow, or not?'

'Go on.'

'She's a trained market gardener. She learned her trade at one of the larger farming estates in Derbyshire. When her master died the estate was split up. In the course of the upheaval one of the Baverstock-Pauls – one of Agnes's sons – came to view the market garden side of things. In the end the price was too high but he had several conversations with the head gardener and told him about Fetternish, about this wonderful tract of land just waiting to be turned to good use.'

'What nonsense! Fetternish is a wilderness.'

'We know that, but the Baverstock-Pauls haven't set foot on Mull for decades. Obviously they passed on to their children an idealised vision of the estate that they never quite managed to reclaim. You know what incomers are like: wide-eyed and simple-minded when it comes to the Highlands and High-landers. They assume that either we all run about in bearskins with our faces painted blue or that we dwell in some kind of earthly paradise.'

She laughed in spite of herself, a little bark of laughter that indicated that she was being drawn in and that he might even get away with it. He pressed on: 'So, when the head gardener declined to follow the star to the north, refused, in other words, to accept any of Baverstock-Paul's nonsense . . .'

'The girl did?'

'Exactly.'

'She swallowed it.'

'Yes.'

'Like a fool.'

'Possibly.'

'What a rude shock she must have had when she got here.'

'I'm not so sure,' Gillies said cautiously. 'I've a feeling that anywhere would be better than where she came from.'

'She's running away, isn't she?'

'Yes.'

'From a husband?'

'Hardly that, hardly a husband.'

'Not the lord of the manor?' Janetta said. 'Please don't tell me that Sir Jasper defiled her?'

'No, not her employer – a boy – a young man whom she will not name.'

'What did he do to her?'

Trying not to be too theatrical, Gillies said, 'I'll leave that to your imagination.'

'Do you believe her?'

'Innis does.'

'No, do *you* believe her?'

'I do now.'

'Now?'

'Why do you think we took her into Tobermory this afternoon?'

It was almost pitch dark in the parlour, for the last of the light had faded and the sullen outline of the moor ridge was lost under advancing cloud. The wind, which had dwindled in the course of the day, was rising again. Gillies Brown's tall tale was endorsed by the wild weather, it seemed, for Janetta cocked her head as if she were listening to the ghost of Catherine Earnshaw crying out, 'Heathcliffe. Heathcliffe.' Gillies was no longer inclined to ask for the lamp to be lit.

'Think,' he said.

Janetta thought.

She said, 'You took her to the doctor's, didn't you?'

'Yes.'

'You took her to see old Dr Kirkhope, not young Dr Cumming?'

'Correct.'

'You wanted to find out if she was telling the truth?'

'Partly that,' Gillies admitted. 'I also wanted an opinion on that nasty eye.'

'What did Kirkhope say?'

'There's been some damage to the retina. He thinks that it will heal completely but he won't be able to tell for sure until the surrounding tissues drain. He'll recommend an opthalmologist in Glasgow if we want to take her down there and pay the cost of a consultation. Meanwhile he gave her some drops. He was amazed at her stoicism. She is, you know, a very stoical young woman; you can't deny her that, Netta.'

'I'm not denying her anything,' Janetta said, 'particularly as I've never met her.' She sat forward. 'What did Kirkhope say about — about the other thing? Is she telling the truth on that score?'

'So it would appear.'

'So it would appear? My God, Daddy, he's a doctor. I mean, he may be tottering on the brink of the grave but he's still a doctor. Doesn't he know? Could he not say for sure if she'd been — you know — ravished?'

'The ethics of the profession . . .'

'Oh, stuff!'

'Netta, I wasn't present at the examination.'

'Innis?'

'Of course not. We aren't related to the girl. You can't expect a doctor, even an old friend like Kirkhope, to betray a patient's confidence.'

'A hint, he must have given you a hint.'

Gillies had knitted the story together with Innis's collusion, two adults concocting a lily-white lie to protect a child. They had done rather well for tyros, apparently: Janetta was certainly convinced. The citizens of Crove would surely accept Fay as the victim of a sexual assault and, embarrassed, would leave her more or less alone. All he had to do now was remove the last vestige of doubt from Netta's mind. She would pass the information on to Mairi Ewing who would tell Maggie Naismith who would find some excuse for visiting Frances Hollander. Before too long the fiction would be half way round the island.

'Hmm,' he said.

'Hmm — what?' Janetta said. 'Did Dr Kirkhope tell you that she had been the victim of an attack?' She got to her feet. For an instant Gillies thought she intended to take him by the ear and pinch an answer out of him. 'Come along, Daddy. Did he or did he not tell you?'

'Innis was upset.'

Janetta emitted a growl of dissatisfaction.

Gillies spread his hands. 'That's all I can say: Innis was upset.'

'And the girl, this Fay person, was she not upset?'

'Now she's here, hundreds of miles from where it happened, I think she feels she has to put it behind her.'

'Oh, stuff!' Netta said again. 'Won't he come after her, this man, this fiend?'

'I very much doubt it,' Gillies said. 'It wouldn't be logical, would it? He's probably exceedingly relieved to see the back of her. After all, even an innocent young woman like Fay Ludlow must represent a threat.'

'Ah! Yes,' Janetta conceded. 'Yes, I see what you mean. It's not as if he were in love with her. He just — just used her for his own despicable pleasure.'

'He won't pursue Fay. He doesn't even know where she is.'

'She wasn't so daft coming to Mull, was she?'

'Not daft at all,' said Gillies.

And there it was: fiction made fact.

By Monday the whole village would know that Fay Ludlow had been the victim of an unspeakable crime and, Gillies thought smugly, the tale would soon spread out to Dervaig and the farms of Mishnish and Calgary, down as far as Ulva or across to Salen, and whenever two or three women and an occasional man met and talked, in Gaelic or in English, Fay Ludlow's personal history would be revised and recreated and no one would dream that she was really Gavin Tarrant's wife.

'You did the right thing, Daddy,' Janetta told him. 'The sensible thing.'

'Nothing if not sensible, that's me.' Gillies paused then said, 'By the way, dear, you won't tell anyone what I've just told you, will you?'

'Would I betray a confidence?' said Janetta, outraged.

'Of course you wouldn't,' Gillies said, and just before his daughter struck a match to light the lamp on the mantel shelf, managed to stifle his grin.

It had been thirteen weeks since her last bleeding. She had suffered none of the sickness that had blighted buxom Marian Kellow's pregnancy in its early months. Apart from a not unpleasant pricking sensation in her breasts she felt not one bit different. She'd had little to do with Marian Kellow before or after Marian's baby was born, however, and what she knew of pregnancy applied more to ewes than women. She might, she supposed, have asked Marian, wife of the shepherd from Peterswell, what signs to look out for, but in her latter days on the Edge she had trusted no one, for she had known only too well what Gavin would do to her if she dared discuss 'her business' with outsiders.

In the early mornings before Innis or Becky got up she would slip into the stone-floored alcove off the kitchen where the wash-tubs were. She would close the door, strip off her clothes and carefully prod her small, conical breasts to see if her milk glands were swelling. She examined herself below stairs too, not the fading yellow bruises on her thighs or the jagged scars on her leg but the curve of her belly, wondering if she really was growing fatter or if it was only her imagination at work. Out in the March winds at Pennypol or in the countryside around Pennymain, however, she was convinced that she could feel a quickening in her belly and thanked God that she was safe in a house of women, far removed from Gavin and the cottage on the lime-stone edge.

In a gloomy big room in the house on the hill above the town where Innis's friend Mr Brown had taken her, the doctor with the craggy face and eyebrows like white parsley had examined her thoroughly. She had been tempted to question him about her condition but had decided to keep quiet a while longer, to deal with one thing at a time. She had said nothing about pregnancy, therefore, while the doctor examined her face and her ill-knit leg and, tutting, gently raised her foot and turned it this way and that. He had asked her who had attended her after her fall and when she had told him 'No one' he had shaken his head and muttered, 'Dear God! Dear God!' as if he thought that all shepherds, or all Englishmen, were barbarians.

She had grown used to limping, to the pains that stabbed her kneecap and ran down her calf like rivulets of scalding hot water. She had adjusted to having to squint out of the blackened eye. She chose not to associate these relics of pain with Gavin or anything that Gavin had done to her, to regard them almost as acts of God, little punishments, little markers that would by some miracle turn into emblems of forgiveness.

It had been Innis's decision not to inform Becky that she, Fay, was Gavin's wife. Becky could barely remember her brother. None the less, she shared his blood and perhaps his character and, like Gavin, always seemed to be a half-step ahead of herself.

Fortunately her job at the big house kept her away all day and Fay saw her only at breakfast and suppertime.

Immediately after breakfast Fay walked over the ridge to Pennypol. She carried a ball of twine, a spade and the hoe that Innis had allowed her to take from the shed. She was eager to get to work; there was good soil under the turf, light enough to be manageable but not so sandy that it would wash away in heavy rains or so thickly packed that it would resist the spade. She had no notion how she would obtain manure, however, for the dung heaps she'd spied on her excursions were unventilated and undoubtedly earmarked for field dressing.

The old plots were surrounded by rusty snarls of wire and broken posts that cattle and sheep had all but rubbed away. There was about an eighth of an acre here, Fay calculated, with more useful ground between the shoreline and the corner of the old calf pasture. Using a pencil stump and an oilcloth-backed notebook that she'd brought from Fream, it didn't take her long to calculate that a garden of this size would demand no more than an average of one man-hour a day to keep in trim. She also reckoned that if she could reclaim another eighth of an acre, say, then she could increase the number of plots from four to eight and make space for fruit bushes and a strawberry bed.

It was all so different from the gardens at Fream which had been laid down a century ago, were defended against prevailing winds by coppices of oak and elm and regiments of privet and beech and had walls and trellises drenched in greengage, plum and apricot, knitted together with honeysuckle and sweet verbena. There would be no room for such sweet profusion here, Fay told herself, no energy to waste on permanence or prettiness.

Concerned about the raking winds that came in from the sea, she decided to plump for vegetables that required no glass or heat in the first stages. She would start with early potatoes, lettuces, broccoli and beetroot before she worked up the back plots for carrots, sprouts and cauliflower. She paced the ground again, staked it with driftwood, straightened the edges and edged out the turf so neatly that she could almost visualise the garden as it would be at summer's end, could almost smell the pungent aroma of leeks and onion sets, the healthy stench that summer-hearted cabbage gave off when wetted by rain. Before that could come about, though, she would need dressings and seeds, for the pouches that Josh had given her had no planting value at all. And she could not afford to delay, not with March, first of the seven growing months, running fast before her.

She slid the spade into the scanty turf with a satisfaction that had been denied her during the months of her marriage. She had taken her turn with the hay like the rest of Cloudhill's servants and had knelt in the long rows with the harvesters when the late potato crop came in, but being a field-hand was not the same as being a gardener's girl and it was not until Gavin had carried her off into the bleak uplands that she had realised how much the orchards had meant to her.

She had ground now, plenty of ground to work with. And if it was sour she would sweeten it, if it was wet she would drain it. And if it would not yield fruit she would plant root crops. And if not root crops then stems or bulbs or legumes. Something, anything to prove to the Tarrants that she could be useful, to justify herself to the Tarrants and to the Quigleys too.

And she *would* do it, would do it with a baby in her belly or a baby on her back. Whatever Gavin had done to her he had failed to smother the green resilient part that responded to the needs of the earth.

Singing quietly to herself, Fay set about preparing the plots for seed.

Maggie Naismith drove the pony-trap that carried the ladies out to The Ards where Mrs Frances Hollander had laid on an afternoon tea for her friends. Maggie had no difficulty in obtaining use of the trap, for her brother, Angus Bell, had once been horseman on Fetternish and still hired out horses to the estate. Angus was now the proprietor of a livery stable in Crove where he employed two boys and a blacksmith and took a keen interest in internal combustion engines on the off chance that some day someone in the neighbourhood might suddenly decide to purchase a motor-car.

There was precious little purchasing of anything going on in Crove in the spring of 1908, however, and there was no cash to spare for new-fangled luxuries. Besides, the roads of the north quarter were in such deplorable condition that only a lunatic would contemplate importing a motor-car from the mainland; so Angus continued to dream his oily dreams and his sister Maggie continued to borrow the Fetternish trap now and then to drive her friends down the narrow peninsula to Frances Hollander's house at The Ards.

The Ards was not so grand as Fetternish. It was snug and sturdy, though, with thick stuccoed walls and square, lead-paned windows. Old Mrs Lafferty, Frances's mother, had 'apartments' on the upper floor where she dwelled unseen and unheard, though, according to Frances, she was still a game old stick in spite of being an invalid. She, the mother, had lived in Paris and Vienna and had travelled extensively in America with her second husband, Macklin Lafferty, owner of a publishing house in Boston. Maggie was much impressed. Even Janetta, an avid reader, was a little dazzled by Frances's literary connections, though she had never heard of Macklin Lafferty or any of his publications.

For the schoolteacher, the housekeeper and the minister's wife, however, every invitation to The Ards was ripe with the promise – never so far realised – that the grand old lady would grace the tea-table and might be persuaded to tell tales of the fabulous continent which, a half-century ago, had swallowed up so many emigrants from Mull that Maggie was convinced that half the folk in America must be distant relatives. Frances did not disillusion her. Although she was inclined to boast on her mother's behalf, Frances seldom talked of the places *she* had visited or the sights *she* had seen, and on the subject of marriage she remained reticent to the point of rudeness.

The servants at The Ards were young and pretty. Florence had been a pastry-cook in London before Frances had lured her into service, Valerie a maid in a country-house in Staffordshire. Their unfamiliar accents added a sedate quality to the serving of tea; and rosewood furniture. Queen Anne cabinets and the animal-skin rugs on the floor fair put the poor old manse to shame.

'The Ludlow girl, have you seen her yet, Margaret?' Frances began.

'Not a sniff,' Maggie answered. 'She keeps herself to herself at Pennypol.'

'Digging, so I've heard,' said Mairi.

'Making a garden,' said Maggie.

'Did Rebecca tell you that?' said Frances.

'Rebecca is not happy.'

'Well, indeed,' said Janetta, 'can you blame her? After all, how would you like a cuckoo settling in your nest?'

'Do they share a bed?' said Frances.

'Pardon?' said Maggie.

'Pennymain is rather cramped, is it not?'

'You know,' said Maggie, 'I never thought to ask about that.'

'Perhaps she shares with Innis,' Mairi suggested.

'That would hardly be the thing, would it?' said Frances.

'Wouldn't it?' said Mairi, uncertainly.

'Nothing wrong with two young girls sharing sleeping quarters,' Frances said. 'I mean, it's done in the best households, at least in the servants' wing.'

'Wing?' said Maggie.

'Doesn't Fetternish have wings?' said Frances.

'Of course it does,' said Janetta. 'Haven't you seen them, Frances?'

'I have never been invited to Fetternish.'

'Oh!' Janetta recoiled slightly. 'I'd have thought Biddy would have made some effort to meet you. She used to be so hospitable.'

'We have met, of course,' said Frances.

'At the manse,' said Mairi.

'Once,' said Frances.

'Have you not invited Biddy here?' Janetta said.

'On several occasions,' Frances answered with a shrug of her round little shoulders. 'Only to be turned down.'

'Good Lord!' said Janetta. 'That isn't like Biddy.'

'There is no money in the house now for entertaining,' Maggie blurted out. 'In the old days she would be having parties and the picnics and fetching folk back after Sabbath to sing and play the piano. That is all over now. Ever since the Baverstock-Pauls' mill was sold Biddy has to sell her wool at market price, just like everyone else.'

'Did Willy tell you this?' said Mairi.

'Willy did not have to be telling me anything,' said Maggie. 'It is as plain as the nose upon your face what has happened.'

'Did Mrs Quigley make nothing from the sale for the mill?' said Frances.

'She accepted a payment below the table.'

'Below the table?' Frances said. 'What does that mean?'

'When it looked as if the Baverstock-Pauls would go into liquidation and Biddy might be dragged into court and forced to sell off Fetternish to pay creditors she accepted a low offer for her parcel of shares. Willy, I think, recommended it.'

'If Willy did, Willy was right.' Mairi said.

'My father doesn't think so,' Janetta said.

'Well, it is true that the manufactory was finally sold as a going concern and the Baverstock-Pauls did not have to face court proceedings,' Maggie said, 'but then neither did Biddy.'

'Well, well, well,' said Frances. 'It's all frightfully interesting. I had no idea that poor Mrs Quigley had faced up to ruin.'

'Ruin?' said Janetta. 'There are worse things to face up to than the loss of a few hundred pounds, Frances. I would not be calling it "ruin". After all, there's still the house, still some rent coming in. She might still do what you've done and sell off some acres for tree planting.'

'Huff! There's no money in that,' said Frances airily. 'I simply sold off ground that had become a burden. What do I want with six hundred acres of undrained moorland? Let Mr Rattenbury get on with planting his pines. I will be long gone before he reaps his harvest.'

'Long gone?' Janetta frowned. 'Are you planning on leaving us, Frances?'

'Leave Mull, leave The Ards? Certainly not. I mean that I will be *dead* and gone before Mr Rattenbury's tree are mature enough to fell.' Frances smiled and with a lisping sweetness that sounded almost loving, said, 'If I did leave Mull, Netta dear, would you miss me?'

'We all would,' said Mairi promptly.

'Indeed, we would,' said Maggie.

Janetta did not answer.

There was something behind the question that she could not put her finger on, something in the lingering glance that Frances gave her, something odd and unexplored that Netta did not wish to examine just yet. She looked from the window at the lawns, at a lump of hillside speckled with rain. It was the sort of nondescript afternoon that made her wish she was far from Crove and Fetternish and the suffocating rural morality that had grown up around her as remorselessly as one of Mr Rattenbury's forests of foreign spruce and pine.

'Netta?' Frances said. 'Don't look so sad.'

'She always looks sad,' said Mairi. 'Even when she was a little girl she was always far too sober for her own good.'

'You didn't know me when I was a little girl,' Janetta said.

'I meant in your youth.'

'I'm not old now, Mairi,' Janetta reminded her. 'I am not old yet.'

'Of course you're not,' Frances Hollander said. 'Why, dearest, you're hardly much older than I am,' and lifting the silver bell from the side of her plate, rang it to summon one of the servant girls with fresh tea and lemon cake.

CHAPTER FOUR

The New Leaf

Her old master had held prayers every morning for field-hands as well as servants. He would trot out of the rear door of the mansion, prayer book in hand, and assemble them under the awning at the end of the rose garden. He would read them a passage of Scripture and have them recite the Lord's Prayer, then he would bless them, hands raised, the tassels of his prayer book fluttering like the wings of a butterfly. On wet days he would open the gunroom at the foot of the tower. In they would troop to perch on the lockers while he preached a little sermon about piety and progress and off they would go feeling if not uplifted at least grudgingly grateful to the old boy for bringing them in out of the rain.

Fay was ten when the old master had died and young Sir Johnny had inherited the estate. Morning prayers had gone by the board, lopped off without a word of explanation. All the religion they had had to go on then, Josh, the Mussons and she, had been Sunday services in the church at Fream. After she had married Gavin and had gone to live on the Edge there had been no religion at all. When the shepherds' wives came by for her on Sunday mornings Gavin would give them a mouthful of blasphemies and send them on their way. After a month or so of such rough treatment they had left Gavin and she alone.

On Mull there were no bells to summon her to worship, only the waves on the shore and the wail of the winds that buffeted the hillside above An h-Vaignich, which, she had learned, was the Gaelic name for the gully that backed Pennymain.

Innis had borrowed the dogcart and had set off for mass in the community hall in Glenarray. Becky had gone up to the big house, for, Sunday or not, Maggie would have need of help in case Biddy and Quig brought the minister and his wife back for lunch. It hurt Fay a little that Innis hadn't invited her to go with her to the chapel; she would not have objected to worshipping with Catholics which was better than not worshipping at all.

Worship, though, was not all Fay had in mind that Sunday morning. She had dug out all the Pennypol plots and needed fertiliser and seeds before she could begin planting. Necessity not loneliness spurred her to cross the wooden bridge that spanned the gully behind the cottage and follow the path to Fetternish House.

She took the dog with her. The spaniel would pop out of the bracken every now and then with a sneeze or a snuffle and a look of panic on his face until Fay called out, 'Go on, go on, boy,' then he would race up the path ahead of her. He waited for Fay at the top of the last hill, though, and glanced up at her, perplexed by his discovery of the tiered lawns and great stone walls of the house.

'Good dog.' Fay fondled his ears. 'Good boy. Stay with me now, stay close.'

The dog trotted at her heels as she crossed the skirt of the lawn to the door in the garden wall and nuzzled his nose into her palm when she came to a halt.

She stared up at the house, all solid and soaring above her. Gable windows, mean and narrow, were crowned by carved stone balustrades. There was a tower of sorts and battlements and a flagpole without a flag. Though it boasted all the trappings of a castle there was something spurious about the place which seemed to have been built not for fortification but for glorification and to claim a piece of history to which it was not entitled.

Fay cupped the spaniel's throat to hold him in check.

She unlatched the door in the wall and stepped into the garden.

Her first reaction was one of disappointment.

There were no gravel walks, no tiled edgings, only a network of turfed paths all muddy and scored and she looked in vain for cloches and cold frames. The shrubs that clung to the south wall were shrivelled and blighted and Ayrshire roses swarmed unchecked into the downy foliage of a Damask Perpetual that should have been pruned weeks ago. Unraked leaves had turned damp and rancid and cabbages and Brussels sprouts rotted forlornly in the sour ground. The only sign of abundant growth was a great dank bed of rhubarb.

'Oh dear!' Fay said, beneath her breath. 'Oh dear! Oh dear!'

Releasing the spaniel, she limped along the pathway by the wall, irked by the sight of so much neglect. If there had been tools – a spade, a rake, even a trowel – she would have set about repair work there and then but no tools were to be seen and no hut that might contain them.

'Good morning, Mrs Tarrant.'

She spun round. 'What? What did you say?'

'No need to shout, lass,' Willy Naismith told her. 'Old I may be but I'm not deaf.' He glanced at the woman who was seated on the bench at his side. 'And Aileen here has such a fine pair of lugs on her that she can hear the seals bark out on the Treshnish. Is that not so, Aileen?'

'Aye, Willy,' the woman said, and giggled.

The bench was tucked under a shelf built out from the wall close to a breast-high gate, screened by a little evergreen, that led into the kitchen yard. The old man, the woman and the bench seemed all of a piece. They had found – or conjured up – a patch of sunlight and the woman's brown, unblemished face was upturned, her gaze fixed on the source of the light.

Fay realised that this must be Aileen, youngest of Ronan Campbell's daughters, the aunt who wasn't quite right in the head. But Aileen Campbell displayed none of the pathetic innocence of the silly boy or the poor, nodding girl who had come to Fream with the potato-pickers every September and even before she opened her mouth Fay sensed that she was dangerously embroiled in her own condition and inexplicably proud of it.

'Don't you remember me?' Willy asked.

'I do, sir. You're Mr Naismith. You were the steward of this house once.'

'I am still,' said Willy, 'nominally at any rate. This lady is Aileen Campbell.' He patted the woman's knee with a gnarled hand. 'Will you not be saying How-Do-You-Do to Mrs Tar—'

'I'm Fay Ludlow now, sir.'

'Aye, of course you are. I've heard the stories that are being put about. Very inventive some of them.'

'Mrs Tarrant seems to think they are necessary.'

'I couldn't agree more,' said Willy. 'He was a surly youngster, your husband. He shot Quig, you know, and damned near killed him.'

'I haven't heard the whole story yet,' said Fay.

'No story. It's the solemn truth,' said Willy. 'Damned near killed him with a blast from a shotgun. It was Donnie, Aileen's son, Gavin was after but fortunately Quig managed to get in the way. Don't go thinking it was an accident. Gavin stole that shotgun and stalked his cousin as deliberately as he might have stalked a deer.'

Aileen, face still tilted skywards, appeared uninterested in the conversation.

'Are you not going to ask me why?' Willy added.

Fay shrugged. 'Resentment?'

'Call it resentment if you like,' Willy said. 'Rage might be more accurate. If you ask me he was just born bad, that one. Mark you, if you'd ever met his grandfather, old Ronan, you wouldn't have far to look for a reason. Know a lot about gardens, do you, lass?'

'A little,' Fay said, then added, 'more than a little.'

She was not unnerved by his questions, for old though he was Willy Naismith still managed to convey a rough masculine charm.

'What do you need?' he said. 'What have you come here to find?'

'Seeds,' Fay said. 'And fertiliser.'

He took one hand from the walking-stick and scratched the point of his nose lightly. 'Is it your intention to turn Pennypol green again?'

'I don't see why not, Mr Naismith. It's rich and fertile ground.'

'That's as may be,' Willy said. 'The point is, whose ground is it?'

'Pardon?'

'Come now, lass, land always has an owner. Pennypol is no exception.'

'Mrs Tarrant – Innis is the owner?'

'Did Gavin tell you that?'

'Gavin never told me who owned anything.' She gave a soft, surprised laugh. 'Now that I think of it he talked as if Fetternish belonged to him.'

Willy shifted on the bench.

Aileen opened one eye and glanced at him.

'Michael Tarrant was always a great one for coveting land,' Willy said. 'It galled him that even after he married Innis he couldn't find a way of tearing off a piece of Fetternish for himself.'

'And Pennypol?'

'It is part of Fetternish now.'

'Oh!'

The woman kept one eye open, as if mention of Pennypol had brought her back from the dream world. The unblinking blue eye in the weathered face seemed sinister and knowing. For a moment Fay was almost as afraid of Aileen Campbell as she had been of Gavin.

'Don't mind her,' Willy said. 'She can't help it. Besides, you may have more in common with poor wee Aileen than you know.'

'What do you mean?'

'Campbell men,' Willy said, 'are brutes, some of them at least. It wasn't Gavin but his grandfather that ruined Aileen. I don't mean he spoiled her. I mean ruined her. He destroyed her wits with his cruelty.' He lifted his shoulders, thin as wicker under a loose Ulster cape. 'However, you'll not have come here to dig at the roots of the family tree. We'll talk instead about Pennypol and how you can find the money to buy what you need.'

'It would be a wise investment for someone. I just don't know who that would be.' She shifted her weight on to her knee and felt a stab of pain in the ends of the bones, a reminder of who she was and what had brought her here. She looked round as the spaniel came trotting up and made water against the leaves of a giant genista that had taken root in a corner near the bench. 'I want nothing for myself,' she went on. 'I need a roof, a bed and feeding but I'm not out to make profit.'

'Profit?' said Willy.

'From the sale of the produce.'

'Where will you sell the produce?'

'At the market.'

'What market?'

'In Crove.'

'There's no market in Crove.'

'In – in Dervaig, is it?'

'There's no market in Dervaig either.'

'Well, Tobermory . . .'

'It's not fish you're selling,' Willy told her. 'You can't sling a sack of potatoes or a parcel of cauliflower on to the pier wall and start crying your wares. Nobody's interested in vegetables. Most folk either grow what they need or trade with neighbours. You'd do well to bear in mind that this isn't the heart of England. We fill our baskets, and our bellies, from the fields not the garden, from the sea not the larder. There is no ready market here for anything.'

'What about Oban?'

'Possibly, but ferry rates are high, even for small cargo.'

Fay pursed her lips. The old man was right. She had come unprepared. She should have paid more attention when Josh and Mr Musson and Sir Johnny had discussed marketing matters. She might know a great deal about plants, seeds and soil but she knew nothing about managing money.

'Doubts, Miss Ludlow?' Willy said.

'I've dug out the plots. They're ready for seeding.'

'So I've heard,' said Willy.

'Who told you?'

'My wife.'

'I don't know your wife.'

'No, but she knows you,' Willy said. 'At least she knows as much about you as any of us. Becky tells her everything.'

'I was under the impression that Becky had no interest in me.'

'Oh, Becky is very interested in you. We are all of us interested in you. You're a fine bit of diversion in a place where not much happens.' Willy scratched the tip of his nose again. 'You mustn't hold our curiosity against us. It can be made to work to your advantage.' He leaned forward. 'Listen carefully, lass: Pennypol belongs to Fetternish by right of lease from Innis who survives on the income from small rents and investments but Biddy, on the other hand, has poured all her profits back into Fetternish.

You wouldn't think so to look at it but Biddy's spent a fortune on land improvements over the years.'

'Why then is it so run down?'

'Markets,' Willy said. 'The poor price for the wool crop, foreign imports and, of course, this bloody island itself.' When he hunched his shoulders under the loose cape Fay thought that he looked like some big, rather ugly bird. 'Mull will devour you if you're not careful. It has no heart, no gratitude. It takes what is given to it but gives little in return.'

Fay raised an eyebrow. 'What do you mean?'

Willy dismissed his own fancy. 'Rubbish, I'm talking. Listen, are you here to see about seed or are you not?'

'I am.'

'Well, Quig's your man. Quig's the one you'll have to talk round. At least you're not some damned speculator who wants to coat the island with spruce trees.' He struggled to his feet, leaning into the stick. Aileen rose too, as if she were attached to him by a hinge. 'Talk to Quig. He hasn't entirely forgotten the days when there was still some breath left in these islands.'

The spaniel lay, chin on paws, at Fay's feet as if the unfamiliar scents of the garden had finally overwhelmed him. She could smell wild onions among the rot, and lavender. Lavender at this time of the year?

'Where is Mr Quigley?' she asked.

'At church with the rest of them.'

'When will he be back?'

'About one o'clock or half past.'

'I will make an appointment to see him then,' Fay said.

'No,' said Willy. 'Tomorrow will be time enough. You'll find him in the factor's office at the back of the house about half past eight o'clock.'

'The factor's office?' Fay said. 'It's to be business, is it?'

'Strictly business,' Willy said. 'Are you ready for it?'

'I'm ready for it,' Fay said, then limped off down the turf walk with the drowsy little spaniel trailing at her heels.

At the door in the wall she turned to thank Mr Naismith for his advice but he and the sinister sister had vanished as if they'd never been there at all.

Becky's gloss on national affairs derived mainly from the pages of the *Manchester Guardian*. The cost of the newspaper subscription consumed a fair portion of the miserable wage that Aunt Biddy paid her but she spent little on clothes and was so adept with needle and thread that make-do-and-mend was more hobby than necessity. The *Guardian* was well worth the sacrifice, Becky reckoned: its articles and editorials fed her sense of injustice. When she dreamed of life on the mainland it was not as housekeeper or wife to a prosperous businessman but as a starving factory worker with pinched features and bitten finger-nails, one of the oppressed masses who might one day rise up and overthrow the government.

Willy did not read the *Guardian*. Willy read *The Times*. It arrived on Mull earlier than the Manchester paper, only two days after publication, and he usually managed to snaffle the household copy before Biddy could lay hands on it. Willy was therefore primed and ready to tease the young cook while she peeled potatoes, pounded on a tough piece of beef or stripped the bones from a cod-fish with a thin-bladed knife. More than once the thin-bladed knife had been wagged angrily in Willy's face, for Becky, though smart, was not smart enough to realise that what the mischievous old Tory roused in her was a passion not of the intellect but of the imagination.

At root Becky was uninterested in the plight of the rural poor or the fate of Scotland as a nation. She was dazzled by the romance of poverty and believed that it could only really be found in soot-smudged Midland towns or the blackened slums of the north of England. Since she had no first-hand knowledge of deprivation she could make what she willed of it and nothing Willy could say would shake her faith in the realities of capitalist oppression.

What riled Becky most in that March month, however, was not Willy Naismith's resistance to proposed social reform or his suggestions that militant suffragettes were little better than ill-mannered louts but Maggie's persistent questions about 'the new arrival'.

The new arrival, the new arrival: Maggie went on and on about the new arrival as if Fay Ludlow had turned up in a basket on the doorstep or been found in the reeds on the shores of Loch Frisa. The nag, nag, wheedle, wheedle, wheedle of Maggie in full flow was more than Becky could endure and Maggie was lucky not to have the thin-bladed knife wagged in her face too, a reaction that might have cost Becky her job, for Maggie was a mainstay of the household, unlike Willy who was regarded as a bit of a clown now and a general all-round nuisance. Maggie's persistent questioning pointed up just how narrow and provincial life in Crove could be and brought home to Becky that this house, this island were far too small to hold a girl of vision and awakening conscience much longer, even if her mother did need to be looked after which, in fact, she was beginning to doubt.

Biddy and Quig were no longer wealthy. The lines of demarcation between servant and master had sagged and slackened. It was not unusual for Quig to eat his dinner off the kitchen table, for Biddy to take a trot round the hall with a feather duster or help Maggie turn mattresses and make beds. Life in Fetternish House, Becky reckoned, was little better these days than a version of cottage life writ large. And it startled her to encounter scraps of the style that Aunt Biddy had once aspired to and which she as a child had accepted as perfectly normal: a rare formal dinner party, for instance, when Biddy donned her silks and adorned herself with the few trinkets that remained in her jewellery box and Quig shoe-horned himself into a dress coat and gleaming pumps and smoked a whole cigar in the library afterwards while Maggie and she, unaided, washed up the dinner dishes in the kitchen sinks downstairs.

Times had changed so radically that Becky did not know quite who or what she was supposed to be, whether she was more servant than relative or vice versa. Rachel, though, had known from an early age that one day she would leave Fetternish and settle on the mainland. 'Come with me,' Rachel had urged. 'Train as a nurse. It's a good life for a young woman and it pays moderately well, you know.' But for all her idealism, nursing in a Glasgow hospital was a dimension of reality that Becky's imagination could not quite encompass.

Fay Ludlow's arrival put matters into perspective, however.

Fay Ludlow slept on the floor of the kitchen, ate with her fingers, washed without soap and limped out before dawn to study the sky, as if she understood something that she, Becky, had not yet grasped, something that was not of the mind or the spirit but lay deeper, without boundary, in the soul.

Becky envied Fay Ludlow her cheerful disposition and resented her stoicism, her sense of purpose and, most of all, her secrets which, Becky felt, were bogus. Spurred on by Maggie's questioning, she decided to test her theory against the truth one Sunday evening when Fay and she found themselves alone.

'Where's my mother?' Becky began. 'Hasn't she come back yet?'

'Not yet,' Fay answered. 'She said she might have to drive Father O'Donnell to Tobermory. He has another mass there in the evening and—'

'Yes, yes,' Becky said. 'I know all about Father O'Donnell's itinerary.'

'The pony has to be rested.'

'What pony? Oh, that pony. Yes, I know about the pony too.'

'I've made some tea. It's fresh in the pot,' Fay said. 'I'd have cooked supper too but I wasn't sure what you'd want.'

'I'll wait for Mother, thank you.'

'What if she goes to call on Mr Brown?'

'What if she does?' said Becky.

'I just thought you might be hungry.'

'Well, I'm not.'

Becky removed her overcoat and hung it neatly in the alcove to the right of the door. Fay's coat was there too, hanging limp and tawdry and as lopsided as the girl herself. She had an impulse to tear it down, toss it at the girl and order her out, order her back to Derbyshire. Fay did not seem put out by her scolding tone and that in itself was a mark against her. The girl was too humble, too ingratiating and obsequious to be genuine. Becky suddenly decided to change her tune and when Fay offered her the teacup accepted it with a smile and said, 'Who shall we drink to, Fay? Who shall we toast?'

'I don't know what you mean.'

'Shall we drink to my brother?' Becky said.

'Your brother?'

'Gavin — my brother, your husband.'

'Oh!'

'Shall we?'

'If you don't mind, I'd rather not,' Fay said. 'Who told you?'

'I guessed.'

'I wanted to tell you but your aunt insisted on keeping it secret.'

'Huh!' Becky said. 'Yes, family pride and all that. You were never raped, were you?'

'Raped?' said Fay. 'No.'

'Who cooked up that disgusting story?' Becky said. 'I mean, honestly, how long did you think I would be taken in by that pathetic lie?'

'I believe your mother intended to tell you quite soon.'

The spaniel had been dozing in his basket in the stone shed

off the kitchen but he was awake now and stood in the darkened doorway staring at her. Becky stared back, defying him to bark, and after a moment he clicked across the floor and lay down meekly in front of the fire.

Becky said, 'How long were you married to my brother?'

'Twenty-six months.'

'Did you love him?'

'I did at first but I don't think he ever loved me.'

'Why did he marry you then?'

'He needed a wife to get a job.'

'Shepherd?'

'Yes.'

'Tell me about my father.'

'I can't,' Fay said. 'I never met him and Gavin said little about him.'

'Odd,' Becky said. 'I always thought that they were close.'

'Perhaps they had a falling out.'

'Over you?'

'Oh, no, no,' said Fay, and repeated, 'I never met him.'

'What's he like?'

'Gavin? He's – he's . . .'

'You don't have to be embarrassed. I can hardly remember him. I'm not going to contradict you even if you tell me he's a monster.'

'Not a monster, no,' Fay said. 'He has a temper, though.'

Becky said, 'My dada had a temper too. I don't remember him very well, though, just that he used to shout at us. Where did you and Gavin live?'

Fay told her sister-in-law about the isolated cottage under the limestone edge. She chose her words with care: the way Becky sat at the table with her chin resting on her knuckles was uncannily reminiscent of Gavin.

'Why are you looking at me like that?'

'Like what?' Fay said.

'As if you were sorry for me?'

77

'I didn't realise – I mean, I didn't intend . . .'

'You're the one who sleeps on the floor,' Becky said.

'What does that have to do with anything?'

'I've never had to sleep on the floor.'

'I don't mind sleeping on the floor.'

'It's demeaning, though. Don't you think it's demeaning? We'll have to find you a proper bed. I mean, I can't allow my sister-in-law to sleep on the floor.'

In spite of the girl's sweet, placatory words, the hand on the table had contracted into a fist. Fay was adept at reading such small signs, for living with Gavin had taught her much. She did not want to quarrel with Becky. She liked living at Pennymain and had no objection to sleeping on a mattress on the kitchen floor. By the time of the harvest month, however, she would have a child of her own to consider and she was afraid that the baby's arrival would make Becky even more hostile than she was now.

'Quig will have a spare cot somewhere.' Becky said. 'I'll ask him to dig it out and cart it down here.'

'Thank you,' Fay said, 'but . . .'

Becky shot to her feet, possessed by the queer, quirky energy that Fay had observed in Gavin, a frightening, purposeful energy that reminded her not of an animal but of a mechanical device or instrument whose workings she did not comprehend. 'There are no "buts" about it,' Becky said. 'I'll have a word with Quig first thing in the morning.'

It was on the tip of Fay's tongue to inform her sister-in-law that she would be speaking to Robert Quigley herself tomorrow morning, but she thought better of it.

'Quig knows all about you, I take it?' Becky said.

Fay nodded. 'Yes, Mr Quigley knows who I am.'

'That's good,' said Becky. 'That'll save me all sorts of tedious explanations,' and turning her back on Fay, set about making supper as if her life depended on it.

＊　　＊　　＊

'I hear,' Quig said, 'that you are looking for a bed?'

'Becky told you?'

'Aye. She seems quite taken with the idea of having a sister-in-law.'

'I'm not so sure about that, sir.'

Though the wood-panelled office was gloomy Fay felt comfortable there. Sacks of grass seed were stacked in corners. Calendars and charts were pinned to the walls and the desk was littered with papers and catalogues. The smell really put her at ease: Quig's office smelled exactly like the cubby where Mr Musson kept his logs and planned the planting year ahead and she was only slightly disconcerted by the collection of stuffed animals that mouldered on the upper shelves and the array of stags' heads and antlers that protruded from the panelling.

'My wife used to shoot,' Quig said. 'Very good at it she was. But none of those trophies is hers. They came with the house, I think, and were probably bought as a job lot at auction. They look as if they have been dead for a very long time, do they not?'

'They do, sir, they do.'

The only light came from a rectangular window high on the outer wall. If the room had been warmer it would have been a perfect place for germination, Fay thought. She could smell a malty odour from the seeds sacks: oats or mixed grass, or barley perhaps. On a muddy canvas tarpaulin on the floor were four or five slices of peat, each with a ferny green sprout rising from it.

Mr Quigley was watching her carefully. He was dark-haired, dark-eyed and his tanned complexion suggested that he was not a man who spent much time indoors. He wore a striped flannel shirt and a quilted waistcoat that had seen better days. His hands, even in the half-light, looked slender and sensitive. He's a cautious person, Fay thought, but one who will listen to reason.

'Are those young trees?' she asked.

'Yes, seedlings. Norwegian spruce fir.'

'Do you intend to plant trees on Fetternish?'

'Perhaps.'

'It takes a long time to make profits from tree plantations.'

'Do you know a lot about trees then, Miss Ludlow?'

'Very little,' Fay said. 'Orchards, fruit orchards, but not forests.'

He nodded. The movement seemed to take a considerable time. She could readily understand why Biddy had chosen this man to be her second husband. He reminded Fay just a little of Josh. For an instant she experienced a pang of homesickness for Fream, where she'd been so carefree and protected. When she looked up at Robert Quigley, though, her homesickness turned into a soft pang of yearning.

'How do you find Mull?' Quig said. 'It must be very different from John Yeates's market garden in Derbyshire.'

'It is, but I expect I'll get used to it in time.'

'Used to being on your own?'

'I am not on my own, sir.'

'You have been working on your own, have you not?'

'Oh, that!' Fay said. 'Did Becky tell you that, too?'

He gave a little cough that might have been laughter.

'Becky would hardly be noticing if you planted cotton from here to Gometra,' he said. 'Willy Naismith told me that you want to grow vegetables in commercial quantities. Is that the truth?'

'Yes, sir.'

'Pennypol will not yield the best of crops.'

'It has yielded crops before, I'm told.'

'Vassie had a kitchen garden there,' said Quig. 'Potatoes and onions, mostly. I am sure that you have something much more ambitious in mind.'

'It would be as well to start simple.'

'What would you need,' Quig asked, 'to start simple?'

He was seated in a chair with wooden arms and a curved leather back that was almost worn through in places. It creaked when he leaned against it.

'Medium dressing,' Fay said, 'rather a lot of it.'

'What do you think of our garden here at the house?'

'She hesitated then said, 'More could be done with it.'

'Aye, a great deal more,' Quig said. 'What does that tell you about the state of affairs on Fetternish?'

'That you are short-handed.'

'That is it in a nutshell,' Quig said. 'Back a year or two we had labour for the asking, but the new trades' rules apply just as much to country labourers as they do to factory workers. We can still find cheap labour when the tinkers come round, but the tinks do not come to Fetternish now.'

'Why not?'

'Because they have never been fond of working with sheep and can make better deals elsewhere these days.'

Though he spoke slowly Quig was just as sharp as Willy Naismith and Fay was not sure that she could keep up with him.

'Do you see,' Quig went on, 'my problem? I can find a few pounds to purchase plants and anything else you might need to make a garden at Pennypol. But that will not be enough, will it? There is the garden here and ground at An Fhearann Cáirdeil that might be cultivated. But we are all workers here, not dabblers, and there is no labour to spare.'

'I hope you don't think I'm a dabbler, Mr Quigley.'

'I do not know what you are,' he said. 'I might be willing to put out a bit of cash to find out but I cannot be giving you an extra pair of hands to help you do it.'

'What about Billy?'

'Billy Barrett? What about him?'

'Could he not help?' Fay said. 'In summer he will have time to spare.'

'Billy is a shepherd.'

'That's not what he says.'

Quig paused. 'So you have been making friends already, have you now?'

'Billy came to me,' said Fay. 'I did not seek him out.'

'You're a girl,' Quig said, 'an attractive young woman, and

Billy – well, he is reaching that age when . . . No, Billy is needed
for the lambing.'

'And after the lambing?'

'School, three terms of school in Oban next year.'

'And what will he do then?'

'Whatever he can.'

'Here on Mull?'

'You are not going to save Fetternish by growing vegetables,
you know.'

'Are cabbages not better than trees?'

He laughed aloud. 'By God, do not be telling me that you are
another reformer like your sister-in-law. I thought you came here
to ask me for help?'

Fay laughed too. 'I did, Mr Quigley. I did. It's just that – well,
in Fream the boys do not leave until they marry and sometimes
not even then. I think it's sad that on Mull they have to go across
the sea just to find work.'

'That is the nature of the Highland economy, and a certain
turn of mind which you cannot be expected to understand. We
want to keep ourselves to ourselves but we also want to be
subsidised for being left alone.' He raised a finger, warningly.
'Do not repeat what I have just said to Becky, for she will bend
my ear with political theories and wind up blaming me for all
Mull's woes. My concern is to keep Fetternish together as a
paying proposition so that my children will have something to
inherit. There is a price to be paid for permanence, for clinging
to tradition, however, and that price is anxiety. Do you want me
to purchase the plants for you?'

'I would be obliged, Mr Quigley.'

'Make up a list of what you need.'

'Fertilisers too?'

'Everything.'

'For Pennypol, or for Fetternish?'

'You cannot cope with two plots.'

'I think I can, sir.'

'I hope' – he frowned before he went on – 'I hope that you are
not going to be running away from us the way you ran away from
Gavin Tarrant?'

'I was driven away, sir.'

'Because you did not get your own way?'

'Because there was no future in my marriage and I – I was
afraid.'

'In case you had children?'

'Yes,' Fay said quietly. 'If I'd had children . . .'

'Gavin would never have let you go, is that it?'

'I did not want them to be punished for my mistake.'

Quig was silent for a moment, looking up at the band of
sunlight in the window as if he felt an urgent need to be outside.
At length he said, 'Willy thinks that it was brave of you to leave
him.'

'What do you think, Mr Quigley?'

'Considering that I still have several old shotgun pellets buried
in my chest,' Quig said. 'I am more than inclined to agree with
Willy.'

He rose from the chair. He was, she saw now, younger than
Biddy. And she felt again an unwarranted desire to please him.
Trying not to blush, she rose too and shook out her drab skirts.
Her eye had started to water again in spite of the doctor's healing
drops and she rubbed at it with her wrist and then with her
handkerchief which only made it water all the more.

'Did Gavin really do that to you?' Quig asked.

'Yes.'

'And worse?'

'Yes, sir, and worse.'

'Do you know, Fay, I almost wish that he would come back
here – Gavin, I mean – that he would come here to look for you.'

'Please don't say that, Mr Quigley.'

'I would like to meet him again. Oh, yes, I would.' He seemed
about to say more but then, with a little grunt, he lowered his
head, extracted a sheaf of seed-merchants' catalogues from the

litter and handed them to her. 'Pick what you need. We deal with Dobbie's in Glasgow, who are very reliable, and with Carfin-layson's in Perth. There is a nursery of sorts out by Connel Ferry that I've heard well spoken of and, if the worst comes to the worst, we can send you over there to see for yourself.' He glanced up at the window again, at the sunlight swirling in the rectangular sky. 'I take it you know that Pennypol is under lease to Mrs Quigley and is in effect part of the Fetternish estate?'

'Yes, sir. I heard that.'

'I cannot pay you a wage, you know.'

'I know that too, Mr Quigley.'

'We will pay for any produce that we take for the house,' he said, 'but whatever is sold commercially will be counted as our profit. I doubt if Innis will charge you for room and board. If, however, she wishes to do so then we will either meet that charge or find other accommodation for you. That is the best offer I can make, Fay, until we see what weight of crop comes in. As for Billy Barrett, if he wishes to help you and his father can spare him then I have no objection. But, be warned, you won't see much of him until after lambing.'

'I understand, Mr Quigley.'

He came around the desk, brusque now, but not fierce. He put a hand on her arm and guided her towards the door.

'Mark off the quantities that you calculate you'll require and then give the lists back to me, or have Becky deliver them. I'll do the ordering for you.'

'Will it take long?'

'No, not long.'

He steered her along a stone-floored corridor away from the hallway that lay at the heart of the house. He opened a door and ushered her out into the sunlight. He continued to touch her very lightly, his palm resting against her shoulder-blade.

They paused on the shallow step and, together, scanned the sky.

'What will it do, Mr Quigley?' Fay asked.

'Do?'

'The weather, I mean.'

'Oh, it will be fine,' he said. 'A fine day ahead.'

'I hope so, sir,' Fay said, then, heart thumping, she left him to hurry off to Pennymain and share the good news with Innis.

CHAPTER FIVE

Out of The Nest

Easter fell in the middle of April. Barrett's flock of lambing ewes obligingly dropped on schedule and young Billy was kept busy pairing off twins, succouring orphans and scouring the heather for sagacious mothers who had taken to the hills rather than endure the indignities of midwifery once more.

The lambs provided company for Fay. Her days at Pennypol were long now that Quig had delivered plants, seed and fertiliser. From the plots she could see the sheep and the men who tended them. Now and then Muriel Barrett also put in an appearance and even Billy's young sisters had been taught how to lug the leggy little creatures without too much 'ooo-ing' and 'aaah-ing' and how to bottle-feed those who were sickly or whose mothers refused them the teat.

Fay enjoyed having Quig striding about close by and Billy crowned by a crook taller than he was. She would watch from a distance when Barrett pinned a ewe for a difficult delivery, a stark little tableaux against the skyline that usually ended with the feeble bleating of a newborn lamb and the deep, indignant baaa-ing of the ewe. Sometimes though she would look up, heart in her mouth, and no sound at all would flutter from the hill and a little grey carcass would be tossed aside for the gulls and crows to fall upon. And she would busy herself with the spade or the rake and not look up again until Barrett and Billy had gone.

In addition to the seeds and plants that she had requested, Quig had added netting, straw, and pea and bean sticks and she had quick-maturing lettuce and early potatoes planted before March was out.

Breaking ground was strenuous work and she fell into bed immediately after supper and was asleep long before Becky came into the room. Quig had found a camp cot and had personally carted it down to Pennymain. The cot had short folding legs and a dark-green canvas mattress so hard that Becky claimed it must be stuffed with sand. For some reason. Becky had readily agreed to the new sleeping arrangements and had even made room in her cupboard for Fay's few possessions.

So her first month on Mull passed swiftly. Her eye healed, the pains in her leg eased and she was happier than she had ever been. Occasionally she would pause to wonder why Mrs Quigley hadn't come down to Pennypol to inspect her work but she told herself that in the flying spring days there were probably too many other things going on for the lady of the house to be bothered with a mere gardening girl.

She had learned from Becky, for instance, that Biddy's children were due home for the Easter holidays and that Quig would be despatched to Oban to meet the train from Edinburgh and accompany them across to Mull on the steamer. She also heard that Rachel, Innis's elder daughter, still at the beck and call of the governors of the Victoria Infirmary, could not be sure until the very last moment when she would be released from her duties. There was some talk of Donnie, Aileen's son, visiting Fetternish too but in the end he decided to wait until summer.

Fay was eager to meet Rachel for she had heard a great deal about her. It had been eight months since Rachel had last been home for she had spent New Year with Donnie and his family in Glasgow rather than risk a crossing in unpredictable weather; unlike Gillies Brown's son and daughters who did not have the time, or money, to make the trip at all. Gillies, it seemed, had arranged to visit them in Glasgow at Easter and would leave

Janetta to occupy the schoolhouse on her own. There was certainly a holiday feeling in the air and the folk of the north quarter shared in it. There were 'trippers' in Tobermory and the first of the season's touring steamers could be seen rounding the point en route to Staffa and Iona. The bunting boats wafted faint strains of fiddle and accordion music across the waters and Fay would pause at her labours and wave her scarf at them, though whether the passengers could see her or not she had no way of knowing.

Fortunately Billy was not so tied up with lambing as all that. He would pop up from behind the wall to enquire what she was planting or, if he had a quarter of an hour to spare, would kneel beside her to help tamp down the onions and carrots.

From time to time he brought her a home-baked scone wrapped in a clean handkerchief or a square or two of sticky sugar candy. On Easter Day, a mite prematurely, he presented her with a hard-boiled hen's egg that he had painted himself. It was almost as if he were courting her, Fay thought. Indeed, if he had been older she would have been flattered by his attentions but Billy was still a boy and she was a woman who was carrying a child. She wondered how Billy would react when her belly became too big to hide under a baggy work-skirt or when, in September, she appeared with a baby in her arms.

Nevertheless, she carried the painted egg carefully in the pocket of her skirt as she trailed up the hill to the top of the ridge and followed the familiar path down to Pennymain. When she reached the cottage she found the door closed and Kilty lying sulking on the doorstep. He growled at Fay's approach, hoisted himself up and padded towards her, eager for attention. She petted the dog absently for a moment then knocked upon the door and waited for it to open.

The young woman was pale and tired-looking but much prettier than her sister. Somehow Fay had expected Rachel to be clad in a starched white cap and nurse's apron and she was rather taken aback by the fashionable hip-hugging skirt and floral blouse.

'Fay, you must be Fay.'

'I am.'

'I'm Rachel. My sister wrote to me about you. So you're my brother's wife.'

'I was,' Fay answered. 'I suppose I still am, really.'

'Come in.' Rachel stepped back a pace, then, to Fay's relief, fashioned a comical sweep of the arm. 'Enter, please do.'

The kitchen was filled with the rich aroma of roasting meat. Pots chuckled on the stove. Pans steamed on the hob. The table was covered with an embroidered cloth and set with the best rose-patterned china, a silver-plated cruet, a crystal water jug and decorated with posies of primroses and early daffodils.

Fay had never seen a scene quite so warm and welcoming and wished that it had been laid on for her, not Rachel.

'Here am I, practically a stranger, inviting you in,' Rachel said. 'What a cheek I've got. After all, it's more your house than mine, since I've been out of the nest and you've just come into it.' To Fay's astonishment, Rachel wrapped her arms about her and kissed her cheek. 'I doubt if my dear sister has done that, has she?'

'Nuh-no,' Fay admitted.

'Well, there you are,' said Rachel. 'That one will just have to do for both of us. Belated but sincere.' She studied Fay with disconcerting candour. 'You're not at all what I expected. I got the impression from Becky's letters that you were – perhaps I shouldn't say it.'

'I think I can guess what Becky says about me.'

'You're Gavin's wife, that's all that counts.' Rachel reached out and touched the crescent of bone above Fay's eye. 'He did that to you? What was he wearing? Knuckle-dusters?'

'No, just his . . .'

'It appears to be healing up rather nicely, though. What did Dr Kirkhope prescribe, drops or powders?'

'Drops.'

'Good, that's good,' Rachel said. 'I'm not surprised that my brother turned out to have a violent streak. I haven't seen him

since I was a little girl, of course, but I remember him only too
well. Becky doesn't really remember him. She probably confuses
him with Dada who, between you and me, wasn't much of a
father in the first place. But Gavin – oh, oh, oh, Gavin! He was
spoiled. Spoiled rotten, as they say in Glasgow. What Gavin
needed were regular thrashings to sort him out but Dada never
lifted a hand to him that I recall. Why on earth did you marry
him? Did he grow up to be terribly handsome?'

'He said he loved me.'

'That old story.'

'No one had ever told me that before.'

'Poor you.' Rachel's accelerated delivery reminded Fay of the
costermongers who came up from Derby for the Buxton fair, fast
and flippant and decidedly more town than country. 'I suppose
he is handsome though?'

'I never thought about whether he was or not.'

'Of course you did,' said Rachel. 'That's all us girls ever think
about. Is he good-looking? Is he in love with me? It's certainly all
we talk about in the home.'

'Home?'

'The nurses' home, where I'm boarded.'

'I'm not sure I'd like to stay with a lot of other girls,' Fay said.

'It has advantages, believe me,' Rachel said. 'Discipline's a bit
on the strict side but then you don't have to go far to borrow a
clean pair of drawers.'

'Oh!' Fay murmured, trying to hide her embarrassment.

'I'm exaggerating,' Rachel said. 'Brought up in the country,
were you?'

'In Fream. That's in Derbyshire. After I married Gavin I went
to live with him in a cottage on the Edge.'

' "The Edge"? Sounds a bit dangerous. How far was that from
Fream?'

'Seven or eight miles.'

'You've seen nothing of the world, Fay, have you?'

'I came here on a railway train.'

91

'Well, at least you didn't have to walk,' Rachel said. 'However, that's enough of the introductions. I do want to hear all about my brother, though. I mean I want to hear *everything* about him, not just the potted version you've made up for my mother's benefit.' She winked. 'We'll have a nice, long, confidential chat before I sail off into the sunset again. All rightee?'

'All right,' Fay said, without much conviction, as the bedroom door opened and Innis, dressed in her Sunday best, came smiling into the kitchen.

'Well, that was very jolly,' Rachel said. 'I'd forgotten how tasty Mam's cooking can be when she sets her mind to it.'

'I did most of it,' Becky said. 'In any case, I expect anything would seem tasty after the muck they serve you in the nurses' home.'

'It isn't muck,' said Rachel. 'Our meals are quite substantial and very nutritious, in fact. We can't all live in the lap of luxury, like you.'

'Fetternish isn't luxurious, not these days.'

'No, I know,' said Rachel. 'I'm only pulling your leg.'

The sisters had gone out on the path to share a cigarette and, arms linked, leaned together by the gate. Fay had gone to bed soon after the supper dishes had been washed and put away. Rachel glanced at the lighted window.

'You don't think she can hear us, do you, Becky?'

'Who? Mam? No, of course she can't hear us.'

'I meant her, the girl.'

'Fay?' said Becky. 'She sleeps like a corpse.'

The night was alive with the sounds of the season and the low brassy boom of the waves on the rocks of the headland. Rachel drew in a mouthful of smoke and let it disperse through parted lips. 'Mother seems quite taken with her.'

'Mother would take to anyone who was pathetic enough.'

'Do you think she's pathetic?'

'Don't be ridiculous,' Becky said. 'She's a parasite.'

'Ah, but is she a *dependable* parasite, that is the question?'

'What do you mean by "dependable", for heaven's sake?'

'Will she stay?' Rachel said.

'Free board and lodging,' said Becky. 'She'll stay until someone throws her out, of course she will. Why do you think she
came all the way up here in the first place? If Gavin – if some
man had beaten me black and blue I don't think I'd have been
chasing off to leech on his folks. It is a kind of blackmail,
really.'

'She claims she has no one else to turn to.'

'I'm not sure I swallow that,' said Becky. 'There's something
going on, but I'm not sure what. All that damned digging, all that
weeding and planting. She works like a demon, you know.'

'Digging in,' Rachel suggested, 'literally and metaphorically.'

'Big words, dearest,' Becky said. 'But yes, I agree with you.'

'If she is digging in then surely she *must* be planning to stay.'

'I'm sure she is: I'm just not sure why.'

'The reason's immaterial,' Rachel said. 'You should be much
nicer to her, you know. A smile costs nothing.'

'Dear God!' Becky exclaimed.

'No, truly, at least you should attempt to be friends with her,'
said Rachel.

'Why? Go on, tell me.'

'In case you ever decide to abandon ship.'

'I don't want to abandon ship. Someone has to look after
Mother,' Becky said. 'I hope you're not suggesting that Fay
Ludlow could ever take my place.'

'Not take your place, no. No one could take your place,'
Rachel said. 'But the island is Mother's life, not ours. I tell you,
Becky, you'd love Glasgow. There are music-halls and dances and
young men by the—'

'I'm not interested in young men.'

'There are good prospects for girls, good jobs going a-
begging.'

'I am not going to train as a nurse, if that's what you're implying.'

'No, no, no. Nursing's not for you. I see that now.'

Becky drew inexpertly on the cigarette. She coughed and blew out a puny feather of smoke. 'I could be a nurse if I wanted to, of course.'

'Of course you could,' said Rachel soothingly. 'You can be anything you want to be, anything you set your mind to, but . . .'

Becky nodded. 'But not here on Mull, is that what you mean?'

'I've always been grateful to you for looking after Mother,' Rachel said.

'She isn't helpless, you know.'

'Oh, I know that,' said Rachel. 'Even so, she isn't getting any younger and I wouldn't feel at ease if she were left alone here.'

'Perhaps Gillies will move in and make an honest woman of her.'

'If only that were possible,' Rachel said. 'But we both know that she won't marry Gillies, not while there's the foggiest chance that Dada is still alive. And Father O'Donnell would have a purple fit if she suggested seeking a divorce on the grounds of desertion.'

'We don't even know where Dada is,' said Becky. 'Perhaps he's dead.'

'I doubt it,' said Rachel. 'He's not much older than Mama. What? About fifty? Men don't die at fifty these days, not unless they're drunkards or are predisposed to inherited tubercular disorders, or—'

'Spare me the lecture.' Becky took a final puff on the cigarette, dropped it on the turf and ground it out with her heel. 'Has it occurred to you that Dada may have sent her here – our little Miss Innocent, I mean?'

'Why would he do that?'

'To get his hands on a piece of land.'

'Oh no. God, no! That's pushing deviousness too far,' said Rachel.

'Well, I for one wouldn't put it past him. Maggie Naismith has told me often enough that all Dada ever wanted was a stake in Fetternish and a few acres of land to call his own,' Becky said.

'Aunt Biddy would never sell, especially not to Dada.'

'Perhaps this is his way of getting a foothold on Fetternish. Perhaps he's sent the girl to spy out the lie of the land. I mean, doesn't it strike you as incredible that she claims she's never met him, not even once?'

'That does seem a bit odd, I'll admit.'

'Gavin and Dada were always so close.'

'She did say, did she not, that Gavin received letters from him?' said Rachel. 'At least that proves Dada's still alive. If you ask me, I think he's gone and got married again.'

'You think he's a bigamist?'

'Marriage is a term that covers a multitude of sins,' said Rachel, 'not all of them actually criminal. No, I reckon he has himself a common wife, perhaps another family in some Border town and couldn't care less about Fetternish.'

'There may not be much *to* care about, not for much longer.'

'That's exactly what I'm driving at,' Rachel said. 'Precisely why I'm not opposed to this girl "digging in" here.'

'She's a usurper, Rachel.'

'Now who's using big words?' Rachel said. 'Look at it this way: if Biddy and Quig do have to sell off Fetternish what will become of you?'

Becky shrugged. 'I haven't given it much thought.'

'Opportunity, that's what you lack. Opportunity – and gumption.'

'Absolute rot!' said Becky. 'I'm cold. I'm going indoors.'

'Listen to me, Beck. Listen. I don't want to see you stuck here when everyone else has gone. If Mother does like this girl and the girl is all she seems to be then Fay Ludlow is the key to getting you out of the nest.'

'I do not want out of the nest, thank you.'

Becky turned away. Rachel caught her by the arm. 'The

island's finished, you know. It's 1908, Becky, not the middle of the eighteenth century. Whatever was great and full of promise is long gone. Dead and buried. You haven't seen what I've seen. You don't know how well people live in the city. Take Donnie and Tricia, for instance. They have an apartment in a nice tenement with big spacious rooms, a bath, a big kitchen. Even Neil has a better standard of living than you do, and his children—'

'Neil? Have you seen Uncle Neil?'

'Once or twice,' Rachel admitted.

'Why haven't you told Mother?'

'It would only upset her.'

'Upset her? Why?'

'Because he's very bitter about the family and he hates Mull. He told me all sorts of things I didn't know before.'

'Like what?'

'Never you mind,' said Rachel firmly. 'The point is that Neil wouldn't come back here for all the tea in China.'

Becky drew away and walked towards the cottage door.

Rachel caught up with her. 'At least think about what I've said.'

'Be nice to little Miss Innocent, you mean?'

'Until we see what she's made of.'

'Sugar and spice?' said Becky sarcastically

'Well,' said Rachel. 'you never can tell, can you? You really never can tell how people will turn out in the long run. Promise me you'll think about it?'

'I'll think about it,' Becky said, and hurriedly went indoors.

Biddy slept in a four-poster bed that she had inherited from her first husband. The over-priced, over-ornate antique fitted so well into the first-floor bedroom, however, that she had never had the heart to have it removed. Quig did not seem to mind and had taken his place in another man's bed without quibble or protest;

after all, the fellow was long dead and gone. If he had known just how many other men Biddy had lain with in the big four-poster before she had agreed to marry him, though, he might have been a deal less sanguine.

Biddy's auburn curls were tucked into a muslin night-cap and a pair of eyeglasses with silver rims were perched on the tip of her nose. A book, Cranach's *Wild Sports of the Highlands*, was propped open on the slope of her thighs. In recent years she had become an avid reader and frequently plundered the collection of books that her grandfather, Evander McIver, had willed to Innis but that Innis had agreed to leave in store in Fetternish House.

Before the children had gone off to school in Edinburgh the library had meant little to Biddy; afterwards, with time hanging heavily on her hands, she had taken to mooching about among the books and had gradually begun to read for entertainment and instruction and, though no one guessed it, to escape the tormenting sense of loss that frequently threatened to overwhelm her.

When the Reverend Tom Ewing had first caught her at it he had cried out in astonishment, 'Biddy, is that a book you're reading?'

'Of course it's a book,' she had answered him. 'What does it look like?'

'What on earth are you doing reading a book?'

'Broadening my mind, if you must know.'

'Not before time, Bridget,' Tom had said. 'Not before time,' at which point Biddy had thrown the volume — a weighty introduction to geology — in his direction and he had retreated to the kitchen, chuckling.

On warm summer nights Quig slept naked. In winter, though, Biddy insisted that he wrap his lean frame in a night-shirt, not for modesty's sake but simply because she had been raised to believe that night chills might lead to more serious illnesses and she did not fancy being widowed for a second time. Besides, she had once taken pleasure in the textures of cotton and cambric, the smooth, mysterious bumps and hollows that the fabrics created and the sensual warmth that her husband had generated. If she had recalled former lovers during uxorious embraces she gave no hint of it, for Quig, though not obstreperous, had never been less than thorough when it came to satisfying her needs.

In the past year or so, however, Biddy's bedtime ritual had become exceedingly compartmentalised.

She would put down her book. Take off her glasses. Remove her night-cap. Unwilling to admit that anything was wrong, Quig would turn down the lamp, snuggle down beside her, blow on the back of her neck or rub his forefinger against the small of her back, all part of the code of married lovers to which Biddy had seldom failed to respond. Now, though, she would flinch and pull away or, depending on her mood, even slap at his hand as if she could no longer bear to be touched. And Quig, puzzled and disappointed, would move silently away into the cold portion of the bed and respect her wishes in that matter as he did in all others.

Tonight Biddy did not put down her book and when Quig reached out to the table lamp she snapped at him, 'Wait, if you please.'

'Are you not finished reading, dear?'

'I want to talk to you.'

'Can we not do that with the lamp out?'

She closed *Wild Sports* with a little snap, drew off her eye-glasses and clicked them into their case, dropped book and case on to the floor. 'No, we cannot.'

Quig was tempted to seek refuge under the sheets but forced himself to sit upright and fold his arms across his chest.

'What is it that's really bothering you, Biddy?'

'The children will be back tomorrow.'

'I know. I am looking forward to seeing them again,' Quig said. 'I will be on the first boat out, never fear, and will be waiting on the platform when the train pulls into Oban railway station at half past eleven o'clock.'

'It isn't the travel arrangements that concern me,' said Biddy.

'What is it then?'

'What are we going to tell them about the girl?'

'Fay?' Quig shrugged. 'The truth surely would not hurt.'

'What if they ask awkward questions?'

'I am sure they will ask awkward questions,' Quig said. 'Christina in particular is bound to ask awkward questions. She never stops asking questions these days.'

'They will want to know who she really is.'

'I expect they will.'

'How are we going to explain her relationship to us?'

For once Quig let annoyance show. 'Good God, Biddy, we don't have to explain anything much. Fay is not a blood relative and Robbie and Christina have barely heard of Gavin. They are certainly not going to waste much time or energy fretting over Fay Ludlow's misfortune.'

He leaned against her, resting the crown of his narrow shoulder against her plump arm. He was relieved when she did not pull away. Tom Ewing, his father-in-law, had warned him that Biddy was probably undergoing a change of – ah – character and that he must be even more understanding than ever. How the minister knew about such things as the cessation of the female cycle was more than Quig could imagine: he doubted if Mairi, his mother, had ever discussed anything as intimate and unpleasant with her husband.

'You like her, do you not?' Biddy said.

'Who?'

'The Ludlow girl.'

'Neither one way nor the other.'

'Oh, come now, Robert, you've been visiting Pennypol every day.'

'Lambing.' Quig felt unaccountably guilty. 'I look in on her when I have a spare moment, it is true, but it is not so much the girl as the vegetables that interest me.'

'Liar!'

'Biddy, for God's sake. She is only a youngster.'

'I saw how you looked at her that first day.'

'How? How did I look at her?'

'With – with . . .'

The word Biddy was searching for was 'longing' but he did not dare tell her. She would have seized on any such statement as a confirmation that he did indeed long for little Fay Ludlow when, in fact, he did not.

What he felt for Fay was impossible to explain to a jealous wife who had never had any cause to accuse him of chasing after other women. Under the circumstances how could he tell Biddy that all he wanted was what he had. If he said that she would assume he was making it up to placate her. The damnable thing about Biddy these days was that there was no arguing with her. She knew perfectly well that he was no Michael Tarrant, no surly seducer who believed that he had a God-given right to take whatever he wanted from a woman.

'I feel sorry for her,' Quig said.

'I knew it wasn't the vegetables.'

'She is young and—'

'And I'm not?'

'That's not it at all, Biddy. Stop putting words in my mouth.'

He risked another rebuff by sliding his arm about her. She stiffened and then, capitulating, allowed him to hug her. He must let actions speak for him, must say nothing that she could turn against him. He listened in silence while she poured out her uncertainty, her disappointment that she had finally left her prime behind her and had entered into the years of long decline. He had heard her complaints before but had failed to appreciate their depth and import.

'When the children arrive tomorrow,' Biddy said, 'they are bound to notice how much I've changed, that their Mama has become an old woman. Robbie already thinks I'm too old to bother with and Christina barely acknowledges that I exist. She'll be all over you, of course, fawning all over you as usual.'

'Biddy, that is a terrible thing to be saying.'

'It's the truth, is it not?'

Quig was seized by a sudden fear that his wife might ruin his loving relationship with his daughter, not out of malice, not even intentionally, but because of what had happened to her when she was Christina's age. He said nothing, offered no denial. He must let Biddy lead. It had been bad before, but never this bad. How could there be anything wicked in loving a daughter he had helped create, a child he had nursed in his arms and cradled in the nights of her fevers; whom he had let go out into the world at an early age only because Biddy insisted upon it? How could Biddy possibly be jealous of her own daughter?

'Is it her you want?' Biddy said.

The pronoun swung before him like a hook.

He had attended four difficult births that afternoon. He had drawn a rotting lamb from the pulpy womb of a ewe that only Barrett's veterinary skills had kept alive. His hands were raw. His forearms burned with the suction of reluctant female openings. His back ached as if he had crawled in the vaginal tract to find and remove the poor dead thing from its puddle of corruption. He did not have the stamina to cope with this ugly twist in Biddy's reasoning.

Resentment curdled into disgust. He flung himself away from her, stabbing an elbow into the mattress, thumping his head into the pillow.

Biddy was taken aback by his anger but could see no justification for it. She tapped him on the shoulder.

'It's true, isn't it?' she hissed. 'You *do* want her. I know how it is with men. Look at me when I'm talking to you, Quig. Can't you even meet my eye any more? Young girls – it doesn't matter who they are. Look at me, Robert, look at me.'

He clenched his raw hands under the sheets.

'Biddy, I have to be up early tomorrow. Stop this nonsense and go to sleep.'

'Nonsense! It isn't nonsense. I suppose you'll be going to see *her* first thing.'

'I am going to the boat,' Quig stated, 'first thing.'

'Oh, yes, and then you'll have your precious daughter to fawn all over you.'

It was too much even for Quig. He rounded on her. He flattened his hand against her chest and pushed her back against the pillow.

'I don't know what it is that has got into you lately,' he said, 'but if you are going to behave like this when Robbie and Christina get here then it would be better if I put them straight back on to the train.'

He pressed his hand against her breast: a wave of elation broke over her. She wanted him to lose control, to jolt her out of depression, to drag her out of herself by brutal and unwieldy force. She wanted him to change as she had changed, to become something other than himself. But Quig was not Michael Tarrant and she was no longer young Biddy Baverstock with an estate to trade away.

She sagged against the pillow, cheeks flushed. She could feel her heart beating hard against his palm. She heard herself say, 'I think I'm going mad.'

'Sometimes I think you are,' Quig told her.

'I don't know what makes me think these dreadful thoughts and say these dreadful things.'

'You are not yourself,' Quig said. 'It is worry about the future.'

Biddy shook her head. Her hair tumbled from beneath the cap and hung across one eye. She hovered between the desire to be loved and a need to be indulged. Quig had been as much of a man as any of the men she had ever known. He had given her a child, which in those daft days had been all she thought she needed to make her happy. But marriage and motherhood and Robert Quigley had all failed to protect her against the stealthy inroads of the passing years, against the horror of growing older day by day.

'I'm sorry, Robert,' she lied. 'I don't know what comes over me.'

He drew her down against him and cradled her as tenderly as he had cradled Christina in the nights of her childhood fevers.

'Are you all right now?'

'Yes,' Biddy said, lying once more. 'Yes, dearest, I'm fine.'

It was just after dawn when Fay came out of the water closet and saw him standing by the gate. It gave her quite a start. She had never seen Quig at Pennymain before; his work was up on the hill with Barrett and the sheep. On the summit of the slope that rose from the flats she could make out the dogcart and realised that today was the day when he would go to Oban to pick up his children.

She wore nothing but a shift and a shawl. She was barefoot and bare-legged, her hair uncombed. She was afraid that when the wind blew against her he would notice the curve of her belly under the cotton shift.

Picking her way across the drying lawn, she went to him. He wore a check tweed suit with pockets at the hip, a collared shirt with a necktie of brightly coloured silk and a homburg hat that lent him a raffish air that did not seem wholly out of character. She had never seen him so dressed up before, neither on the hill nor in the house. He watched her cross the grass and step over the soft brown earth of the flower border that she had raked the evening before last. She drew the ends of the shawl about her to cover her breasts.

'You're an early bird this morning, Mr Quigley.'

'I am having to go to Oban to meet my children,' he said. 'It struck me that perhaps there is something you need while I'm there.'

'What would I need that I can't get in Crove?'

'For the gardens, I mean.'

She did not have to think about it but she wanted to prolong the moment, for the morning air was clear and the sun had just lifted over the brim of the hill and the ridge had a great long slant of calm russet light upon it and six or eight bullocks were stolidly grazing in the band where light and shadow met.

'No, I don't think I need anything for the gardens, thank you, Mr Quigley.' She hesitated. 'Do you always go to Oban to meet your children when they are coming home?'

'They hardly need me to do anything for them now but my daughter expects it and I'm not one for flouting tradition,' Quig said. 'Besides, it gives me some time with them, just the three of us.' He looked down at his shoes. 'So there is nothing you will be needing then, Fay?'

She leaned on the gate. The warming breeze buffeted her breasts and swelled the shawl around her. 'No, thank you,' she said. 'Nothing.'

He nodded, gave a little bow, turned and went away.

She watched him stride up the straggling path that led to the track that led on to the Dervaig road. He clambered into the cart, brought the pony round and drove off at a fair lick.

Only then did it occur to her that Mr Quigley had come far out of his way to call upon her and as he vanished behind the ridge into the slanting sunlight, began to wonder why.

He sailed over from Tobermory on the *Claymore*, a little steam packet that carried mail to and fro among the islands. If the train from Edinburgh arrived on time, however, the children and he would catch MacBrayne's big paddle-wheeler, the *Grenadier*, for the return crossing.

He bought Biddy a box of the perfumed chocolates that she liked so much and waited rather self-consciously under the glass dome of the railway station with the box, wrapped in glossy paper, in his hand.

He did not much care for railway stations. He did not much care for Oban, come to think of it; a town of meetings and partings and, these days, a crossroad to markets that were hardly worth the name. He waited for the signal to clack and the engine to appear. He was always tense when Robbie and Christina were in transit. He would waken sometimes in the night with the shriek of brakes in his ears and the crash of metal grinding away in his head and it would take him a minute or two to realise that he was dreaming and that his children were safe in their beds in schools in Edinburgh.

He let out a little sigh when the locomotive finally hove into view and steamed to a halt against the platform.

Robbie emerged first.

In the three months since last Quig had seen his son, the lad had definitely grown taller and had shed the last traces of boyishness, so much so that the school cap looked fairly ridiculous on him now.

Robbie handed down a suitcase, then another.

The battered luggage had travelled forth and back from Edinburgh more often than he, Quig, had done; then his daughter stepped down to the platform, his treasure, Christina. Only she was not his Christina, not the same quiet, polite child to whom he had waved goodbye only a dozen weeks ago.

Her voice cut through the hiss of steam in an affected bray and when her brother, with a stoicism that did him credit, offered her a hand, she batted it away. 'I'm not helpless, Robbie,' she cried. 'Now where is he? Is he here? I do hope that he is here and that we will not have to sprint for that blessed tub again. God, what a place; will you take my case? Where is he? Oh heck, there he is, grinning as usual – ah well, it's only a week; I suppose I can survive a week without going mad.'

Still cawing, she ordered her brother to advance with all the superciliousness of a sergeant-major bullying a recruit into the front line.

Her hat also seemed far too small, Quig thought. It was jammed on the back of her head and suspended from the elasticated chin-band in a style that would have had her in detention in a trice in the scholastic institution from which she had temporarily escaped. What was even more alarming than her cultivated untidiness was the rate at which his little daughter had grown. She was no longer dainty or delicate. She seemed enormous, almost monstrous, bulging out of her cream-coloured shirt front like a corseted dowager.

Bristling with disapproval she strutted down the platform towards him.

Quig tucked the chocolate box under one arm and held out both hands to welcome her. 'Good to see you again, dearest. Pleasant journey?'

She brushed past him and swinging from the hip snapped her fingers at her brother who struggled along the platform, wrestling with two suitcases and an awkwardly shaped hat-box.

Quig swiftly relieved him of the hat-box and the pair followed Christina out of the station. He glanced at Robbie who pulled a long face but did not dare utter a word except 'Hello, Dad,' as they trailed the girl along the harbour towards the pier.

Christina called over her shoulder, 'Watch out for my hat, if you please. I would be obliged if you would be more considerate of my possessions, Papa; the one decent *chapeau* I own and I do not want it ruined. Come along, come along, I'm dying for a spot of lunch.'

Robbie leaned towards him. 'What is it that's happened to her, Dad?'

And Quig, groaning, answered, 'God knows.'

If Quig had thought to ask Biddy she might have informed him that 'glands' had wrought the sudden transformation in their daughter's character and appearance, but since she had tumbled into the slough of despondency that lay, as it were, at the end of the valley of fertility, Biddy was not given to off-the-cuff explanations. Christina might be sprouting in all directions but Biddy was shrivelling, her body as well as her brain occupied by a legion of demons whose task was to pluck out handfuls of her beautiful auburn hair, score wrinkles in her ample flesh and, worst of all, twang away on her nerves.

She had heard and read about 'the change', of course, and the emotional disturbances that accompanied it but she simply could not believe that it was happening to her; that nature, having driven her crazy once before, would be so cruel as to do it all over again.

The arrival of the children distressed her beyond measure; an uncomplicated event that occurred regularly three times a year suddenly became threatening. Any sort of novelty, any alteration to drab routine now seemed menacing. Perhaps that was why she had taken such a spite at the Ludlow girl and accused dear, devoted, docile Quig of lusting after the pathetic little creature. She did not truly believe that her husband would ever deceive her with another woman – certainly not with his own daughter – but jealousy was part of the lubricious mix that slopped about in her head at all hours of the day and night.

She sought relief in reading, driving the printed words into her brain like nails in the hope of shoring up her reason with plain, hard fact. She read dull books on geology and miner-alogy, on obscure diseases of cattle, on apiary, on instinct in animals and the importance of sanitation in relation to public health. When all else failed she buried herself in James Brown's massive treatise on the planting and management of forest trees, a tome which her grandfather had annotated in pencil and from whose marginal comments she drew a perverse kind of consolation.

Her grandfather had died of distemper of the brain. Her sister had never been right in the head. Her father? She still could not decide whether he had been mad all along, or merely wicked. Now, out of nowhere – or, rather, out of Derbyshire – had come news that her nephew was similarly tainted. All of which suggested that she, Biddy, might be heading down the road to mental derangement instead of merely growing old: a prospect that was curiously comforting.

She did not get out of bed until after nine.

She went straight down to the kitchen and scrounged a

headache powder from Maggie Naismith and then spent a considerable time in the bathroom doctoring her appearance.

She rinsed her hair with Chevallier's Restorer, removed her almost imperceptible moustache with Boudet's Depilatory and attacked her complexion with Kittoe's Lotion and a fine carmine rouge. When she was finally dressed – no lady's-maid employed to help her now – and surveyed herself in the cheval-glass tears started into her eyes at the mess she had made of herself.

If she had not been so hungry she might have hidden in the library and refused to come out. But 'the change' had not so far affected her appetite. She returned to the kitchen and ordered Becky to put up a plateful of scrambled eggs and home-cured ham and serve it in the dining-room where, in a spirit of revenge against her decaying body, she did full justice to the breakfast.

The grandfather clock in the hall sonorously ticked away the minutes.

All too soon she would have to square up to her handsome son and gorgeous daughter, whom she regarded now as latter-day copies of Michael and she. Christina had all the arrogance and ambition that had once given *her* power over men, and Robbie was the spitting image of the lean, handsome young shepherd who had sauntered over the hill from Fetternish on a sultry August afternoon twenty-five years ago, a resemblance that no one, least of all Quig, seemed yet to have noticed.

There were a million things to do before the children arrived but she had no strength of will, no desire to break the inertia that held her in thrall. Her headache had eased but had not gone away. Rouge dried on her cheeks and her upper lip stung. More hair had come out in the comb again. Come summer she would probably be as bald as Gillies Brown and condemned to wearing an ill-fitting wig for the rest of her life.

She sobbed to herself in the empty dining-room for twenty minutes or so, then, discovering a little pool of willpower that had not quite dried up, forced herself from the table, flung open the door and stalked across the hall and out into the clear April daylight which, to her surprise, was already waxing towards noon.

The front lawn needed its first cut of the season. The gravel drive had not been raked in months. The three tall pines that marked the start of the path to An Fhearann Cáirdeil appeared gnarled and ragged in the wake of winter. And at the top end of the driveway Willy and Aileen were waiting with the mute forbearance of the very old and the very stupid, waiting for Robbie and Christina to arrive in three hours' time. Willy leaned on his stick, Aileen clung to his arm; a grotesque couple with nothing but time on their hands. Would she wind up so devoid of impetus that she would squander three or four precious hours staring vacantly into space? Biddy wondered. The prospect angered her: she was tempted to shout at Willy and Aileen, to order them to move along and stop taunting her with their appalling patience.

Instead she turned into the kitchen yard and crossed into the walled garden where, to her disgust, she found herself face to face with her rival.

Fay said, 'You're looking very pretty today, Mrs Quigley, if you don't mind me saying so.' She put down the pot and trowel and, wiping her hands on her canvas smock, stood up. 'Is there something you're looking for specially?'

'What are you doing here?'

'Mr Quigley said I could—'

'Mr Quigley? I thought it would be Quig by this time.'

Fay assumed that there were no secrets between the lord and lady of the manor, though she found it difficult to associate Quig with this elegant and imposing woman. She had seen little of Mrs Quigley, had not yet encountered her in patched corduroy breeches or a knee-length riding skirt. This morning Mrs Quigley appeared very much a *grande dame*. She wore no hat or topcoat, not even a cape, but her cheeks were rouged and her hair freshly curled and her dress was more like a ball-gown than the sort of thing you would slip into for a morning stroll.

Only the fact that she had Quig's express permission to dig in the walled garden gave Fay the courage to speak out so boldly.

'I have come for the strawberry plants.'

'Strawberry plants?' said Biddy in a deep, angry sort of voice. 'We have no strawberries here.'

'You do, Mrs Quigley.' Fay held up the earthenware pot. 'See.'

Biddy peered into the pot, head held back and her nose in the air as if she thought that it might contain something nasty. She glanced at Fay. 'Your eye has almost healed.'

'Yes, ma'am.'

'You look the better for it.'

'Thank you, ma'am.'

'I can see what he sees in you.'

'Gavin, do you mean?' Fay said.

'Yes. Gavin. I mean Gavin.' She took the pot from Fay's hand and gently stroked the sad little leaves. 'Is this really strawberry?'

'It's strawberry all right,' Fay said. 'Latest of All, I think.'

'Latest of All?' Biddy said. 'Hah! I remember when I first came to Fetternish how we used to boil up a great flood of jam every summer. In those days we had gardeners to take care of everything, of course. It's not dead, is it?'

'No, it's been fruiting away quietly without any proper attention,' Fay said. 'Latest of All can survive quite well for years if it's under a wall.'

'I thought the strawberry beds had been rooted out,' Biddy said. 'It must be five years since I last tasted a fresh strawberry.'

'Perhaps Mr Quigley has been eating them,' Fay said.

'Did he tell you that he had been eating them?'

'He told me to come here and see what plants I could find.'

'Can you make them grow?' Biddy said.

'It's open ground at Pennypol and Sovereigns or Scarlets would probably fare better but I think I can secure some runners for next season, if we're lucky.'

'Ah, but you *are* lucky,' Biddy said. 'I think you're very lucky to have made a friend of Mr Quigley.'

'Should I not have made friends with Mr Quigley?'

'Oh, as you wish, as you wish.' Biddy slackened her shoulders and let her arms hang down by her sides as if, Fay thought, she were listening to inaudible music and might soon begin to sway in time to it. 'My daughter's coming home today. You will not be seeing much of Mr Quigley after she arrives. How thin he has to spread himself these days, among all you women.' She glanced at the strawberry pot again and then, again, at Fay. 'Have you planted your crops at Pennypol?'

'Everything is in and growing.'

'I know nothing about gardening,' Biddy said. 'I left all that to my mother. She used to pull a fair haul of potatoes from the plots at Pennypol but I was always more interested in barley and oats and cultivating grass for cattle.'

'When did the sheep arrive?'

'Over thirty years ago,' Biddy answered. 'Before that it was cattle, just cattle, as far as the eye could see.'

'Perhaps the cattle will come back one day,' Fay said.

'No, the grazings are ruined for cattle, and the sheep – well, what money is there in sheep when you can ship mutton from abroad cheaper than you can ferry it from the isles? Why did Gavin strike you so violently?'

'I think I disappointed him.'

'Did he break your leg too?'

'I fell.'

'He pushed you, did he not?' Biddy said.

He had, in fact, kicked her from the bed when he could not raise the strength to enter her. He had dragged her to the stone floor and then, as if he were breaking kindling, had stamped on her leg until the bones had snapped.

The walled garden seemed sombre even in the clear Easter light, the tower canted at a precarious angle against a cloudless sky; all such a far cry from the tiny cottage on the Edge where Gavin had shown her no mercy.

'It was an accident,' Fay said.

'You're loyal, I will say that for you,' Biddy told her. 'Perhaps that's the best thing to be in this day and age.'

'I don't know what you mean, Mrs Quigley.'

'I am sure you don't.' Biddy glanced round. 'If you like you may try to resurrect this garden too but not – let me repeat – *not* until my son and daughter have gone back to school.'

'When is that, ma'am?'

'One week from today.'

'You don't want me to meet them, do you?'

'No,' Biddy said. 'I would prefer it if you do not.'

'May I ask why?'

'No, you may not,' said Biddy sternly and, gathering in her dress, swept off without another word, leaving Fay puzzled and perturbed to get on with unearthing the strawberry roots.

CHAPTER SIX

Little Nobody

Sunday was a very special day for Innis: the Bishop of the Isles was coming to Tobermory to conduct an Easter service, which was flattering for Mull's tiny Catholic community and a feather in the cap of Father O'Donnell.

The visit caused no end of excitement and a patching up and pressing of Sunday-best clothes but there was worry too that one's confession would not be dramatic enough to satisfy the august personage of a bishop who was no doubt used to absolving more sophisticated sins than drunkenness and occasional blasphemy.

Innis left early on Sunday morning and to Fay's surprise Rachel decided to accompany her.

Gillies Brown, whose ecumenical instincts were decidedly in advance of the times, had promised to join the ladies at the service. Although he was a Presbyterian, on four or five occasions when Father O'Donnell had been storm-bound on Mull Gillies had laid on supper at the Mishnish Hotel and had dragged the Reverend Ewing along to add a bit of ballast to the evening.

Becky scoffed at all the fuss and declared that the bishop was just an old buzzard in a fancy hat who had been appointed to a diocese that nobody else wanted. Her cynicism irritated Fay who would have been only too glad to receive an Easter blessing from such a holy man. She did not argue with her sister-in-law, though. She distrusted Rachel and Rebecca's affability and had no desire to provide them with critical ammunition that might be used against her. Besides, the Quigleys would be at church in the village and she had no wish to risk bumping into Biddy's children on the road back from Tobermory.

Pennypol would just have to do for a little nobody, Fay told herself, and, with bread and cheese and a small brown paper bag filled with sugar and tea, walked down to the plots to celebrate Easter, alone.

The lambed ewes had been moved to a meadow beyond the stream. There was no sign of the Barretts on the hill, not a soul to be seen that forenoon, not even a steamer cleaving up from Staffa or a fishing smack nosing round the headland. The sun glinted on empty water, the waves broke upon an empty shore.

The seeds that Mr Quigley had given her were germinating nicely, however, and if she could prevent the rabbits from eating the shoots in twelve weeks or so she would be taking off turnips, leeks and potatoes ready for market.

She had even prepared the strawberry bed, deep-digging a south-facing strip of ground close to the drystone wall to accommodate the runners she had redeemed from Fetternish. It was such a pretty morning that she soon lost all sense of time. Her awareness of self slackened. The sly and subtle underside of her nature slipped away and Josh and Gavin, Fream and Clouds-hill seemed very far off.

She kindled a driftwood fire against the gable wall of the cottage and boiled water in the blackened kettle that Innis had given her. She brewed tea and seated herself on the grass. She rested her head against the stones and felt the sun upon her face. She cupped her hands across her belly and tried to envisage how the seed that he had planted in her would unfold. 'Turnips, leeks, parsley, potatoes – and baby,' she murmured and then, smiling up into the sunlight, closed her eyes and fell asleep.

*   *   *

Quig left them at gate of the manse. Almost the entire Fetternish clan were going to lunch with the minister and his wife, all except Becky, in fact.

Quig did not much care for Becky. She struck him as petulant and opinionated, changed in much the same way as Christina had changed. He was too simple, he supposed, to understand what got into young girls when they crossed the bridge into womanhood. This past half-year or so he had had to learn to adjust to changes in Biddy too. Mother and daughter had parted enemies at Christmas but embraced as allies at Easter. He did not know whether to be sorry or relieved at this unexpected turn in the relationship. He felt sorry for Robbie, though, who had no option but to duck when his sister and his mother rode their high horse together.

Leaving poor Robbie to suffer in his stead Quig made his apologies and escaped down the main street.

He drove rapidly back to Fetternish, grabbed a bite to eat, changed into his work clothes and set out at once for Pennypol where he knew he would find Fay Ludlow and have her, at least for a little while, all to himself.

Fay opened her eyes. She had no idea how long she had been asleep or how long he had been watching her but knew that he had been looking at her legs.

She blinked.

Quig shifted a pace to the left to put himself between her and the sun.

'I brought you something,' he said.

'What did you bring me?' she said.

'A buttery.'

'What's that?'

Quig put his hand into his pocket and brought out a breadroll wrapped in a sheet of newspaper.

She leaned forward and inspected the soft, oily roll lying on the newspaper in his cupped hands. His wrists were thin but not bony, his forearms downed with dark hair. He had a kind face, not wrinkled like Mr Musson's or Mr Naismith's.

Inclining herself forward, she allowed him a glimpse of her breasts.

She held herself in that position, looking not at him but at the bread. She could see the butter used in the baking lying sleek within the dough, the curls of pure butter with which the roll had been spread.

'Take it,' he said, 'if you want it.'

She took it and bit into it.

'Is it good?' he asked.

'Yes, it's good.'

He lowered himself on to his heels, crumpled the sheet of newspaper into a ball and placed it on the embers of the fire that spilled warmth into the sunlight.

Out beyond the bay a boat was visible, a tall-masted yacht with three sails. Fay watched it draw towards the point, its bows dipping deep into the blue sea.

She ate the buttery, drank a mouthful of tea, wiped her hands on the grass.

Quig was twice her age, or more.

He watched her, apparently without calculation.

He said, 'How far on are you, Fay?'

'Far . . .'

'How far on is your pregnancy?'

She felt a little shock like a kick within, as if the foetus had responded to the question before she could think of an answer. She opened her mouth, found nothing to say, no denial or protestation. She had been plotting how she would respond if he tried to kiss her and all the time . . .

'I didn't think I was showing yet?' she said.

'You aren't,' Quig said, 'but you will be very soon.'

'How did you know?'

He shrugged. 'I was brought up on an island called Foss where there were plenty of births of one kind or another. Even as a lad I could read the signs. I developed an instinct for knowing without knowing, if you see what I mean.'

She glanced down at her stomach and frothy laughter rose within her. She was glad that someone knew the truth. She was relieved that it was Mr Quigley even although he would not dare kiss her now.

She laughed at her own silliness.

'I think it will be with us late in August,' she said. 'Perhaps September.'

'Have you told Innis about the baby?'

'I've told no one yet.'

'I must be asking this question,' he said: 'it is Gavin's child, is it not?'

'It can be no one else's,' Fay said. 'I know what they think of me in the big house and what Becky says, but I've lain with no other man than my husband.'

'Does Gavin know that you are carrying his child?'

'No.'

'What if he finds out?'

'I can't imagine what he'll do,' she said. 'It's because I can't predict what he'll do that I ran away. I was feared that he would be jealous of the baby and do it the sort of harm that he did to me.'

'When you broke your leg, who set it for you?' Quig asked.

'Gavin.'

'With what?'

'Torn sheets and baling wire,' Fay said. 'He didn't want me going out and telling anyone what had happened. He fitted the bones back into place and cut away the torn skin, poured gentian on it to stop it suppurating and bound it up tight. He refused to let me go out of the house until I could walk upright again.'

Quig sat back on his heels. 'Was it about that time that you conceived?'

'No,' Fay said, 'further into the winter.'

117

'He's a devil, you know.'

'I know.'

'His father was much the same.'

'I never met his father.'

'I wonder where Michael Tarrant is now,' Quig said. 'I wonder what mischief he is getting up to. I find it strange that he and the boy parted company. They used to be very close.'

'Perhaps Gavin was too much for his father too.'

'Aye,' Quig said. 'Maybe there was not room enough for both of them to be in the same place at the same time.'

'Mr Quigley?'

'Hmm?'

'What if I have a boy, a boy like Gavin?'

Quig squinted out to sea, watching the tall-masted yacht sag and tilt as the breeze off the point caught it.

'Well' – he gave a faltering chuckle – 'I don't think we will be heeding Willy Naismith's advice and taking him down to the jetty in a canvas sack and throwing him into the ocean. If it is a boy – or a girl for that matter – we will just have to wait to see what sort of person God has given us. Tarrant or Campbell or Quigley, you can never tell what a person is made of or what they will make of themselves.'

'Do you really believe that?' Fay said.

'Yes, I do,' Quig said.

He did not draw away when little Fay Ludlow pushed herself into his arms.

As a child Christina had been encouraged to visit the servants' quarters but, unlike her brother she had shown no inclination to desert the upper part of the house for the friendly atmosphere of the kitchens.

She had preferred to shiver in the drawing-room or curl up with the dogs – there had been dogs in those days – before the fire in the great hall rather than consort with servants. Five years of infant education in the schoolhouse at Crove had not diminished her belief in her natural superiority, though she had been careful not to make enemies of the sons and daughters of fishermen and farm labourers. When she finally escaped to the boarding school in Edinburgh, however, she had shed not a single tear and felt completely at ease with the daughters of merchants and brewers, doctors, lawyers and colonial civil servants.

If it were possible to prove that one could be born a snob then Christina Quigley would have been proof enough and with the arrival of the spectacular glandular eruptions that marked an end of adolescence she was revealed in all her glory as what she had always been: a right little pain in the backside.

Becky was gutting a rabbit when Christina came thumping downstairs to the kitchen. Tuesday, four days into the holiday: even loyal Maggie Naismith had been heard to mutter disparagingly about 'the lump' upstairs and in private had given Willy a fair imitation of Christina's latest line in airs and graces.

When the door burst open and Christina bowled into the kitchen, however, Maggie, true to form, was all simpering and obsequious.

Boning knife in hand, Becky had a sudden urge to be sick.

She kept her back to her cousin while Christina helped herself to coffee from the pot that simmered on the stove.

Carefully Becky bent the rabbit's head back against its shoulder and with her pinkie slid an eyeball back into place.

Christina hoisted herself on to the ledge of the dresser.

'Well now,' she said in saccharine tone, 'is this not cosy? I do so love being home with my friends. It's what one misses at school.'

'Does one?' Becky said.

'Maggie, dear Maggie? How *are* you these days?'

'I am well, Miss Christina, thank you.'

'I hear that you have made an interesting new friend.'

'If you mean Fay Ludlow' – Becky glanced round – 'she's no friend of mine.'

It had only been a matter of time before Christina caught the rumours about Fay Ludlow and curiosity got the better of her. No doubt, Becky thought, Tom or Marie Ewing or possibly Gillies Brown, before he'd left for Glasgow, had said something they shouldn't have.

'Fay who?' Christina said. 'Oh, you mean the girl my father has taken on. No, no, no. What possible interest would a gardening girl have for me? Besides, I wasn't talking to you, Rebecca. I was talking to Maggie. I meant *your* new friend, Maggie, the lady at The Ards.'

Becky put down the boning knife and pushed the slithery corpse to one side. She leaned against the chopping block. She too was interested in Frances Hollander and pricked up her moist young ears to hear what Maggie Naismith might have to say about her.

Maggie wiped her hands on her apron and preened a little before answering. 'Frances? Yes, I do not think it would be stretching a point to say that I am her friend. Frances has been to America, of course, and that will be making all the difference.'

'How will that be making all the difference?' Christina said.

'She does not go picking her friends from among the rich.'

'Like Mama, do you mean?' said Christina.

The accusation was false, Becky thought, a calumny. She might have no regard for landowners but she was not entirely blind to reality. Her aunt may have pawed at the rungs of the social ladder when she was younger but these past eight or ten years – half Becky's lifetime – Aunt Biddy had steadfastly refused to court middle-class magnates in the hope of replacing the contracts that had been lost when the Baverstock-Pauls had sold out the manufactory in Sangster.

'I don't think your mother picks her friends that way,' Becky said.

'What do *you* know about it?' Christina said.

'More than you do,' Becky retorted. 'I'm here on the spot to see what's going on.'

'What do you mean? What *is* going on?' The merest trace of alarm tipped Christina's question. 'Maggie, what is going on?'

'Nothing, Christina, nothing,' said Maggie hastily.

'Oh, tell her the truth, for heaven's sake,' said Becky. 'There are all sorts of things going on that you obviously know nothing about.'

'What, for instance?'

'Haven't you heard?' said Becky.

'Heard? Heard what?'

'About Mr Rattenbury.'

'Who is Mr Rattenbury?'

'The fellow who bought most of the land around The Ards,' said Becky. 'You're not very observant, are you?' She had no qualms about pursuing her advantage over her cousin. 'I thought that's why you were asking Maggie about Mrs Hollander. By the way, she isn't "Lady" Hollander.'

'Isn't her husband a peer of the realm?' Christina said.

'There is no husband,' said Becky. 'Ask Maggie if you don't believe me. Have you ever seen a husband, Maggie? Come to think of it, have you ever seen the mother?'

'I – I . . . Have you no work to be getting on with?' Maggie stammered.

Christina slid from the ledge of the dresser. She was taller than Becky, heavier than Maggie. 'Let the work wait,' she said. 'Tell me about your friend Mrs Hollander. Has she no husband?'

'I have not seen Mr Hollander,' Maggie admitted.

'So there is a Mr Hollander?' said Christina. 'Is he not a peer?'

'Of course he's not a peer,' said Becky, 'in spite of what certain persons in Crove would like to believe. He's a mystery, another damned mystery. We have lots of them around here these days, Christina.'

'Do you? How interesting!'

Becky felt no warmth towards her cousin but just for a moment there was a certain indefinable spark between them. 'I have heard,' she went on, 'that Frances Hollander keeps her mother a prisoner in the attic.'

'That,' Maggie blurted out, 'is not true.'

'Have you seen *her* then?' said Becky.

'No, but I . . .'

'Never mind the mother, what about the husband?' Christina said. 'Is he dead, alive, separated, a soldier, a sailor, a – a what?'

Silence: between them they had rendered old Willy Naismith's chatterbox wife speechless.

'Well, Maggie, aren't you going to tell us?' Christina persisted.

'I do not know what he is.'

'I thought Mrs Hollander was your friend,' said Christina.

'She – she is an acquaintance, that is all.'

'Not an intimate friend, then, not your confidante?' said Christina.

'She is entitled to keep – not to speak of . . . What business is it of yours?'

'You don't know, do you, Maggie?' said Becky. 'You don't really know anything about Frances Hollander. I'll bet my bottom dollar, though, that she knows all about us.'

'Are you going to chop up that rabbit,' Maggie snapped, 'or do I have to do it myself?'

'The rabbit isn't going to run away,' Christina said. 'You still haven't told me – either of you – who Mr Rattenbury is or what he has to do with Fetternish.'

The housekeeper glanced helplessly at Becky.

'I do not know.'

'I do,' said Becky. 'It's as plain as the nose on your face what Mr Patrick Rattenbury wants.'

'What?' said Christina.

'I think perhaps you'd better ask your mama to explain.'

'Please,' Christina said, 'please tell me.'

'All right then. If you insist,' said Becky. 'He aims to buy Fetternish.'

'What!' Maggie exclaimed.

'Buy Fetternish?' said Christina. 'How — how do you know?'

Becky smiled triumphantly. She had put one over on the housekeeper who thought she knew everything, and on Christina who really knew nothing at all.

She reached behind her and lifted the boning knife.

'I read it in the *Guardian*,' she said.

'I really would prefer it if you talked to your father,' Biddy said.

'No, I want you to tell me,' Christina said. 'Is it true? Is this man, this Patrick Rattenbury going to buy Fetternish?'

'He has made certain approaches,' Biddy admitted.

'What sort of approaches?'

'To purchase several hundred acres at An Fhearann Cáirdeil.'

'You're not — oh, I mean you're not going to sell, Mama, are you?'

Biddy was seated at the piano, the lid of the instrument closed. She was dressed in a worn tweed skirt and a patched flannel shirt and Christina thought that she looked totally out of place among the faded gilt furniture.

'We may have to, darling, that's the long and short of it.'

'Sell Fetternish?' Christina shouted. The prospect of being cut adrift from an island estate that she had always detested suddenly filled her with horror. 'What about — I mean, what will be left for us, for Robbie and me?'

'Look, I would prefer it if your father and Robbie were here.'

'Does Robbie know what's happening? I mean, have you told Robbie and kept it from me? That's not fair. That is just not fair.'

'Robbie knows no more than you do,' Biddy said. 'Nothing is settled. Nothing has been discussed in any detail. In fact, there has been no formal offer from Mr Rattenbury. He has merely indicated by letter—'

'How? How do you "indicate" something like that?'

'Frances Hollander mentioned it to your father.'

'Oh! Oh-hoh! So that's it! It's all being done in whispers.'

'Please, Christina, don't shout. The servants will hear you.'

'The servants *told* me, for heaven's sake.'

Christina lowered her voice and sidled closer to the piano bench. There was not a lick of powder on her mama's brow or a dab of rouge on her cheeks and she looked, Christina thought, quite old. She felt a sickening little wave of fear at the realisation that her beautiful mama might soon resemble Willy Naismith.

'What does he want with Fetternish, this Mr Rattenbury?'

'To plant trees.'

'Trees?'

'Timber,' Biddy said. 'Norwegian spruce, I believe.'

'Is there money to be made from trees?' Christina did not wait for an answer. 'If there is money to be made from trees why don't we plant them ourselves?'

'We have no capital,' Biddy said. 'Do you know what capital is?'

'For God's sake, Mama, of course I know what capital is.'

'It would cost a great deal of money to drain the ground and fence it and purchase a sufficient quantity of seedlings for a plantation.'

'Can we not borrow the capital?'

'From whom?'

Christina had no answer, though she understood her parents' dilemma. Lord knows, she heard enough talk about yields and investments at school, for some of the older girls were almost as interested in financial matters as they were in forging romantic associations. She wished now that she had listened more attentively when dormitory conversations had turned to broker-age and banking and borrowing procedures. For a single, brilliant moment she imagined herself as the saviour of Fetternish, bringing home a banker or a broker to save the day but the bright little bubble of fancy burst before it could take proper shape.

Biddy said, 'You really should not be concerning yourself about these matters, Christina. I will take care of them.'

'Will I have to leave school?'

'Of course not.'

The female bond that had united them for the best part of a week slackened. Mama was putting her in her place again, pushing her back into adolescence. She thought of Becky expertly dismembering a rabbit and rolling pastry for a pie, wondered if in days to come she too would be reduced to being a servant, or a wife.

'Why haven't you told Robbie what's happening?' she said. 'I mean, why did I have to hear it from Becky?'

'Robbie will be told in due course.' Biddy laid a hand to her brow as if the question had brought on a headache.

'You mean Robbie will be consulted, and I will not?'

'He is the heir to Fetternish. He has a right to be kept informed. Besides, he is older than you.'

'And he's a man, of course.'

Struggling to control an urge to stamp, shout and demand equality, Christina spread her elbows on the lid of the piano and tried to think what to say next. In fact she did not know who she wanted to be equal *to*, certainly not Robbie who would eventually inherit what was left of this soggy piece of Mull and this creaking house and, along with it, the burden of caring for Mother and Father when they became old and helpless.

She did not envy Robbie his responsibility. Perhaps, she thought, it was time to talk to Robbie, though, to discover if he had given any thought to the future, or if his head was still filled with stupid Latin verbs and rugby football.

Christina said, 'Who is Patrick Rattenbury anyway?'

'An agent, I believe,' said Biddy.

'An agent for whom?'

'I have no idea, dear.'

'Doesn't Dada know? Becky says that an article about Fetternish appeared in an English newspaper – the *Guardian*.'

'The *Guardian* article did not mention Fetternish.'

'You saw it, you read it?'

'Of course,' Biddy said. 'Patrick Rattenbury is not the only land-purchase agent who is going the rounds right now. The article was a general one about forestry as an investment for the future.'

'Did the Hollander woman really sell off part of The Ards?'

'She leased out most of the estate, I believe.'

'A lease?' said Christina. 'Ah, so you wouldn't necessarily have to sell?'

'We may not have to do anything at all.' Biddy massaged her temples. 'We do have some rents coming in, though not many, and wool prices may pick up again. There are always fat lambs to sell in the back end of the year.' She managed a smile and, reaching out, rubbed Christina's arm consolingly. 'I'm sorry you had to be bothered with this just when we are getting on so well.'

Christina ignored her mother's request for reassurance.

'Have you met Frances Hollander?' she enquired.

'At church, only at church.'

'You don't like her, do you?'

'She's . . .' Biddy hesitated. 'Something about her does not seem right.'

'What about Mr Rattenbury? Haven't you met him?'

'Not yet,' Biddy said. 'No, dear, not just yet.'

Quig did not think that he was doing anything wrong by taking Robbie down to Pennypol to meet Fay Ludlow.

He realised that he should not have responded to Fay's advances and was wary of being alone with her. She was by no means as helpless as he had supposed her to be and reminded him a little of the orphans to whom Evander McIver had given shelter on Foss. He could not deny that he had enjoyed the moment of intimacy. It had brought back times before his marriage to Biddy when he had taken Aileen on to his knee to listen to her chirrup and rave. He had always been caring, responsible and trustworthy, which, now that he thought of it, had been a heavy burden of virtues for a young man to bear.

It was too late now to change: he had held little Fay Ludlow in his arms without desire. He feared only that she would fail to understand that he wanted nothing in return for sympathy.

He was more than twice her age and quite old enough to be her father.

She had never had a father, of course, nor a lover.

She had talked to him about a young man, Josh. She missed Josh, she said. She missed her little cot in the attic of the cottage at the end of the long garden in Fream. She had no one now, she said, to care for her.

He had held her too close for too long: not only was she still another man's wife, she was carrying another man's child. He must not let compassion blind him to reality. And the reality was that he was a married man and had troubles enough of his own.

'Do you fancy a walk, son?' he said.

'I thought you were still at the lambing?' Robbie said.

'No, lambing is almost over. Barrett can take care of what's left. We can go over that way if you wish, though, or out by An Fhearann Cáirdeil.'

'Or down to Pennypol?' Robbie said.

'Well, if that is what you fancy, yes.'

'Will Aunt Innis be there?'

'Where?'

'Looking after her.'

'After . . .'

'I've seen the girl, you know.'

'Have you now?' Quig said.

'From the hill, with Billy. Billy's awfully smitten with her.'

'Is he indeed,' Quig said. 'It is just his age.'

Robbie did not miss the irony: he laughed and said, 'Billy tells me the English filly thinks you're spiffing. He's terribly jealous.'

'Billy has no reason to be jealous of anyone, least of all me.'

Robbie hoisted himself from the worn leather couch in the great hall and tossed aside the week-old copy of *The Times*.

'It's all rather rum, really,' he said.

'What is?'

'Employing a girl, you know, when we're going quietly broke.'

'I did not employ her. Innis took her in. All I've done is buy her a few tools, a bit of seed and one or two plants. No point in her doing nothing all day long.' Quig paused, frowning. 'Who told you that we are going broke?'

Robbie put a hand on his arm and, to Quig's consternation, punched him lightly on the chest.

'Common knowledge, Dad. Common knowledge.'

'We are not going broke,' Quig said.

'I believe you, though thousands wouldn't,' Robbie said and, still grinning, punched his father's chest once more. 'Come along, let's toddle down to Pennypol so that I can see for myself what the cat dragged in.'

'The cat?'

'Figure of speech, Dad, just a figure of speech. Are we going, or are we not?'

'We're going,' said Quig.

There was little enough to do at Pennypol save keep weeds at bay and wait for the first green shoots to appear. Rabbits, though, were a hazard. They would devour anything green almost as soon as it showed. She had thwarted them by fixing up the galvanised wire netting, complete with staples and stakes, that Quig had ordered from a nurseryman near Oban. Billy had helped her erect the circular fence, no great labour, really, for the mallet was light and Billy was strong for his age and claimed to have done quite a bit of fencing in his time.

She was keen to secure the plots at Pennypol before she started on the garden at Fetternish House. Once she had made a start there she hoped Quig might be tempted to come and help her whenever he had an hour to spare. She loved the idea of working with Quig. He would dig and she would hoe and together they would bring the old garden back to life. She would have to be quick, though, for the baby was growing rowdy within her. When autumn came Quig would have to tend the garden all by himself for a while.

Rachel had gone back to Glasgow on the same day that Mr Brown had returned from visiting his son and daughters. He had come for supper last evening to cheer Innis up. He had talked at length about the Yeates family and about Fream and seemed to know more about its history than Fay did.

There had also been a picnic on the lawn at Fetternish House. All the Quigleys' friends had been there. Fay had not been invited but she listened with interest while Innis told Mr Brown all about it and wondered how long it would be before she was accepted into the family and if the arrival of the baby would help or hinder her progress in that direction.

It was a fine, bright morning, with high scudding clouds. Boats were out in force, fishing craft and yachts, the blue water beyond the limit of the bay both busy and benign as Easter receded and spring began to give way to summer.

She had left Kilty at home this morning. Innis had brought him into the kitchen as soon as Becky had gone to work and Fay, running later than usual, had not had the heart to call him to her. She missed the spaniel's company, though, and was glad when she spotted the Barretts heading in her direction.

Then she realised that it was not the Barretts but Quig and his son, that Mrs Quigley's orders notwithstanding she was about to meet the heir to Fetternish face to face.

She was kneeling in the strawberry beds, turning the dead-looking leaves in search of mildew when the men appeared. She stayed where she was and watched Quig and the young man descend the rough side of Olaf's Hill.

The young man wore a spotless white shirt and baggy flannel trousers and looked much more city than country.

Fay got to her feet. She steadied herself with a hand on the wall.

As she watched them cross the old calf pasture with its litter of nettles and thistle stalks, her stomach lurched with fear and excitement. She had an urge to run and hide but bravely stood her ground.

He advanced towards her, grinning.

She experienced the lurch in her stomach again and a sudden awful wave of nausea that made her want to retch.

Robbie Quigley held out his hand.

'Miss Ludlow, is it?' he said. 'I am pleased to make your acquaintance.'

She felt her throat close in panic.

'Fay, are you not going to say hello to my lad?' Quig said.

She could not answer, could not respond.

She was struck dumb by the uncanny resemblance that Quig's son bore to her husband. She understood now why Biddy had tried to prevent this meeting, for Robbie Quigley and Gavin Tarrant looked less like cousins than twins – and she, little Fay Ludlow, held the key to Biddy Baverstock's dark secret right in the palm of her hand.

SEVEN

A Woman Against the Light

He had done his work thoroughly and well. He had ridden round most of the north part of the island within a month of being offered the contract. His preliminary reconnaissance had been made four years ago but nothing had changed since then and he had no need to revise his original estimates.

The first plantation of Norwegian spruce would come away quickly after thinning and in eight or ten years' time would be an irresistible attraction for any proprietor with land lying idle and a bit of cash to spare. All he would have to do then would be to collect his commissions from Louden, Lafferty and Spruell and settle down to manage the new estates. That was still in the future, however; meanwhile he intended to obtain a hold on Fetternish before the summer was out so that laying and drainage could begin in the autumn and seedlings brought in for planting in the spring. As yet he had no clue just how many acres he would be able to wrest from Bridget Quigley on behalf of his clients or even if mixed woodland would be a viable proposition on the great table of land at An Fhearann Cáirdeil.

There were hundreds of wasted acres close to the seashore too which with sheltering stands of maple, evergreen oak and yew to protect them would probably support the newer conifers and call a halt to the north quarter's decline. He was not particularly interested in reclamation as such – he was too mercenary for that – but he had picked his way over the debris of so many deer forests, grouse moors and sheep runs – money-making schemes that had foundered through lack of enterprise or plain bad management – that anything that held the promise of permanence had to be an advance on the here and now.

It was not the misuse of land that irked Patrick but the squandering of money on dreams that anyone with a sound head for business and a smattering of geological knowledge could have spotted as doomed from the outset.

Mull, in fact, was no bad place to plant timber. The base-rich soils of Carsaig Bay already supported woodlands and along the shores of Loch Spelve there were pretty strips of larch and alder. Pines backed a few farmsteads. Rowans huddled against the wind in the long, bare valley of Glenarray, and on the rough peninsula of Laggan scrub birch thrived.

The north quarter was less promising, however. Its even green terraces had been ruined by over-grazing and bracken had swarmed out of the gullies to pollute every patch of pasture that laziness or lack of capital had pushed back towards its natural state – a state that some fools interpreted as a sign of the earth's indomitable powers of regeneration but that Robert Patrick Rattenbury regarded, more realistically, as inexcusable waste.

He had written several times to the Quigleys and had received letters in return, letters that expressed vague interest, that did not, as it were, close the door upon his request for a meeting. He was not disheartened by the Quigleys' caution or the slow pace of proceedings; he had learned long ago that a soft approach worked best when it came to catching monkeys.

The old woman was less patient than he was, though, and he wasn't in the least surprised when she sent for him again.

He travelled from Perth just as fast as train and boat could carry him and, prepared for a prolonged stay, arrived on Mull on the first Monday in May.

He preferred saddle to cart and kept one of his own horses in livery at Ardenshiel on the outskirts of Tobermory, along with several items of surveying equipment that he had used in laying out The Ards. He wasted no time in town but rode out to Mrs Hollander's house at once.

Barely an hour after the *Claymore* had set him down upon the Tobermory pier, he arrived at his destination in a flurry of fine rain. His billowing black oilcloth cape was wet and his breeches spattered with mud. He carried the rest of his belongings in a huge waterproof bag strapped to the saddle. He intended to change before the interview and would have done so too if Mrs Hollander had not urged him to make haste.

Frances had been looking out for him from the front steps. She was dressed in a style that jibbed with her rough country environment but Patrick knew that the clinging gown of fawn cashmere trimmed with white silk passementerie had not been put on for his benefit.

He swung out of the saddle and handed the reins to the servant-girl Florence who, among other virtues, had learned how to care for horses. He watched the girl lead the animal away, then, with his travelling bag slung over his shoulder, greeted Frances Hollander, and followed her indoors.

Muddy boots and oilcloth cape notwithstanding, she led him directly up the carpeted staircase to the second-floor landing where she paused and in that lispy, breathy way she had, whispered, 'I do not think she is well, Mr Rattenbury. I trust that you will not detain her a moment longer than is necessary.'

It was on the tip of Patrick's tongue to remind Mrs Hollander that he had been sent for and had not just dropped in in the hope of finding her mother at home. He said nothing, though. As a rule it was best not to interrupt Frances in the middle of one of her impersonations: at that moment she was performing her Dutiful Daughter act which, he thought, was a bit rich given that she, Frances, wanted nothing more than to have the old dragon pass away just as soon as God was ready to receive her.

Not for the first time he wondered how Frances would react if he clasped her dainty little head in his hands and crushed a passionate kiss on to her lisping little lips. Smiling at his conceit, he unbuttoned his cape, swept it from his shoulders, and swiftly climbed the three carpeted steps that led to the door of Madam Lafferty's apartment.

He glanced round.

Frances nodded.

He knocked, and entered.

Quig said, 'Unless I am much mistaken that will be a healthy crop of early potatoes. When will you be taking them up? June?'

'No,' Fay said. 'I'll leave them until the third or fourth week of July. It will run them into the main crop but I should manage to get them up before I become too heavy for stooping.'

Quig refrained from comment. She seemed no more than a little thick around the middle but she was beginning to huff and puff when she hefted up the barrow or swung a spade.

Biddy had been huge by the fifth month of her first pregnancy but had been so eager to bear a child that she had endured all the discomforts without a word of complaint. How different it had been with Christina; everything had gone awry with Christina. Biddy had moaned for seven solid months, had suffered aches and pains in every limb and organ and, to her chagrin, had even broken out in a rash.

Fay had a smooth unblemished complexion. Even the bruises around her eye seemed like cosmetic shading. He could not imagine Fay wasting time at a dressing-table strewn with paint pots and powder puffs. Everything about her was natural and unaffected. He even liked the way she sweated, a fine moist film dappling the slope of her breasts between the collar and the base of her throat.

'What weight do you expect to take in?' he asked.

'Nine or ten tons per acre. What will a ton fetch at market?'

Quig had already consulted a back issue of the *Oban Times*. 'Twelve to fourteen pounds at last season's prices.'

'If there's no glut, we should do well from our quarter-acre then.'

She wiped her throat and the upper part of her breasts with a cotton handkerchief. She had strong, rounded arms, not at all weak. There was nothing waif-like about Fay, nothing to foster pity. He would not be able to hide behind that excuse for much longer. She might have been one of Evander's orphans or one of the old man's young mistresses who had dropped babies easily and innocently out on the green sward of Foss.

Foss would suit Fay Ludlow well, he thought.

Foss would shelter her condition from prying eyes, would shelter them together, he and she.

'Our seed potatoes,' Fay was saying, 'are in the rows at the top of the plot. They're Duke of York and can be run on as a main crop next year if we can't sell them as earlies. I'll store them in chitting boxes in the cottage, if that's all right with you – with you and Mrs Quigley.'

'That will be just fine,' said Quig.

She was so eager for one season to follow another, for the future to unfold. What would have happened if he had met her before he had married Biddy? There were too many imponderables in that calculation to satisfy his growing sense of regret for all the sacrifices he had been asked to make.

The five years that separated him from Biddy had never seemed relevant until this last half year. He acknowledged that it was the cycle of nature that had changed his wife but he could not help but be hurt when she blamed him for the misery that had come down upon her. How could he pretend to be old? He still felt strong and hopeful. Biddy's imaginary infirmities, her depression, her conviction that her life was over and done with had become a dunning force in his life too. Of course he would care for her, look after her interests, would kow-tow to her less than reasonable demands if that was what she required of him, but he would not allow her to drag him under too.

'Has he gone home?' Fay said.

It took Quig a moment to realise that the subject had changed.

'What?'

'Your boy, has he gone home again?'

'This is his home,' Quig said. 'It is here he lives, with – with us.'

'To school. I mean, has he gone back to school on the mainland?'

Their concept of the mainland was surely very different. To him the word defined everywhere that was not Mull. To Fay, though, it was all the places that she had left behind.

'Days ago, weeks ago,' he said.

He had met with her several times since the end of the holiday. He had even asked her up to the house when Biddy had been away in Tobermory to give him advice about the walled garden. Why had she had not mentioned her meeting with Robbie before now?

God knows, Robbie had mentioned Fay often enough. He had talked about her in the moonstruck, slightly suggestive way that boys do when they are impressed by a girl that they know they should not be impressed by. Robbie had even added a postscript to one of his weekly letters – Quig suspected that the letter was no more than an excuse for the postscript – to ask after 'The Fair Maid of Fetternish', a casual enough enquiry that had driven Biddy into a frenzy of anger and had brought on a headache that had sent her off to bed in the middle of the day.

'He did not come down this way again,' Fay said.

'No, he . . .'

'I thought he might have come to visit Innis. Isn't he fond of her?'

Quig had no reason to suppose that Robbie harboured any animosity towards any of his relatives. He was a young man, self-concerned but not selfish, who had grown up with aunts and cousins all around him.

Unlike Christina, Robbie had never been afraid of Aileen. He would clamber up beside her without a qualm when she was seated on the long sofa in the hall and would even put his arms about her and give her childish kisses now and then. When instinct finally told him that Aileen was 'different', he took to providing her with attentions of a gentler sort, just as he, Quig, had done on Foss twenty years before.

'It is a strange question to be asking, Fay?'

'I just thought that when he did not come down to Pennypol . . .'

'In summer you – we will see more of him,' Quig said.

'He will be home for the summer then?'

'He will, he and his sister, and their cousin Donnie and his family.'

'It will be a busy summer for you at the big house,' Fay said. 'I'll be all swolled up by then and nobody will want to look at me.' She gave a little grunt. 'Does Robbie know who I am?'

'I am sure that he does.'

'Did you tell him about me?'

'Why are you so interested in Robbie?'

Quig tried to make the question light and teasing but there was a tiny piece of grit in his throat that he could not disguise. He could not bring himself to tell her that Biddy had ordered Robbie to stay away from Pennypol. He should have taken the bull by the horns and explained the situation to Robbie, but there was a little snarl of fear in him that Robbie would steal Fay from him.

'I'm not interested in Robbie.' Fay swabbed her throat with the cotton handkerchief. 'I mean, I'm more interested in you.'

She did not look at him. She stared at the sea. Odd, he thought, how everyone stared at the sea when they were trying to hide something or hold something back. He glanced down at the swoop of land than ran towards the shore and his alarm receded.

'Why is it that you are interested in me?' he heard himself say.

'Because we are partners.'

'Partners?'

'Or will be when the harvest comes in.'

He shook his head. 'I do not know what to be making of you.'

Fay laughed and stretched her arms as if she had just wakened from sleep, stretched them behind her and then above her head. 'There's nothing to be made of me, Mr Quigley,' she said. 'I can look after myself now, I reckon.'

'I think that may be true,' Quig said, 'but what will you do when the baby comes? And after the baby comes?'

'Stay here,' Fay said. 'Oh, yes, stay here on Fetternish – with you.'

'With Innis, do you not mean?'

'Aye,' the girl said. 'With Innis: that's what I meant to say.'

Her hair hung in a heavy tangle across her brow. Her eyes were a colour that he had never seen before, not green like Biddy's or ice blue like Aileen's but a queer sort of hue that reminded him of cornflowers. He wanted to hold her again as he had done before, to taste the perspiration that dewed her upper lip and feel the warmth of her young body packed with new life.

'I had better be pushing on,' he said.

'Yes, Quig,' she said, 'you'd better,' and picked up the hoe again.

She looked less like a queen than a czar. Czar of all the Russias was a title that would have suited her very well, Patrick thought. She was monumentally massive and occupied the carved wooden chair in the window bay with all-conquering arrogance. He had never been afraid of women but there was something about Mrs

Dorothea Lafferty that undermined his self-confidence: when he entered her presence he felt a little tightening of the scrotum and a faint retraction in the adjacent parts as if the mere size and scale of her, drenched in all her finery, challenged not just his authority but his manhood.

At one time, years ago, she must have been magnificent. Even now, in her sixties, the great boned bulge of her bosom suggested a smothering sexuality. The slant of eyes, her high plucked brows, the broad, moist, glossy mouth and arched cheekbones that were still just discernible under ruffles of fat were not so much ruins as reminders of a beauty that in its heyday had rocked many a courtly banker back on his heels. But the fast life had taken its toll: she was huge now, her limbs swollen with a gouty disease that broche silk and tucked muslin and a weight of gold and silver jewellery served to emphasise, not disguise.

She occupied the chair in monarchical fashion. Her ringed fingers cupped her knees and her knees were splayed out under her skirts in a pose, Patrick thought, more architectural than human. An embroidered neck-roll hung from the chair back and at her feet was a tiny footstool upon which she might rest her ankles when the pain in her joints gripped sore.

Sullenly she watched him cross the carpet from the door.

He was tempted to execute one of the grand Shakespearean dips that he had seen performed upon the stage of the Lyceum but Frances had warned him that illness had made her mother-in-law uncommonly sensitive to anything that smacked of mockery. Determined not to be brow-beaten by the magnificent old reprobate or show how much she impressed him, he contented himself with a concessionary bow.

The window bay was raised six or eight inches above the level of the floor: the light from the lead-paned window was behind her.

'Madam,' he said. 'Good-day to you.'

Her voice had no trace of Frances's winsomeness. It was low-pitched and dry, moderated by an accent – or accents – that hinted at Boer and Yankee yet still held echoes of the Glasgow tenements out of which she had crawled forty or fifty years ago.

She said, 'Was the boat on time?'

'It was.'

'Then why are you late?'

'I'm not late,' Patrick said.

'You have kept me waiting.'

'Madam, I have not.'

The smile was hardly a smile at all, a mere tilt of the side of the lip, but her eyes told him that she appreciated his resistance. If she had been younger he reckoned that she would have eaten him alive.

'Hasn't she replied to your letters yet?' the woman said.

'Mrs Quigley? No, there has been no further correspondence.'

'No suggestion that you meet?'

'None.'

'She's the devil to deal with, that one.'

'Her children have been home for the holiday,' Patrick said.

'Her children! Is she so lacking in sense that she would put her children before her children's future?'

Patrick did not quite grasp the point. There was no mystery what Dorothea Lafferty wanted, though: she wanted as much land as she could lay her hands on. She wanted Fetternish and Mishnish and Pennypol and would take Leathan and Mingary and Calgary too if they ever came on the market. But still he could not fathom why Dorothea Lafferty, a woman of great worldly experience, had settled in this far corner of Mull.

Planting was cheap, large tracts of land could be had for less than equivalent acreage in, say, Inverness or Haddington, with no tussles over game preservation or the building of in-roads to delay progress. There were plenty of vacant properties for Louden, Lafferty and Spruell's forestry workers and, once timber-growing had been established, there could be no recanting on the proprietor's part. Even so, Mull was no place for a woman like Mrs Lafferty and it was on the tip of his tongue to ask what sort of future Frances could look forward to stuck away in such uncouth surroundings — but he wasn't bold enough to put that question either.

He said, 'We have eight hundred acres to be going on with and, on general estimate, about nine hundred on the peninsula north-west of Fetternish House.'

'I've heard that the moor may be right for spruce trees if the planting is large enough to make it practical?'

'I believe I told you that,' said Patrick.

'So you did. So you did.'

The twitching smile became a grimace. He watched her shift her bulk, ponderously lift each knee with both hands to place her ankles on the footstool. She was no whining hypochondriac but a genuine cripple. He wondered if she had retired to Mull to hide her decay from friends and lovers or, more probably, to sustain some vestige of independence. She grunted and settled her weight forward, resting her forearms on her thighs.

He stood awkwardly before her, hat in hand, cape draped over his arm. This was not a social call: this was business and it would be conducted quickly.

He said, 'I think the only thing to do is to call upon Mrs Quigley.'

'She won't thank you for that. She's a burr, by all accounts.'

'A burr?'

'Prickly.'

'What do you suggest I do then?' said Patrick.

'Frances has befriended the Quigleys' housekeeper.'

'Well, that's a start.'

'Please do not interrupt.'

'I'm sorry.'

'Frances has befriended the housekeeper and has a fair inkling of what's going on inside the house. The husband, Quigley, has been employed to manage some of our estate's affairs.'

'Employed — on what basis?'

'*Pro rata*,' the woman said. 'It's nothing, just make-work. Frances asked for his help in assessing the worth of a couple of our old cottages.'

'I've seen them. They're ruins and worth nothing.'

'I know that,' Mrs Lafferty said. 'He will also club our sheep in with his when it comes time to sell. The Quigleys' shepherd has helped out with lambing already and, to save you asking, there were twenty-six head born alive.' She lifted one hand into the air and waved it, making the gold and silver rings glint in the pale sunlight and the bracelets on her wrists tinkle like Spanish wind-chimes. 'The stock isn't important. What is important is that we have a connection with the man of the house — and he will introduce you to his wife.'

'It seems to me,' Patrick said, 'unnecessarily devious.'

'We are dealing with peasants. Deviousness is all they understand.'

This, Patrick knew, was false. He had dealt with Highlanders for most of his professional life and had always found them fair and honest. True, they were keen on bargaining and cautious in their dealings with southerners but he did not hold that against them. Again, he wondered where Mrs Lafferty had come from, in what peculiar milieu her character and her fortune had been formed.

'If I were to meet Quigley,' Patrick said, 'if I were to bump into him by chance, let's say, do you suppose that he might accelerate the process of negotiation?'

'Sure,' the woman said. 'Sure he would.'

'Is that what you had in mind when you asked me here today?'

She leaned back suddenly, arrested not by his perspicacity but by some internal disturbance, some new thread of pain.

He watched her legs tremble, saw her skirts shiver, heard the heel of her slipper knock rapidly and rhythmically against the footstool. She remained radiant against the light, however, massive and opaque in her distress. It occurred to him then that the cotillion-like steps that passed for land dealing were all that were keeping her sane and that land purchase, tree-planting, an acquisitive manoeuvring for family property were the last stand of a woman whose greed had finally brought her to the brink of the grave.

She pressed down firmly on her trembling knees.

She said, 'Do I not pay you enough?'

'You pay me very well,' Patrick said. 'I'm just not sure what you are paying me for. You have my surveys and costings. The Ards is laid out, drained and fenced and planted. What do you want from me now, Mrs Lafferty?'

'Fetternish.'

'Unlet and derelict and going out of cultivation?'

'I do not have time to argue. I want you to get me that land.'

'I understand that,' he said. 'It's never been my intention to neglect your interests, madam. I have brought my belongings with me. Be assured that I'm here until the lady of Fetternish surrenders her land for tree-planting.'

'Spruce trees.'

'Wherever possible, yes, Norwegian spruce.'

'A sea of green boughs,' Mrs Lafferty said. 'I would like to see a great waving sea of green boughs again before I die.'

'Fifteen years?' said Patrick. 'Ten at best.'

'And I would like to live there.'

'What?' Patrick was caught off guard. 'Where?'

'In that castle, in her great house on the headland.'

'I didn't realise that the house was to be part of the lot.'

The quirky smile was pain-free.

'I want everything that Biddy Baverstock has, everything she owns.'

'I thought her name was Quigley?' Patrick said.

'It matters not a goddamn what she calls herself,' Madam Lafferty said.

Her lips had been numbed by the glycerine and powdered carmine. Her mouth folded in on itself and formed a line, straight as a plumb-string, across the centre of her face. She had almost given herself away, had just caught herself in the nick of time. He had a shadowy sense that the transaction was not about land or trees or the laying down of legacy for future generations but was all about the past, only about the past, and that he was merely a pawn in the final moves of a game that had begun long ago.

'I will establish myself as soon as I can,' he said. 'I'll do as you suggest and meet with the husband and, through him, the wife. I cannot guarantee that you'll have your nine hundred acres by this weekend, but have them you will, madam. Once we have an agreement on the land we can begin to negotiate for what stands upon it. Are you sure that you want the house too?'

She heaved herself up on columnar legs. The effort was majestic. She was not tall, he realised, no more than average height for a woman, but she dominated not just the window bay but the entire room.

Patrick lifted a hand and shielded his eyes.

'Everything that Biddy Baverstock owns or has ever owned I want taken from her,' Madam Lafferty said. 'I want all of it for myself.'

'Then all of it you shall have,' said Patrick.

The presence of forestry workers had not passed unnoticed in Crove. The men were billeted in Dervaig and seedlings and equipment unloaded at Calgary so that all the traffic bypassed the village and Frances Hollander's spruce plantation seemed, in a manner of speaking, to have sprung up overnight.

Some of the older boys had skiffed across the river from time to time to admire the huge Clydesdale horses that hauled the laden drays and, later, dragged heavy sharp-tongued ploughs across the hillside.

The boys relayed the latest news to Mr Brown who mentioned it to Janetta who, as her friendship with the lady of The

Ards ripened, wrung fresh information from that source and conveyed it back to her father. He, in turn, transferred it to Tom Ewing who compared notes with Mairi who carried the latest to her son, Quig, who passed it on to Biddy – who declared that she had no interest whatsoever in what was happening on the other side of the loch.

News also continued to emanate from Miss Fergusson's shop as new ground was drained and fenced and lightly ploughed over.

'What are they planting?'

'Spruce, I think.'

'Huh, the salt air will kill white wood before three winters.'

'Some larch too, for protection.'

'There is a woman who does not know what she is doing.'

'She is by way of having more money than sense, I am thinking.'

'Aye, that is what I am thinking too.'

'There is nothing for us in it, is there now?'

'No, nothing for us at all.'

When the first letter was delivered to Fetternish Biddy was not surprised.

It came not from Frances Hollander but from a firm of land agents in Perth. Biddy had never heard of Louden, Lafferty and Spruell, and neither had Willy. Willy was sufficiently interested, however, to interrogate his wife about the woman who had bought The Ards and when that failed to elicit anything more interesting than frivolous gossip, he had written on the q.t. to his oldest son, now in his fifties, who was senior cashier in the Royal Embassy Insurance Company in Edinburgh.

He, the son, had written back to inform his father that Louden, Lafferty and Spruell had been registered as a private development company as recently as 1905 but that as far as he could discover had developed nothing so far except a single site on Mull.

Willy was not satisfied; he longed to learn more about the woman who had dazzled his wife; in particular how Frances

Hollander came to be associated with a spanking new development company in Perth.

Before Willy could lick his pen-nib and unfurl another sheet of foolscap, Biddy received a communiqué from Robert Patrick Rattenbury which went some way to explaining what Louden, Lafferty and Spruell were after, which, it seemed, was nothing less ambitious than coating the whole of Mull's north quarter with Norwegian spruce trees.

Seated with Aileen on a rug on the lawn, Willy would peer at the headlands that fell away to the south and debate whether or not an ancient emptiness was preferable to an ocean of new timber; whether or not forestry would bring life — by which he meant people — back to Fetternish and how future generations would judge the landowners who had sold off their pastures to provide raw material for furniture merchants, box-makers and paper manufacturers; if, in the history that had yet to be written, Biddy and Quig would be regarded as progressives or would be condemned as destroyers of a way of life that had existed only in dreams.

Willy would have no part in it. He lacked the juice to interfere in progress now, though the will to do so was as strong as it had ever been.

Biddy was skulking in the library on a day when she should have been out and about. Willy opened the door and let himself into the room. Ignoring his mistress's scowl of displeasure, he scraped out a chair and seated himself upon it.

'Biddy,' he said, 'you're going to have to do something.'

'What can I do? She is here to stay by the look of it.'

'About Rattenbury's letters, I mean.'

'Oh, the letters.'

Willy had done enough reading to last a lifetime and his eyesight was barely up to browsing through *The Times* these days. He peered at Biddy, waiting for her to say something intelligent.

'Where's Aileen?'

'In the kitchen, eating her dinner,' Willy answered. 'Don't

change the subject, Biddy. I know you're thinking about it, otherwise you would not have asked Quig to fetch in sample seedlings. Do you have any idea what the hard cash offer will be?'

'No.'

'What's holding you back?' Willy said. 'Are you thinking that it isn't your land to give away? That you are bound to hold it in trust for Robbie? That Fetternish is somehow a part of Mull's history and has to be preserved intact?' He shook his head. 'That's just nonsense, sheer nonsense. You came into possession of Fetternish by chance, by luck, if you like: good luck followed by ill. It's no more yours by right than it was Austin Baverstock's. He bought this estate with trade money and he treated it like a toy.'

'He did not treat me like a toy.'

'I didn't say that, Biddy.'

'I wish Austin hadn't died.'

'If Mr Austin had not died you would not have been free to marry Quig.'

'No, and I wouldn't have all these troubles piled upon me now.'

'Biddy, for God's sake, what's come over you?' Willy said. 'Have you lost all your spunk?'

She peered at him, fierce and unrelenting.

Once he had feared that he would go out like Ronan Campbell, descend into madness, be cast off by the family, abandoned, imprisoned and left to die alone. Maggie would not let that happen, of course; Maggie was the power below stairs. Maggie was also an islander born and bred and had no idea how the world wagged or what changes a woman like Frances Hollander might bring to the sleepy communities of the north or what damage her money might do.

Biddy pinched her eyelids with her fingertips.

'What will happen to us, Willy, if I do sell out?'

'You don't have to sell out. You can trade off a piece to save the rest. God, woman, what do you want all that trashy ground *for?* It's no use to man nor beast. What do you hope to do with it? Howk up the stones, drain it, build fences, lay hedges and reclaim it as arable? Never in a thousand years would you be able to find the cash. And who else would want it? Another Austin Baverstock, another Edinburgh romantic?'

'Where will we go?'

'Nowhere, I tell you. You'll have the best part of three hundred acres left, more if you hang on to Pennypol and Pennymain. You'll stay on here in the house and hardly notice that anything has changed.'

'Is that true?'

'Biddy, what's come over you? Do you think I'd tell you lies?'

'Everyone lies to me these days — one way or another.'

'Well, I don't,' Willy said. 'I wouldn't know how to lie to you even if I wanted to. Look,' he went on, 'there's no guarantee that Robbie will want this place. He isn't a farmer. You picked a different line for him to follow. You set him off down the road to being a doctor or a lawyer or, if the worst comes to the worst, a teacher like his cousin. And Christina — well, she is a young lady of breeding and will no doubt marry a gentleman and live in a fine house in Morningside or Corstorphine and have umpteen babies. What I'm saying is that neither of your children are farmers and you mustn't let your feeling for Fetternish cloud that fact. They don't have dirt under their fingernails as you did when you were their age.'

'What are you telling me, Willy?'

'At least talk to this man, this Patrick Rattenbury.'

'What good will that do?'

Willy threw up a hand in exasperation. 'No good at all, perhaps. But at least give him an opportunity to put his case before you dismiss him. Try, woman, for God's sake, try, otherwise you'll lose the lot.'

'Save what I can, is that what you are telling me?'

'Yes,' Willy said. 'Save what you can while you can.'

Biddy appeared unconvinced. She turned her head away. In profile she seemed soft and young again.

Willy sighed.

'Why does Quig never talk to me as sensibly as you do, Willy?'

'Perhaps he does and you just don't listen.'

'That's no answer.'

'No, it isn't,' Will admitted. 'What Quig does he does as well as any man alive, but he is not city sharp.' He gave a tight self-deprecating snort of amusement. 'Quig wasn't "educated" by the Baverstocks the way I was – and you should be damned glad of that, Biddy, believe me.'

He studied her carefully, hoping for some of the rough teasing humour that she had brought with her out of Pennypol. There were times when Willy wondered what Ronan Campbell had really done to his daughters and why Vassie had gleefully committed him to the madhouse at Redwing and danced a jig on his grave.

'Save what I can,' Biddy said.

'While you can,' said Willy.

'I'll see him,' Biddy said. 'I don't know what good it will do, but I'll see him.'

'Will you inform him, or shall I?'

'I'll write to him soon.'

'Not soon,' said Willy. 'Today.'

'I assume he's still at the Perth address.'

'No,' Willy said. 'As a matter of fact, Biddy, Rattenbury's here.'

'Here?'

'Outside in the yard, talking with Quig.'

'Quig brought him here without my permission?'

'Yes,' Willy said. 'Brought him in the dogcart from the Hollander house.'

'Oh, God! Oh, God!' said Biddy.

'What do you want to do?'

'Oh, God! Oh, God!' She closed her eyes and touched a trembling hand to her hair. 'Oh, God, Willy, what shall I do, what *shall* I do?'

'Have him shown in, I reckon,' Willy said.

And took her hot and bothered little groan as a 'Yes.'

EIGHT

The Charmed Circle

One thing to be said for the stubborn Scots is that the parochial tradition dies hard in all walks of life and in none more so than the provision of education. Janetta Brown did not require a crystal ball or a consultation with local divinator Aileen Campbell to predict that the legislators would take little account of experience when the new education acts came into force and in the autumn of 1903 she left Mull to acquire a certificate that would entitle her to do what she had been doing for the past fifteen years, namely teach.

During her absence a certain Miss Somerville was imported to assist Gillies. Miss Somerville lodged in the manse and in a ten-month tour of duty contrived to make an enemy of everyone in Crove. Even Gillies, a man not prone to violent emotions, had been ready to throttle the dictatorial old spinster and had been overjoyed when she finally marched off and Janetta had returned to the fold.

A year in Dundee's teachers' training college did not alter Janetta's approach to education. It changed her outlook in other ways, however.

She did not consort with her fellow students or yield to the blandishments of one or two young gentlemen who attempted to pay her court. She chummed up instead with a young woman named Belinda Struthers, of whom she became rather too fond.

After Netta had returned to Crove Belinda had bombarded her with letters, threatened to give up her own career and come to live on Mull; became so dramatic and presumptuous, in fact, that Netta had broken off the correspondence with a curt and callous letter which, though Belinda knew it not, had been written in tears, so many tears that Netta's nose had been red for days and everyone had assumed that she was coming down with a cold.

Some months later Janetta had received a note from Belinda to inform her that she had found another friend, had gone to live in Dorset with her friend and realised now that her feelings for Janetta had been no more than childish infatuation.

Since that sad episode Janetta had cautiously preserved what was left of her heart wrapped in flannel in a bottom drawer, as it were, together with Belinda's letters and the little silhouette that she, Belinda, had sent her just before the last cruel exchange.

Frances Hollander was so sophisticated and polished, however, that Janetta was caught off guard and did not realise the true nature of the emotions that Frances roused in her magisterial breast until the warm May afternoon when Robert Patrick Rattenbury first walked into her life.

Dandy MacArthur and his grey-haired son were not trawlermen or netters but ran a little boat from a mooring at the mouth of the loch and brought in line-caught sea-trout or buck mackerel and now and then cod or an illegal salmon which they sold from a tiny smoke-filled shed behind their cottage at the end of the main street. It was late afternoon when Janetta left the schoolhouse and set out to buy fish. Fish was cheaper than beef or mutton or the stale cooked meats that Miss Fergusson sold and that evening she bought two whole plaice, and with her purchase wrapped in newspaper had just started back down Main Street when she spotted the American buggy drawn up outside the McKinnon Arms.

The horse was still in the shafts, long leather reins looped around the leg of a wooden table that Mr Patterson, current proprietor of the Arms, had put outside in the vain hope of attracting female customers.

Janetta stopped dead in her tracks.

She swapped the packet of fish from left hand to right and glanced almost furtively up and down the street.

There were few folk to be seen. Children were indoors eating supper. Hens pecked listlessly at the blossom that had blown from the cherry tree in the grounds of the United Free church. Angus Bell's blacksmith was wrestling with a long iron tee-bar that a carrier had delivered that afternoon. The front door of the Arms was wide open and the yeasty odour of the bar leaked into the evening air.

Janetta had never set foot inside the McKinnon Arms and had no intention of doing so now. She was teased by curiosity, though, by a desire to find out what Frances might be doing in such a low-down place.

She slipped the packet of fish into her pocket, crossed the street and walked around the buggy in a half circle.

The horse was not one of Angus's docile beasts but a handsome stallion that did not seem to belong between the shafts. Janetta hesitated then walked back towards the railings of the Free church, turned and came back along the narrow pavement that flanked the pub. She was so intent on appearing uninterested that the man was upon her before she noticed him. He had an oilcloth cape thrown over his shoulder and the type of hat that she had not seen since her spell in Dundee; soft curled hair; long eyelashes; the sort of dark, flashing eyes with which the heroes of her bedtime reading were unrealistically endowed.

He appeared suddenly from behind the buggy.

He had a heavy, sausage-shaped valise tucked under one arm and a stiff cardboard document case in one hand.

'Madam,' he said. 'My apologies. I did not see you there.'

'Nor I – nor I you, sir.'

She had seldom felt so awkward, not even when Belinda Struthers had taken her hand when they walked on the silver strand on a day's outing to Newport; that had been awkwardness of a different order, not so much embarrassing as jolting.

'I saw – I thought – Mrs Hollander's . . .' Janetta began.

'Buggy.'

'Yes, I thought she might be here.'

'I can't imagine what Mrs Hollander would be doing in a public house, least of all a public house like this one,' the man said. 'Are you a friend of the Hollanders?' Janetta had an urge to run off like a mischievous pupil. 'Hold on a moment. Are you, by any chance, Miss Brown?'

'I am. Do I know you, sir?'

'I'm Patrick Rattenbury. I've heard a great deal about you.'

'I'm afraid,' Janetta said, 'I've heard little or nothing about you.'

'That's all to the good,' Patrick Rattenbury said.

'It is?'

'It means that you may judge me without preconceptions.'

'Oh, I do know who you are or, rather, what you represent.'

'And what might that be?'

'Trees,' Janetta said stupidly. 'You're the tree fellow, aren't you?'

He had strong white even teeth and a long, columnar throat that vibrated against the stud of his collar when he laughed.

'I suppose you could say that.'

She would have excused herself and moved on but he had put down the bag and the document case and showed every sign of wishing to continue their conversation.

'Is that,' Patrick said, 'fish?'

Janetta jerked her hand from her pocket.

Laughter loitered about his lips and he reminded her a little of Quig, though he did not have Quig's rather plodding air of gravity. He was quick and relaxed at one and the same time. She felt sure that his intelligence would more than match her own. She hesitated, then ruefully extracted the newspaper-wrapped packet from her pocket and held it up.

'Supper,' she confessed. 'Plaice.'

'Is there a fish merchant in the village?'

'MacArthur's, second last cottage on the far side of the street.'

'Do they also sell fresh butcher-meat?'

'No, it's best to shop in Tobermory for fresh meat.' She paused. 'By the sound of it, Mr Rattenbury, you intend to stay in Crove for a while?'

'For a month at least, possibly longer, but with the best will in the world I can't see myself bedding down in the McKinnon for more than a night or two.'

'Can't you stay with Frances – with Mrs Hollander?'

The last trace of laughter vanished. For an instant he seemed almost hostile. She wondered if she had stumbled upon some impropriety.

'It would,' Patrick said, 'not be politic.'

'Politic?'

'For a gentleman to stay in a house with so many ladies.'

'I see,' Janetta said, though she didn't, not clearly. 'We would take you in at the schoolhouse, sir, but there's no spare room at all, I'm afraid. There's always the manse. On a temporary basis, the manse might do. Reverend Ewing has taken in lodgers before. Or Fetternish House. Have you met the Quigleys?'

'As a matter of fact,' Patrick said, 'I have.'

'Is it a project you'll be working upon?'

'Yes, a project.'

'Biddy might well be willing to put you up. There's no scarcity of rooms in Fetternish House.' She knew she had said too much, had rushed in like a fool simply to impress him. 'Perhaps that would not be convenient to your work.'

'Probably not,' he said. 'I'm here for the moment and will take my time looking about for a lodging. You are the schoolteacher, aren't you?'

'My father and I teach school here, yes.'

'Frances thinks very highly of you.'

'Really! Oh!' was all Janetta could think of to say.

'I'll spare your blushes,' Patrick said.

'No, what did Frances—' Janetta bit off the question. 'We are friends, of course, and I think highly of her too. Very highly.'

'She is certainly lively,' Patrick said. 'And unusual.'

'Unusual?'

'I mean, not, perhaps, the sort of person one would normally expect to find in a rural community.'

'I see.' Janetta put the packet of fish back into her pocket and rubbed her fingers on the skirt of her overcoat. She would have to put the coat outside to air before she wore it again. She had been careless, and carelessness annoyed her.

She said, 'Have you known Frances for long?'

'She's more of an acquaintance than a friend.'

'And her mother? Do you know her mother?'

'Hardly at all.'

'We – I have never met her mother.'

'Perhaps one day you will have that pleasure.'

Down at the livery stables McCaig, the blacksmith, was beating on the long iron tee-bar that he had manhandled into the forge. The sound was clear, rhythmic and ringing in the cooling air, the sort of sound, Netta thought, that one's heart might make if it were amplified through a copper horn.

She felt detached, separated from the Charmed Circle, from Maggie and Mairi, unable to pursue a quest for information that could be passed along to her female friends. She would say nothing about her meeting with Mr Rattenbury or relay the few scant crumbs of gossip that had come her way. From now on she must remain loyal to Frances – and to Mr Rattenbury. She was curiously relieved that there was a man in Frances's life and that she had met him before the others, had had him, albeit briefly, to herself.

'I must not detain you,' Janetta said. 'You will have much to do.'

'Not so much, really,' Patrick said. 'However, I'd better get this chap to the stables before he begins to kick up a rumpus. He doesn't appreciate being used as a mule, I may tell you.'

'He is your horse then?'

'He is indeed.'

'Very handsome,' Janetta said.

'But not to be tampered with,' said Mr Patrick Rattenbury and, a moment later, took a polite farewell and let Janetta — and the plaice — go home.

She served the fillets with a sauce of lemon and white peppercorn and a side dish of finely sliced bottled beetroot. It was, her father declared, a dish fit for a king. With a glass of mild ale to help it down, he soon made short work of it and of the rice and raisin pudding that followed.

He had taken off his coat and rolled up his shirt sleeves. It was his habit to wash away the ink stains and chalk dust after a day in the classroom. The hair on his forearms stood up and he smelled pleasantly of soap.

Janetta could not remember what her father had been like when he had been young. She thought of him as a constant and unchanging presence and it surprised her every time she studied the faded old photograph that he kept in a box in the dresser drawer, a photograph of Mother and he in formal dress with a potted plant in the background. She could not relate to the woman in the photograph at all and even the man, so youthful and fresh-faced, seemed like a total stranger. Sometimes she wondered if she would have been attracted to him if she had been a young teacher in Glasgow thirty-five or forty years ago, or if she would have found his breezy manner irritating.

'I met a man,' she said.

'You did?' Gillies said. 'Just like that?'

'I mean, of course, a specific man — a Mr Rattenbury.'

Gillies put down his spoon and shifted his empty pudding plate to one side. He rested his elbows on the table. 'Rattenbury, the tree fellow?'

'He's looking for lodgings in Crove.'

'So he plans to stay for a while, does he?'

'It would appear so, yes.'

'I wonder if Biddy's thinking of selling out.'

'Selling out? What on earth are you talking about?'

'Rattenbury spent all yesterday afternoon at Fetternish,' Gillies explained. 'Quig brought him over from The Ards. Apparently Biddy was quite upset.'

'How do you know this?'

'Becky told me.'

'Becky told you?' said Janetta. 'When?'

'Yesterday evening.'

'Did Mr Rattenbury spend the night at Fetternish?'

'I don't believe he did.'

'He must have slept somewhere.'

'With your friend, with Mrs Hollander, perhaps?' Gillies said. 'I don't mean . . . I meant spent the night at The Ards. The important thing is that he and Biddy appear to have entered into negotiations at long last.'

'Is Biddy really going to sell the estate?'

'It's certainly on her mind but I doubt if she's reached a decision yet. Much will depend on the terms of the offer, I expect. Didn't your friend Mrs Hollander tell you what was floating in the wind?'

'It's private business; ladies do not discuss such matters.'

'Didn't she say anything about Mr Rattenbury?' No answer was forthcoming. 'He's a land agent, you know, here to buy up land for tree-planting.'

'What's wrong with wanting to grow trees?'

Gillies was puzzled by Netta's inability to grasp the economic implications of the situation, by her unwillingness to acknowledge that her friend Frances Hollander was not as flighty as she pretended to be.

He had talked at length with Becky yesterday evening. To some extent he shared the girl's indignation at the recent turn of events which he saw as signalling the end of a cycle now that the little lairds of the north quarter had become so unpinned from progress.

Forestry might well be the best solution to the problem of decline. If the foresters did come they would bring their wives and children and in ten years or so would be an established part of the community.

And the school would survive.

'I know what you are thinking,' Janetta said. 'He's not her sweetheart. He refuses to lodge at The Ards because he considers it impolitic.'

'Impolitic? What the devil are you talking about?'

'Mr Rattenbury.'

'Haven't you heard a word I've been saying?' Gillies asked. 'Honestly! Is that all you can think about, little bits of female gossip? What's at stake here, my dear daughter, is a great deal more than a reputation or two. Your Mrs Hollander is here to grab what she can. Has that not become apparent to you yet? She is a go-getter, a carpet-bagger . . .'

'What does that mean?'

'Ask your friend — or ask Rattenbury. No doubt they will be only too willing to educate you in commercial jargon and bring you up to date on the schemes of nefarious capitalism.'

'Becky has obviously turned your head with her parrot talk,' said Janetta stiffly. 'Nefarious capitalism! I never heard such rubbish. Frances isn't in the slightest interested in acquiring land, especially a wasteland like Fetternish. Dear heavens, Daddy, don't you remember how hard it was to keep the brambles and bracken from eating up the cottage when we lived at An Fhearann Cáirdeil?'

'Of course I remember.' Gillies was piqued; an evening which had started pleasantly was deteriorating into another session of argy-bargy. He enjoyed discussion, relished debate, but found it difficult to cope with Janetta's fixation on Mrs Frances Hollander, a woman for whom he had no time at all. 'God knows, I put in enough hard labour with sickle and shears to keep the damned jungle at bay.'

'I wonder what it's like now?' Janetta said.

'Much as it was,' said Gillies. 'By which I mean that the cottages haven't fallen down yet or been swamped by the undergrowth. Take a walk out there. See for yourself.'

'I have more to do with my time, thank you.'

Gillies paused, then said, 'This tree fellow obviously impressed you.'

'What makes you say that?'

'You didn't even ask what he was doing here, did you?'

'He – he's surveying.'

'Surveying what?'

'Stop badgering me, Daddy.'

'What's he surveying, tell me?'

'I – I don't know.'

'Have a guess then, an inspired guess, apply a little deductive—'

'All right, all right!' Janetta exclaimed. 'It has to be Fetternish, otherwise he wouldn't be negotiating with Biddy.'

'Correct,' Gillies said. 'Where does your friend Frances Hollander fit into this puzzle picture, I wonder?'

'I'm sure she knows nothing about it.'

'Oh, come now, Netta.'

She did not hang her head, did not bow to his sagacity.

She sat upright at the table, taller than ever, leaner than ever in the milky light from the window. Common sense had already cost her victory. She had lost the argument and, at any moment, would be forced to vocalise her fears.

'All right, Frances may be his employer. *May* be, I say, *may* be.' Daddy uttered not a word, did not smile, did not rub it in. She pulled her shoulders back. 'What if she is? I mean really, what if she is? What does it matter? It's none of our affair what becomes of Fetternish. I'd expect you to disapprove of any moves to change this god-forsaken place, of course, to bring improvements, no matter who came up with them, how sound they may be or how well financed.'

To her surprise her father simply shrugged. 'On the contrary.'

'You mean, you approve?'

'I do not necessarily disapprove.'

'Oh, for heaven's sake, Daddy, what *do* you mean?'

'I mean, dear, that tree-planting will bring work and work will bring workers, and they will have children.'

'The school,' Janetta said. 'You're only thinking of the school?'

'Of course I am. It won't matter to me, of course. I'll be dead and gone or at least retired before long, but you . . .'

'Me?'

'You have thirty or forty good teaching years left in you.'

'Good teaching years? Here? In Crove?'

'If there's a strong community then the school will stand,' Gillies said. 'So, if it takes trees to sustain a strong community, then let there be trees.'

'Thirty or forty years . . .'

'What's wrong? Isn't stability what you want?'

She got up, rising all in one piece as if her limbs had turned to wood.

'I do have to consider your future, Netta,' Gillies said, 'since you won't have a husband to look after you.'

'*Good God!*' Janetta bellowed. '*My good God!*'

And stalked out of the room and slammed the door, while Gillies, by no means chastened or surprised, reached calmly for the remains of the rice pudding.

There was a clear dividing line between informality and intimacy, a line that Frances never crossed. She had hired the girls, Florence and Valerie, because they were kindred spirits, not because she found them attractive. They had each other to keep them from wearying for the bright lights of London. They were very efficient, readily accepted orders and generally removed from Frances's shoulders the burden of pretending to be a housekeeper.

Valerie brought up Dorothea's specially prepared meals. Valerie fastened the big linen bib around the old woman's neck, cut up her meat, cored her apples and peeled the sweet little oranges of which she was so fond; oranges shipped directly from London in straw-packed crates along with grapes, dates, marzipans and special consignments of coffee and, two or three times a year, a hamper stuffed with walnuts, pecans and almonds, all treats for which Mrs Lafferty had developed a taste in the course of her travels, that brought back memories of happier days and allowed her to while away the long hours of her self-imposed imprisonment by nibbling, gnawing and sucking.

For all her greediness Mrs Lafferty was not mean or niggardly. She liked to share her treats with the servants and took pleasure in spoiling them.

She would keep Valerie by her for hours on end, not reading but eating, as if educating the girl in oral satisfaction had become a personal crusade. She would discourse for half an hour or more on subtle differences in flavour between grapes grown in a hothouse and those gathered from the vine in, say, the commune of the Médoc. She would urge the girl to test one grape against another and would watch the girl's white teeth close on the fruit and see the juice run, trickling, down the side of her lips and would say, 'Do you see? Do you see, child, what the difference is?'

Valerie, more diplomat than epicure, would answer, 'Hummm: yes, ma'am, I do. I really and truly do,' which somehow always satisfied the old woman.

There were days when pain unaccountably slackened its grip and Madam Lafferty would manage to feed herself with a big silver spoon and a big silver 'pusher'. There were even days when she could grasp a horn-handled steak-knife and hack at a slice of roast beef or a small tender sirloin and squint smugly at Valerie and wink too perhaps and, dripping on to the bib, would stuff her mouth full of the mangled meat and chew and chew and chew until every last drop of nourishment had been extracted from it.

It was not one of Dorothea's better days when Frances joined the old woman for lunch in the spacious upstairs apartment.

Lunch for Frances was a bowl of consommé and a slice of brown bread *sans* butter. She could whack away a cream tea with the best of them but had some scruple about gorging herself at every meal, for she disliked the bloated feeling that followed a period of indulgence and, being dependent upon Dorothea not just for food but clothing too, did not want to become so fat that her wardrobe would have to be replaced or, at best, re-seamed. Besides which, Frances could not abide to watch the old woman struggle and slobber. She found age disgusting and prayed that she would die while she was still young enough to be mourned more for her looks than her legacy.

Valerie was seated on the footstool beside Madam Lafferty's chair. The table had been lifted up into the window bay and Frances accommodated on one of the rag-backed chairs that had been shipped over from the last house in Boston.

She cradled a porcelain soup bowl in her left hand and dipped her spoon with her right so that her only connection with Dorothea was the bread plate which, so far, the old woman hadn't touched.

Dorothea was lunching on a whole roast fowl that Florence had cooked to perfection and Valerie had carefully dissected. Valerie had been allocated the legs and, urged on by her mistress, nicked and nibbled away between loading the old woman's fork with fragments of breast.

'Now there's a fine figure of a man for you.' Dorothea chewed strenuously. 'He would break your heart, that stager, if you were to give him the chance.'

'Not my heart, Mama,' Frances said.

'No, not your heart. We all know about *your* heart.'

'Does he remind you of Macklin? Is that why you like him?' Frances asked.

'Macklin! Hoh!'

'Iain then?'

Frances was being provocative; no better way of passing the time than by being provocative, for in that area at least she and the old woman were evenly matched. She watched the jaws slow and then, like a faulty engine, start up again. Valerie speared a piece of white meat on the tines of the fork and placed the fork against the edge of her mistress's plate. The fat hand groped for the fork, closed around it and brought it to her mouth.

'What do you think of Quigley?' Dorothea said.

'Aren't you going to answer *my* question?'

'It doesn't deserve an answer,' Dorothea said. 'Quigley – what do you make of him? The husband, not the wife.'

'The wife, I hardly know the wife.'

'Better friends with her housekeeper, aren't you?'

'It's my way of keeping in touch.'

'Does she appeal to you?' Dorothea said.

'Maggie Naismith? Please, Mama!'

'The teacher then: Brown?'

'One question at a time is good fishing.'

'Larry's father used to say that.'

'Then I must have picked it up from Larry,' Frances said. 'Do you want my opinion on Quigley, or on Netta Brown?'

'Quigley.'

'He is not a happy fellow, Mr Quig is not.'

'What leads you to that conclusion?' Dorothea said.

'You only have to look at him. Hangdog, if ever was.'

'Henpecked, do you think?'

Frances finished the consommé, licked the spoon and handed bowl and spoon to Valerie who put them on a tray on the floor behind the footstool.

'He's an islander,' Frances said. 'I don't understand islanders.'

'It's men you don't understand, whether they be islanders or whether they be not,' said Dorothea. 'Tell me about Quigley, though.'

'He might be useful,' said Frances.

'He took Patrick Rattenbury round there without protest, did he not?'

'Straight off,' said Frances, 'not a quibble nor a quit-claim to it.'

'I am hearing Larry's father again,' Dorothea said.

'Pillow talk tends to stick,' said Frances.

'Pillow talk? How much of that was there between you? Precious little!'

'More than you might think, Mama.'

'I don't want to talk about Larry – or your peculiarities.'

'Shall we talk about Iain then?'

The old woman sucked her teeth and laboriously picked a fleck of fowl meat from an incisor with her fingernail. 'There is nothing to say about Iain. It's what he would have wanted.'

'I doubt it,' Frances said.

'You did not know him as I did.'

'I should hope not, indeed,' Frances said. 'I'm still bewildered, though, why you are putting yourself to all this trouble and expense to honour the memory of a man who did not love you.'

'Oh, love me he did,' said Dorothea. 'Besides, what else have I got to do with my time? Where will I be as comfortable as I am here? In the Hôtel de Ville? In the Ritz or the Savoy? I've no desire to be laughed at by snotty young bellhops. I'd rather be here.' She paused and gripping the fork tightly in the palm of her hand forced her fingers to close round the shank. 'I feel closer to him here.'

'That,' said Frances, 'is horse feathers.'

'Larry—'

'I knew it would come down to Larry.'

'Larry will love it here.'

'If he ever decides to show up,' said Frances.

'He promised you he'd come this summer, didn't he?'

'Yes, but you know how much Larry's promises are worth.'

'Why won't you give him what he wants?'

'A divorce?' said Frances.

'Children.'

'I can't have children.'

'You mean you won't have children.'

'Same thing, Mama,' Frances said. 'In any case, you're one to talk about bearing children. In spite of all the gentlemanly attentions that came your way you only managed to produce Larry. Larry! I ask you!'

'He should never have married you.'

'He was desperate to marry me.'

'He didn't know what you were?'

'Yes, he did. He just refused to accept it.'

Frances watched the gobbet of white meat advance towards her mother-in-law's mouth and disappear.

The hand slid down again and Valerie diligently removed the fork from the weary fingers. Dorothea began to chew at the tit-bit with the same self-absorbed determination as she ground away at everything else in her life.

Frances was well aware that Mull's north quarter was the last place on earth that Larry Hollander would ever wish to settle. He relished the outdoor life but liked adventure more. There were no adventures to be found on this grey coast and the ghosts that Dorothea sought to exorcise or embrace were quite different from those that held the Quigleys in thrall, the sticky traditions of suffering and endurance of which an incomer had better beware.

With a twinge of revulsion she watched the old woman dribble and Valerie wipe the trickle from the unwholesome cheek.

Frances got to her feet.

Lunch was not over. Lunch would not be over until every last bit of the fowl had been consumed. She would not be permitted to leave until her mother-in-law gave sanction, nor would she attempt to do so. She had nothing to do downstairs, no one she cared to call upon until school was over and Janetta Brown was free to walk with her along the riverbank or beside the sea loch.

'Where are you going?' Madam Lafferty said.

'Absolutely nowhere,' Frances answered. 'I'm just looking out of your window, if you don't mind.'

'Looking at what?'

'He's doing something with the sheep.'

Dorothea surged and writhed but the chair was too narrow and her spine too stiff to allow her to turn of her own free will. For once Valerie seemed unwilling to interrupt the feeding process to push the chair into a more advantageous position.

'Who?' the woman demanded. 'Who is it?'

'Barrett, I think.'

'He's moving them to a greener site, ma'am,' Valerie said. 'The lambs are big enough to crop now and need more grass.'

'We all need more grass,' said Frances. 'I wonder if Barrett can find me greener pastures. What do you think, Mama? Shall I ask the good shepherd to move me on too?'

'Yes,' the old woman said, 'if you're willing to live on grass and fresh air and let a ram mount you properly at the right time of the year.'

Frances laughed. 'I think not,' she said. 'No, Mama, I really do believe that I prefer to stay where I am and await the coming of Larry.' She glanced down at her mother-in-law. 'That is what we're waiting for, is it not?'

'Of course it is,' said Madam Lafferty and, settling her bulk into the confines of the chair, signalled Valerie to charge her fork once more.

The boundary had been fenced with brand-new stobs and strands of heavy-gauge wire; a fine job done, Quig suspected, not by local contractors but by a couple of forestry workers from Dervaig.

The Hollander plantation, now in its third season, lay west of the shore line, tucked behind the grassy ridge that separated The Ards from the high ground of Fetternish. Nothing could be seen of it from any vantage point, yet Quig was always aware that the brushy little conifers were sprouting away on the parks where once the Clarks' sheep had grazed.

He had no objection to being hired out to the Hollanders. There was little enough involved. He had purchased winter feed and straw for lamb bedding in case April was excessively wet or cold but the straw lay unused in the open barn at the rear of The Ards and Barrett had managed the lambing more or less by himself.

Quig waited at the end of the old meadow at the tail of the glen that ran between the edge of the sea loch and the hills that dipped steeply down to Dervaig.

Nettles were sprouting, the broom was full yellow and in the gentle warmth of early afternoon he could hear the crackle of seaweed drying on the stones of the beach. He watched ewes and lambs amble over the stony ground at the top of the dip, the dog crouched low behind them.

The Hollanders' house was situated on a saddle at the head of the glen. Whoever had designed the house had had a fine sense of perspective, for, framed by hills and sky, the house appeared larger and more noble than it really was and had none of Fetternish's pretentious towers and turrets to spoil its lines. It was painted burned pink and snow white, with glossy black edgings to windows and doors, whereas no man in his right mind would have dared lay a brush on the rugged granite of Fetternish.

Barrett had taken off his jacket and rolled up his sleeves. He wore an old tweed cap pushed back from his brow and the pipe in his mouth emitted little gouts of smoke, like the funnel of a steam locomotive. He carried a long crook, hallmark of his trade, and tapped and nudged at the heels of the lambs who had grown enough in the past few weeks to be both nimble and curious. A fair racket rose from the ragged flock but there was no scattering or panic. The sheep would be given a day or two in what remained of the home park before being driven out on to the hill. There was less of the hill than there had been before the plantings but there would be grass enough to fatten up the Hollander lambs before the autumn sales.

In two or three weeks Barrett and he would round up the lambs for docking and castration but there would be none of the wild chases that there had been in the old days when Mull flocks had been thrown wide over heather hill and dale and the ewes had been crafty and canny. There would be fewer unexplained losses too, fewer torn corpses to feed the buzzards that circled overhead or the hirpling crows or the swaggering blackbacks that followed the trail of wool tufts and glossy droppings.

Progress, Quig knew, had its advantages.

The dog came up to him, glanced at him, let its tongue loll out in greeting and continued past on its stealthy business. It eased the last of the ewes through the new gate in the new fence. Barrett closed it behind them. Ewes and lambs drifted out into the park or bobbed away towards the burn line and, even as Quig watched, fell to quiet grazing.

Barrett took the pipe from his mouth and spat. He wiped his chin on a bare brown forearm. Though he was not yet forty, his hair and brows were streaked with grey and he looked older than his years; the days when he had been known as Boy Barrett were long, long gone.

There should have been a son with him, Quig thought, a replica of Barrett in his young manhood, but the older boys were employed in the Glasgow shipyards and he doubted if they would ever return to shepherding.

'You are looking very glum this afternoon, Quig,' Barrett said. 'Is there something the matter with Mrs Hollander's ewes that I have not been noticing?'

'What could be wrong that you would not be noticing?' Quig had been thinking, vaguely, of things other than sheep. 'They are looking better now, as a whole, than they were a year ago.'

'It was feed they were needing,' Barrett said. 'That is all.'

'She will be for selling them off, you know.'

'Well then, she will be getting the best price she can for them. When?'

'At the back end. Fat lambs to Dalmally, perhaps to Glasgow.'

'She could have a flock here, you know,' Barrett said. 'There will be grass enough for three or four hundred ewes, even with the trees round about.'

'Aye, but there will be more trees to come,' Quig said.

His work finished, the dog waited on the near side of the park close to the bracken, ears pricked for a further command. Barrett stared out at the sea for a moment, then removed the pipe from his mouth, put two dirty fingers between his teeth and uttered a high, chirping whistle that brought the dog racing to him.

'Soon it will be all trees, I am thinking,' Barrett said. 'Will it be trees on Fetternish too, Quig, that is the question we are all asking ourselves?'

'If it is,' said Quig cagily, 'it will mean employment for Billy and his kind for many years to come.'

'And for me?'

'There will always be room for sheep.'

'I seem to recall having heard my father say that about cattle.'

Quig knew only too well what Barrett meant: once it had been cattle, then it had been sheep, soon there might be nothing but trees as far as the eye could see. There was no stopping it, no point in burying your head in the sand. He would not live to see the end of the next cycle in the island's economy, though Robbie might – Robbie and Christina and Billy Barrett, Fay Ludlow too if she stayed.

He put his hand into his pocket and brought out the brown envelope.

He handed it to Barrett.

'What is this? I have been paid this month already.'

'It is extra, a bonus.'

'From her, from Mrs Hollander?'

'No, it is from me,' Quig said. 'I receive a fee for this wee bit of extra work so it is only fair that you should be sharing it with me since it is you who have had the extra effort. Take it.'

'I did not expect to be paid.'

'Are you turning down good money now, George?'

'I am turning down nothing of the sort.' Barrett took the envelope, folded it and put it away, unopened, into the back pocket of his breeks. He patted his hip and nodded. 'Muriel will be finding something to be spending it on, I am sure.'

'If the Lady Hollander sells more ground,' Quig said, 'and I am sure that she will, then we will have seen the last of sheep in these parts. If the right sort of drainage is put in and fencing and some protection from the winds then there is no reason why the old parks will not be spouting out spruce or larch or pine in forty years' time.'

'Forty years!' Barrett said softly. 'God! What a thought that is.'

'Forty years of steady employment for lads of Billy's age.'

'We are not foresters. We are sheep farmers here.'

'We can change, can we not?'

'She is selling too then, is she?'

'Biddy?' Quig shook his head. 'She will never let Fetternish go, not entirely.'

'How much of it?'

'It is far too early to say.'

'But she has met with the man, this Rattenbury who is doing the buying?'

'Well you know that she has,' said Quig.

'It was not my intention to pry,' Barrett said.

'Aye, well, you have every right to be curious,' Quig conceded. 'It is not just the landowner who will benefit from change and I would not be wanting to see the place laid to rack and ruin for the want of investment.'

'How did she – how did Mrs Quigley take to the man?'

'Well enough. He is persuasive without being pushing.'

'Like a shoe salesman,' Barrett said.

'Aye, just like a shoe salesman,' Quig agreed.

'Would it be local labourers who would tend the plantings?'

'There would be foresters brought in at first but the ditching and digging would be done by our lads.'

'Because they are cheaper?'

'That is the reason right enough,' said Quig. 'Even so, the wage would be more than a crofter can make, or a shepherd for that matter.'

Barrett stared out to sea again, then, lifting his shoulders high, let them drop in a gesture of resignation. 'Well,' he said, 'when I saw the girl at Pennypol I thought that we had something coming back to us at last.'

'What do you mean, George?'

'Something starting.' Barrett shrugged again. 'I should have been looking in the other direction, should I not?'

'You would be needing eyes in the back of your head to see where the future is coming from.' Quig put a hand on the shepherd's shoulder. 'Would you be for having it the way it used to be, George?'

'Aye, would I not now?' Barrett answered. 'Like a shot, I would.'

'I would too,' Quig said. 'I would give anything to go back to Foss.'

Barrett angled the tip of the crook, cocked his wrist and described a great shallow circle in the air.

'In a hundred years perhaps all this will be gone,' he said.

'No, it is us who will be gone,' Quig said. 'The land will still be here.'

'Well, there is some comfort in that, I suppose, although I will be damned if I can see what it is.' Barrett let the tip of the crook drop and laughed under his breath. 'God, Quig, it would be a fine thing to be young for ever, would it not now?'

'A fine thing,' Quig agreed, then, glancing up at the position of the sun, said, 'It is time I was on my way home, George. High time,' and leaving the shepherd and the dog behind, set off along the shore road for the long walk round to Pennypol where he knew that Fay would be waiting to welcome him with wide-open arms.

CHAPTER NINE

Blessings in Disguise

'I must say, Mrs Quigley, I am a trifle surprised.'

'Why is that, Mr Rattenbury?'

'I had thought that your husband would be joining us.'

'Apparently he has other things to do,' Biddy said.

'More important things than selling land?'

'Ah, but I'm not selling land, Mr Rattenbury.'

'None the less it seems you aren't averse to escorting me out to Friendship Farm to look over the site?'

Biddy hesitated. 'I see no harm in it, particularly as you have neither your theodolite nor your field-book with you.'

'I do not require a field-book,' Patrick said. 'I'm quite adept at keeping figures in my head.'

'You are very sure of yourself, sir,' said Biddy.

'I've no reason to doubt my abilities as a surveyor.'

'But not sure enough to make me an offer on the spot.'

'No, not that.'

They walked on. He had not taken her arm. She would not have flinched if he had. There was excuse enough for it on the track out to An Fhearann Cáirdeil which had grown rough and weedy in the years since the Browns had left the area. The saplings had grown taller and the leaves of the little birches that sprang up without aid or attention shivered in the wind that came in from the sea. The scrub was dense enough now to blot out the great looming peninsula of Ardnamurchan that dominated the horizon to the north-west.

Biddy felt unusually well. She had no megrim, no anxiety, no sense of persecution or oppression. For the first time in months she felt alert. She was well aware that this handsome and urbane man was really just another wheedling charlatan, not so very different from the suitors who had wooed her in her widowhood and whose sole aim had been to lay hands on her land and to whom bedding her would have only been a small additional reward. She had resisted them, denied them what they wanted. Even amiable, energetic Iain Carbery, who had given her so much pleasure and who, poor soul, had fallen head over heels in love with her and betrayed his masters for her sake, had not been 'right' for her in the end.

There were times though, particularly in this past year, when she thought of the robust and doting sporting gentleman with wistful longing. He would not have cut her off or allowed her to languish unfulfilled as Quig had done. If she thought wistfully of Iain Carbery, she thought longingly of Michael Tarrant, who had taken her wilfully and spitefully and regardless of consequence. How often had she walked this path by herself, lonely and desolate. Today, however, she had a gentleman companion to distract her from morbid imaginings and revitalise her sense of self. She was glad that she had kept the Hollander woman at arm's length and had refused to rush into negotiations with the company that coveted her land. Her truculence had brought her a suitor, a handsome agent with charming manners who reminded her what it was like to be young.

'You will not have been down this path before, Mr Rattenbury?'

'Not here, not exactly here.'

'Have you walked the boundary on the Tobermory side?'

'I admit that I have.'

'With your measuring chain?'

'I used a survey map to take my distances.'

'In a word, you have been sizing us up for some time.'

'That is hardly a secret, Mrs Quigley.'

'This company you represent . . .'

'A group of private individuals.'

'Whatever it is, I take it Frances Hollander found their offer satisfactory?'

'She – like you – had land to spare.'

'That,' Biddy said, 'was not my question.'

'Louden, Lafferty and Spruell are a perfectly legitimate concern, you know. They aren't speculators. They have no motive except the acquisition of land upon which to establish plantations of timber. They have connection with nurseries in Perthshire and considerable experience in financing long-term cash crops.'

'Mr Rattenbury, you are in danger of repeating yourself.'

'Of course, we've been through all this before, haven't we?'

He walked closer when the track narrowed. Inches separated her shoulder from his, her hip from his flank.

'You ask about Mrs Hollander,' Patrick said. 'She holds no shares in Louden, Lafferty and Spruell, if that is your point?'

'I am pleased to hear it.'

'Really?' Patrick Rattenbury said. 'May I ask why that is?'

'I regard her as an intruder not a neighbour,' Biddy said pompously. 'Did you negotiate with her too?'

'Initially, yes.'

They were approaching the end of the track. The mountains massed dark and distant behind the birch leaves beyond the chasm that marked the edge of Biddy's holding. Patrick laid a hand on her arm and brought her to a halt.

'Why are you so opposed to Frances Hollander? Is it because she's pretty?'

'Pretty?' Biddy was taken aback. 'What does that have—'

'She's not like you,' Patrick said.

'Meaning that I – that I'm not . . .'

'She is slight and flighty,' Patrick said. 'That's between you and me, of course, not something I would shout from the rooftops. I have no difficulty in dealing with her, however.'

'Dealing with her?' Biddy said.

Although he had taken his hand away Biddy did not move forward. She was rooted like a larch filled with the thrum of the wind. Perhaps all she had needed to make her well again was a man to stand up to her.

'How did you deal with her, sir?' she heard herself say.

'Directly.'

'Will you deal with me in a similar fashion?'

'Emphatically not.'

'How will you deal with me, Mr Rattenbury?'

'Cautiously and astutely. I treat people as I find them.'

'And how do you find me?'

'Prickly,' he said. 'Prickly and astute, cautious to a fault.'

'Is it wrong of me to be cautious?'

'In your position, I would expect no less.'

'My position? What is my position?'

'A beautiful woman has to be more careful than one who is merely pretty.'

'Oh, so that is how you intend to play me, is it? With flattery?'

'I don't intend to "play" you at all, Mrs Quigley. I intend to persuade you by reason and sound argument that it would be in your best interests to consider the proposals I will put to you.'

'In respect of the land?'

'In respect of the land.'

'How much of my land do you want, Mr Rattenbury?'

'As much as you care to surrender.'

'Surrender? That's an odd word to use.'

'Sell, if you prefer it.'

'I'm not being coy, you know,' Biddy said. 'It's necessity that drives me to entertain your proposals at all. If times were less uncertain we would not be having this conversation.'

'That would be regrettable.'

'Please understand that I am far from desperate.'

'I do not suppose for a moment that you are.'

'I want it to be clear between us that I will not be easily persuaded.'

'In that case I'll have to make sure that my offer is up to scratch.'

'And that what you are offering for will be worth it,' Biddy said. 'Now, Mr Rattenbury, shall we move on?'

'By all means,' said Patrick.

They sat together in the shadow of the wall that Vassie Campbell had built to keep the sheep from invading her cattle parks.

It seemed to Quig that the wall had been there for ever, like the prehistoric fort at Dun Fidra where – so Innis had told him – Aileen used to hide, or the standing stone at Mingary where she had left gifts for elves and fairy folk. Even on Foss, when he, Quig, had been her guardian, Aileen had dwelled with ethereal sprites constantly at her elbow but in the last half-dozen years it seemed that she had forsaken her belief in a world unseen and had been rendered dumb and hollow by its lack.

He spoke to her of Aileen and told her things that he had told no one else. How he had both loathed and loved the mad Campbell sister. How Aileen's son Donnie and he had once been closer than brothers but had grown apart when Donnie had become educated and important and had lost his soft island accent and all respect for the culture that had fashioned him. Spoke of his fondness for his son, a fondness so strong that it was almost weakness. Told her how much he loved his daughter, Christina, and feared that she was about to follow her cousin Donnie into that realm where shame replaces pride and one tries so hard to shed the old ideals that innocence – or was it naivety? – had preserved for a thousand years.

Rabbits scratched at the mesh-wire fencing. Buzzards circled high overhead. The spaniel lay asleep in a pool of sunlight. The black cattle, the handful that remained, grazed passively along the distant foreshore. Behind the wall, away from the plots, weeds grew tall and the moor sizzled in the warmth of the afternoon sun.

On the grass the smoke-blackened kettle let out a last little gasp of steam from its snub spout and the tin billy-cans leaned one against the other just as he leaned on Fay or, rather, as she leaned on him. He rested an arm about her shoulders, her arm draped across his chest while he rambled on. She was not old enough to console him with anything more profound than silence and intimacy.

He took the weight of her easily against his shoulder. He could smell heather in her hair, the sea on her skin. She was his responsibility yet not his responsibility. He could not be expected to love her as much as she loved him.

'Ow!' she said. 'Ow!' and sat up suddenly.

He sat up too. 'What? Fay, what is it?'

'It moved,' she said. 'The baby moved inside me.'

Quig laughed. He was not alarmed. He remembered all too vividly Biddy's sleepy fantasies, her glee, the realities of her pregnancy.

'Is it not early for that?' he said.

'I don't know, do I? No. Wait. There, there it is again.'

She sat upright, tugged at her smock and bodice and laid herself bare across the midriff. He could see the undersides of her breasts and, almost comically, the outward thrust of her stomach, arched and pale in the warm afternoon sunlight.

'There! There! Feel it, feel it, Quig.'

She reached for his hand and slapped it down upon her stomach, pressing it down on the smooth, taut flesh.

He spread his fingers and gently let his hand rise and fall in the rhythm of her breathing. A line of fine golden-brown hair ran downward from her navel, bisected by another line of hair, darker in hue. He was tempted to touch her there, to feel that intimate fabric against his hand.

And then it kicked, a pronounced agile little leap against his palm.

'Good God!' Quig grinned. 'I am thinking you are right, Fay.'

She pressed both hands over his and held him there. She did not glance at him, did not perhaps realise what it meant or how the trusting gesture might be construed by any man but Quig.

'There?' she said, very quietly. 'Do you feel it?'

'Yes, yes,' he said. 'Right under my fingers.'

She let out a series of tiny whoops, gleeful and rejoicing. 'Well, well, well.'

Reluctantly he slid his hand from her stomach.

'Very soon,' he said, 'you will have to be telling Innis the truth.'

'Tell everyone, I suppose.'

'Innis first of all.'

'Will you come with me?' she said. 'Please, Quig. I want you to be there when I tell her the news.'

'Where is Innis?'

'At home, at Pennymain.'

'All right.' Quig got to his feet and offered her his hand. 'We will do it now.'

'Now?'

'Why not now?'

'Why not, indeed,' said Fay.

Innis knew that there would be trouble as soon as Becky got home but hoped that her excitement at Fay's news would protect her from her daughter's anger.

Surely nothing could mar her delight at Fay's announcement. The prospect of having a new baby in the house shone about her like a halo; an infant to play on the kitchen floor and toddle on the grass, a child to accompany her to the beach to discover for the first time sand and sea and the great high vault of the sky.

With the girl seated at the kitchen table in the cool afternoon light and Quig standing by the stove, Innis felt as if she had been tugged back from the shadows of the night and, though she didn't close her eyes or clasp her hands, she offered up a prayer of gratitude to God for bringing her a grandchild.

She kissed Fay, hugged her, assured her that she and the baby would always be safe on Pennymain.

Only Quig's frown set bounds on her pleasure.

He seemed to be reminding her that she would have to cope not just with Becky but with Rachel and Biddy too. How could she possibly explain to them what a new baby would bring to this house, what it would mean to her to have Gavin back – Gavin without Gavin – and a chance to make amends for all her past mistakes?

'What?' Becky shouted. 'Expecting? Oh, yes, now I see it all. You scheming little cow, coming here with a baby in your belly and a smile on your face. Well, tell me this, just whose child is it?'

'It is Gavin's of course,' said Innis.

'Stay out of this, Mother, if you please.' Becky flung her apron across the kitchen floor and, hands on hips, scowled ferociously at Innis. 'You, Fay Ludlow or whatever you call yourself, what lies have you been telling us?'

'No lies,' said Fay.

'You knew you were carrying a child when you came here, didn't you?'

'Yes.'

'We've only your word for it that this is Gavin's doing.'

'It is,' said Fay steadily. 'Believe me.'

'Why should I?' Becky ranted. 'I know what it's like for people like you.'

'People like me?'

'Got yourself pregnant to find a place. Like a cuckoo, stealing somebody else's nest. Well, you're not going to kick me out.'

'Becky!' Innis protested. 'Nobody is going to—'

'It could be anybody at all sitting there looking as if butter wouldn't melt.' Becky strode around the table to the basin in the sink and poured water into it. She plucked a cake of soap from the rack and, rolling up her sleeves, began to wash her hands, soaping and rinsing them as thoroughly as if she were about to perform surgery. She spoke over her shoulder, shooting the words out like arrows.

'I was willing to give you the benefit of the doubt, Fay, but I'm not willing to stand by and see you make a damned fool of my mother.'

'I am not for putting her out, Becky,' Innis said.

'What' — Becky rinsed her forearms again — 'if it came to a choice between her and me? It would be her, I suppose, because of the baby. You've never really understood me, Mam, have you? I mean, just because I won't accept all your mumbo-jumbo, all your grovelling to the priest . . .'

'That has nothing to do with Fay,' said Innis, 'or the baby.'

Now that it had come to it she felt oddly gratified at her daughter's reaction. She had been too soft with Becky, softer than she had ever been with Rachel. Her friendship with Gillies had offended her younger daughter and her commitment to the Roman faith had bewildered and distressed her. In spite of her apparent passivity there was anger in Innis too and a not entirely unmalicious satisfaction that Becky was being forced to learn a valuable lesson at last, a lesson not compatible with loyalty or motherly love.

'Piety is everywhere in this damned house,' Becky said, 'like a bad smell.'

'Becky, I'm just going to have a baby,' Fay stated, 'that's all.'

'Gavin doesn't know, does he?'

'No.'

'You're a selfish little devil,' said Becky, 'that's what you are.'

'No, you are the one who is selfish,' Innis heard herself say.

'Selfish! Me! I'm stuck here with you when . . .' Becky did not have the temerity to complete the sentence. She grabbed a towel from the hook by the sink and rubbing her hands and arms with it, turned. 'I suppose you're going to look after her and keep the baby here?'

'If that is what Fay wants,' Innis said, 'yes, I am.'

'Just one big happy family!' Becky exclaimed. 'God! We were never a happy family. For a start families have fathers. Families do not have bloody lovers traipsing in and out. You're not a widow, Mother, you just chased my dada away so you could be with Gillies Brown.'

'That is a lie, Becky.'

'Well, if it is what do you expect? You've never told Rachel or me the whole truth about anything.' Becky tossed the towel into the sink and then, habit being stronger than temper, retrieved it and hung it neatly back on its hook. 'Now you seem to think you can make everything turn out rosy by having this creature drop a pup in your lap. No. No. No.' She stiffened, her fury cooling and solidifying. She pulled a chair from the table and seated herself. 'What if it turns out that it's not Gavin's child, that she's not even Gavin's wife?'

'I am,' said Fay.

'Prove it.'

'I have the papers . . .'

'Papers! Papers can be stolen. Papers can be forged.'

'Your mother believes me.'

'My mother is a fool,' said Becky. 'I'm sorry, but you are, Mam. All this stuff about charity and loving kindness is just a method of getting what you want.'

'Don't you believe I am who I say I am?' Fay asked.

'What does it matter what I believe?' Becky leaned on the table. 'There's only one person can prove you are who you say you are and that the child you're carrying isn't a bastard.'

'No,' Fay said. 'No.'

'My brother's the only one who can tell the truth about you.' She sat back. 'I think it's about time that we wrote to Gavin and found out his version of what happened in Derbyshire.' She looked at Innis. 'Might be a different sort of story entirely when the truth comes out, Mother, and then you might not be so damned keen to trade me off for somebody else's baby.'

'You mustn't tell Gavin where I am,' Fay said.

'Why not? What have you got to hide? If you've told us the truth then my brother will confirm it.'

'He – he'll come here.'

'I wouldn't be surprised,' said Becky.

'He'll punish me.'

'He has every right to punish you,' said Becky, 'after what you did to him.'

'He has no right to punish her,' Innis said. 'Do you think, Becky, that Fay put those marks upon herself?'

'Someone else could have . . .'

'I know what Gavin is,' Innis stated, 'and you do not. It is not a thing I would be saying lightly against my own son, Rebecca, but he was a vicious child and by all the evidence has grown into a vicious man.'

'What if he—'

'He hates us. You have heard that he hates us. If he discovers that we have taken Fay in then it will not be thanks you will be getting for telling him.'

'He wouldn't harm us.'

'Oh, but he would. At least,' Innis said, 'he might. There is no sense in taking that risk.'

'You want her to stay here, don't you?' Becky said.

'I want you both to stay here,' said Innis.

'I don't want to stay on Mull any longer,' Becky said. Anger had drained her: she was still too young to ride the wave of indignation without tears. 'Everything's changing, Mother. Everything's going to pigs and whistles and I don't want to see you left high and dry. I don't want to see you hurt.'

'You must not write to Gavin.'

'But what if he—'

'Promise me.'

'Very well. If that's what you want.' Becky got up, not angrily now but with a weariness that appeared to signify capitulation, a surrender to common sense. 'When will you tell Aunt Biddy? Or do you want me to do it?'

'I will tell her,' Innis said.

Becky looked down at Fay. 'I'm not doing this for your sake, you understand. I'm doing it because it's what's my mother wants. If I ever find out that you have told us lies . . .'

'I haven't, Becky,' Fay said. 'Why would I lie to you?' Then, without warning, she burst into tears and held out her arms to Innis, begging to be comforted, while Becky, grim-faced, slipped unnoticed into the bedroom to find her notepad and pen.

Quig continued to bide his time. By tomorrow word of Fay's condition would be all over Fetternish and Biddy would chastise him for not telling her first. Even so he said nothing over supper, nothing afterwards. Biddy, in fact, went into the drawing-room and played the piano for the best part of an hour, played so loudly that the dusty air of the house trembled with marches, polkas and Viennese waltzes, and Willy Naismith, roused from his lair downstairs, clambered up into the hall to enquire, rather peevishly, what the devil had got into Biddy to make her suddenly so melodic.

'I have no idea, Willy,' Quig answered.

'She'll not have had his offer in yet, so it can't be that,' Willy said.

'What offer?' said Quig. 'Whose offer?'

'Rattenbury's.'

'Rattenbury was here again today?'

'Did you not know? Did Biddy not tell you?'

'She said nothing to me about it.' Sprawled on the worn couch that occupied space in front of the fireplace, Quig stared at Willy who, hand cupped to his ear, was trying to close out the racket from the drawing-room. 'Was he here for long?'

'She took him out to An Fhearann Cáirdeil, I think.'

'Did she tell you why?'

'She told me nothing. Never does these days.'

'How do you know where she went with him then?' Quig asked.

'Saw them go. Aileen and I.'

'There is not much that goes past you, William, is there?'

'No, not much,' said Willy modestly.

'Will you be having a dram to keep me company?'

'Not here,' Willy said, frowning. 'That din would turn the whisky sour in my mouth. By God, she's giving it big licks tonight.'

'It keeps her happy, I suppose,' said Quig.

'She never seems very happy to me.' Willy lifted his shoulders as if to apologise for the question before he put it. 'Is it Fetternish that's getting her down, Quig, or is it just the sad and sorry state of growing older?'

'You have known her longer than I have. What do you think?'

'Is it money?' Willy said. 'If it's money, I have a piece put aside. I would be willing to make you a loan, or a gift if need be.'

Quig was touched. 'Well, you had better be hanging on to what you have, William,' he said. 'By the law of nature Maggie will be here when you are not and might have need of a shilling or two to see her through.'

'I'm not departing just yet, you know.'

'I am beginning to wonder if you will ever depart at all.' Quig tried to make light of it. 'Anyhow, it would not be right for us to be taking your savings, Willy, though I am grateful to you for the offer. If it is just money that has Biddy on tenterhooks then it might be no bad thing for her to be selling off ground.'

'What's it worth?'

'Come on, Willy, you know what it's worth.'

The old man nodded. 'For land that has never been under cultivation and a clutter of near-derelict cottages — six shillings an acre would be my guess.'

'Yes,' Quig agreed. 'And eight would be generous.'

The chords from the drawing-room became more pedantic as

Biddy changed key and plunged into a sonorous sentimental ballad about mermaids and dead sailors that had once been a favourite of the crowd at Wingard Hall concerts and had earned her much praise. There was no praise tonight, however, for neither Quig nor Willy were in any mood to applaud her *fortissimo* performance.

'Rattenbury will offer no more than he has to,' Willy said.

'Do you know the man at all?'

'No, I do not,' said Willy. 'But I have met his kind often enough.'

'What is it you are meaning by "his kind"?'

'Sharpers,' said Willy. 'Agents, land-dealers, brokers, dabblers on the market, that sort of thing.'

'Do you think that Rattenbury's a dabbler?'

'Oh, no. He is too polished and professional to be a dabbler. I've seen many like him when I served the Baverstocks in Edinburgh. Wool trading occupied the best of them in our circle but there were others too, men whose income depended almost as much upon their wits as their expertise.'

'Are you saying that Rattenbury is not to be trusted?'

'I'm saying – I wish she'd stop that infernal racket – I'm saying that he will not be easily put off if he has a client eager to buy your land. If Biddy does decide to sell make sure she isn't deceived by his charm.'

'Biddy's no fool when it comes to money.'

'Am I not the one that knows that?' Willy said. 'But she . . .'

'Go on.'

'How can I go on when that noise is rattling in my head.' He eased round and aimed himself at the corridor that led to the staircase. 'Anyway, what need is there to go on? I've been going on at this household for far too long and you'll not be wanting to be bothered with my blathers right now.'

'Willy, are you trying to tell me that Biddy is attracted to this man?'

'I'm telling you that she's aimless, that's all.'

'Aimless?' Quig nodded. 'Aye, come to think of it that is the word that has been on the tip of my tongue. Aimless. Once there is food enough on the table, clothes enough in the chest and fuel for the fires then it is amazing how quickly aimlessness sets in.' He gave a little grunt. 'To be telling you the truth, Willy, I have been feeling a wee bit aimless myself this last year or two.'

'Well then,' Willy said, 'perhaps Rattenbury's deal is a blessing in disguise.'

'It is not the blessing that worries me,' Quig said.

'I know,' said old Willy Naismith, 'it's the disguise.'

'Have you any thoughts on that score, Willy?'

'None whatsoever,' Willy said and, grimacing, shuffled off into the darkened corridor and took himself back downstairs.

Quig was in bed before Biddy. He had shed his night-shirt for the summer and slept as naked and uncluttered as he had done when he was a lad on Foss. He had brought a glass of whisky and water up with him, for he was nervous and needed something to occupy him while he waited for his wife to appear.

Eventually, about half past ten o'clock, she came into the bedroom.

'Oh, there you are,' Quig said. 'What is that you are carrying?'

'What does it look like?' Biddy said.

'Books,' said Quig. 'Are you not sleepy?'

'I would like to read for a while, if you don't mind.'

'No, I don't mind.' Quig sipped from the glass and wished he had added a little more water into the whisky, for the fumes made him feel oddly light-headed. 'I thought, though, that we might be having a bit of a chat.'

'About what?'

She placed the books on the rug by the side of the bed. She unpinned her hair, dropped the pins into a dish on her dressing-table and, still with her back to him, plucked cotton wool from a bowl and began to wipe powder from her cheeks. Her complexion seemed to grow redder as she cleansed away the lip rouge and mascara. She wore a full-skirted evening gown, not quite her most brilliant, and had an air of pretence about her, of play-acting. It had been several years since his wife had indulged in airs and graces and Quig began to wonder if Willy was right, if it had indeed been aimlessness that had pushed her back into her shell.

He was loath to admit that he did not understand the woman he had married, for at one time he sincerely believed that Biddy and he were one of a kind, separated only by gender.

He watched her over the rim of the glass as she went to the basin on the table by the window curtain and poured water from the ewer. She unhooked her gown at the bodice and then at the side, peeled it down to her waist.

Holding a towel over her undergarments, she splashed her face with water and rubbed it vigorously with a square of cloth, one of many unguarded moments that made up a marriage and strengthened the bonds of intimacy. But tonight there was nothing seductive or demure to it; as far as Biddy was concerned, he might not have been there at all.

She finished undressing and turned to face the big four-poster.

'You were playing very enthusiastically, dear,' Quig remarked.

The lace at the collar and cuffs of her nightgown was slightly frayed. Through the thin material he could see the outline of her body, her full breasts, dark oval nipples and a hint of the shadow between her thighs. She looked better, he thought, the less she wore, for her figure was not nearly so gargantuan as she believed it to be.

'I have not heard you play like that for a long time.'

'I'm no pianist, Quig. I'm a thumper, that's all.'

She seemed not withdrawn, not disengaged but she was certainly not flattered by his comments. If there had been less tension between them he might have strayed into amorousness and, ever the optimist, hoped for a response.

Clearly Biddy was in no mood to entertain him.

She swept the nightgown around her flanks, tugged back the bedclothes and got in beside him. He felt her weight depress the mattress. He was glad that he had remained flaccid. It would have been altogether too embarrassing to talk of Fay – and Rattenbury too, perhaps – while he was aroused.

Biddy put on her reading glasses. Reaching out, she hoisted a hefty green cloth volume from the little pile on the rug by the bed. She wriggled, punched at the bolster behind her head and then, settling, opened the book at the Table of Contents and ran her finger down the page.

Quig cleared his throat. 'What is it that you are reading?'

'A treatise on nurseries to start with.'

'Nurseries?' Quig said. 'Babies?'

'Trees, forest trees.'

'Oh!'

The lamp burned with a soft yellow hiss and, after a moment, Quig realised that it was accompanied by a soft little hum of concentration from his wife.

He lifted the whisky glass, sipped, put the glass away again.

What would it be like to have Fay Ludlow in bed beside him? he wondered. The speculation was more tender than erotic. She would not be reading nor humming to herself and he would be encouraged to caress her, to lay his hand on her stomach, accept the embrace of her eager young arms.

He sighed.

Biddy glanced at him.

'Sorry,' he said.

Biddy went back to her book.

He took his hands from behind his head, scratched the irascible stubble under his chin, rubbed his cheeks, fingered the tip of his nose.

'Can you not be lying still?' said Biddy.

'Sorry,' he said again.

With exaggerated patience Biddy closed the book over her thumb and pinched off her glasses. She glowered down at him from behind one rounded shoulder. 'What's wrong with you, Quig? Out with it. Did Willy tell you that I had a visitor this afternoon?'

'Actually,' Quig said, 'it was something Innis told me.'

'Innis? What did Innis tell you?'

'Fay is expecting.'

He was resting on his left arm, looking up at her. He noticed how she hesitated, how her eyes flared open then closed, closed and opened once more before becoming scornful.

'I can't say I'm surprised,' Biddy said, at length. 'Why did Innis tell you?'

'Well,' Quig said, 'she thought we should be kept informed.'

'Why didn't Fay tell you herself?'

'Innis is her mother-in-law. She is entitled to be first to know.'

Crisply Biddy said, 'So you aren't the father?'

'What a ridiculous thing to be saying, Biddy. Of course I am not the father. It is perfectly clear now that she ran away from Gavin Tarrant to protect her baby.'

'What is not clear, not to me,' said Biddy, 'is what you see in her.'

'I do not see anything in her, nothing of that sort.'

'She's just another lame duck, I suppose,' said Biddy. 'Why is it, Quig, that you attract lame ducks? What is it about you that brings them flocking? The girl worships you and next thing she'll be wanting to call the baby after you.'

'I do not think that would be wise.'

'Wise? Good God, Robert! Wise?'

'It is due late in August or early September.'

He had expected her to be irked but not scornful. He certainly had not expected her to turn against him. On the other hand, she turned everything against him these days.

'Innis is very pleased,' he said tightly.

'Oh, yes, there will be no getting rid of her now,' Biddy said.

'Rid of . . .'

'Your little friend, your succubus.'

'My what?'

'Fay. Fay.' She pronounced the name raucously, like a crow. 'She has bought herself a berth in Pennymain for as long as she chooses to stay. Baby, indeed! Another Campbell bastard!'

'Biddy, I wish you would not talk like that.'

'Are you defending her?'

'No, not exactly,' Quig said, 'but the child is not a bastard. It was conceived in wedlock, remember.'

'Unlike some.'

'What do you mean?'

'Nothing.'

She flicked open the book and pretended to read again. She was no more reading than flying, though. He had no notion what thoughts occupied her head at that moment and the only clue to her mood was one raised eyebrow.

He wondered if she was getting at him: he never thought of himself as a bastard, though, like Fay, he had never known who his father was. His mother refused to address herself to the old days, to the time before Evander had taken her to live with him on Foss. He knew that Evander was not his father – Mairi had told him that much – but which of the travelling men, the drovers, tinkers and packmen she had consorted with in her youth had sired him remained unknown. Perhaps she herself did not know, or did not care to remember. It mattered not to Quig: Evander McIver had been as much of a father to him as any boy could want.

He squared himself against the pillow and folded his arms.

His chest was thin and almost hairless and the few hairs that there were looked almost white in the lamplight. It had not occurred to him that he, like Biddy, might change with age. He felt a soft, swift surge of panic.

'Is that all you have to say, Biddy?'

'What do you want me to say? That I'm delighted? I'm not.'

'Why do you have such a down on the girl?'

'She has trouble printed all over her.'

'I think,' Quig said, 'that is your imagination.'

'Is it my imagination that she clings to you like a limpet?'

'If she does,' Quig said, 'it is because she needs a friend.'

'Oh, you just want to be her friend, do you?'

'Yes,' Quig said. 'I like her.'

'It's a pity that Gavin Tarrant got there before you.'

'Biddy, for God's sake!'

She closed the book at last. 'Isn't it true that you want her?'

'No, it is not true.'

He had seldom defied her. When he had been obliged to correct her he had done so cautiously and politely, steering her away from ill-considered decisions as gently as possible, guarding her feelings. He had become skilled in marital diplomacy, in repairing rifts in their relationship but he had all but run out of patience. He had gone just once too often to the well.

He heard himself say, 'What did Rattenbury want with you?' The auburn eyebrow rose higher still. 'Willy told me. It is not the sort of thing you can be keeping secret, Biddy.'

'I didn't intend to keep it secret.'

'Are you planning to sell land without telling anyone?'

'I would tell you. Of course I would tell you.'

'Would you?' Quig said.

He realised that he had within himself qualities that he had not known were there: stealth and slyness, the sediment of patience.

'I hardly know the fellow,' Biddy said. 'Rattenbury, I mean.'

'It seems that you are intent on rectifying that situation.'

She opened her mouth, put her tongue against her upper lip and then, thinking better of it, shook her head and said nothing.

Quig said, 'How much did you show him?'

'All of it.'

'Pennypol too?'

'No, only the stretch of rough pasture at An Fhearann Cáirdeil.'

'Will that be enough for him?'

'He is a businessman. He needs land for tree-planting. He will take what he can get. What I – what we are prepared to give him.'

'He will have every acre of Fetternish, including this house, if he can get his hands on it.'

'I haven't decided to sell anything yet. Patrick has made no firm offer.'

'And when Patrick does?' said Quig.

'I will consult with you.'

'Will you, Biddy?'

The tell-tale glow started up from her bosom and swiftly reached her throat. Comical in its rapid spread, it had been the source of many friendly little jokes over the years; 'Biddy's epidermal barometer', Tom Ewing had called it. Tonight it was not in the least comical. Quig watched the crimson flush envelop his wife's cheeks, and felt sorry for her. He had felt sorry for her too often in the past, however, and pity had become almost as demeaning as derision, respect a mere blind habit.

'Of course I will,' she said. 'Of course.'

'That's good,' said Quig and, kissing her curtly on the cheek, turned on his side to sleep.

CHAPTER TEN

Something Unexplored

Janetta was not entirely happy with the person she had become since Frances had begun to take an interest in her but she could not deny that she was flattered by the woman's attentions and even found herself daydreaming of her in class from time to time and had to bear down to keep her mind on her job. That was the trouble with teaching: she had to be the constant factor in the classroom, the metronome that dared not lose a beat, no matter if her nose was stuffed up or she had the shivers or a touch of cramp or if she just hankered to be outside listening to the larks rising and the gulls crying, riding in the buggy with Frances or walking on the deserted beaches that Frances had discovered.

Classroom, schoolhouse, church, the village shop, Main Street, a ceilidh in the Wingard Hall, an occasional trip into Tobermory, now and then a picnic or a lunch at Pennymain or Fetternish House: those were the parameters of Netta's existence and when she was disgruntled or restless she would take herself down to the classroom, strike chalk upon the blackboard and refresh the list of verbs and multiplication tables that seemed to fade with ever-increasing rapidity these days.

She had never been much of a one for Nature Study, though she had learned the names of local birds and animals from books and could even identify the squashy little creatures that dwelled in the rock pools. She had never been inclined to walk on the

sand, however, or clamber over the rocks or dip her long pale feet
in mysterious green pools and had never once tucked her skirts
into her drawers and paddled in the sea.

Then, on a hot Saturday afternoon in late May, Frances said,
'Let's go bathing.'

It had not occurred to Janetta until that moment that Frances
had deliberately disbanded the Charmed Circle by breaking the
pattern of Saturday meetings and separating her from Mairi and
Maggie.

'Let's bathe today, Netta. It's so hot, I'm boiling up.'

'Bathe? Bathe where?'

'Here, of course,' said Frances. 'Isn't it beautiful?'

'Well, yes, I suppose it is.'

'You do surprise me sometimes,' Frances said. 'Honestly, I'd
have thought that with all the reading you do you'd have
developed a little more aesthetic sensibility. Don't you find this
place enchanting?'

'It's all right,' Janetta said.

She was reluctant to admit that she did find the little bay
enchanting.

It was one of many little coves tucked into the stretch of coast
between Fetternish and Calgary. She had lived on the remote
headland of An Fhearann Cáirdeil for so long that she had begun
to believe that the whole of Mull sat on a table of black,
precipitous rock, gashed by gullies and surrounded by impenetrable vegetation. She had been awed by the magnificent sunsets
and had relished the clear, hard winter mornings when it seemed
that you could see to the edge of the world, but she had never
had an urge to explore, and on those occasions when her father
had led the family off on 'expeditions' she had stayed at home to
get on with washing or mending or bookwork.

On the little bay that nestled into the hills on the tip of the
Hollander estate the granite outcrops were pink and russet,
sculpted into clean, acute shapes that gave protection from the
breeze. The Barretts' whitewashed cottage across the mouth of

the sea loch was visible from the top of the track but by the time that Frances had eased the buggy down to the fence even that landmark had disappeared and soon they were alone on the thumbnail of soft white sand, screened by the gigantic granite slabs.

'I haven't brought a bathing costume,' Janetta said. 'To tell you the truth it's not something I possess. Perhaps I could just put my feet in.'

'Nonsense!' Frances said. 'It's all or nothing, Netta.'

'In that case it had better be nothing.'

'Are you afraid of the water?'

'Yes.'

'Oh, you coward, you.'

'I can't help it. I am.'

'I thought you would be brave and hardy. You look brave and hardy enough to me. Oh, come on, Janetta, a little dip will cool you down.'

Their voices were muffled by the rush of the waves. Beyond the rock prow hovered three or four gulls and on the far horizon, framed like a print, three tiny fishing smacks nosed north in convoy.

'Well, please yourself,' Frances said. 'I'm going in.'

'Do you have a bathing dress with you?'

'I don't need one.'

'Can you swim?' Janetta asked.

'Of course I can swim.'

'I can't.'

'You'll just have to watch me then.'

Janetta turned away as Frances took off her cartwheel hat and threw it down on the sand, unbuttoned her summer dress and, hopping on one foot, stepped out of it. From the corner of her eye Janetta noted that she wore no petticoats, only the latest in directoire knickers. When Frances seated herself on the sand, her back to the big rock and began to strip off her stockings, Janetta swung round and stared back up the footpath to the fence as if

she expected to find several curious pupils or prim Innis, or her
father or, worst of all, Mairi and Maggie gathering to observe her
embarrassment.

'There!' Frances leaped to her feet. 'Netta, are you sure . . .'

'No, I'll – I'll stay here and guard your clothes.'

'Guard my clothes? From what?'

'In case someone happens to come by.'

She heard Frances's mocking laughter and then a loud whoop
as she scampered into the waves.

'Oh, God! My God! But it *is* cold. Lovely, lovely and cold.'

Janetta had never seen a grown woman undressed before, for
she did not count the young girls and fat mamas who sneaked
out of the bathing huts on the sands near Dundee all wrapped up
in caps and flounced skirts.

'Come in, oh, do come in, Netta.'

Janetta was tempted. She did not want to be thought a
coward, or a prude. She was both excited and frightened by the
realisation that sooner or later Frances would emerge from the
sea clad in nothing but her skimpy undergarments. She was also
concerned that Frances might catch her ankles in a tangle of
weed and be dragged beneath the surface or that a cramp might
suddenly seize her and she would sink down into the sand that
floored the bay and never be seen again.

Janetta sat down and unlaced her half-boots.

Frances was ten or fifteen yards from shore, paddling back
and forth across the narrow inlet, head held high above the
water: fine delicate white shoulders, fine slender white arms, a
glimpse of her breasts when she waved.

Janetta tucked her skirts carefully into the band of her
under-drawers. She rolled down her stockings and stuffed
them into her boots. She stood up and looked apprehensively
at the sea.

'Oh, you coward, you custard-pie.' Frances dog-paddled into
the shallows. 'Do you want me to hold your hand?'

'*No.*'

Janetta walked down the slope, the sand warm between her toes.

She had long, pale feet with neatly clipped nails and scrubbed heels. Her legs, though thin, were shapely; no one outside the family had ever seen her legs before, let alone the region just above them that might be anatomically classed as thigh. She clutched the bunch of skirt and petticoat at her waist and walked into the water with a chopping, determined stride that did not even falter when the waves swooped about her ankles and clasped her calves.

She heard Frances call out, 'There now, isn't it exhilarating?' but did not look up. She stared down at her limbs, distorted by the clear water and saw, without flinching, little fish dart away from her great bare feet and a tiny crab, no larger than her toenail, float by in a light, soft swirl of sand.

The sea was cold, cold and somehow solid. It pressed, resisting, against her flesh. She uttered a tiny gasp of surprise at the weight of it and its coldness and, hoisting her skirts higher, advanced cautiously into the surge.

Frances rose before her like a water nymph.

Janetta could not help but remark the small firm breasts and upright nipples. Cold, she thought, cold did that to you: she thought of her own breasts, flat and uninteresting, how even her nipples grew taut on cold winter mornings when she washed at the basin; how sometimes when she wakened in the night she would touch herself there with her thumb for the small, tense pleasure it gave her.

She let the water ride up over her knees and touch her thighs, while Frances scrawled great foaming half circles in the water with her arms.

'Do you like it, dearest?'

'Yes, I do. It is fine.'

Frances waded closer. The water fell away from her. She seemed to be made of silk, all sleek and shining. She cupped her hands and splashed Janetta and Janetta splashed her in return.

They waltzed in the shallows in a series of little whirlpools, advancing and retreating, in and out of their element; then, abruptly, Frances said, 'Oh, enough!' waded out of the water and walked unselfconsciously up the slope.

Janetta felt the air on her back, the weight of the sea pressing upon her, felt that if she swung round quickly she would find the toy-tiny fishing smacks gathered at the mouth of the cove as Frances, still wet, lay down on her clothes, rested her head on the rock and put her arms up and fluffed at her hair.

'Didn't you enjoy that?' Frances said.

'Yes.'

'I told you it would be fun.' Frances patted the sand. 'Come here and let me dry your legs.'

'What – with what?'

'My dress.'

'You'll spoil it.'

'No I won't.'

'Have you done this before?'

'Many times.'

'In America?'

Frances laughed. 'In America too. Only there we wore nothing at all.'

'We? Your husband and you?'

'Larry, yes, but . . . Oh, never mind. Come, let me dry you.'

'I'll do it myself.'

'I won't bite, Netta, I promise.'

'No, really, I . . .'

'Don't you like people doing things for you?' Frances stretched out her hands. 'Come along, let me pamper you just for once.'

Janetta fumbled at her waist and released her petticoat and skirt, let them fall about her bare wet legs.

'They will dry by themselves.'

Frances laughed again. 'Spoil *me* then? Come along, dry my shoulders.'

'This – this isn't right.'

'Isn't it? What's wrong with it?'

'I wish you wouldn't tease me.'

'I'm not teasing you. I just want you to dry my shoulders.'

'Frances, I'm – I'm not a man.'

'If you were a man,' Frances said, 'I wouldn't let you. I'm made just the same way as you are, dearest.' Frances got up. Her skin was sticky and grained with sand and she had lost her silken quality. 'If I were a man, my darling, I would know what to do next. This is what I would do next.'

She raised herself and with an arm about Janetta's waist, kissed her.

Her lips were soft, salty.

Janetta waited, arms hanging heavily at her sides.

Frances came again, lifting up, kissing her.

'Isn't that what you would do to me if I were a man?'

'I don't know,' Janetta said.

'Oh, Netta, Netta, what a fibber you are.'

'I think,' Janetta said stiffly, 'that I will go back to the buggy now.'

'Ah!' Frances said. 'Ah! So I can't persuade you to admit to the truth.'

'If it's a truthful answer you want from me, Frances, I believe I'll need time to consider it,' Janetta said and, picking up her boots and stockings, set off up the path to wait by the buggy.

Ten minutes later Frances joined her and, chatting lightly about everything and anything, drove her back to the outskirts of Crove.

'What are you doing sitting in the dark?' her father said.

'Nothing.'

'Netta, have you been crying?'

'Of course not.' She averted her face. When he made to light the lamp, she said, 'Don't, please.'

'If something's wrong, tell me.'

'I went out to the beach today,' Janetta said.

'With the Hollander woman?'

'Yes, with Frances.'

'Did she say something to upset you?'

'No, I stayed too long in the sun, that's all. My face is scorched.'

'Oh!' Gillies said. 'Well, I've seen plenty of scorched faces before now.'

'I'm afraid that I'll peel.'

'There's a bottle of Littlejohn's Lotion somewhere if I can just remember where I put it.'

'Perhaps it's in the kitchen cupboard,' Janetta suggested.

'I'll see if I can find it, shall I?'

He went into the little kitchen, lit a candle and groped about in the cupboard beneath the stone sink. He found the old brown bottle and shook it, then, still shaking it, returned to the living-room.

'Netta?' he said. 'Netta?'

But Janetta, scorched or not, had taken herself off to bed.

Everyone knew that Paterson, landlord of the McKinnon Arms, had a paying guest in one of his upstairs rooms; a fact well worthy of comment, for not even the drovers, the few that were left, would doss down in the McKinnon Arms these days.

The bedrooms in the Arms were not exactly unsanitary but they were old, very old. It was said that Boswell and the great literary gentleman Samuel Johnson had spent a night in the Arms in the autumn of 1773 but there was no printed evidence to confirm or refute the allegation and even Miss Fergusson had not been around *that* long.

For a day or two after his arrival rumours abounded that Mr Rattenbury was also a literary gentleman and intended to put everyone into a book he was writing. Though the good folk of

Crove considered themselves unique and fascinating and firmly believed that a competent author would be able to fill several volumes with accounts of their doings, the rumour was quickly scotched, not by common sense or modesty but by a series of even wilder speculations that suggested that Mr Rattenbury was a wanted felon or even a spy; that the long oilskin-covered rolls that he had carried up to his room contained not maps but the components of a new long-range weapon that he had been commissioned to test out in secret in case there was another war with the Boers, or possibly the Germans.

'He is a bloody land agent, that is all he is,' John Paterson told everyone who would lend him an ear. 'He is here to buy land for more tree-planting. He is a friend of Mrs Hollander's and he has been here before. If you do not believe me take a look for yourself at the spruce trees across the loch and tell me if you think that they planted themselves. He is the man who bought the land that brought the foresters to Dervaig. If my guess is correct, he will be bringing the foresters to Crove next, or at least to Fetternish, for he has been seen talking with Mrs Quigley and riding about with Quig himself.'

'Is that the way of it, do you tell me?'

'That is the way of it, I tell you.'

'Why is he not lodging with Mrs Hollander?'

'Because he is more comfortable staying at the Arms.'

'Did he say that?'

'No, I did.'

On Sunday morning the no longer quite so mysterious Patrick Rattenbury appeared from the side door of the Arms and joined the trickle of worshippers who were making their way up to the kirk.

By five minutes to eleven he was seated in a pew on the left side aisle where visitors and strangers were ushered so that the congregation could squint at them without appearing rude and Reverend Ewing could locate them with his hawk-like eye and fix them for a welcoming comment or two. By five minutes past eleven, not a man, woman or child in church doubted that Mr Rattenbury was who Paterson said he was, for the chap was too handsome to be a criminal, too friendly to be a spy, and far too well groomed to be an author of books.

By a quarter to one o'clock, however, the communal imagination had more to work upon, for Mr Rattenbury was observed in conversation not just with the Lady Hollander but with Biddy Baverstock Quigley and then with Miss Janetta Brown, who, unlike the other two, was a woman of impeccable moral character who should have known better than to blush and flutter her eyelashes at a land agent from Perth, even if he was well dressed, well spoken and handsome.

Shrewd observers of the social scene, Messrs Brown and Ewing among them, also detected a certain lack of warmth in the greeting that Janetta gave to Mrs Hollander outside the church, not hostility exactly but coolness, as if one or both of the ladies had decided that reserve was the order of the day; or caution, perhaps, in respect of the new arrival who, to judge by the signs, was not quite such a stranger as all that, not at least to the ladies.

Maggie Naismith was fizzing. Mairi Ewing was amused. Biddy was upset. Frances Hollander no less so when Janetta Brown managed to corral Mr Rattenbury and lure him away with her, not quite arm-in-arm but as near as dash-it-all, on a little promenade all the way up to the iron railings outside the 'other church' — where, it being only one o'clock, Barclay Boag was just getting his second wind — and back again to the locked front door of the Arms.

By this time Mr Brown had gone in to lunch in the manse with Mr and Mrs Ewing. Biddy, her husband and her housekeeper had ridden away in the dogcart, presumably heading for home, and the Lady Frances Hollander, all on her own, had shown just how unladylike she really could be by driving off in the American buggy as if pursued by wolves.

The sun shone down on the locked door of the Arms and in

the lane by the side of the building hens clucked and scratched and bathed in the dust of ages.

Patrick said, 'I'm very grateful to you, Miss Brown, for your advice concerning my quest for permanent accommodation.'

'Perhaps you prefer the company in the Arms?'

'Company? What company?'

Janetta grinned. 'Yes, you do have a point.'

'It's necessity that keeps me in Crove, not a love of raw nature.'

'Is that how you see us, Mr Rattenbury, as ignoble savages?'

'You mustn't put words in my mouth, Miss Brown. It isn't the citizens of your village that I object to so much as its insects.'

'Fleas, I suppose?'

'Fleas and black flies,' said Patrick. 'However, this is hardly a fit subject for a pleasant Sunday afternoon. Tell me a little more about the stables.'

'They are lying vacant but, I believe, are in good order.'

'Are there not other properties to be had?'

'There are,' Janetta said, 'but I doubt if any would suit you.'

'Why not?'

'Friendship Farm, for instance, is too far out.'

'Is that not where you stayed when you first came to Mull?'

'How did you know that?'

'I am not entirely a stranger to the north quarter,' Patrick said. 'And you are quite a famous person in the parish.'

'I would hardly say that I was famous.'

'Oh, but you are. You have the reputation of being an excellent teacher.'

'Really!' Janetta was flattered in spite of herself. 'From what source did you hear such nonsense?'

'You're being overly modest, Miss Brown.'

'Perhaps I am,' Janetta said. 'Yes, at the risk of conceit, the teaching of young persons is the one thing that I do rather well.'

'There must be other things that you do well?'

Shaking her head, Janetta said, 'Precious few, I fear.'

'Mrs Hollander — Frances — holds you in very high regard.'

Janetta's lips closed into a thin line of disapproval. 'Does she?'

'High regard, tinted with affection.'

'I have every respect for Frances,' Janetta said. 'But I am only one of several friends that she has made since her arrival. We are not particularly — close.'

'Are you not?' said Patrick evenly.

'No, Mr Rattenbury, we are not.'

Janetta did not fully comprehend what trait she had just denied, for the nature of her feelings for Frances had changed in the past twenty-four hours.

'I would invite you to eat with us, Mr Rattenbury, since it is wearing past dinner-time, but my father is not at home and . . . you understand?'

'All too well,' Patrick said with a bow. 'No doubt Paterson will dust me off a slice or two of roast beef if I ask him politely.'

'Poor soul,' said Janetta. 'I will make a dinner for you very soon.'

'I will hold you to that, Miss Brown.'

'Janetta.'

'The stables you spoke of sound promising. I take it they belong to Fetternish and may be available for rent on a short-term basis.'

'Biddy will take what she can get, I am sure,' Janetta said. 'They have several apartments and are, I believe, furnished. You could move in immediately and have ample room for your horses, and your housekeeper too.'

'I have no housekeeper. I don't travel with servants.'

'At home, surely, you have servants?'

'I live with my parents,' Patrick said.

'Do you indeed?'

'It's a small price for a hard-working bachelor — and a dutiful son — to pay for his creature comforts. My parents aren't so young as they once were. All three of my sisters have married and moved away to Edinburgh. I have no objection to caring for my mother and father. I like living in the house in which I was born. And when the time comes – as, alas, it must – when my parents are no longer with us then ownership of the house will fall to me.'

'Is it a large house?'

'Large enough.'

'In Perth?'

'Near Perth, in the village of Dunning.'

'Have you never been tempted to marry, Mr Rattenbury?'

'Tempted certainly but no, I've no wife, and no children – that I know of.'

'Surely you would know if . . . Oh, I see.'

'It was a joke, Janetta, in rather poor taste.'

'It is not a joke to some people,' Janetta said. 'I have been in Dundee and I've seen what men get up to there.'

'Ah, but that's Dundee for you,' Patrick said. 'In Perth we are much more circumspect.'

'Have you known Frances for long?'

'Four years, give or take.'

'Do you know her well?'

'No, not well. To tell you the honest truth I've no particular desire to get to know her better,' Patrick said. 'Does that shock you?'

'I am not easily shocked,' Janetta said. 'I had thought, however, that men would find Frances hard to resist.'

'She is attractive, I suppose,' Patrick said, 'but there's something lacking in Frances, do you not find?' He paused. 'No, perhaps you don't.'

He knew, knew about the kiss. Frances had told him about the kiss, had told him that she, Janetta, had not drawn back. She tried to remain calm; she had already begun to knit a fresh set of emotions around this man but what had happened yesterday had complicated the pattern and there were too many feelings in her now that remained unexplored.

She said, 'Have you met the husband?'

'Frances's husband? No, I've not had that pleasure.'

'Is there — I mean, I assume that there is a husband?'

'Without doubt,' said Patrick. 'Has she not told you about him?'

'It's not a subject she cares to discuss,' Janetta said, 'not with me at any rate. She is very open and candid in some respects, in others not candid at all.'

'He's an American.'

'I rather thought he might be.'

'His name is Larry Hollander. He's very wealthy, though not, I gather, in his own right.'

'What do you mean?'

'Ah, so you haven't been introduced to his mother yet.'

'*His* mother?' Janetta said. 'Not Frances's mother?'

Patrick smiled. 'Is that what she's led you to believe, that La Belle Lafferty is her mother? Not so. Mother-in-law.'

'But the name . . .'

'Larry is Mrs Lafferty's son by her first husband.'

'And who was he, the first husband?'

'I have no idea. Wealthy, that's all I know about him.'

'And her second husband, the publisher?'

'Also wealthy.'

Janetta frowned. 'Who is *she* then? Frances, I mean?'

'I really have no idea,' said Patrick.

Janetta glanced up the main street at the watchers.

She had never thought of herself as an object worthy of attention. She had lived the best part of her life in this closed rural community, had established a position here and earned a reputation for rectitude, yet, she realised, she had never become one of them. Dented by recent events, her integrity suddenly seemed as fragile as an eggshell. What did Patrick see when he looked at her? A prissy rural schoolteacher with no figure to speak of and a face like a horse who had become so desperate for affection that she would even allow a woman to kiss her on the lips?

'You're frowning,' Patrick said. 'Are you angry with me?'

'No, but you have given me much to think about.'

'I'm tempted to say that I'm just an instrument of changing times,' Patrick said, 'but I'm not so pretentious as all that, or so filled with my own importance.'

'Why are they here, the Hollanders? I mean, why did Frances choose Crove? We were muddling along quite nicely without the intervention of strangers.'

'I have made you angry.'

'Oh, I am always angry.' She managed to stop scowling. 'It is the manner of me, I suppose. I scowl all the time in the classroom.'

'A fearsome sight, no doubt.'

'Can you not be seeing that for yourself?'

'I see nothing of the sort,' Patrick said. 'Do not do yourself down, Janetta.'

She could not decide whether he was teasing or patronising her. Could not accept that a land agent, a friend of the Hollanders, might pay her a compliment. She felt a little prickle of sweat start across her brow under her hat-band and the Bible in her hand suddenly seemed as heavy as lead.

'Well,' she said, far too brightly, 'I have said my piece. If you *are* interested in finding accommodation, the stables might be just the place. That, of course, is a matter between you and Biddy, and nothing to do with me.'

'None the less,' Patrick said, 'I am very grateful to you for going out of your way to offer me a helping hand. I doubt if anyone else in these parts would have done so. Still, I'm used to being the villain of the piece and it's comforting to know that I have at least one friend in the village.'

'I will invite you to eat with us, you know. Will you come?'

'With pleasure.'

'My father will be there too.'

'Of course,' said Patrick. 'I look forward to meeting him.'

'And now,' said Janetta, 'I must go. Will Wednesday suit?'

'Wednesday,' said Robert Patrick Rattenbury, 'will suit very well.'

They rode together along the road to Dervaig and east over the pass.

Ben More and Ben Talla lay off in the distance looking grand and mystical in the morning haze. The stony white road stretched before them, running erratically down into the broad green glen where the chapel stood. In this little tin-roofed community hall in the middle of nowhere Innis had married Michael and, years later, her daughters had been confirmed. The congregation was now very small and Innis was one of the few who could remember the old days when Father Gunnion had administered the elements.

She coaxed the pony forward and steered around the glacial boulders that strewed the track to Glenarray. She was pleased to have her daughter-in-law with her. Although Fay spoke with a strange accent and had not been raised in the old faith, she was a better companion that Becky had ever been.

There was no soul in Becky, who claimed that she had not asked to be born and saw nothing magnificent in the prospect of death; no meeting with Our Lady or Our Lord, no God to castigate or approve and put you down again, winged or wingless, among the chosen. How, Innis wondered, could such a joyful and innocent child have grown up into such a cynical young woman? She would love Rachel and Rebecca with that uncomprehending part of her that had fretted for them since they had first drawn breath but the little hurts that they had inflicted upon her had accumulated until she could hardly bear Becky's sourness.

With Fay it would be different; in spite of all she had been through Fay still glowed with the grace of God.

'What is that mountain?' Fay asked.

'That is Ben Talla.'

'How high is it?'

'I cannot be saying for sure.'

'Thousands of feet high?'

'Two or three thousand at least,' said Innis.

The girl wriggled beside her, turning this way and that on the seat. Innis sensed her excitement at being in this new place with mountains and wild moorland all around. There was newness within her too and in time the child that was not yet born would ride with them to chapel. She didn't voice her pleasure at that prospect, for she didn't want Fay to regard her as a possessive old fool.

Fay looked up. 'Eagles?' she said. 'I've never seen an eagle before.'

'There are no eagles here,' Innis said. 'Those are buzzards. See how they find the currents of air above the rocks. Listen, you will hear them crying.' Fay seemed to have lost interest in the birds. She placed her hands across her stomach as the cart rolled downhill.

She said, 'Is this the road you brought Gavin to church?'

'Gavin preferred to stay at home with his father on Sundays, and he was gone before he reached the best age to be confirmed.'

'Why do you never ask me about him?' Fay said.

'I have heard what you have to say.'

'Are you frightened of hearing more?'

'Frightened? No, I am not frightened,' Innis said.

'If he came back, would you be frightened of him?'

'That is a strange question,' Innis said. 'Is he coming back?'

'I hope not,' Fay said. 'I don't want ever to see him again. He's all pride, all pride and anger. Quig told me that Gavin's grandfather was like that.'

Innis slapped the reins against the pony's rump, nudging the animal around a boulder as big as a bullock. She leaned down and watched the wheel click and slide against the boulder's flank then, with the way ahead clear, sat back. She did not care to think of Ronan Campbell, drunkard and braggart, a brutal husband

and father, for she feared the taint that lay in Biddy and Aileen –
in her too perhaps – and might be passed on to her grand-
children in times to come.

'Is that who Gavin takes after?' Fay said.

'I do not know who he takes after.'

'*His* father, maybe? Your husband?'

'No, not Michael.'

'Gavin was never kind to me,' Fay said. 'He cared for the
master's sheep better than he cared for me. He married me only
to get charge of the flock and to secure the cottage for himself.'

'Michael never struck me,' Innis said.

'What would you have done if he had?'

'I do not know.'

'Would you have left him? Would you have run off?'

'I had children to consider, and a settled place here on Mull.'

'You would have stayed, wouldn't you?' Fay said. 'You'd have
borne it with fortitude, I think.'

'I loved my husband.'

Fay was silent for a second or two, eyes fixed on her hands, on
her belly.

She gave a little sigh. 'But you love Mr Brown, don't you?'

'Gillies and I . . .' Innis began.

'Mr Brown would have looked after you. And Quig, you had
Quig to look out for you too. Your husband would never have
dared strike you, not with Quig there to protect you,' Fay said.
'I've never had anyone to look out for me. When Gavin married
me I thought I'd found a man who would love me and look out
for me, but I hadn't. Oh, if only I'd had half your fortitude,
Mammy, I might have stayed on at the Edge and endured it.
When I thought of the baby, though, a baby in that house, of
what Gavin might do . . .'

'Enough, Fay!' Innis said sharply. 'I am not one to blame you
for running away from him. It is the baby that matters now.'

'Is that why you want to keep me here, just for the sake of the
baby?'

'It is nothing of the kind.' Innis felt a qualm of guilt pass through her at the thought that the accusation might be true. 'Did I not accept you before I knew that you were carrying my grandchild?'

'You did.' Fay nodded. 'It's true, you did.'

'Is that why you did not tell me at once?'

'I wasn't sure,' Fay said. 'No, I wasn't sure in myself. I needed to find out if I could trust you.'

'Are you sure now, dearest?'

'Yes.'

Innis slipped the reins into one gloved hand and laid her arm about the girl's shoulders. There had been no tears, no obvious plea for pity; yet Innis sensed that her loyalty had somehow been put to the test, that this small, defenceless stranger – hardly more than a child herself – had reached out to her. She must let Gavin go, let her loyalty to Michael melt, put all her foolish hopes behind her for the sake of this girl and her child.

She drew Fay to her, let her rest her head against her shoulder as they jolted down the steep brae that led to Glenarray.

The river twisted below. There were sheep on the low ground and cattle still roamed the moor fringe higher up and the chapel's iron roof glinted in the sunlight.

'Is that it?' Fay said lazily, not shifting her position.

'Aye, that is our meeting place.'

'It's lovely, lovely and peaceful,' Fay said. 'Will I be able to pray, Mammy? Will they let me kneel beside you?'

'Of course they will,' said Innis.

'Oh, I am so happy,' Fay said. 'So happy that I've you to take care of me, you and Quig. Nothing bad can happen to me now, can it?'

'No,' Innis said, 'nothing bad can happen to you now,' and gripping the reins tightly, began the final descent down to the floor of the glen.

*   *   *

Rather to Janetta's surprise her father and Mr Rattenbury got on like a house on fire. Supper passed off in a clatter of conversation between the men while she nervously attended to saucepans and pots and carved the roast of beef that she had asked Mairi to bring her specially from the butcher in Tobermory.

She had also baked a Camden pudding, rich with dates and walnuts, which she served with whipped cream and a little porcelain jug of whisky liqueur, a dish so sweet and tasty that it finally brought conversation to a halt while Patrick, and her father too, paused to savour the flavours and murmur their appreciation.

'Wonderful!' Patrick declared. 'Simply delicious!'

'Isn't it?' said Gillies. 'By gum, but she'll make some man a famous wife.'

'Daddy!' Janetta protested, almost blushing.

'She believes,' Gillies went on, 'that nobody wants to marry a schoolteacher. Have you ever heard anything more ridiculous, Mr Rattenbury?'

'Daddy, please stop it,' Netta said and, to cover her confusion, gathered up the plates and crusts and rushed back into the kitchen with them.

She could still hear the conversation, though, for parlour and kitchen were cosily situated and there was no door between.

Her father's voice, raised up, had a perky impudent tone that indicated that he was thoroughly enjoying himself. Patrick's voice was not cool and not cautious but so smooth and warm that it sounded the way fine tweed felt to the touch. She was irritated by her father's obviousness, though, by the fact that he had dared bring up the subject of her matrimonial status.

She infused tea into a teapot that she had spent a half-hour scouring and polishing. Next she filled a small muslin bag full of ground coffee that had been foisted upon her by the minister's wife who seemed to believe that serving both tea and coffee was a mark of class, though how Mairi Ewing knew what passed for class in Perth was more than Janetta could imagine.

She soaked the bag in hot water and squeezed it over an earthenware bowl, soaked it again and squeezed again. When she held her nose over the bowl and caught a whiff of the opulent aroma, though, she had to agree that coffee did add a certain air of sophistication to the spartan apartment. She crushed the bag in both hands as if it were lavender and gazed at the reflections in the window.

In the angle, faintly, she could make out a corner of the dining-table. Patrick. Patrick seated in a chair that had always been empty. Sometimes she had imagined what it would be like to have Frances seated there but she'd never had the gall to invite the lady of The Ards to tea, let alone supper. It would have seemed too much like a confession – or perhaps an admission of the distance that lay between them.

Laughter roused her from her reverie.

She started guiltily, wondering if they were laughing at her.

She dropped the muslin coffee bag into a saucer and looked at her hands, lean and long-fingered and stained brown. She washed them at the sink, returned to the dresser, poured boiling water from the kettle into an electro-plated jug that had never been used before, and added the thick, oily essence from the bowl. The little kitchen filled with the unfamiliar aroma of coffee.

The men laughed again.

Netta shook her head, closed her eyes, pulled herself together.

'Devils?' her father was saying. 'Oh, indeed, yes, they were devils all right, but no worse than other kiddies. It was hard for Netta to have to mother them and have no mother herself. But it did them no harm to be out on the Point. Have you visited An Fhearann Cáirdeil, where we used to live?'

'I have,' said Patrick. 'I went by there the other day, in fact.'

'Biddy showing you round?'

'Yes, a magnificent spot, if rather lonely.'

'Too cut off, too remote,' Gillies said. 'If the cottages were a mile from Tobermory instead of three miles from Crove I've no doubt Biddy would have found a tenant by this time. That's the problem. There's more to it than the mere lack of a sound base to the economy.'

'It's the same in many parts of the Highlands,' Patrick said. 'It must suit you, however.'

'What? Oh, properties that nobody wants?' Patrick said. 'They're becoming a drug upon the market, rather. However, there's money about and people to whom the Highlands still suggest romance.'

'Romance?' said Gillies. 'I can't see it. I suppose I believed it once upon a time, but no longer. Now it's all hard fact, hard matters, and a hard struggle to keep the rural communities from sinking into the mire of progress. You wonder – at least I do – if there will come a day when there will be nothing left here but a collection of broken walls and fallen roofs like some of the old black house hamlets or the ruins of the Pictish brochs.'

'There,' said Patrick, 'there, you see.'

'Hmm? What do I see?'

'I think you are still a romantic at heart, Mr Brown.'

'Or a pessimist.'

'Same thing, Father,' said Janetta who, having collected herself again, inched into the living-room bearing a laden tray. 'Tea, Mr Rattenbury, or coffee?'

CHAPTER ELEVEN

Wildfire

'Tea, Mr Rattenbury,' Biddy said, 'or would you prefer something stronger?'

'Tea would be very nice,' Patrick said, 'but may I suggest that we hold off until we have completed our business.'

'Of course,' Biddy said. 'Have you brought me your offer?'

'My clients' offer.' Patrick corrected her, mildly. 'No, there is some way to go before I can present you with a formal proposal and set a per-acre price.'

'Why are you here then?' Biddy asked, equally mildly. 'Is it, perhaps, a social call? I would like to think that it is.'

It was mid-afternoon on Thursday. Patrick had arrived unexpectedly and had been fortunate to find Biddy at home.

She had planned to accompany Maggie into Tobermory that afternoon to shop for a length of good winter-weight cloth in the little haberdashery in Columba's yard. The store was one of the few on the island where consignments of quality cloth turned up from time to time and word of a recently arrived shipment had spread quickly. Maggie, however, would not sacrifice a 'big washing day' for anything and she'd had Becky at the tubs since half past eight o'clock.

On ropes across the kitchen yard and on the grass of the lawns sheets and blankets were draped like bunting and Becky, red-cheeked but somewhat less than rosy, had been taking a breather when the horseman had come galloping over the hill. He had thundered up to the front of the house, spraying gravel in all directions, had reined the stallion in front of her and slipped nimbly from the saddle.

'Is your mistress at home?'

'If you meant my aunt, then I am thinking she is.'

'Tell her that Patrick Rattenbury is here.' He had offered Becky the reins. 'Give my horse a rub down, will you?'

'Damned if I will,' Becky had said. 'Do I look to you like a stable-boy?'

'No, stable-boys have better manners. Is Mr Quigley about?'

'I doubt it.'

'In that case tell your mistress I'm here. I'll attend to the horse myself.'

To Becky's astonishment her aunt had been up and out in seconds, had scurried around the house until she found the Rattenbury person on the green by the gable where he had unsaddled the horse and was rubbing the sweat from his flanks with handfuls of grass.

At this point Becky had been summarily dismissed and had gone sulking back to the puddles and tubs in the kitchen yard to complain to Maggie about the manners of so-called gentlemen.

Prudently, Maggie had dried her hands, changed her apron and put a kettle to boil in readiness for a summoning bell. But there had been no summoning bell, no sound at all from upstairs.

'In point of fact,' Patrick said, 'I'm here to do a little business on my own account.'

'Are you, indeed?' said Biddy.

She was not at her most alert yet. She had been dozing in the sunlit library with a great folio of botanical prints flopping on her knee.

Becky's abrupt appearance had startled her. She had been mulling over Quig's changed attitude and mentally experimenting with the possibility that she might take revenge on her husband by selling the whole place out from under him.

Pictures of swollen green leaves and coarse trunks in jungle settings in the book on her knee had stirred a vague kind of sexual yearning in her and Patrick Rattenbury had not been a million miles from her thoughts when her niece, even more petulant than usual, had flung open the door with a, 'Oh, so there you are,' and had announced the agent's arrival.

'I believe,' Patrick said, 'that you have several vacant properties on Fetternish. I wonder if you would be prepared to rent one out to me for, say, a six-month period?'

'Ah!' said Biddy. 'Oh!'

'I'm told that the old stables are partly furnished and may be suitable for immediate occupancy.'

'Who told you that? My husband?'

'Miss Brown, the schoolteacher.'

'Janetta?' Biddy said. 'I was not aware that you were on any sort of terms with Netta Brown?'

'I dined with her father and she last evening.'

'Did you?' said Biddy. 'Well, Gillies is renowned for his hospitality.'

'Concerning the stables . . .'

'Have you seen them?'

'Not yet.'

'They are large, too large, perhaps, to suit a single gentleman.'

'And his horse,' Patrick reminded her.

Oblivious to humour at that moment, Biddy frowned.

She was seated in the sagging armchair that she'd had Quig bring up from the cellar some months ago, a chair that had been her mother's favourite in the last years of her life. It was not the sort of piece that would fit into any other room, not even the great hall, but its broken springs and clotted horsehair were accommodating and comfortable. She was no longer indifferent to creature comforts and assumed that in a year or two she would become just as sluggish and lackadaisical as Vassie had done latterly.

Rushing out to greet Patrick Rattenbury had left her slightly breathless and her colour, she knew, was high.

She resisted tampering with her hair.

'Why,' she said at length, 'would you want to reside on Fetternish?'

'I have to "reside" somewhere,' Patrick said.

'Has Frances Hollander no properties for rent?'

'In actual fact, no, she does not.'

'I must ask you, Patrick: is this a ruse to persuade me to sell my land?'

'When it comes to persuasion,' Patrick said, 'I am much less devious than you give me credit for. It will be the terms of the offer that will persuade you. Cash, profit, that sort of thing. The truth is that I need somewhere to stay before the fleas and the bad food in the Arms turn me into skin and bone.'

'You are a long way from skin and bone.' Biddy did not intend the remark to be humorous or suggestive. 'I assume by what you've said that you intend to stay on Mull for some time.'

'I do.'

'What, however, if I reject your clients' offer? What then?'

'I will submit another on their behalf.'

'And if I reject that one too?' said Biddy.

'There are other landowners, other bits of ground that might suit our plans.'

'What are these plans?' said Biddy.

'I thought I'd made that very clear,' said Patrick. 'Forestry.'

He sat on a narrow high-backed chair of painted beech that Austin had claimed had once belonged to a German prince. Biddy had never bothered to find out if it was true or not, but she admired the princely manner in which Patrick Rattenbury occupied the rackety antique, his buttocks perched on the edge of the tattered seat, his ankles crossed, knees spread. Under the smooth cloth of his riding breeches she could see the shape and strength of his thighs and, recalling the muscular agility of her long-ago lover, Iain Carbery, experienced an indefinable yearning that linked past and present.

So far she had remained true to Quig; but had she been happy being true to Quig? That was another question entirely.

Patrick Rattenbury was no disdainful young gamecock. He was close to her age and exhibited all the confidence of a man who had taken his pleasure without tumbling into the pitfall of matrimony. What if he did want her only to hew off a piece of Fetternish and help earn his commission? What did that matter now that the world about her was crumbling and her own sweet days were numbered? Who would know or care if she allowed the passion in her heart to leap up again, that wild fire that had been all but snuffed out by financial worries and Quig's blundering neglect?

She was *not* too old to fall in love again.

She said, 'How much of Fetternish *do* you want?'

'Eight hundred acres to the north-east.'

'An Fhearann Cáirdeil?'

'Yes.'

'I suppose you will tell me that it would hardly be missed?'

'Well, would it?'

'No, I suppose in honesty it wouldn't,' Biddy said.

She did not know why she had steered the conversation back to matters that had already been discussed, to have him repeat facts that she had already stored in her head. She was delaying, holding back, playing the old game. She did not want to appear too eager to grant his request. The very thought of having Patrick Rattenbury installed in the old stable building, a half-mile from her doorstep, fostered all sorts of fond imaginings, however, together with the notion that she might teach Quig a lesson by having a 'friend' to spend time with, to balance out his friendship with the Ludlow girl: she had always been able to justify her wilfulness.

'What else?' Biddy said.

'Else?'

'What other parts of Fetternish would you like to lay hands on?'

'There's a stretch of moorland behind the farm at Pennypol that might convert to forestry.'

'On the shore?'

'Behind the shore.'

'Have you sampled it?'

Patrick shook his head. 'I am not one to rush things, Mrs Quigley.'

'Are you not now, Mr Rattenbury?'

'Do you think it might ease matters if we reverted to Bridget and Patrick?'

'I have no objection to reverting to Biddy and Patrick.'

'Or at least to letting me have a look at the stables?'

He had given her the lead. He had done it promptly and with style, Biddy thought. She knew that Patrick was flirting with her, that it was no whim, no charming spasm or accident of interpretation; he was as seriously interested in her as she was in him.

She felt her limbs grow light and slender, blood race faster through her veins and her brain, dulled not by age but by her husband's ineptitude, become sharp and calculating once more.

She stretched out her hand to the bell on the table.

'Shall we have tea first, Patrick?'

'No,' he said, thrusting himself out of the chair. 'No, Biddy, let's do it now.'

'Shall we walk,' she said, 'or would you prefer to ride?'

'We'll walk, I think,' he said.

'And keep the horse for another day?'

'Yes.' He laughed at last. 'And keep the horse for another day.'

It was not unusual for Frances to throw a tantrum. As a rule, she fumed only in her bedroom or, if Florence or Valerie were about, would take herself out of house to stamp her feet and scream until all her frustration had been discharged, after which, flushed but calm, she would reappear and be her sunny little self again.

Dorothea was not deceived by the character that Frances presented to the world at large. She had watched her daughter-in-law pass through many different phases in the course of their life together and nine years of mutual distrust had not softened Dorothea's attitude to the unnatural woman who had lured her son into marriage. She was honest enough to acknowledge that Frances and she did share one common bond: that she, like Frances, had given away her heart far too freely and far too often.

She was waiting now for Frances to fall as she herself had fallen, for Larry to pick up the pieces, for everything to come together again. Every tantrum, every fresh outburst, therefore, signalled the possibility that Frances was a little closer to capitulation, that this time her resilience might not be up to it and that she would either return to Larry's bed or, better still, agree to a bill of divorcement.

Frances's mid-summer tantrum was as unexpected as it was loud.

When she heard the girl's wails echo through the house Dorothea experienced a sudden relaxation of pain and an urge to get up and go downstairs.

She called out for Valerie who had been loitering on the landing.

'What's wrong with her this time?'

'Don't know, ma'am.'

'What's she shouting about?'

'Can't make it out, ma'am.'

'Find my sticks. I ain't sitting tight and letting her racket spoil my lunch.'

'Are you a-going downstairs, Mrs Lafferty?'

'Where the Saint Christopher do you think I'm going? Of course I'm going downstairs.'

'It's a long way down, ma'am.'

'Not nearly as long as the way up, girl, so fetch my sticks *tout de suite.*'

Frances was in the morning-room which was wide, airy and

bright. It had been furnished in accordance with Dorothea's instructions with blonde modern pieces, pastel cushioning and a hint of Paris chic in the choice of wallpaper and carpeting. She had locked the door before she had thrown herself down upon the silk-upholstered sofa to drum her heels and beat her fists into the cushions and set up such a wailing that she could be heard halfway to the beach.

Dorothea made it downstairs in five minutes, during which time Frances's cries diminished into violent sobbing.

'Is the door locked?'

'Yes, Mrs Lafferty.'

'Do you have the key I gave you?'

'Yes, ma'am.'

'Well, don't stand there like Tom Dooley. Open it.'

Valerie unlocked the door, flung it open and stepped quickly to one side as Dorothea hobbled past her and propelled herself into the room.

Startled but not embarrassed, Frances looked up. She was on her knees or, rather, draped half on the carpet and half on the sofa in a pose of maidenly distress that was part of every actress's repertoire.

Dorothea fixed the base of her crutches firmly into the carpet and took all her weight upon her arms. 'And what's wrong with you?'

'I don't wish to be disturbed.'

'Then you should have gone outside like you usually do.'

Frances shifted against the sofa and stretched out her arm. She did not look elegant but she did seem vulnerable. Her nose was pink, her eyelids puffy, her hair plastered to her forehead in moist, crinkled bangs.

'What is it? Tell Mamma.'

'I do not wish to discuss it.'

'Valerie, close the door.'

Valerie closed the door.

Dorothea slung her arms across the padded tee-pieces and

hung there, suspended. She had been faster, more nimble in the old days: on that day in the spring of '96, for instance, when she had bounded up the hotel staircase to find Iain Carbery – her last, best love – lying as Frances was now, half on, half off the sofa with the side of his head blown away and the stink of powder still rife in the room.

'Come on now, chicken, tell Mamma what ails you?'

'It is, frankly, none of your business.'

'Sure, it's my business.' Odd how her accent billowed about: pure Boston for Larry, pure Chicago for Macklin; with Iain she had usually been as Scottish as oatcakes or mince collops. 'Everything you do, honey, is my business. If you're down in the mouth then it's my business to find out why.'

'She took him home.'

'Pardon me?'

'She' – Frances sniffed – 'she took him home for supper.'

'What,' said Dorothea, 'dead on a pole?'

'I don't see what's funny about it.'

'And I don't know what the heck you're talking about.'

'Janetta. She took Patrick home for supper.'

'God Almighty! Is that what this tragic performance is all about? Some feller. No, wait, it ain't just any old feller, is it? It ain't Patrick Rattenbury's fickleness that's got you hopping mad. It's her, isn't it, it's the schoolmarm?' Dorothea's laughter shook her bosom. She swayed and braced one aching foot on the carpet. 'It's the schoolteacher. You've fallen for the goddamned schoolteacher, and she's given you the iffy.'

'Do you know how vulgar you sound?'

'Sure, I know how vulgar I sound,' Dorothea said. 'What did you do to scare this one off? You're losing your touch. Lack of practice taking its toll?'

'I,' Frances said, 'love her.'

'Balderdash!'

'What would you know about falling in love?'

'Some,' Dorothea said. 'But then again, only with men.'

'At least *my* lovers don't go shooting themselves in the head.'

Dorothea was not offended, for even malicious remarks about the manner of his dying helped restore Iain to her for a moment or two.

'Anyhow,' she said, 'Iain didn't kill himself for love. He killed himself because he was dying anyway. He went out quick to save me suffering.'

'Well, I'm not going to kill myself,' said Frances.

'More's the pity.'

Frances was recovering. She tucked her knees under her and, very deliberately, seated herself on the sofa and folded her arms.

'How long are you going to stand there, Mama?'

'As long as I have to,' Dorothea said. 'I ain't going to fall down.'

'I'm all right now. I was upset when I heard.'

'How did you hear?'

'Letter from Maggie Naismith.'

'Is that all she did – the teacher, I mean – invite him home for supper?'

'Yes, but we can all guess what's behind it, can't we?'

'Can we?' said Dorothea. 'You scared her, didn't you, Frances? You told her you loved her.'

'No, I did not.'

'What was it this time? A kiss, another damned kiss in the wrong place at the wrong time. She was never for you.'

'You don't know her as I do. In fact, you don't know her at all.'

'Perhaps not,' said Dorothea. 'That's not the issue. The issue is that you'd better leave her alone. She's the local *schoolteacher*, for God's sake. These people aren't going to understand what you're doing to her or what you could possibly want to do with her.'

'I just want to be her friend.'

'You don't really love her, Frances, do you?'

'I believe I do.'

'You're bored, that's all.'

'Of course I'm bored. I'm *bloody* bored.'

'You don't have to stay here. You can leave any time.'

'And go where, with what?' said Frances.

Dorothea's strength was giving out. The ache gnawed at her joints and pain slithered in her wasted muscles. Her chest hurt. She would need to get back upstairs soon, take two of her pills and lie down. Her smile was puckered.

'Go anywhere,' she said. 'I'll pay your fare to the mainland. How's that?'

'You won't get rid of me as easily as all that. No, Mama, I prefer to wait for Larry.'

'What if he doesn't come?'

'Larry always turns up sooner or later.'

'Whether he does or not,' Dorothea said, 'you'd better cut out this nonsense with the schoolteacher.'

'What nonsense?'

'You know what I mean. I don't want you cracking up on me and ruining what little I've got left of my respectability.'

'Power, you mean,' Frances said. 'Power, not respectability.'

'I won't have you wrecking my plans, Frances,' Dorothea said, 'not over some skittish schoolteacher who's apparently taken more of a shine to Patrick Rattenbury than you consider right. Besides, all she did was cook him supper. She hasn't gone to bed with him yet, has she?'

'How do I know what she's done, or what she plans to do?'

'What *did* you do to her?'

'I gave her a sign of my affection.'

'You scared her.'

'She has nothing to be scared of. She loves me. She just won't admit it.'

'She doesn't even know what you mean by "love". I reckon you've scared her off for good and all, like that woman in Antibes, what was her name?'

'Claudette.'

'That's the feller,' Dorothea said. 'You were lucky her

husband didn't find out what was on your mind or he'd have murdered you on the spot.'

'You don't understand any of this, do you, Mama?'

'I'm here to do business. I don't want you wrecking my plans with your perverted seductions. If you do . . .'

'What? You'll cut me off without a penny?' Frances hunched her shoulders and cupped her hands over her ears. 'Ooooh, shiver, shiver. I don't *have* a penny, in case you hadn't noticed, not a damned red cent. But I will have. When Larry decides that he wants to marry again then the only way you'll get me to sign a bill of divorcement is to pay sweet for my signature.' She rose from the sofa and stretched her arms above her head. Grief, anger and frustration had all evaporated. 'What would you say if I decided to fall in love with Patrick Rattenbury? What would you do if I entered into an affair with your land agent?'

'That isn't going to happen,' Dorothea said.

'It might.' Frances cocked her head coyly. 'Teach you a lesson, wouldn't it, Mama? Teach my teacher a lesson too.'

'Patrick Rattenbury knows what you're made of.'

'He *thinks* he knows what I'm made of. I'm sure I could change his mind.'

'Bluff,' Dorothea said. 'Bluff, bluff, bluff.'

'Are you sure, Mama?'

'I'm certain,' Dorothea said. 'What did you really do to her?'

'I kissed her.'

'And I presume she was disgusted, as any decent woman would be.'

'Oh, no.' It was Frances's turn to smile. 'She liked it. I know she did. She liked it and that's what she's afraid of.'

The pain had become almost unbearable. She craved the relief that her morphine pills would bring: four, not two; four, and a long sleep, a sleep so deep that she would not have to face her daughter-in-law again before nightfall. When Frances moved to support her, she shrugged one crutch from the floor and slowly rotated her hips, bringing herself round to face the door.

'Valerie,' she called out. 'Valerie, open the goddamned door.'
Then, with only the servant to help her, she crabbed out into the
hallway and hauled herself up the staircase to lie, like one dead,
on the bed.

No one, not even her father, could have guessed how much nerve
it took Janetta to walk out to the Fetternish stables.

She had been upset by Patrick's abrupt departure from the
McKinnon Arms and the fact that he had given her no
explanation and no warning.

She had, of course, no right to expect it of him. There was
nothing between them, no obligation on either side, yet she
could not help but feel that he had been, at best, impolite. He
had been served supper at the schoolhouse several times and had,
as it were, made himself thoroughly at home. Even on his last
visit he had said nothing about moving from the inn to the
stables, nothing about reaching an arrangement with Biddy
Quigley.

Frances too had been giving her the cold shoulder. She had
been hurt by the woman's sudden indifference. Could it be, she
wondered, that Frances had lost interest in her? Had she totally
misinterpreted the nature of their friendship? Had Patrick been
in cahoots with Frances all along, perhaps, and she was somehow
being used simply to further the Hollanders' ends?

In class she was snappish.

At home she was sullen.

Patrick had been gone for six days before she lost patience
and, as soon as supper was over, put on her hat and gloves and
made for the door.

'Where are you off to, dearest?' Gillies asked.

'I am going for a walk.'

'A walk? Well!'

'Am I not entitled to go walking if I feel like it?'

'Of course you are. Will you be late?'

'No, an hour at most.'

'If you happen to bump into . . .' Gillies began, then changed his mind, cleared his throat and lifted his newspaper to cover his *faux pas.*

It was around eight o'clock when she reached the stables.

It was a beautiful summer's evening, the sky clear, the sun still high, the shadows of the broom bushes and a clump of beeches dense and defining in the shallow glen where the stables stood. The buildings were of stone and, unlike most of the other properties that Biddy owned, rose tall against the skyline: two tall storeys crowned by a mortared chimney-head. There was a forge of sorts, stalls, sheds, a pump in an open yard and, as everywhere on Mull, a litter of discarded implements and broken carts decaying in the weeds behind an old manure pile.

The house itself was stark even on a bright June evening. There were no lights, no signs of life.

Janetta wondered if the information that Becky had passed to Innis and Innis had passed to her father was in fact false, if Patrick had taken lodgings elsewhere or had left Mull altogether.

She walked on, upright and purposeful, hiding her trepidation.

On the cobbles that bordered the yard she noticed fresh horse manure. In the yard itself a bucket filled with clean water, a spill of cornmeal and then in the big stall to the left of the carriage sheds she found Patrick's unruly stallion, peacefully stabled for the night. Why he should be stabled when a fenced paddock lush with buttercups lay just over the knoll was more than she could fathom. Rakings from the stable, a musty pile of last season's hay, a rake and a fork, another bucket, new and shiny, by the door of the dwelling house, then – and this surprised her – five shirts and five pairs of stockings hanging from a rope strung between two wooden posts: whatever else Patrick Rattenbury might be, he was clearly self-sufficient.

She glanced up at the chimney-head; a faint wisp of smoke rose against the untrammelled sky. Her chagrin dwindled,

replaced by admiration for the speed with which Patrick had
settled in to the Bells' old dwelling and how swiftly he had begun
to mark out his territory.

She did not knock upon the door, though, but waited for him
to find her.

She heard him whistling, a tuneful melody complete in all its
notes. She stepped away from the door. She did not wish him to
think that she had been prying. The whistling continued,
growing neither louder nor softer and seemingly sourceless, like
the calling of peewits or the crying of a vixen.

She turned, and turned, spinning on her heels.

The whistling ceased.

Patrick said, 'Well, well, if it isn't my schoolteacher.'

He had come around the corner of the gable. His shirt was
knotted by the sleeves around his neck and he was naked, quite
naked to the waist. He wore patched riding breeches unbuckled
at the knees, no boots or stockings, and carried a long-shafted
mallet braced across his shoulder like a shotgun. His chest was
matted with hair, curled damp with sweat, and a cloud of insects
had followed him out of the wilderness.

'I came to see if you needed anything,' Janetta said. 'Apparently you do not.'

Patrick laughed. 'Not unless you happen to have a packet of
fresh fish in your pocket, Janetta,' he said. 'Even if you don't, I'm
delighted to see you. I haven't encountered a soul all day long, not
even the estimable Quigley, and I could do with a little civilised
company. Come in, come in while I clean myself up a bit.'

'No, I . . .'

'Oh, come along,' he said. 'See what I've made of the place.'

'I think – now that I see you're – I think I should head home.'

'Netta, Janetta, what are you afraid of? For goodness sake,
there's no one within five miles . . .'

'Two miles.'

'Two then, if you must be accurate – two miles to tattle on
us.'

He put down the mallet, resting the shaft against the wall. Within the stall the stallion let out a feathery snort and then a bray.

'At least he's pleased to see you,' Janetta said.

He smelled, not unpleasantly, of the moor, the way her brothers had smelled when they had come trekking home after a long evening of races and chases in the scrub behind An Fhearann Cáirdeil. His hair was damp and lay in little Roman-esque fringes across his balding brow. His body was downed with hair: Janetta had not realised that a well-to-do gentleman from Perth would have so much body hair, for she had assumed that something in his lineage or upbringing would have rendered him as smooth and well pressed as his clothes.

She wondered what he would think of her if he could see her unclothed: all lean and long-shanked and flat-chested. She doubted if he would be in the least impressed, or moved by the untamed impulses that roused the brute heroes of cheap fiction to behave without honour or scruple.

'Aren't you pleased to see me?' Patrick asked.

'I wasn't sure that I'd be welcome.'

'Not welcome? Why ever not?'

'Was I supposed to guess where you'd gone?'

'Ah!' The exclamation had no more weight than a sigh. 'My fault, my tactical error. I wanted to wait, you see.'

'Wait? Until I'd forgotten who you were?'

'Until I could invite you – and your father too, of course – to dinner.'

'Patrick, I do not believe you.' She meant it. 'I think that you simply didn't want to be bothered with a schoolteacher and his daughter now that we have served our purpose.'

He shook his head. 'Unworthy, Janetta,' he said. 'Not worthy of you at all. Really, that's so petty. Not all the world wags as it does in Crove.'

'What's wrong with Crove?'

'Not a thing.' Patrick loosed the knot at his throat and rubbed the shirt over his chest and belly. 'You are just so – what? – sensitive to slights and suggestions that you always take things the wrong way. Actually, you're not so very different from townies, but more, more . . .'

'Barbaric?'

'There's nothing barbarous about good manners,' Patrick said. 'And, I confess, my manners were not up to my best intentions. Come in, I'll make tea and then I'll take you home.'

'Take me . . .'

'On horseback.'

'I'm not going . . .'

'Oh, stop fretting, Janetta. Do come inside.'

He took her hand, claimed her hand in fact, and dragged her after him.

She should have resisted, but there was a force to him that she could not deny and the wide, empty sky under which she had dreamed so often of a man who would take her hand in his and lead her off was no longer wide and empty.

Meekly she allowed him to lead her into the house.

The Bells' kitchen was large and plainly furnished, without dankness or dustiness to suggest that it had lain empty for several years. There was crockery on the table, jugs, pans and a kettle on the shelves, an armoury of utensils that Janetta guessed had been donated by Biddy, or perhaps raked together by Quig who was more considerate and competent than his wife.

'It's far too spacious for me, really,' Patrick said. 'There are three bedrooms upstairs and another room across the corridor.'

'It used to be a family house,' Janetta said.

'Perhaps it will be again,' said Patrick.

She blinked. 'What – what do you mean?'

'If all goes well and Biddy eventually decides to sell us land for tree-planting then the company will need all the properties it can find to house its workers.' He released her and went to a rack where a clean white towel was draped. 'What did you think I meant?'

'Nothing. I'm just making conver . . . Did she give it to you cheap?'

'I'm tempted to say for an old song but that wouldn't be quite correct.' He slung the soiled shirt into a wicker basket in the corner by the washing basin. 'It needs some degree of modernisation, of course, mainly drains and interior plumbing. Even in Dunning few of us are obliged to go out to the pump to draw water these days. And as for sanitation . . .'

'I would prefer not to know about sanitation,' Janetta said. 'I remember the inconvenience of rushing outside on a black winter morning.'

'Of course. At An Fhearann Cáirdeil. Now the cottages there *have* gone to rack and ruin. One would be hard pressed to find a forester who would be willing to move in there.'

'Will you renovate them?'

'I'm not renovating anything just yet,' said Patrick. 'Strictly speaking, none of that is my affair. I'm employed to find, survey and purchase land, not to manage a forested estate.'

'But you could, could you not?'

He dried himself carefully. She watched his hand move in the half-light, stroking the muscles of his chest. He had a slight belly, the beginnings of a paunch but that was the only sign of ageing. She thought of her own flesh, pared down and brittle as cane. He pulled a fresh, unironed shirt from a rail before the hearth and drew it over his head.

'Oh, I could, certainly. I have, in fact. I set up the plantation at The Ards and brought in a team from the nursery on the Duke of Anstruther's estates to work the contract.'

'Do you know the Duke of Anstruther?'

'Archie? Oh, yes. A bit of a blether and none too bright but he has a good team of managers and advisers and so much land that it would be hard for him not to make money. His father was sensible enough to establish a nursery thirty years back and Archie inherited it as a going concern. And "go" it does, believe me. He raises from seed and is the best in the north-east, at least

his seedsmen are, not Archie himself. He has a huge stock of
seeds and seedlings from all over the globe, ornamentals as well
as timber-producing varieties and a thousand acres or more of
transplants. It's a highly successful operation and enormously
profitable.'

He buttoned the shirt and, turning away from her, tucked it
into the waist of his breeches.

'Is that what you hope to do here?'

'What? Turn profit? Naturally,' Patrick said, 'though not for
myself, alas.'

'I mean develop a nursery.'

'Mull isn't the place for it. Oh, we can make trees grow even in
the acid soil of the upper moorland, for there are ploughs that
will dig deep and a technique for drainage that . . .' He turned
again, and raised his eyebrows. 'I'm sure you're not in the least
interested in any of this.'

'I'm a teacher. I'm interested in learning everything.'

'Your father wants it to happen.'

'I know. He fears for the future of the school.'

'And you, Janetta, do you want it to happen?'

'Will you stay here if it does?'

Patrick paused, not offended or even surprised. He was no
boy, no arrogant youth; he had been flattered before no doubt,
more often perhaps than Janetta cared to dwell upon.

He said, 'Is your answer dependent upon my answer?'

'No, I do want it to happen.'

'If Bridget Quigley sees reason and sells my clients a portion
of her land then I will be here for at least a year, probably longer.'
He paused again. 'I take it that you have no influence with
Biddy?'

'What makes you think that I have?'

He lifted one shoulder and spread his hands. 'I heard that your
father and Biddy's sister were close friends, that's all.'

'Innis and Biddy are not, however.'

'Not what?'

'Close friends.'

'Indeed!' Patrick said. 'Now that is interesting.'

'Why should such a petty little piece of Crove gossip interest you?'

'I suppose I deserved that,' Patrick said. 'For your information it isn't Mrs Tarrant or Mrs Quigley who really interests me.'

'Who is it then? Frances?'

'Phooh! Frances!' He came across the stone floor towards her, padding on bare feet. 'Frances may be pretty but she is cheap and flighty and it would be a sorry sort of fellow who would fall for her dubious charms.'

He stood before Janetta, looking directly into her eyes, saying nothing.

Mesmerised by his silence, she felt empty of every emotion except expectation. He did not touch her with his hands. He leaned forward and kissed her on the brow.

'There,' he said. 'Now, I'm going to brew us up a quick pot of tea, put on a clean pair of stockings, and take you home.'

'Are you?'

'Yes, I am,' said Patrick Rattenbury.

And did.

CHAPTER TWELVE

Balancing the Books

The last of Willy Naismith's duties as steward was to collect the mail from the teak-wood box nailed to the fence at the top of the driveway.

The box had been a bone of contention between Fetternish and the Post Office since the autumn of 1905 when the route had been assigned to Hermann, the German. Hermann was not German at all, in fact. Born in Reute in the Tyrol, he had been transplanted at an early age to Oban where his father had set up as a cabinet-maker. Hermann had shown no aptitude for carpentry. At fourteen he had gone to work as a porter on the railway before joining the postal service. An officious little chap with an eye on the managership of the county sorting office, he might well have attained his ambition if he had been a bit more patient and a bit less libidinous. Hermann could not keep his hands off the lassies, however, and the lassies were having none of it. Consequently, Hermann was given the option of resigning or of taking up a vacant post on Mull; he chose the lesser of two evils.

The Quigleys' mail-box and a dozen like it were Hermann's revenge on the good folk of Mull for participating in his downfall. He had hardly been on the island ten minutes before he invoked an obscure piece of legislation that debarred delivery of mail direct to the recipient's door if the recipient resided more than one mile from a paved highway. Nobody on Mull had a clue about postal legislation and Hermann was soon running Barclay Boag close as the most unpopular man in the north quarter.

He was assaulted several times and frequently manhandled by irate farm-hands, and the baiting of Hermann quickly became something of a sport in the remoter areas of the parish. In response to the crisis Hermann purchased a very large, very fierce elkhound named Lindorf that trotted alongside the bicycle, tongue lolling, day after day, and ate Hermann out of house and home night after night.

Lindorf was worth every penny as far as Hermann was concerned, for Hermann's dog struck terror into the hearts of every man and beast along the nine-mile route.

Collies that could rip a fox apart, beagles that could swallow a hare whole, savage lurchers, psychopathic mongrels, and terriers that were, as a rule, all heart slunk away from Lindorf with their tails wrapped between their legs or, catching wind of his approach, would streak for home to cower under the master's bed, or, if caught in the open, would light out for the sea loch and take their chances with seals and sharks and killer whales rather than risk an engagement with the postie's ferocious friend.

Willy Naismith had no respect for Hermann – and no fear of Lindorf.

Willy had a secret weapon of his own: her name was Aileen.

Aileen and he would stroll up the driveway every morning about half past nine o'clock, arm-in-arm like an old married couple, and await the coming of the postman and his dog without a trace of fear or trembling.

When Hermann appeared, puffing, over the brow of the hill, Willy would flip open the door in the front of the mail-box and stand to one side, canted a little into his stick, and Aileen, her icy blue eyes glittering, would crouch down and spread her arms and in the tiny, crooning voice with which she addressed all God's creatures, would beckon and cajole Lindorf to come to her.

'Here, pussy, pussy, pussy,' she would say. 'Come to your mama then, pussy, come and be seeing what I have got for you.'

Lindorf might be Norwegian, but Lindorf wasn't daft.

He would stare into Aileen's arctic-blue eyes and retreat: retract might be the better word, for his fine curled tail would flatten against his rump, his compact body would become even more compact and he would sink down on to his belly by the wheel of the bicycle, uttering not a 'woof' or bark or whimper that might be taken as a sign of aggression, for in the Campbell woman, tiny and gnome-like, he apparently detected a force that he knew he could not match.

'He is very sensitive, is he not?' Willy said, on first meeting the dog.

Hermann grunted.

His English was nigh perfect, his Gaelic coming along, but he would not risk an utterance in any language in case he, like the elkhound, be set upon by the unknown and unseen forces that Aileen Campbell represented.

'Will you not order him to let the lady tickle his ears?'

Hermann grunted again.

Willy smiled. Willy said, 'Well, there you are, Hermann, there's the mail-box all open and waiting for you. As I understand it you're constrained under Post Office law to put the letters into the box and close the door of the box tightly. Aileen will be watching just to see that it's done right.'

Hermann propped the bicycle against the fence and fumbled in his satchel. The packet of letters, newspapers and catalogues for Fetternish was bound with a withered rubber band. He stretched out and offered the packet to Willy.

Willy shook his head. 'In the box, sir, if you please.'

Still kneeling, braced on one set of knuckles like a tracker, Aileen tipped her head back and with a contortion of the neck that seemed to render it boneless, watched Hermann step over and around her and swiftly project the mail-packet into the cavity.

'And close the door,' said Willy.

With one extended forefinger, Hermann closed the door.

'There now,' said Willy. 'Aileen, let the poor doggie go.'

So the pattern was set and, thereafter, when Hermann and the bicycle and the elkhound came over the hill Willy and Aileen would be waiting, whatever the weather or the old man's state of health, waiting by the open mail-box, with Aileen crouched and cajoling and Lindorf cowering and Hermann saying not a word, not even 'Good morning,' in all the weeks and months that followed.

'The post's arrived,' Willy called out as he hobbled to the big Jacobean table in the centre of the hall. 'Five letters, two newspapers, the *Lady's Journal* and a seedsman's catalogue that's been on the road for a fortnight.'

He cocked his head, listened for a response, of which there was none.

He glanced down at Aileen who was close behind him, finger and thumb pinching the hem of his overcoat.

He said, 'Where are they all today, I wonder?'

He expected no reply and got none.

He put the mail on a silver-plated tray, manoeuvred himself into position then swung down, gathered Aileen up and hoisted her on to the table.

She giggled and held on to her hat.

'*Pooo-st*,' Willy called again, and waited.

Maggie and Becky must still be out in the yard filling up the drying lines with the week's small wash. Quig would be down at The Ards or, more probably, helping Barrett round up the sheep preparatory to shearing. Biddy? He couldn't imagine where Biddy might have gone, for Maggie had told him that she had been up and in the bath by ten past eight and at her breakfast by half past and she certainly hadn't passed Aileen and him at the road end.

'Oh, well!' Willy murmured to himself after a full minute of silence.

Aileen looked at him expectantly, eyes alert and glittering.

That portion of her brain that drifted in and out of shadow as the moon drifts in and out of cloud was obviously shining brightly. Willy glanced at the corridor that led to the stairs, plucked a letter from the tray and handed it to Aileen.

She took it, peered at the handwriting, sniffed the sealing. 'Donald,' she said.

For someone who could neither read nor write it was a remarkable feat of deduction. Willy had no notion how it was done, only that it was no trick or illusion. With few exceptions Aileen could accurately identify the sender of each piece of mail that arrived on Fetternish; only obscure items from government departments or Edinburgh lawyers defeated her.

He returned Donald's letter to the tray and handed her another. She stroked it, sniffed it, peered at the printed address. 'Man from Oban. Seed.'

'An account?' said Willy, but Aileen's sixth sense stopped short of bills.

He gave her a third letter from the tray, and she stiffened. She held it across the flat of her hand for a moment then visibly recoiled, thrusting the letter away. 'Bad,' she said in a voice so frail that it might have been a dying breath. 'Bad, Willy, bad, bad.'

He did not like to see her distressed and took the letter from her. He did not recognise the spidery handwriting and the franking stamp was too smeared to be legible. The letter was addressed to Miss Rabbecka Tarrant of Fetternish House. It was by no means the first item of mail that Becky had had delivered care of the Fetternish box; in the past month her sister Rachel had taken to writing to her here instead of Pennymain.

'Where did it come from, Aileen? Can you not tell me?'

'Bad!' Aileen said again and, before he could stop her, hopped down from the table and headed for the staircase to seek refuge in her room upstairs.

Willy fingered the letter, thoughtfully.

He was sorely tempted to steam the envelope open but had a

vague notion that tampering with mail was a criminal offence and wouldn't put it past Innis's daughter to report him to the Sheriff's office. He heard Aileen's hoofs drumming on the floor of the gallery, the thump of her bedroom door. Knowing that she was safe for the time being, he snatched up his stick and hurried downstairs, taking the unopened letter with him.

'None of your blasted business, Willy,' Becky said. 'You don't have any say over me and if you don't like me receiving letters here then you'd better complain to my aunt about it.'

'It's him, isn't it?' Willy said.

'Him? Him? Who do you mean by "him"? I'm not psychic, you know.'

'Gavin.'

'Now why would I be writing to a brother I haven't seen in years?'

'I don't know,' Willy said. 'Sentiment, perhaps.' He paused. 'Or pique.'

'Pique?'

'You don't like her, do you?'

'Oh, I see,' said Becky. 'You think I've written to my brother to come and pick up his bride, is that it?'

'That's it,' said Willy.

'I wouldn't know where to find Gavin, even if I wanted to.'

'Did Rachel put you up to this?' Willy said. 'Did she tell you to write to Gavin at the Yeates' estate?'

'What if she did? What business is it—'

'Dear God, girl!' Willy said. 'Did you tell him that his wife is hiding here? Did you tell him that she's carrying a child?'

'Surely he has a right to know where his wife is and that he's about to become a father.'

'So you did write to Gavin?'

'What if I did?'

He had cornered her by the hedge that backed the lawn. She had been spreading pillow-slips to dry in sun. She wore a huge apron, one of Maggie's cast-offs, and a dress with bunched sleeves that she'd rolled up to the crown of her shoulders. She looked, Willy thought, like one of the painted wooden dolls that Christina had had as a child, a youthful Mrs Noah.

Becky had become even more wooden when he had held out the letter and guilt was written all over her.

Willy had no inclination to be merciful.

'Why?' he said.

'Because he's my brother, my blood.'

'Blood's the word,' said Willy. 'God, Becky, you don't owe Gavin any loyalty. You can barely remember him.'

'I don't believe he's as bad as people say he is.'

'You mean,' said Willy, 'you don't care. You want rid of her. You want Fay Ludlow out of your house. You're jealous of the attention Innis gives her and when the baby comes you reckon you'll have your nose put completely out of joint. What do you expect Gavin to do?'

'Take her away, take her back with him to Dorset or Derby or wherever she came from. She isn't *our* responsibility. She can put on the poor lip and squeeze out all the tears she likes but she does not belong here with us.'

'Gavin may not want her back,' Willy said. 'Didn't that occur to you?'

'He won't leave her here,' Becky said. 'She's his wife. And he won't do her any more harm. My mother won't let him. Besides, this is the twentieth century and there are laws . . .' She held the letter against her apron, pressed flat to her breast, confused now and perhaps a little ashamed.

Willy said, 'Open it.'

'I will not. I'm entitled to my privacy.'

'Open the letter, Becky, and tell me what it says.'

'Or what? You'll report me to Aunt Biddy? You won't get any support from her. Aunt Biddy doesn't like the Ludlow girl any more than I do. In case you hadn't noticed, she's been making eyes at Uncle Quig.'

If he had been younger he might have caught her by the shoulders, pinned her against the hedge and tried to shake some sense into her silly head but she was stronger than he was now and considerably more agile.

'All right, Becky. Keep the letter to yourself, but do one thing for me: tell me if Gavin intends to come here.'

'Why?'

'Because if he does, he will do damage.'

'How can you be so sure?'

'You saw Fay's face, her leg?'

'We only have her word for it that my brother was responsible.'

'Just tell me if he's coming, and when.'

Becky's cheeks dimpled, not a natural smile but a grimace. She sensed that she had obtained power over him and, like Biddy, she relished the rich taste of power in her mouth. He might have been able to negotiate with Rachel who was more mature and more experienced but he could not negotiate with Becky whose effulgent ego would not allow her to listen to reason.

'I'll say nothing about the letter in the meantime,' Willy said. 'I will tell no one what you've done if—'

'I knew there'd be a condition.'

'If,' Willy went on, 'you tell me what Gavin has to say for himself.' He prodded downward with the point of his stick, bracing himself for a turn-about; and then the thought struck him. 'Have you received letters from Gavin before?'

'Oh! So there is something you don't know?' Becky said smugly. 'Did Auntie Aileen miss out in her sniffing and prying? How do you know he hasn't been writing regularly to Rachel?'

'Has he?'

'You may think yourself a clever old stick, Willy, but you can't stop my brother writing to my sister in Glasgow.'

'Will you open it for me?'

'No,' Becky said, with a shake of her puffy sleeves. 'But if you promise not to tell anyone, anyone at all, that I've written to Gavin then I'll let you know what Gavin has to say for himself.'

'All right.'

'Promise you'll not say a word to a soul in the meantime?'

'I promise.'

'Cross your heart.'

'Cross my heart,' said Willy, feeling rather like a fool.

'Of all the times to be doing this to us,' Quig said. 'I cannot for the life of me imagine why she would be so stupid.'

'She doesn't know what he's like,' said Willy.

'Do you think that she will tell you the truth about the letter?'

'Who knows?' said Willy. 'I just want to know if he's on his way, that's all.'

'I hope that he does come,' said Quig. 'I will be ready for him.'

'Ready for him?' said Willy, frowning. 'You're not going to do anything rash, Quig, are you?'

'I will not let him take her away against her will.'

'Have you a fancy for the girl yourself?'

Quig shook his head brusquely.

Willy said, 'Becky claims that the girl's been making eyes at you.'

'That is just another of Becky's stupid fancies.' Quig hesitated. 'It would be better if we did not say anything to Biddy, however, under the circumstances.'

'What circumstances would those be?' said Willy.

'Biddy has it in mind to sell off a piece of Fetternish and she will not be wanting anything to queer her pitch at this time.'

'Is it near to being settled then?' Willy said.

'I have not been told,' said Quig.

'Wouldn't you advise her to sell?'

'I do not want to see Fetternish sliced up and given away,' said Quig.

'Hardly given away,' said Willy. 'She'll get a fair price for it, I'm certain. When it comes to money Biddy is never rash.'

'Aye,' Quig said, 'and she is enjoying the attention.'

'Rattenbury, do you mean?' said Willy.

'She has him in the stables now, and she's charging him next to nothing in rental. I had to go down there with Barrett and make the place all spick and span before she would allow him to move in. She is treating him like a king.'

'It might be just a shrewd piece of business,' Willy said.

'And it might be that she is flattered by his attentions.'

'Biddy would never allow herself to be *flattered* into selling Fetternish, or even a part of it. No, no, I've known her too long to think that of her.'

'She's changed, Willy.'

'So I've noticed,' Willy said. 'There's far too much change going on around here to suit a reactionary old goat like me.'

He leaned into the stick and looked out at the sea, always at the sea: even if you hated water as much as he did, you always turned your eyes to the sea. He was weary, suddenly weary of it all, perhaps because the walk down to Pennypol had proved to be too much for him. He would have to walk all the way back too and that prospect increased his fatigue.

'Where is she? The girl, I mean.'

'I sent her home,' said Quig. 'She is not resting enough. I sent her home to lie down for a while.'

Willy looked at the plots, at green tops and sprouting leaves set out in rows so neat that Vassie Campbell would not have recognised them. All vegetables, all marketable crops, with nothing fancy here except some strawberry plants over by the long wall. He shook his head. 'There won't be enough to make a living out of,' he said. 'Is this your hope of salvation, Quig? Market gardening?'

'Of course it is not,' Quig said. 'It is just a sort of crofting, that is all. I have put money into it just to keep her happy.'

'Why would you want to do that?'

'Because . . .' Quig shrugged. 'Because, I suppose, that has been my lot in life and it is very hard to shake off old habits.'

'Oh, so you are a martyr now, are you?' Willy said.

Quig chuckled, not loudly. 'Aye, you have been around too long, Willy Naismith, and there is no hiding anything much from you. No, I am no martyr, nor do I have any inclination to make myself into one. But I will not be letting Gavin Tarrant take her away with him, no matter what I have to do to stop him.'

'If Fay's to be believed he won't come here.'

'It will not be shame that will keep him away.'

'Probably not,' said Willy. 'But will it be pride that will bring him back?'

'I tell you this,' said Quig, 'I will be ready for him whatever brings him here. I will be looking over my shoulder every minute for that dark head of his appearing over the horizon. In the meanwhile I will not be letting Fay out of my sight.'

'That might be difficult.'

'Everything worthwhile is difficult,' said Quig, without a trace of pomposity. 'Anyhow, since you have been good enough to warn me, Willy, I take it that you will keep me informed just when we might expect a visit from young Mr Tarrant.'

'If Becky tells me, that is,' said Willy.

'And if she does not?'

'Aileen and I will be on the hill.'

Quig chuckled again, totally without mirth. 'Like a pair of Pictish scouts watching out for the Vikings.'

'Something like that,' said Willy.

She had packed the picnic basket with her own fair hands and carried it out of the house tucked under her arm.

Billowing along in the morning sunlight she felt as light as a piece of thistledown, not in the least stealthy, though she'd been careful to slip out by the side door and circle through the bushes so that no one would see her.

Mistress of the house of Fetternish and mother of two grown

children she might be, but deep down she was still Biddy Campbell, the girl from Pennypol whom all the men lusted after, whom all the men adored.

Her confidence unfurled like a fist of young fern, grew green and sappy again in the heat of the summer's day. She was delighted at the manner in which Patrick had helped her shed the sundry plagues and sad distempers of middle age. Had helped her realise that she was not old after all, not old the way Willy was old, not like her stuffy sister who relied on prayers and painted statues to keep her from brooding on the dull existence she had chosen for herself, with a lover who was no lover at all, and daughters who despised her.

She had put on a summer dress, floral and filmy, with just a light elasticised stomacher beneath her underskirt. She no longer felt constricted, or lumpy, or fat, or frumpy, and when she caught sight of Patrick down at the pump in the yard her voice rose an octave and she called out to him and waved and held up the wicker basket and ran downhill towards him, floating like a zephyr: floating . . . and falling . . . falling head over tip . . . falling and sprawling into the rank grass among buttercups and ox-eyes and the coarse stems of ragwort, into the nettles that sprouted on the mound of the Bells' old dung-heap.

She was weeping when he reached her. She was lying full-length upon her stomach with her arms stretched out before her, cheek and brow smeared with dirt, her floral dress stained with grass.

The picnic basket had strewn its contents down the hillside. Fragments of roast chicken, slivers of smoked mackerel and several bread rolls coloured the dusty ground, along with cracked cups, plates and the two half-bottles of white wine that she had sneaked out of the cellar last night.

Biddy lay helpless where she had fallen, tears streaming from her eyes.

Patrick reached her and, kneeling, lifted her up.

'Are you hurt? Is anything broken?'

She clung to him and wept, abashed, into his shoulder.

He had been drawing water from the pump, the fine old pump that tapped an eternal well-spring deep under the rock. He was wet with the water that sprayed from the rim of the spout, his forearms wet with the spray that came from the joint of the handle: old things, old memories of her days at the stables with Angus Bell and Maggie and the ostler's family. Patrick was as wet as she was, and his voice had a moist, lugubrious quality, as if her pain made him want to weep too.

He patted her upon the back, as gently as if he were winding a baby.

'Are you sure?' he said. 'It was a dreadful tumble, Biddy. Perhaps I should take you into Tobermory and have the doctor—'

'No,' she said, in panic. 'No, just – just hold me for a moment, please.'

His shirt was open to the waist. It was not one of the rough wool shirts that farm-hands wore but cotton, a decent and expensive garment like his twill breeches, his hacking jacket, the wardrobe of a gentleman. He had a handkerchief too, clean and folded, which he produced with the dexterity of a conjurer and before Biddy could stop him wetted a corner with the tip of his tongue and, still holding her, began to dab away the smudges and smears that marred her brow.

'What on earth were you doing, running like that?'

'Coming – coming to see you, to surprise you.'

'You surprised me all right,' said Patrick, still dabbing. 'You gave me the fright of my life. Are you sure there's nothing damaged?'

'Fairly sure,' said Biddy.

'Perhaps I should look you over.'

'What?'

'Come, I'll help you down to the house and take a look at your ankle.'

'Will you?'

'In case you've broken one of the small bones, or torn a tendon.'

'And if I have, what will you do then?'

'Shoot you, most probably,' Patrick said, and with his face very close to hers, wiped the moistened corner of the handkerchief across her parted lips.

It was no go with the walled garden. Quig had known it from the outset. He had encouraged the girl only to lift her spirits and give her something to hang on to. The walled garden was dead, a victim of his neglect. He felt no inclination to dig it up and relay it, however, for this was not his house now, not his garden and he had lost the urge to foster and restore it for someone else's benefit.

Fay would be lying down in the cool back room in Innis Tarrant's cottage. She would be breathing gently through her mouth, her stomach extended under the sheet that Innis would have pulled over her.

She was safe there, asleep in the afternoon.

He seated himself on the rustic bench and contemplated what Fay might have done with the garden if only there had been enough time, if only she had entered his life before he had surrendered his belief that he could make Biddy happy and leave Fetternish a better place: a brave, daft dream, one that was bred into every islander who wanted to keep his paradise intact without the intervention of capitalists and adventurers.

He sat with hands between his knees, listening to the sound that was no sound, to the infernal stillness of decay. He had never felt so hollow, so despairing and so bitter before.

The news that Willy had carried down to Pennypol had disturbed him: not the notion that he might wake up one morning to find Gavin Tarrant strutting down the drive and baying for blood but that he might wake up one morning to find that Fay had gone, for the English girl had brought him the promise of new beginnings.

Forty years ago Evander McIver had chosen him out of many to protect the others against their own weaknesses. He had been told that he was a tower of strength and that come what may he would not bend or break. He was breaking now, though, crumbling under the weight of change, soured like the garden around him and smothered by all the promises that had been made on his behalf.

Fay would be lying in Innis's house, safe by the altar that Innis had erected to her Church and her God. He wondered what Innis prayed for these days, marvelled that the half-wild, wilful little girl whom he had almost fallen in love with had grown into such a calm, unfazeable woman.

Innis had Gillies Brown to look after her. Aileen had Willy Naismith. Becky had Rachel. He'd had a loyal daughter once but it seemed that she had lost her loving ways. He still had Robbie, a good boy, but he must let Robbie go soon, could not drag Robbie back here and saddle him with Fetternish. He, Quig, he had no one now, no one except the girl from Fream who, when it came to it, might want her young half-mad husband more than she wanted him.

He got up and went into the house through the kitchen.

'Maggie, where's my wife?'

'I don't know, Mr Quigley.'

'Becky, have you seen her?'

'Not me.'

He nodded and went upstairs.

He crossed the hall and entered the corridor that led to the office.

On the left was a big locked closet that he had not looked into for five years or more. He went into the office, took a ring of keys from the desk drawer and fingered through them until he found the little blunt key that would open the cupboard where Biddy kept her guns.

It was a decade or more since she had given up shooting, letting it go as she had let so many things go, out of apathy, out of laziness; another talent sacrificed to vanity and anxiety.

Quig unlocked the closet and stepped inside.

There was just enough light to let him see the rack of three hunting rifles of which Biddy had once been so proud. He had never been a shooting man. He left vermin control to Angus Bell and a couple of boys from the village who would come up occasionally and pop away at the rabbits or blow out the rooks from the rookery in the stand of trees near the stables.

There were no shotguns in Biddy's little collection, only rifles.

He took one down and worked the bolt, inspected the mechanism. He propped the rifle against the wall and reached up to the shelf deep in the cupboard. As he did so he felt the prickle of pellet scars that crimped the muscles of his chest and ribcage and the twitch of the old wound in his shoulder. Imagination perhaps, just imagination: thinking of Gavin had brought it on. He found the rod, the rags, a rusty tin of oil, a box of cartridges still sealed and dry.

He brought them down, locked the cupboard, carried the tools, the cartridges and the rifle into the office and put them on the desk.

He locked the door of the office and set about preparing for Gavin's return, for a chance to balance the books at last.

'Does that hurt?'

'Just a little.'

'And this?'

'Hardly at all.'

'No damage done then.'

He knelt before her as Willy had done in the old days when he, the servant, would take off her hunting boots and massage her feet. There had always been a hint of impropriety in Willy's ministrations but he knew better than to overstep the mark and she had enjoyed the touch of his big hands upon her, intimate and gentle yet perfectly discreet. Now, though, the intimacy was charged with sexual feelings that she did not attempt to deny.

She stretched out her leg, pointed her bare toes and tugged her skirts a little higher so that he could see the roundness of her knee if he wanted to.

She was seated on a kitchen chair, Patrick on a stool at her feet.

She might have been Cinderella and he Prince Charming, except that this was no fairytale and there was nothing romantic about her intentions or, she thought, about his.

She watched his fingers curl under her ankle, felt pressure increase. She squeezed her thighs together and let her foot revolve away from him, then, leaning forward, pointed, frowning, at her calf.

'There, I think, just there is where the pain is.'

He did not glance up.

He was playing the game with studious concentration; so much studious concentration that Biddy began to wonder if he even realised what was going on.

Of course he did! Of course! Patrick was a man of the world, not a man of the cloth. He had watched women take off their stockings before, and a lot more besides, Biddy reckoned. She was hot. A little dew of perspiration gathered on her upper lip and two unfortunate patches under her arms. Fortunately her calves were smooth, smooth-shaven and dry. When he rubbed his hand along the muscle, ostensibly feeling for tenderness, it was all she could do to stifle a gasp.

'If we had ice, I could put a cold pack on it,' Patrick said.

'Is it swollen?'

'No, it doesn't seem to be. Something stretched, I fancy, not something torn.'

'Have you done this sort of thing before?'

'Once or twice,' Patrick said.

'Really!'

'My mother suffers fearfully from rheumatism.'

'Your mother?'

'My father used to do it for her but he doesn't have the strength in his fingers that he used to have. My mother prefers it to be firmly done. She claims that she only feels the benefit when it hurts.'

'How odd!' said Biddy, pointlessly.

'Not odd at all,' said Patrick. 'I've also had a lot of experience with horses.'

'Horses?'

'Strained fetlocks, mainly.'

'Are you comparing me to a horse?'

'Not at all,' said Patrick, 'apart from which you don't have any swelling of the flexor tendon or clap on the back sinews.'

'You are comparing me to a horse.'

He laughed, ran his hand once over the lower part of her leg, making her shiver. He hoisted himself from the stool and tapped her shin with his forefinger. 'You'll live, Biddy,' he said. 'But I wouldn't go skipping down steep braes like a young thing, not for a week or two at least.'

Disgruntled by his flippant manner, Biddy drew down her skirts. Her stockings still hung on the chair back but she did not reach for them. She had given him enough of a show to be going on with and she was not about to put herself in a position to be compared to some other beast of the field. She pursed her lips and picked a flake of mud from the lap of her dress. At least he had been civil enough to fetch her in a bowl of water; perhaps she should count herself fortunate that he hadn't taken her out to the pump and hosed her down.

'Can you walk?' Patrick said. 'Try it.'

She lowered her weight gingerly on to her feet and paddled them on the stone floor. She was perfectly all right, really, and had no pain or tenderness to speak of. It was, she supposed, her dignity that had been bruised and no cold pack or veterinarian's liniment was going to cure that.

'If you feel up to it,' Patrick said, 'perhaps you'd care to accompany me out on to the moor.'

'What for?'

'I have something to show you.'

'Do you? And what might that be?'

'We could take the picnic with us, if you like.'

'What's left of it,' said Biddy.

'I salvaged the chicken pieces. They're quite palatable, most of them.'

'What is this – this thing you have to show me?'

'You'll see,' said Patrick. 'Are you up to it?'

'I'm up to it,' said Biddy eagerly.

The appearance of the Lady Hollander on the edge of the school yard at the commencement of the dinner break created a stir of interest in the pupils.

Holidays were in sight and there was a general feeling of relaxation that Janetta, try as she might, couldn't bring under control. When the whooping and shouting ceased in the yard, therefore, she went out of the classroom like a shot from a gun, the bell in one hand and a big, plump chalk-duster in the other. She scowled and, like a heron stalking a pool, squinted this way and that in search of trouble.

Trouble usually took the form of a fight between boys or squabbles between girls but there were none of the familiar signs, no ring of onlookers, no yelps or shrieks or long straggling lines of children streaming towards the riverbank which served as an arena for serious fisticuffs. The village children, who went home for a meal, had formed a peculiar little file and were sidling towards the fence at the back of the Wingard Hall as if something in the lane had alarmed them. The stay-at-school brigade backed away from the lane too and were staring in that direction as if unsure just what the nature of the threat might be.

Gillies came out of his classroom and stood behind his daughter.

He put on his glasses, took them off again.

'What's going on?'

'I don't know,' said Janetta. 'You, Peter Malone, what's going on?'

'Buggy, miss.'

'Buggy? Are you being impudent?'

'In the lane, in the lane, buggy, the lady's buggy, miss.'

Then Janetta saw Frances emerge from the lane's end and glimpsed the long American buggy and the passive pony which was emphatically not given to devouring small children. It was unusual, though, and anything unusual represented threat. In spite of her maturity, Janetta shared the children's suspicion that the Lady Frances Hollander might have come to do them harm.

'Oh, it's only your friend,' Gillies said. 'She's obviously looking to have a word with you,' and diplomatically retreated back into the classroom, taking the handbell and the duster with him.

Frances looked prettier than ever in a brand-new day-dress with a jacket-like bodice and an open tunic overskirt. The bodice emphasised Frances's tiny waist and brought to Janetta the unwelcome memory of Frances clad in practically nothing, her small, perfectly formed breasts bobbing in the waves.

In contrast she was grey and grubby with chalk dust.

Frances also wore a huge tricorne hat and carried a long-handled lace-lined parasol. Small wonder, Netta thought, that the children stared. But this was her domain and she resented Frances's intrusion and its effect on the innocent waifs of the parish of Crove.

She stopped suddenly and spun round.

'Go on, children,' she snapped. 'Go on. There is nothing here for you.'

They broke ranks and scattered, giggling, and Janetta in control again felt a little like giggling too.

'Frances,' she said. 'What brings you here at this hour?'

'I had to talk with you, dearest. I had to explain.'

'Explain? What is there to explain?' She turned, surveyed the school yard with an eagle eye, turned again. 'Do you wish to step inside?'

'No, I – I thought – if you can, if you are free – able – we might walk a little.'

'I do not have long. I've a lesson to script.'

'Script? Oh, yes, I see. Well, perhaps another day.'

'Ten minutes,' Janetta said, 'that's all I can spare.'

Frances smiled, relieved. 'Shall we walk a little then?'

'By all means,' Janetta said, 'but please do not take my arm.'

'Are you afraid of me?'

'I'm afraid of losing face before the children.'

'I'm sure they would think nothing of it.'

'Who knows what they would think? They aren't so innocent as you imagine, not the older ones at any rate.'

'I will not take your arm,' Frances said. 'I want to, though. I want to take your arm and hold you still long enough to explain.'

'Explain what?' said Janetta.

'I – I misjudged you. No, not you,' Frances said, 'the moment.'

'What *are* you talking about?'

'Us. Our friendship.'

Janetta looked round. Not all the pupils had dispersed. A few of the older girls, mesmerised by the sight of the lady of The Ards arrayed in all her glory in their school yard, were loitering nearby.

Janetta jerked her head. 'In the lane, by the buggy.'

She followed Frances into the tunnel between the cottages' peeling walls, into the odours of boiling beef, cabbage and fried fish. She felt clumsy in her plain skirt and starched shirt and tried to remind herself that she had earned her place in this tiny society and Frances had not.

'What is it, Frances? What do you wish to say to me?'

'I behaved so badly. I understand why you want no more to do with me.' Frances's little voice quivered like a fiddle string. 'What I did was unforgivable, Netta. I don't know what came over me. The sea, the sand, I suppose, and having you all to myself in the sunshine, so carefree and easy.'

'I am not,' Janetta said, 'so carefree and easy as all that.'

'I realise that now,' Frances said. 'I misjudged you.'

'So you keep saying.'

When Frances reached out a hand, Janetta pulled back.

'Can't we be friends, Netta, dearest?'

'I'm not sure what being your friend entails.'

'Well, no more of that – that . . .'

'Kissing,' said Janetta. 'Is that the word you're looking for?'

'Simple affection, pure friendship. I'm too impulsive for my own good sometimes, aren't I? Have you never been kissed by a friend before?'

'No,' Janetta lied. 'Never.'

'If I promise,' Frances said, 'not to misbehave will you come back to me?'

'Back . . .'

'I mean,' Frances put in hurriedly, 'will you be my friend again? Come to tea at The Ards, go walking with me. I miss you, Netta, really and truly I do.' She cocked her head coyly, the gesture outlandishly exaggerated by the size of the tricorne hat. 'Do you not miss me even a tiny bit?'

'I can't honestly say that I do,' Janetta said.

'Oh! Oh, dear! Oh, my!'

'Stop it, Frances,' Janetta said. 'I'm not impressed by your theatricals. I've no doubt that you're sincere but you've a strange way of showing it. In spite of the fact that we are as different as chalk from cheese I do enjoy your company.'

'Come back then, let's have it as it was. I need a friend.'

'What about Maggie and Mairi?'

'They are merely acquaintances. They're not like us.'

'Us?' said Janetta. 'What makes us so special?'

'We have a special affinity.'

'Is that why you've shaken them off? Maggie's hurt—'

'Maggie has a husband to console her,' Frances interrupted.

'Ah!' Janetta said. 'So it's a husband that makes the difference. What about your husband, Frances? Will he not be coming back to be your husband again? When he does what will happen to our "friendship"?'

'It will make no difference to Larry.'

'Well, it makes a difference to me,' said Janetta.

Janetta saw the tip of Frances's tongue protrude between her teeth almost as if she were about to spit daintily on to the ground.

'It's Mr Rattenbury, isn't it?' Frances said.

'Patrick? What does he have to—'

'Patrick! I knew it. You used me to worm your way into Patrick Rattenbury's good books, and now you want rid of me?'

'How could I possibly have used you,' Janetta said, 'when we have never been together, the three of us. Mr Rattenbury may be your mother-in-law's agent but you don't own the rights to *his* friendship any more than you own the rights to *my* friendship. As for Patrick, if he prefers me to you . . .'

'Prefers? Prefers? Oh, that is a hoot, I must say.'

'At least friendship with Patrick' – Janetta drew back her shoulders – 'is the sort of friendship I can understand.'

'Do you think he's in the least interested in you, dearest? No. Oh, no. I can tell you that Patrick Rattenbury will do you more harm than I would ever do. If you think I put on airs to impress you then you've obviously not encountered your beloved Patrick Rattenbury with his buttons undone.'

'That's a shocking thing to say.'

'You're easily shocked then,' Frances told her. 'I'll tell you who is *not* shocked by your Mr Rattenbury: Mrs Bridget Quigley is not shocked by him. On the contrary, she is delighted by those very qualities that you have overlooked.' Frances opened her parasol, causing the pony to shy. 'Well, run off to Patrick then. Go on, run into his arms – or into his bed for all I care. You'll regret it. Mark my words well, Netta, you *will* regret it.'

She gave the parasol a twirl, making the lace edges bobble, and then darted forward and kissed Janetta on the mouth, a sliding little kiss too hasty to have meaning at first; then the tip of Frances's tongue came out and tracked a moist little smear of saliva across Janetta's cheek and chin.

Janetta rocked back on her heels and shot up a hand to protect herself.

Hoisting the parasol high, Frances stepped back and up into the buggy.

'*Adieu*, Janetta,' she said. 'When Patrick has taught you a lesson, I'll be waiting just across the river to comfort you. Remember that, my dear one. I'll be waiting.'

Janetta was too thunderstruck to reply. She felt a strange drag of the heart as Frances, smiling and dimpled, tossed the parasol into the wagon bed and snatched up the reins; a weird, weak feeling of anxiety, almost of regret, as the lady of The Ards wrenched at the brake handle and the buggy trundled forward.

'Bye-bye, dearest,' Frances called out as she steered the pony into the narrow lane and away out of it, round in a loop into the main street in a cloud of grit and hen feathers. 'Bye-bye.'

Stiff as a ramrod, Janetta turned on her heel and walked back to the safety of the schoolhouse.

'What did that woman want?' her father asked her.

'Nothing of consequence,' Janetta said, tight-lipped, and stalked past him into the empty classroom and pointedly slammed the door.

On a crown of heather in the midst of a rough circle scythed out of the bracken, the instrument looked like the sort of modernist effigy to which her pedantic nephew Donnie, with his passion for metaphor and symbol, might have been tempted to bend the knee.

'What is it?' Biddy asked.

'What does it look like?' Patrick said.

'Is it a generator of some sort?'

Patrick held her by the arm, keeping their distance while the machine whirled and whirred on three stout metallic legs. Brass cups attached to a horizontal arm flickered and flung back the sunlight; a wheel – two wheels – were attached by a linking chain and a finely crafted box was bolted to the frame. Even from thirty yards off Biddy could clearly hear the click and *whoof* of the metal arm and the soft, rushing sigh of the cups as the breeze drove them round.

'No, not a generator,' Patrick said.

'A pump then,' Biddy said. 'Or, wait, a device for testing the weather.'

'Ah, now, that's shrewd of you, Biddy.'

The sight of the wind-generated machine propped on her land suddenly brought home to her what it would mean to lose Fetternish. There was something too brittle, too geometric about the piece, and its restless fluctuations made it seem alive. She was glad that Patrick had brought her here, that she had not been left to stumble on the mysterious object alone.

He did not hold her back to protect her, however. He held her back to admire his handiwork and, after a couple of minutes, guided her forward through the waist-high fern into the cropped circle.

'It's a wind gauge,' he said. 'It measures the speed of the wind and its various shifts in direction. I designed it.'

The sight of the odd little machine had distracted her from the pleasure of being alone with Patrick in the wilderness. The sagging roofs of the deserted cottages at An Fhearann Cáirdeil were hidden behind clusters of rowan, blackthorn and elder and no habitations marred the long flank of the moorland that stretched away brown-tanned and scarred into the distance.

Biddy tried to appear more interested in the device than in its inventor.

'It's very simple, really,' Patrick said. 'In the lower part of the box there are four gear wheels and a gimbal and in the upper part a drum loaded with graph paper and two fixed pencils. One pencil traces the wind's direction and the other records variations in wind speed. I have to change the drum daily, of course, and the pencils quite frequently. I tried an inking system but that proved to be too messy. It's not so complicated as it sounds.'

'Did you also build the machine?'

'No, that was done by an instrument-maker.'

'How clever you are, Patrick.'

'Necessity is the mother of invention, and all that,' he said, pleased at her compliment. 'I'd let you examine it more closely but I'd rather not tinker when it's in motion, if you don't mind.'

'I believe I've grasped the principle,' Biddy said. 'Wind speed and direction will dictate the variety of trees that you can plant here, I suppose.'

Patrick released her arm and stood now, hands on hips, admiring the activity of the machine. 'We have forty-four species and sub-species to choose from, not counting hardwoods. Foreign conifers have to be protected to some extent by bands of native hardwoods, you see. It's all very scientific these days.'

Biddy did not inform him that she had read up on the basic tenets of forestry in her grandfather's library, for such information as she had gleaned would probably seem out of date to an expert like Patrick.

She disliked the whirling devil that he had planted on her land without so much as a by-your-leave. If she consented to sell or lease the land even larger machines would appear in the form of traction-engines, pumps and drain-laying equipment. In showing off the wind gauge Patrick had unwittingly given her a glimpse of the future. She could not shut her ears to the instrument's greedy whirring, the *whoof-whoof-whoof* of its cups. Although its power derived from the wind, there was something so alien and so devouring about it that Biddy turned and quickly moved on.

It took Patrick a minute to realise that she had left him.

He came after her, more amused than concerned.

'I didn't expect you to be impressed.' He put a hand upon her shoulder to steady her. 'You must admit, however, that it's more interesting than peering into clay dishes filled with soil samples.'

She was still bare-legged like the waif from Ludlow or the tyke that she, Biddy Campbell, had been when Mam had made them walk to Crove with their shoes tied around their necks. She had shoes on now, shoes worn without stockings, which made her feel loose and daring.

Patrick paused to pick up the picnic basket and followed her lead.

She waded through the deep bracken that flourished along the edge of the moor until she found what had once been a sheep path that led to the top of the gully and a steep but not sheer drop into the sea. She had come here often in the past, with the dogs, Odin and Thor, snuffling along in front of her and had felt free then, so terribly free.

Flotsam had accumulated in the cove below, a monstrous tangle of roots and broken timbers, skeletal creels and herring boxes, the swollen carcass of a sheep, not one of hers, from which salt water had washed off the fleece.

She moved round, Patrick still following, until she couldn't see the base of the cove and the carcass of the sheep but only the great grey-green waves rolling in and sea-pinks nodding on the edge of the gully.

'Here,' she said. 'We will sit here and eat.'

He smiled at her dictatorial tone but obediently seated himself on the grass without demur. Biddy sat opposite him, her legs drawn up under her skirt, and watched him work loose the straps of the picnic basket.

Biddy said, 'Do you know how many acres I possess? I expect you do.'

'Two thousand four hundred and twelve.' He went on fiddling with the awkward strap. 'I acquired that figure from your return in the blue book. I assume that it's accurate.'

'My husband — my first husband — had our holdings surveyed twenty years ago. If you feel inclined, you may have them measured again. Eight or ten acres have gone missing in the interim: the cottage at Pennymain and some ground around it are made over in perpetuity to my sister.'

'And Pennypol?'

'No, that is still part of the estate, for the time being.'

'What does that mean: for the time being?'

'There are' – Biddy hesitated – 'complications about Penny-pol.' She drew her knees in with one hand. She did not find the position comfortable and was conscious of a certain strain in her flanks. 'Tell me, just how much of Fetternish do your clients want?'

It was Patrick's turn to hesitate. 'All of it.'

Biddy was surprised that she felt no surprise.

She said, 'Including the house, my house?'

'All of it,' Patrick repeated. 'I dare say we could come to some arrangement about your sister's lease.'

'Buy her off too, do you mean?'

'There is, I assure you, no scarcity of money.'

'Did you look up my return in *Landowners*?' She did not wait for his reply. 'If so, you'll have noted that there are only two asterisks against the entry which, as you know, means that the information is only approximately correct. Approximately, Pa-trick, not substantially. But you'll also have noted the gross annual value and know that I am vulnerable?'

'I have seen worse,' said Patrick. 'In Ross-shire—'

'Do not try to patronise me, please.'

'The value is not high,' Patrick admitted. 'In fact for the acreage you hold it's ridiculously low.'

'Valueless, practically valueless,' said Biddy.

'Well' – he opened the lid of the hamper – 'I'm here to offer a solution.'

'You are here to negotiate a purchase at a rock-bottom price, are you not?'

Patrick looked down into the basket without focusing.

He said, 'I must do what's best for my clients, Biddy.'

'I can keep going, you know.'

'Paying out for repairs to empty buildings, ground tax, wages, insurance, the upkeep of the big house . . . Biddy, I ask you: how long can you hope to survive living beyond your means?'

'I have a reasonably decent flock of breeding ewes.'

'And a wool market at its lowest ebb in thirty years. And a market for fat lambs that makes it hardly worth while shipping them to Oban let alone Perth or Glasgow.' He closed the lid of the hamper and leaned on it as if it were a lectern. 'Oh, yes, you *can* go on. You can struggle on for years while the land deteriorates even further, while the bogs creep closer and the bracken climbs through the cracks, and the house, your fine house, develops roof leaks that you can't afford to repair, and the beams rot and the floors warp and the windows hang loose in their frames. Before your children are our age there will be nothing of Fetternish left to sell.'

'Now is the time, is that what you're telling me? Now or never?'

'Soon,' Patrick said. 'Soon – or never.'

She put her hand to her hair, swept it down to her neck and around the crown of her shoulder as if her hair were still as long as it had been once.

'Someone wants me out, Patrick, don't they?'

'Louden, Lafferty and Spruell . . .'

'No, someone, one person. Tell me who it is?'

'I assure you that there's no conspiracy . . .'

'Please, Patrick, tell me who wants me out?' Biddy said.

'My client's offer will be sufficiently generous to allow you to buy a house in Tobermory, or a town-house in Edinburgh to be near to your children. Wisely invested, the balance will enable you to live comfortably for the rest of your life. Fetternish is a diminishing asset, Biddy, and the longer you delay your decision the less it will bring you.'

'Fetternish is my only asset,' Biddy said. 'Someone wants to take it from me.'

'No, no,' said Patrick. 'That's not the case at all.' He brought himself forward on to his heels and reached out for her hand which, reluctantly, she yielded. 'You must not imagine things, Biddy. No one is out to steal your land. It's a business venture, that's all. You have my word on that.'

'And what's your word worth?' Biddy heard herself say. 'I've been lied to, cheated and deceived by too many men to accept the word of a man I hardly know.'

'That,' Patrick said, 'is why I have not put an offer on the table just yet.'

'So that my price will come down?'

Biddy was sulking now, sulking like a petulant schoolgirl, just like her daughter Christina. She was aware that she was behaving badly, not at all like a woman of business, and despised herself for doing so. Beneath her uncharacteristic posturing, though, was a motive too strong to ignore: if only she could keep Patrick here, keep him dangling, then he might come to want her as so many men had done in the past – and then, she thought triumphantly, the price will go up and Mr Patrick Rattenbury and his shadowy client will have the tables turned on them. She had always done what was best for Fetternish: now, perhaps, it was time to do something just for herself.

She brought his hand into her lap, holding it between both of her own.

'I'm sorry,' she said. 'I should not be doubting you.'

'You have every right to be cautious,' Patrick said. 'I would think the less of you if you weren't cautious.'

'Is there someone else?'

'Someone – what do you mean?'

'A buyer?'

'Biddy, really! No.'

'I think there is,' she said. 'What's more I think I know who it is.'

To his credit Patrick did not flinch. He let his hand rest lightly between her palms in the silky nest of her lap. He knew only too well what she was doing and how he must respond, knew that all the nonsense about there being a silent and sinister partner was guesswork, that she was doing no more than leading him on.

She was clumsy at it, out of practice. He supposed that she had lost touch with the nature of her own sexuality during the years of her marriage. She wanted him to woo her, court her and, in the end, to take her so that she would have the pleasure of conquest and with it an excuse for selling off her land. He was also absolutely sure that she wanted rid of the vast, uncultivated wilderness that had claimed so much of her attention.

He disentangled his hands and before she quite knew what was happening, caught her by the shoulders and brought her forward. She rolled on to her knees and leaned her breast against his forearm as he kissed her mouth. He had put his lips to no woman's lips for three or four years now and had not been tempted to do so. He had loved once, twice, and had left one, two, broken hearts behind him but he was not so cold that he did not desire her or ignore the heat with which she returned his kiss.

Her cheek was scalding, her breast within the bodice of the dress swollen with the essence of her passion. He adjusted position, settled, balanced, and drew her down across his knee.

She was too large, too heavy for the manoeuvre to be accomplished smoothly but once she lay there, shoulders against his thighs, her face upturned towards his, he had to check the sudden rush of blood that urged him to take her there and then. It was not love or hunger, a need for satisfaction or even appeasement that drove her but confusion – and the more confused Biddy Baverstock Quigley became the more it would suit his purpose.

He let the edge of his desire show by bridging her breast with his finger and thumb, not stroking; a static promise of more to come. He kissed her mouth again.

She sighed, she groaned, and – quite abruptly – there was an anguish in her, a desperation, that caught him off guard.

He drew away, his hand first, his mouth.

He eased her from his thighs, upright into a sitting position. She looked stunned, quite stunned. Her sea-green eyes were large with tears. Although he was embarrassed, almost ashamed, he had enough sense not to apologise.

'I can't,' Biddy said. 'I can't, Patrick. Not yet.'

He cleared his throat and rolled back from her. 'I had no right to assume . . .'

'It isn't my husband. It isn't that. It's me. I'm not ready. Not yet.'

Twice she had said it and he had no doubt that she would say it again before the afternoon was out. He knew what *Not yet* meant in the language that women like Biddy Quigley spoke.

She had not been lost, not been desperate. He had been tricked into feeling ashamed. She was manipulating him, squeezing him just to see how pliant and malleable he would be when it came to dealing in pounds and pence. He felt better at once: he knew precisely how to deal with women who traded their sex for profit and with whom there was no possibility of love.

'Do you wish me to take you home, Biddy?' he enquired.

She shook her head and, forcing a brave expression, reached out and flipped open the lid of the picnic basket.

'No,' she said. 'Not yet.'

She had been shaken by Frances's visit to the school yard for she knew that she had made an enemy out of a friend.

Even now, though, she could not perceive what Frances wanted from her, how their intimacy would be expressed or what experiences lay beyond the loving kiss. She got through afternoon lessons on habit and discipline but the effort cost her dearly and she was soggy with tension before her father brought in the bell for her to ring.

She rang it loudly, clamorously, and watched the class empty with an orderliness that was rare enough to be remarkable.

She put down the bell on the desk, wiped the board, dusted her hands and, stiff and straight and purposeful, walked out of the classroom, out of the door and across the grass to the lane.

Stepping up her pace, she headed up the main street and away along the road to Fetternish or, rather, to the track that would carry her to the stables.

Long-legged, stiff-legged, she ran the final few hundred yards.

The stallion was not stalled. He was attached to a long tether in the field that had once been a paddock. He looked up when she passed and whinnied and tossed his great handsome head.

'Patrick?' Janetta trotted into the yard. 'Patrick. Where are you?'

She wanted him to come out to her and take her into his arms.

She wanted him to hold her, to feel the inexplicable assurance of his maleness, to have him erase for ever her doubts about herself.

'Patrick?'

He did not appear.

She waited, breathless, by the pump.

'Patrick. Please. Patrick.'

She was weeping now, not copiously.

She went forward to the door of the house and found it ajar. She pushed the door open. 'Patrick?'

Bands of sunlight angled across the kitchen. There were no plates upon the table, no cups, only a bowl filled with water, and a discarded towel.

Janetta moved forward, her shoes scuffling on the stone, moved forward to the chair where, draped across the spar, the stockings hung. Milk-white, expensive stockings, the sort that only ladies wore. On the seat, a lady's garters, crumpled as carnations.

'Patrick,' Janetta whispered. 'Oh, Patrick. Oh, God, no,' then, hands locked across her chest, she turned and stumbled out of the kitchen and set off, broken and shambling, for home.

CHAPTER THIRTEEN

False Witness

Apparently he had been in Tobermory for two or three days before he made his move. Tom Ewing had bumped into him on the pavement near the harbour but Tom's eyesight was not what it was and he had failed to recognise the man whom he had once known so well.

Few others even noticed the chap who lingered outside the trinket shops on the one-sided street and made several purchases of bangles, rings and brooches and, in the haberdashers, bought a bolt of tartan cloth fine-woven by the famous Salen crofters. In particular he was not visible during the afternoon when Innis or Biddy or Maggie Naismith were liable to be in town. He lodged in the Mishnish Hotel and, like any ordinary tourist, dutifully walked out to Aros House to look at the trickling waterfalls and climbed to the lighthouse on Ru-na-Gal to admire the panoramic view. He even booked a seat on the hotel's waggonette for a 'circular excursion' and in company with a dozen other visitors marvelled at the grandeur of the lochs and mountains as if he had never seen them before.

On Wednesday evening after an early dinner he emerged from the hotel dressed in a hand-cut lounge suit and a squat little bowler hat, lit a cigar and strolled casually off towards the hill that climbed steeply out of town in the direction of Glengorm. Glengorm was not his target, though: at the first crossroads he swung left, at the next he took the right fork and finally, increasing his pace and tossing away his cigar butt, headed out along the back track towards Fetternish.

It was a sullen, sultry evening with no break in the low-lying cloud. Midges swarmed above the peaty streams and the mountains across the Sound of Mull were the colour of old soot. He walked the six miles in just over an hour, sweating a little in his suit. The sea, when he came in sight of it again, was curtained by rain and flat as a cow-pat as far as the eye could see. He paused on the top of the knoll where the track straggled out of the wilderness, stuck his thumbs in his waistcoat pockets, and looked down at the house for a full five minutes before he picked his way down to the curving drive and, at a quarter to nine o'clock precisely, arrived at Biddy's big front door.

He tugged on the iron bell-pull and awaited an answer from within.

To his surprise, Biddy opened the door herself.

He said, 'What's happened to Willy then? Is he dead too?'

'My God! Dear God!' Biddy exclaimed, her hand flying to her bosom, her cheeks turning scarlet. 'It's Michael Tarrant, come back at last.'

Biddy would have preferred to be alone with the man who had once been her lover but Quig was stubborn and refused to quit the drawing-room. It was left to Maggie to bring up gin and glasses, sliced lemons and a jug of cold water.

Maggie entered the drawing-room. She stared at the man, the stranger who was no stranger, but did not drop him a curtsey or even give him a nod. She clattered the tray down on the table in the window bay and, still staring at him, said, 'Have you been down to Pennymain to see your wife and daughter yet?'

Michael gave her a greasy smile. 'Fine you know I haven't, Maggie, or you would have heard about it before anyone else.'

'I do not hear everything that goes on here,' Maggie retorted.

'Aye, well, if that's the case times have changed in more ways than one.'

'Did you deliberately wait until you knew she'd gone home?' Maggie said.

'Who is it you're talking about?' Michael Tarrant said.

'Your daughter Becky.'

By way of an answer he spread his hands in a gesture less helpless than indifferent.

His face had no shape to it now. His dark, droop-lidded eyes were insolent not inscrutable. Michael, Biddy realised, was fatter than she was, fat enough for the line of his jaw to be lost in a roll of pink-shaven flesh and his chin to have sunk down and merged with his neck. What had been strong about him now seemed weak, what had been handsome was ugly, and his expensive hand-cut suit could not hide his paunch. She had recalled him as lean, almost emaciated; now she was confronted by a portly middle-aged man who was less well-preserved than she was. He seemed unconscious of his girth and was not embarrassed by it.

'That will be enough, Maggie,' Biddy said. 'Quig, dearest, will you do the honours, please?'

'Honours?' said Maggie. 'He comes here before he goes home to see his wife and daughter. What is honourable about that, I am wanting to know?'

Michael crossed his knees and placed his bowler hat — which nobody had thought to take from him — on the floor by his chair.

'I'll drop in on them tomorrow,' he said. 'Put the word about, if you like, Maggie. I would be obliged, though, if you wouldn't rouse your husband and send him hot-footing it down to Pennymain at this hour of the night.'

'I will not be taking orders from you, Michael Tarrant.'

'Biddy, please be good enough to tell your housemaid—'

'Housekeeper,' Maggie blurted out. 'I am the house*keeper* here now.'

'No one will give you away, Michael,' Biddy said. 'Becky will be here first thing in the morning, however, and I can't guarantee that she won't find out that you've been to call on me.'

'I'm hoping,' Michael said, 'that I'll be here to greet her myself.'

'What do you mean?' said Biddy.

'Surely you're not going to turn an old friend away with darkness coming down and the rain sweeping in?'

'Don't you have a vehicle, a trap, a gig, to take you back to . . . where?'

'The Mishnish,' Michael said. 'And no, I walked from Tobermory.'

'You walked? Why?'

'Just to see what you have done with the place in my absence.'

'And what have I done with it?'

'Precious little,' said Michael. 'Where are all the sheep?'

'The sheep are pastured at Pennypol,' Quig said. 'Barrett takes good care of them.'

'I trained young Barrett well, did I not?' said Michael.

Maggie said, 'If you are scrounging a bed for the night, Michael Tarrant, would it not be more fitting if you went to your wife and let her put you up? Or are you frightened that she will turn you away?'

Quig turned from the table where he had mixed gin and water into two of the tall glasses. He handed a glass to Biddy and another to Michael, then he continued across the drawing-room and took Maggie gently by the elbow and guided her towards the door. He paused long enough to whisper in her ear before he eased her out into the hall and closed the door behind her.

'What did you say to her?' Michael asked.

'I told her to make sure that Willy does not spoil your surprise.'

'That's damned decent of you, Quigley, damned tactful,' Michael said, 'but then you always were the tactful one, were you not?' He sampled the gin, raised an appreciative eyebrow. 'Konig's, no less.'

'Only the best in this household,' Quig said, and to Biddy's annoyance, returned to his seat in the window bay.

Aileen was curled up in front of the fire in the downstairs parlour that Willy and Maggie had shared for all of their married life.

Willy was dozing. *The Times* was spread open on his lap and his eye-glasses were sliding down his long nose a quarter-inch at a time. Aileen was studying the tiny blue and yellow flames that flowered and withered in the slices of peat in the grate. There was really no need for a fire in such sultry weather but it had been lighted to warm Willy's old bones. Aileen would stare into the fire, any fire, for hours on end, just as she would study the movement of the sea or the pattern of the wind in the tall grasses, but her daydreams, if she dreamed at all, were too dense to be comprehensible.

She was startled when Maggie burst into the room. And Willy, grabbing his glasses and the newspaper, sat up so abruptly that the room spun round and round and he had to let his head fall back against the cushion to steady it and bring his wife into focus.

'He's come back. He's come back. He has not been to see Innis, however. He is sitting upstairs drinking Quig's gin and flirting with the mistress as if he—'

'Wait, wait, wait, wait,' said Willy. 'Calm down, woman, calm down.'

'Michael Tarrant has come back. He is up in the drawing-room at this very minute chatting to Biddy as gaily as if he had never been away at all.'

'Where's Quig?' Willy said.

'He is there too.'

Willy nodded.

'You do not seem surprised?' said Maggie accusingly.

'I expected someone to arrive eventually,' Willy said.

'Michael, Daddy Michael, Daddy.' Aileen had returned her

gaze to the peat slices hanging in the grate a moment after Maggie had entered the room and the little soft chanting seemed to be for her own amusement only. 'Daddy, Michael Daddy, Dad, da, da, da . . .'

'Be quiet, Aileen. Willy, tell her to be quiet.'

'*Dad-de-de-da-da-de, dad-de-da-de* . . .'

'Sweetheart,' Willy said, 'that's enough for now.'

Aileen uttered a little chuckle, coy and almost wicked in its way then stretched full-length upon the rug and covered her left ear with her hand.

'I will have to go and tell Innis,' Maggie said.

'Innis? No, no. Tomorrow will be time enough.'

'It will be the girl he has come for,' Maggie said. 'That damned little devil Gavin could not even pluck up the courage to come for her himself.'

'Are you sure it's the girl Tarrant's come for?' Willy asked.

'What else would tempt him to come back after so many years?'

Willy said, 'Where is he right now?'

'I told you. In the drawing-room, drinking our best gin.'

'Then,' Willy said, 'that's where he wants to be.'

'What do you mean, Willy?' Maggie asked. 'If he has not come here to take the girl back to her husband what other reason could he . . .' She drew up, stiffening. 'You cannot be thinking that he has come for Biddy?'

'I'm thinking nothing,' Willy said. 'I advise you to do the same.'

On the rug at Willy's feet the girl-woman murmured softly: '*Da-da-da, dada.*'

If it had been his house he would have ordered the lamps lighted and the curtains drawn to close out the gloom. He had never been fond of the sea and the views from the windows of the huge front room in Fetternish House had always made him feel small.

He liked the house much less than he liked its situation: a commanding site in the midst of two thousand acres of land that he, and he alone, considered prime. He would not have been averse to having the house thrown in for good measure if it had been in his power to whisk the whole estate away from her, would not have been averse to having Biddy tossed into the pot too, even now.

She was older than he remembered her, running a bit to seed, but she was still elegant and opulent, still transmitted the fiery, tangled sort of fecundity that he had once found so maddening and had enjoyed in his rough, tangled sort of way. It had not been all pleasure, however. Biddy had been the bolt on the door of Pennypol and when he had failed to wrest that piece of the property from his wife or, rather, from his wife's cantankerous old mother, he had surrendered to other aspects of desire, had merged one into another so that Biddy and prime grazing land became one and the same.

In hindsight he realised that he had been too taciturn for his own good. Living with Ada had changed him for the better. Thanks to Ada and her daughters he had learned to speak up for himself.

On the whole he was satisfied with the man he had become and it was to test the validity of the man he had become that he had volunteered to return to Mull to sort out the mess that Gavin had made of his marriage. And to see Biddy again, of course: he recalled their affair as a gilded communion and was ready to take her on again now, even with her husband sitting in a corner with, as it were, his thumb in his mouth.

Quig said, 'I suppose it is because of Gavin that you are making this visit?'

'It is,' said Michael. 'He was all for charging up here himself but he could not leave his flock at this time of the year. It's a big flock he has charge of and Yeates is a hard taskmaster and not forgiving.'

'Forgiving?' said Quig. 'Forgiving of what?'

279

Michael could not see Quigley clearly; he seemed as dusty as the room itself and merged into the gloom like a piece of unpainted furniture.

Quig went on, 'Are you living down in that part of the world, too, Michael? Are you close to your boy?'

'No, I'm not. Fact, I don't know Yeates at all. I've heard about him from Gavin, though. I can imagine the kind of man he is.'

'So' – Biddy cleared her throat – 'you don't work in Fream?'

'I see she has been telling you about me, this girl,' Michael said. 'No, I don't work in Fream. I work near where I was born in the Ettrick Pen.'

'Do you still live with your mother?' said Biddy.

'She died years ago. I'm a farm manager now. I have charge of four thousand acres, two thousand breeding ewes and four shepherds.'

'To whom does this farm belong?'

'Mrs Ada Reese.'

'Who is, I assume, a widow?'

'Aye, a widow,' Michael said.

He was not so thick-skinned as he had imagined himself to be. Biddy had already found a weak spot. He could not think why the question offended him, but it did. He would say nothing about Ada Reese, about the marriage that was a marriage in everything but name.

'And is Mrs Reese looking to expand?' said Biddy.

'Expand?'

'Into a more progressive form of agriculture, say?'

'What?'

'I assume,' Biddy went on, 'that Mrs Reese has money.'

'I'm not here to borrow, if that's what you're thinking.'

'I thought,' said Quigley, 'that you were here to persuade Gavin's wife that her place is at her husband's side.'

'I've never even met the girl,' said Michael.

'You know, of course,' said Quigley, 'why she left him?'

'She was flighty. She had another man who egged her on.'

'Is that what Gavin told you?' Quig said.

'I've seen nothing of Gavin for seven years.'

He put the glass to his lips and would have taken a swallow if at that moment he had not caught Biddy's eye. He sipped, watching her as she watched him — warily. He had thought to surprise and impress her with his aplomb but already found himself on the defensive.

'Have you not now?' Quigley said. 'Why is that, I wonder?'

'He preferred to strike out on his own.'

'You weren't sorry to see the back of him, were you, Michael?' Biddy said.

'I know what you all think of him but he's different now.'

'He's a flockmaster now, I believe,' said Biddy.

'A shepherd, yes.'

'Is there no room for him on this farm you manage?' said Quigley. 'I mean, is Gavin not a good shepherd?'

'I did not say that.'

'Would Mrs Reese not employ him?' Quigley said.

'If you asked her nicely,' Biddy added.

'What does this have to do with why I've made this long and inconvenient journey? It's not just Yeates who is in the middle of the season, with shearing and doping to be done. Do you think it's easy for me to leave my post? Perhaps things are still done as slack here as they always were . . .'

'When you were shepherd?' said Biddy, mildly.

'I am here to see the girl, that's all.'

'On Gavin's behalf?' said Quigley.

'Aye, damn it, on Gavin's behalf.'

'Do you know where to find her?' said Biddy.

'She's at Pennymain, is she not?'

'Staying with your wife,' Biddy said.

Although the bowler lay at his feet, Michael felt pressure against his brow as if the hat were still pressed on his head. He ran a hand over his thick, grey hair and wiped his palm on his lapel.

Nothing was going as he'd hoped it would. The situation was more complicated than he had expected. He had lost thrust, lost impetus. It had not dawned on him that Biddy might have changed too and no longer be as impetuous as he remembered her. He had learned a lot about women from Ada and her daughters. Once he had got rid of Gavin and had settled down with Ada Reese then everything that had happened on Mull had taken on a fresh perspective.

'Who told you that Fay was here?' Quigley asked.

'Gavin told me.'

'How did he find out?' said Quigley. 'She left without a word. She came to us because she had no one else to turn to and because she thought that Gavin would never look for her here. It seems, though, that someone betrayed her.'

'Perhaps this other man, this sweetheart of hers told Gavin.'

'Josh would not betray her, no matter what Gavin did to him,' said Quig.

'You seem well informed about matters you claim to know nothing about.'

'As you are, Michael,' Biddy reminded him. 'As you are.'

'It's a matter for Gavin and this wife of his, that's what I say.'

'Then why is Gavin not here to speak for himself?' said Biddy.

'I volunteered to do it for him.'

'To do what for him?' said Biddy.

'Negotiate on his behalf.'

'You were always a bit of a negotiator, Michael, now I think of it.'

Biddy's irony was lost on him. Shrugging his thick shoulders, he said, 'I have a duty to do what's best for my son.'

'I am sure that you do,' said Quigley. 'But what is best for Gavin may not be the best thing for his wife. He beat her, did you know?'

'A tap or two to teach her her place, what's wrong in that?'

Biddy raised a hand, thought better of it. 'It's Innis you'll have

to convince. Innis you'll have to deal with. The girl has nothing
to do with us. Does she, Quig?'

'No,' Quig said, out of the gathering darkness. 'Nothing to do
with us.'

The habit of early rising had not left him, though sometimes in
the winter months he would lie for an extra half or so, snuggled
under the feather quilt against Ada's flanks and, if she was awake
and wished it, would slip himself into her to set her up for the
day.

Mostly, though, he was up by five and on the hill by half past
to keep the shepherds on their toes and lend a hand with lambing
and shearing just to remind these uncouth Border lads that he
was more than just a fancy-man. He would supervise the dip, the
cutting out, the gathering and, of course, the drive. He took care
of all sales and would hold off for top price for the wool crop or,
his pocket bulging with banknotes, would outbid the local
breeders for a quality ram or a parcel of sturdy young ewes.

Daylight wakened him. He had been given a bed after all, a
bed in a room so far up in the house that gulls roosted on the
window ledge and he had to stand on tiptoe to see the terrace
and the lawns below.

The sun came up to the front of the house. He found that
strange, just as he had found sunsets in the Ettrick Pen strange
when he'd gone back there at first: the sun pitching about in his
head and shadows coming at him from the wrong direction. He
was back in the west now, however, and as he washed and shaved
at the basin on the table in front of the attic window he felt a
stab of apprehension at the realisation that he would soon have
to face his wife and the daughter whom he had abandoned all
those years ago.

He put on the shirt that he'd worn yesterday, the tweed suit,
the bowler hat and went down the back stairs into the kitchen to
forage for a piece of bread and butter and perhaps a glass of ale

to keep him going. He doubted that he would find breakfast waiting for him at Innis's house, neither breakfast nor the welcome mat.

He entered the kitchen quietly.

Quigley was seated at the table, drinking tea.

'I thought you would be for making an early start,' Quig said. 'I will be walking down with you, if you have no objection.'

'I do have an objection,' Michael said. 'I'd rather talk to her on my own.'

'Talk to who?' Quig poured a fresh cup for Biddy's guest. 'Innis or Fay, or is it Rebecca you are so anxious to have a word with?'

'What is it to you, Quigley?' Michael said. 'It's my family that are involved in this, and you're not my family.'

'I could be saying that I am more family to them than you have shown yourself to be these past sixteen years,' Quig said in the soft, sing-song voice that disguised his animosity. 'I will not be doing that, however, for you will be having troubles enough without me taunting you.'

'Gavin did not intend to shoot you.'

There was egg on the plate, a bright yellow smear of yolk. Quig folded a slice of brown bread, mopped up the yolk, put it in his mouth. He was just naturally smug, Michael thought, the way all islanders were smug, as if they considered themselves endowed with matchless charm and a depth of insight denied to mainland folk.

Quig chewed and politely swallowed before he spoke again.

'Gavin would have shot any one of us that afternoon,' Quig said. 'He would have pulled the trigger on you too if you had been foolish enough to stand in his way.' He pushed away the plate and picked up his teacup. 'If you are for breaking your fast, Michael, do it now. There is bread and butter and cheese, and the tea is fresh. If you are hungry I will fry you an egg and some ham.'

'Bread will do fine.' Michael seated himself at the table. He did not see the need to remove his hat. He said, 'Biddy's looking well. How are your children?'

'Well, they are well.'

'At school?'

'Yes, in Edinburgh.'

'Out of harm's way,' said Michael.

'It was not my doing.'

'I didn't say that it was,' said Michael, 'but when you or your missus are miscalling me for putting Gavin out into the world you'd do well to think what you have done to your children.'

Quig watched Biddy's guest butter and fold a second slice of bread.

'Who was it who gave her away, Michael?'

'What do you mean?'

'I was not me and I do not think it was Biddy.'

'I don't know what you're blathering about.'

'I know that it was Becky. I think she is jealous of the girl.'

'Women,' Michael said, 'do get funny ideas.'

'Biddy thinks you're here to buy us out.'

'Does she now? Where would I be getting that kind of money?'

'From your new wife.'

'She is not my wife. How can she be my wife?' Michael said. 'I'm here for no other reason but to settle the differences between my son and this girl he married.'

'Whom you have never met?'

'That's the truth,' Michael said. 'I told you I'd put Gavin out to work on his own account but I did not say I had lost touch with him. He wanted his independence.' He paused then went on, 'There was a bit more to it than that. He was attracted to one of Ada Reese's daughters.'

'What did he do to her?'

'Nothing. She disliked him, that's all.'

'So you sent him away before he queered your pitch.'

'He went of his own accord,' Michael said. 'If I had sent him away, would you blame me?'

'No, I would not blame you.'

'They're a trial and a burden, our children, aren't they now?'

Quig did not answer.

There was something in his eyes, though, in the shape of his mouth that suggested to Michael that all was not well with Quigley. He wondered what the lad, Robbie, might be getting up to in the city of Edinburgh and thought ruefully of what grief a young man with some money behind him might cause to his parents and what fun he might have for himself. He mulled over the notion of the wild young rip tormenting Biddy with his antics – like father, perhaps, like son – and would have followed that line of enquiry if Quigley hadn't stopped him.

Quig said, 'She will not be giving you a divorce, Michael.'

'What did you say?'

'Innis. She will never agree to divorce you. You will be wasting your time asking her.'

'Is that why you think I'm here?'

'It isn't for the sake of the boy, I am sure, not just for the sake of the boy.'

'That shows what kind of a father you are.'

He was blustering now; Quigley had found him out. He might have expected it from Naismith. Willy Naismith had had contacts in the Borders. But he hadn't anticipated that Quigley would see through him so easily. Quig was right, though. It was a lost cause but he knew that he must try to persuade Innis to grant him a divorce, for if he did not legally marry Ada Reese he would not receive all that was due to him in the shape of two thousand acres of best Border land.

'Are you not a Catholic too?' Quigley said.

'I am nothing.'

'You were married as a Catholic, were you not?'

'Is she – is Innis still as devout as ever?'

'More so,' Quig said. 'Did Becky not tell you?'

'The schoolteacher, Gillies Brown, was after getting under her skirts before I left. Did he back away? Did he take cold feet? I was hoping . . .' Michael stopped himself in time. 'I thought he might still be keen to take her on.'

'There is nothing between them but friendship.'

'Hah!' Michael said. 'Hah! I've heard that tune played before and it was as false a tune then as it is now. God, Quigley, are you telling me Innis Campbell has survived all these years without a man in her bed?'

'I am telling you just that.'

'It's hard to believe, knowing how ardent she was with me.'

'Perhaps,' Quig said, 'you spoiled her for other men.'

'Perhaps I did, come to think of it.' Michael Tarrant preened for a moment. 'Aye, perhaps you're right at that.'

'Is this woman you have found for yourself insisting on marriage?' Quig said. 'Is it that you have not told her about Innis?'

'Ada knows about Innis. I didn't deceive her.'

'She must be fond of you.'

'She is. She adores me.'

'I have had a bit of that myself,' Quig said.

'And look what it got you,' Michael said.

'Yes,' Quigley said. 'Look what it got me.' He got up. 'If you leave now you will find them all at home, for Becky does not start work until eight. I will leave you to do what you have to do since it is your responsibility. I will walk down with you as far as the Pennymain turn-off though, since I am going that way in any case. It will be a thrill for you to be meeting your daughter again,' he said, 'and to be meeting your son's wife for the first time.'

'I know she's expecting if that's what you're hinting at.' Michael swallowed the last of the tea and crammed another slice of bread and butter into his mouth. He wiped his mouth on the back of his hand and brushed crumbs from his lapels. 'How do I look?'

'Impressive,' Quig said. 'It was Becky who told him about Fay, was it not?'

Michael tapped the side of his nose with his forefinger and winked.

'No names,' he mumbled, 'no pull.'
'Shall we be going now?' Quig said.
'Aye, why not?' said Michael.

The heat made her sluggish. She was well enough, she supposed, but carrying robbed her of energy and the sultry weather made her anxious. She could feel the baby rolling in her womb as if it too was struggling to breathe. She thought about it constantly while she tended the plots at Pennypol, turning the soil with the tip of a hoe or promenading up and down the rows with a heavy watering-can. The crops needed to be kept moist at this crucial stage but lugging the watering-can over from the burn was exhausting and she was forced to rest between each trip and was afraid that she would not be able to give them enough for their needs.

The strawberry plants were rooting nicely, though. She checked them regularly for mite and leaf rot and remained hopeful that there might be fruit before the end of the season, though the likelihood was that the plants would not bear until next year. She knelt by the beds by the wall, hands supporting her stomach, and stared at the runners and worried that she had planted them out too early: wondered too what 'it' would be like and if in some future season she would be able to feed it mashed strawberries sweetened with a little sugar and mixed with cream and if when she held the spoon to her baby's lips she would see happiness in its eyes.

There was something innocent about strawberries, a quality that no other fruit possessed. They were not hard like apples, grainy like pears, not tart like gooseberries or rasps. She craved the sensation of a strawberry on her tongue, its flavour as subtle as a mid-summer's day kiss.

It was very early when the man appeared from the gully behind the cottage.

She had not left for Pennypol and was feeding Innis's hens.

She had scattered the meal and was standing with the bucket resting against her hip when she noticed the hat bobbing behind the hedge.

She held the bucket tightly and the hens set up a gabbling around her, pecking at her feet, begging to be fed. She dipped into the meal and absently scattered a handful, dipped and scattered, while she watched him round the hedge and stop outside the gate: a cocky, portly, upright man, not very tall, in a loud tweed suit and the sort of hat that seed salesmen wore.

He leaned over the gate and groped for the latch.

Then he stopped and looked at her, looked at her hard.

She knew who he was, though he was not what she had expected, not from the little she had heard of him. There was no mistaking the twist of the mouth, however, the faint, weaselling hint of scorn like something carved in soft wood. The man was fat and middle-aged. His head rode on top of his collar as if it had been squeezed out of a tube, and his hat perched on his thick grey hair like a pea on a hilltop. There was nothing comical in his manner, though, nothing that made her want to smile.

She felt the 'it' within her flop over, and an acid burning in her throat.

'Mamma,' she said. 'Mamma,' she cried out.

Innis came running from the kitchen door.

Agnes MacNiven was George Barrett's sister-in-law: that is she was married to Peter MacNiven who was one of Muriel's brothers.

She was also the district midwife.

She was not a midwife in the traditional sense of the word, however, not someone who by dint of experience and proximity was called upon to deliver babies and who had about as much anatomical knowledge as the average ten-year-old.

Anything less like an old wise woman than Agnes MacNiven would be hard to imagine. After her own bairns were half grown

Agnes had taken herself out of the road-mender's cottage at Leathan and had sailed to Oban every other Friday for three long years to be trained in what her husband proudly referred to as 'Obstreperous Nursing'. In due course she had obtained a certificate, had been placed on the payroll of the county of Argyll and endowed with the sort of scientific status that even Dr Kirkhope in his heyday had never quite attained.

She worked hand in glove – or hand in something – with young Dr Cumming. He, it seemed, had a magical touch when it came to coaxing women into and through pregnancy, but his practice was centred in Salen and with the best will in the world he could not be everywhere at once. He relied on Agnes to spot a case of pre-eclamptic toxaemia or the danger signs of twenty other female malfunctions out there in the wild.

Agnes was popular, strict but caring, and had the best legs in the north quarter, if, that is, your definition of limb quality rests on bulk.

Agnes cycled everywhere.

She had an antique Raleigh boneshaker with solid rubber tyres, a saddle the size of a soup cauldron and a set of handlebars that would have shamed a Highland cow. She would pedal the contraption up hill and down dale with a conviction that Hermann the German could not match and had been spotted more than once zooming down the long, bumpy brae into Dervaig with both hands off the handlebars while she powdered her nose or reapplied her lip rouge or gave herself a squirt with either disinfectant or lavender water depending, one assumed, on her next port of call.

Fortunately, but not fortuitously, Robert Quigley encountered her not on a down slope but near the summit of the hill that linked Leathan to Dervaig.

Agnes was bowed forward, pumping the pedals, her round-brimmed hat down over her nose, her eyebrows knitted with concentration. In the pannier at the back of the saddle her black bag and sterilising basins were strapped under an oilskin cover, her coat draped over the handlebars like a buffer.

'Hoh!' Quig said. 'You are in a hurry this morning, Agnes.'

She braked the Raleigh's front wheel and, as if coming out of a trance, jerked her head up and brought the bicycle to a halt.

'I am in no hurry at all, Robert, as it so happens. What is it that you are doing sitting here on a rock looking as if someone has stolen your scone?'

'I am waiting for you.'

'Is that a fact?' said Agnes.

She was not even breathing hard, he noticed. She hitched her skirts and cocked one sturdy limb in its ribbed green stocking over the crossbar and slid easily to the ground.

Quig got to his feet. 'There is a girl who will be needing your attention soon.'

'What girl?' said Agnes. 'And what is the husband of the lady of Fetternish doing coming all this way just to tell me about her?'

'She is an incomer. Her name is Fay Ludlow. She is staying with Innis Tarrant at Pennymain,' Quig said. 'She is in her seventh month.'

'How far into her seventh month?'

'I cannot tell you that,' Quig said. 'I am not even sure that she will be able to tell you that herself.'

'Is she having pains?'

'No, she says that she is not.'

'Are you looking out for her because you are her employer?'

'Och, come away with you now, Agnes. Do not pretend that Muriel has not been telling you about what has been happening at Pennypol.'

Agnes grinned; her cheeks were more like apples than any apple he had ever seen. 'Is it the gardening girl we are talking about?'

'It is.'

'I though that she was a patient of Dr Kirkhope.'

'She is a patient of no one,' Quig said. 'But she will be needing the services of your good self in the near future and I thought it would be best if you were introduced to her beforehand.'

'Is that a fact?' said Agnes.

'She is very heavy, or seems so to me. I have a notion that she might have mistaken the date of conception and the baby is due sooner than we think.'

'It is not your child we are talking about, is it?'

'Of course it is not my child.'

'Why then are you meddling, Robert?' Agnes said. 'Why is it not Innis who is calling me in? If what I have heard from Muriel – and I am not one to go repeating gossip, as well you know – if what I have heard is true then you have had this girl under your wing for weeks.'

'She is Gavin Tarrant's wife.'

'That is also what I heard, yes,' said Agnes, 'among a lot of other weird stories that seemed to be coming from the school-house.'

'Gillies was misinformed.'

Agnes did something with her legs, a sort of ballet step, Quig thought, though he had never seen ballet performed in his life: a big, wide kick that carried her on to the saddle and, at the same time, straightened up the bicycle.

'I will go down there now, if you wish,' Agnes said. 'Will the girl be at Innis's house or will she be at the gardens? Will she be willing to let me examine her?'

'I would not go now, not immediately,' Quig said.

'I have time. I am not due to be in town until nine o'clock.'

'Town?'

'Dervaig. I have plenty of time.'

'No, do not go now,' Quig said. 'If you have a moment or two to spare this evening, however, I would be obliged if you would drop in then.'

'You seem to be very concerned about Gavin Tarrant's wife?'

'I am concerned, that is true.'

'Why?'

'I feel responsible for her.'

'You feel responsible for everyone, Robert, that has always been your trouble.' Agnes took a powder dish from her pocket, opened it, dabbed at her nose with a circlet of pink lint, admired herself in the little mirror in the lid of the dish, then snapped the reticule shut again. 'I will be dropping in at Pennymain shortly before supper. Will you see to it that she is there?'

'I will. I will,' said Quig and stepped hastily back as the midwife and her bicycle spurted forward and, a moment later, vanished over the brow of the hill.

In her innocence Innis had supposed that she would never see her husband again. She'd prayed for his return, but had never really believed that God would listen to her selfish request. Now Michael was here, seated in a chair in the kitchen: *his* chair, the chair that he had occupied with such authority during the period of their marriage; the chair that she had left untouched for the best part of a twelve-month after he had gone and which would have been left untouched and unoccupied still if Gillies had not settled himself into it one chilly autumn night, and put paid to the first phase of her yearning and her guilt.

Now Michael was back, legs crossed, hat on the table, Innis realised that God *had* answered her prayers and had done so in a manner beyond her imagining, for the man in the chair *was* Michael but not *her* Michael.

Her husband had been as lean as a reed and hard as bone; the man before her now was fat, not pleasantly plump like Biddy but coarse. He was not hard-bitten after all, not masculine and commanding. He had exchanged those qualities for the kind of sly, swaggering conceit that her father had possessed before drink had dragged him down. She wondered if Michael had also taken to the bottle or if mere self-satisfaction had caused him to swell.

She sat in a chair at the table with her hands folded in her lap, looking at him, hearing the familiar voice utter unfamiliar phrases. The pernickety hesitations in his choice of words were symptomatic of the man he had become and not the man she had fallen in love with. Through the half-open door of the bedroom she could see the demure blue colour of Our Lady's gown and the glimmer of the candle that she had lighted barely a half minute before Fay had called out to her.

Tucked out of sight in the palm of her hand were her rosary beads. She felt oddly secure and redeemed as she listened to Michael's demands.

'. . . for the sake of the child, if not for any other reason, you must come back with me, girl,' he was saying. 'Whatever Gavin has done to you in the past, he regrets it now and he'll be good to you. He has whitewashed the house, inside and out, so he tells me and he has put up a partition to make a special room, a separate room, for the baby.'

'Why did he not come himself?'

'If you want the truth . . .'

'I do want the truth,' said Fay.

'If you want the truth, he was afraid to come himself.'

'Afraid? Gavin afraid? I find that hard to believe,' Fay said.

Innis did not intervene. Fay was tough-minded enough to take care of herself, unlike Becky who seemed to have become childishly gullible in her father's presence. She fluttered, simpered, offered tea, a dish of boiled eggs; votive offerings, Innis thought, to a father she could hardly remember. It was all too clear that Becky had betrayed Fay by writing to her brother at Fream.

Innis let the beads trickle under the ball of her thumb.

'I persuaded him to let me come instead,' Michael said. 'You know what Gavin's like as well as I do, girl. He can't always see the other side of things and he flies off the handle far too easy.'

'I'll not go back with you,' Fay said. 'I'll not go back to being his wife.'

'Look at you,' Michael said. 'That big belly on you is his doing. What's inside that big belly of yours is his.'

'No, it's mine.'

'That won't be the way a court of law will see it,' Michael said.

'A court of law costs money,' Fay said, 'and Gavin has no money.'

'I have money,' Michael said. 'I'll lend him money. It's not right to deprive a child of its father.'

Becky nodded agreement. 'Or a father of his child.'

Michael turned, canting his head back almost, Innis thought, as if he had forgotten that his daughter was in the room. He glanced at Becky, saw nothing that interested him and turned again to Fay.

'You see, she agrees with me. She sees the sense in what I'm saying.'

'She would,' said Fay.

'What's that supposed to mean?' Becky snapped.

'Who put you up to it, Becky?' Fay said. 'Was it your sister, or did you decide to get rid of me all by yourself?'

'Leave my sister out of it,' said Becky.

Fay said, 'I wasn't taken in by your smiling faces, Becky. I knew all along you wouldn't let the matter rest.'

'Wouldn't let you take over, you mean.'

Michael watched, smiling faintly. He had groomed his thick, grey hair with water and his newly shaven jowls glistened pink. He raised his left hand. The ring Innis had given him as a token of fealty had been removed, sold perhaps or pawned, or given to another woman.

'Now, now, girls,' he said. 'I've not come here to waste time listening to you bickering. I've got to get back home by the weekend and want everything tidied up and settled before I go.'

'There's nothing to settle,' Fay said. 'I'm staying where I am.'

'If you stay,' said Becky, 'then I'm leaving.'

'That's for you to decide,' said Fay. 'And Mamma.'

To Innis Michael said, 'Don't tell me you'd let a stranger take the place of your daughter?'

'She is your daughter too, Michael,' Innis said.

'She is, she is, I know that,' Michael said impatiently.

'Take me with you, Dada,' Becky said. 'I'm sick of this place. Take me with you. I'm a cook, don't you know, a housekeeper? I'm sure you could find me a position with your employer or even in your house.'

'No, no room in my house,' Michael said. 'Your place is here, Rachel.'

'Becky, I'm Rebecca.'

'Aye, my mistake.'

'My God!' Becky said. 'Doesn't anyone want me?'

'Anyway, it's Gavin's wife I'm here to collect, not a cook and bottle-washer,' Michael said impatiently.

Her husband had never learned that the best way of getting what you want is by waiting for it, Innis thought, by focusing your intentions like the beam of a hurricane lantern. For an instant she felt almost sorry for him.

Fay said, 'He can't take you in with him, Becky, 'cause he has another wife and maybe another family in the Borders.'

Even before he answered Innis knew that Fay's accusation was true. She had known it all along really and a piece of her, a single irritated cell, despised him for reneging on his marriage vow. He had led her to Catholicism, and for that she would always be grateful to him. She had entered the Church with an open heart and had given back whatever the Church demanded of her. Beyond that was the mysterious God in whom she believed, a jealous and righteous and forgiving God, a God with a Son, a Son with a Mother, a trinity that was both transcendent and immanent within her and that shaped and held her as a cup holds water.

For all her goodwill, all her piety, Innis could not forgive him. It was not Michael's fallibility or human frailty that reduced him in her eyes but his dogged pursuit of aggrandisement.

'I don't have another wife.' He could not even lie properly: his face flushed, not in a flash like Biddy's but with a stealthy suffusion of blood that spread up from his neck like a rash. 'I'm –

I'm Ada's farm manager. I can't take another wife when I'm married already. I'm not going to risk going to the jail for any woman. What sort of an idiot do you take me for?'

'What is the name of the woman you – who employs you?' Innis asked.

'Ada. Mrs Reese.'

'Is she a widow?'

'She's older than I am. She's an old woman, near enough,' Michael blustered. 'She depends on me to run things for her.'

'And she is duly grateful, no doubt,' said Innis.

'Why are you badgering my dada?' Becky said. 'It doesn't matter what he's done. What about her, what about this one and her big, fat belly? What are you going to do about her, Mam?'

'Fay may stay as long as she wishes,' Innis heard herself say. 'I will not let you take her back to Gavin on the strength of a few idle threats.'

'Idle threats! By God, Innis, I haven't even begun to threaten you yet.' He sat forward. 'What are you going to do when Gavin turns up? He'll not be put off by soft answers, Innis. I'm the only one he'll listen to. If I tell him to leave this 'un to stew in her own juice, baby or not, he'll do it. But there's something I want in return.'

Innis said, 'I cannot give you a divorce.'

'Good God, woman, it's been sixteen years since I last climbed into your bed. What are you holding on for? I'm not coming back, you know.' The chair creaked under his weight. He closed his fists on his thighs, elbows cocked. His voice was stern and serious, as if he were delivering a homily. 'Are you telling me that you and Gillies Brown haven't been intimate?'

'I am still your wife, Michael. I will always be your wife.'

'Everyone knows about you and Brown. Answer my question.'

'Gillies is no more to me than a friend.'

'Don't you realise that a petition for divorce citing him as an adulterer would ruin him? No matter what the outcome, his career would be ruined as soon as we went into the court.'

'Why do you keeping talking about the court?' said Innis. 'You know that you cannot take me to court, and that you will not. You have had no more dealings with lawyers than I have, Michael. What would you do when all the other things came out, all your secrets?'

'If you mean Ada . . .'

Innis shook her head. 'You have not changed so much as I thought you had. You are still after advantage and advancement, Michael. Will you get it from this poor woman since you cannot have it from me?'

'Ada is not a poor woman.'

'I'll wager she's not,' said Fay.

Swelling up like a bantam cock, he rounded on her. 'Keep your mouth shut, girl. What do you know about the likes of us? You were lucky to find a husband like Gavin, aye, and if he gave you a smack now and then it was no more than you asked for. You're nothing but a bastard out of the workhouse. Nobody wanted you then and nobody would ever have wanted you if Gavin hadn't taken you on. Aye, and look where it got him.'

'Dada,' Becky blurted out, 'don't speak to her like that.'

He glared at her. 'What's wrong with you? You wrote and told Gavin where to find her. You begged him to come and take her away.'

'I don't want her here, that's true,' Becky admitted. 'But you don't have to humiliate her.'

'What a rat's nest of a place this is.' Michael heaved himself angrily out of the chair. 'I'm home for a quarter of an hour and I've three women ganging up on me as if I'd done something wrong.' He swung towards Innis, forefinger stabbing the air. 'It's all your doing, Innis, you and your bloody charity, your bloody religion. You've poisoned my own daughter against me. Is this to pay me back for having gone away and left you? Well, by God, I will have a divorce out of you, and if I can't make you yield then I know someone who will.'

'If you mean Gillies . . .'

'I mean Gavin.' He tugged at his waistcoat, adjusted his lapels and plucked his hat from the table. He put it on, not casually but with care. Wearing the hat seemed to calm him and tamp down his anger. 'I wasted half my life on you, Innis Campbell, and I will not waste the other half because of you. Aye, it's true: I do want to marry Ada Reese. And I want her' — he stabbed a forefinger at Fay — 'to come back with me so that Gavin will have a proper wife and a proper home. Some of us still know how to take care of our children, you see. You, girl.' He tucked away the finger and waved, beckoningly, with his fist. 'I want you packed and ready to leave with me on Friday morning.'

'No,' Fay said.

'She has a life here now,' Innis said. 'It is here she will stay.'

'Then I'll see you in a court of law, Innis.'

Logically she knew that he would not dare take her to law, would not pursue a petition of divorcement. The cost alone would cripple him. Besides, he had too much to be ashamed of, too much to hide. It would not be her reputation or Michael's that would be most at risk by the posting of the bill, however, but Gillies's. At the first whiff of public scandal the School Board would dismiss Gillies from his post, of that there was no doubt at all.

'Friday morning, girl,' Michael said, going to the door. 'Be at the pier with all your belongings at half past eight o'clock.'

'Dada, what about me?' said Becky.

'What about you?'

'Are you not going to take me too?'

'No, Rachel, I'm not,' Michael said and rolling his portly hips went out into the garden and through the narrow gate without once looking back.

'Where are you going, Patrick?' Biddy said. 'Are you leaving without saying goodbye?'

'I'm only going to the mainland for a day or two,' Patrick

answered. 'I've some things to attend to and I'm anxious to see my mother who has been unwell.'

Biddy did not enquire further about his mother's health. Having Michael Tarrant in her house had shaken her and she had hurried out to the stables soon after Quig and Michael had left for Pennymain.

It was still early, not yet seven, and she had hoped to find Patrick in bed or lingering over his breakfast.

She had not expected to find him saddling up the stallion in the yard.

'Is it your clients you're going to see?' she said.

'Yes.'

He busied himself with straps and buckles, holding the horse motionless with one gloved hand over its muzzle.

She said, 'Will you present me with a firm offer when you come back?'

'I can't present you with an offer until I know what you're selling, Biddy.'

'Eight hundred acres.'

'Ah, you're *selling* eight hundred acres, are you?'

He cinched the saddle strap, swung his valise up and buckled it against the saddlebag. The valise was scuffed with much travel, with all the comings and goings that distinguished a man of the world from a man of the land.

In a mad moment she longed for him to sweep her up and carry her away to the mainland, to Perth or Edinburgh, to his house in Dunning, never to see Mull again; but hard on the heels of that spat of longing came fear of being separated from Fetternish, of being sucked into a sea of strangers who had no knowledge of and no vestige of respect for her.

'I am. Yes, I probably am,' Biddy said.

'Probably?'

'Before I decide one way or the other you must tell me who wants Fetternish. Does Michael Tarrant have a hand in it?'

'Tarrant, your sister's husband? Whatever gave you that idea?'

'He turned up yesterday evening. Is Michael Tarrant one of your clients? Is he a partner in Louden, Lafferty and Spruell?'

He put an arm about her shoulder, not amorously. She leaned into him but did not surrender. He drew her closer, or tried to. She felt angry, angry and aroused, one emotion acting against the other.

She said, 'I'm only trying to make sense of all this, Patrick.'

'I take it that your brother-in-law did not make an offer for the house?'

'No, I doubt if he has that sort of money at his disposal.' She felt rather than heard Patrick sigh. 'I have to be sure, however, that Michael Tarrant is not involved and will not benefit. I'll sell – yes, sell – eight hundred acres at An Fhearann Cáirdeil, Patrick, but only after I meet your client face to face.'

Patrick looked down at his feet. He was riding out in shoes, she noticed, not boots. He had tabbed his trouser legs against his ankles with canvas puttees, like Hermann on his bicycle. Conflicting emotions rolled within her, little ripples of amusement frothed among the doubt and calamitous uncertainties and soothed her desire as sand absorbs the momentum of the waves.

At length he said, 'I give you my word, Biddy, I've barely heard of Michael Tarrant. My employer is simply a business person.'

'Person?'

'Man.'

'Well, tell him that I'll sell the piece of ground at An Fhearann Cáirdeil . . .'

'Good.'

'. . . only after I have met him face to face.'

'Biddy!'

'Those are *my* terms, Patrick.'

'I'm not sure that my client will agree to them.'

'Then your client will just have to look elsewhere for land.'

'I thought we were getting along rather well,' Patrick said. 'It's my fault, I suppose, for allowing my head to be ruled by my heart.' He glanced up. 'Who is this Michael Tarrant, in any case?'

'No one, apparently,' Biddy said.

How could she tell him that Michael Tarrant's appearance had destroyed her dream of rediscovering true love in the debris of the past. Michael had been her secret, one of the vague, sentimental secrets that she could not reveal.

'Will you put my proposition to your client?' she said.

'It isn't a proposition, Biddy: it's an ultimatum.'

'Call it by any name you like,' Biddy said. 'Will you do it?'

'Do I have an option?'

'None,' said Biddy.

'Very well,' Patrick said. 'I'll do it. Now' – he fished a hunter from his side pocket and consulted it – 'I really do have to leave you, Biddy, or I'll miss the boat. Please don't think badly of me. You knew from the first that I had a job of work to do and it's not entirely my fault that you've been deceived.'

'Deceived? Have I been deceived?'

'I shouldn't have . . .'

'What? Say it?'

He shook his head and then, to her astonishment, caught her in his arms and kissed her. The brittle shell of her common sense split and she rubbed against him, pressing her breasts and thighs against his body. But the moment he let her go and swung himself up into the saddle, the heat drained from her and she watched him ride out of the stable yard with a curious feeling of relief as if, all things considered, she was doing the right thing at last.

Janetta heard the hooves thudding on the grass of the yard. She rushed downstairs from the schoolhouse to find Patrick dismounting at the doorway.

As soon as she saw him she knew that he was going away, that her stiff-necked behaviour had finally frightened him off.

It did not occur to her that he might be escaping from Biddy or that there was any hypocrisy in his appearance on her doorstep at twenty minutes to eight o'clock on a fine July morning.

She leaned back against the doorpost and folded her arms. 'Have you come to apologise?' she said.

'Apologise?'

'For ignoring me.'

'Oh, really, Netta! How can you say such a thing? I've been busy, so busy, and now I'm off home for three or four days. My mother's unwell.'

'It is not serious, I hope?'

'She fell and bruised her spine. She's confined to bed and is very tetchy, so my father tells me. I'm obligated to turn up at her bedside and act like a dutiful son. No, that's unfair. I want to see for myself how she is and how my father is coping. I'm sure you understand.'

'Does Biddy understand?'

'Biddy?' He frowned in bewilderment. 'What does Biddy have to do with it? What *is* wrong with you, Janetta?'

'I'm jealous, I suppose.'

'Jealous of Biddy? You've no reason to be.'

'I know you've – you've been with her.'

'Of course I've been with her. I'm trying to do business with her.'

'The same sort of "business" that you are trying to do with me?'

The windows of the schoolhouse were open. With the best will in the world, her father would not be able to resist listening in to her confession. She no longer cared what her father thought of her, though, what anyone thought of her. If she wanted Patrick for herself then she would just have to prove herself more compromising than the fine lady of Fetternish and less perverse than the lady of The Ards.

'I felt I had to come,' he said. 'I felt I had to explain.'

'I should think so too,' said Janetta. 'It's the least you could do.'

She continued to lean against the doorpost, legs braced under the skirt, arms folded across her flat bosom. She had not even put up her hair and she looked, she thought, like a slattern. Perhaps Patrick was drawn to slatterns. Perhaps he even preferred slatterns to sluts like Biddy Baverstock Quigley.

As if he had read her thoughts, he said, 'Oh, I see, you think that because Biddy Quigley and I . . . No, no, Janetta, that's not the way of it at all.'

'She will eat you up like a kipper, you know.'

'Well, she may try,' said Patrick, 'but if she does she'll find me more of a mouthful than any fish she's had before. What about you, Miss Brown, are Perthshire men not to your taste?'

'Certainly they are.' She felt almost mesmerised by her own disenchantment. She was sick of falsity, of tedium, of being respected rather than loved. 'One man in particular.'

'What would you like?' Patrick said.

'Pardon?'

'From the mainland, from Perth: a gift, I'll bring you a gift. What would you like, schoolmistress? Anything you fancy.'

'An ebony ruler,' Janetta said, without hesitation.

He laughed. 'That's an odd sort of present to ask for.'

'I've always wanted a genuine ebony ruler.'

'With a brass edge?'

'The best that your money can buy, Mr Rattenbury.'

'That's it,' Patrick said. 'That's all I need to know. I'll be back here by Tuesday, all being well.'

'No matter when you come back' – Janetta favoured him with a smile – 'I will be here.' Then, before he could attempt to kiss her, she turned on her heel, went back indoors and watched from the upstairs window as he rode away down the lane.

'You're throwing yourself at him, Netta,' her father said.

'Oh, yes,' Janetta answered. 'Oh, yes, I most certainly am.'

'Divorce,' Gillies said, as calmly as you like, 'is an empty threat and not even a remote possibility. On what grounds would Michael sue for divorce, Innis? Desertion? He deserted you, remember. He did not at any stage request you to join him, did he? Yes, the marriage is over and a judicial separation, recognised by probate, would be a satisfactory solution as far as a court of law is concerned. But such a judgement wouldn't allow your husband to marry again, and from what you tell me that's his sole reason for seeking a divorce after all these years.'

'He would petition on the grounds of my adultery,' Innis said.

'Ah, then we are dealing with more complex issues,' Gillies, unruffled, continued. 'I assume that he isn't living with this woman, Ada Reese, in a state of chastity, a fact that wouldn't be too difficult to prove. So, we would have a petition based on the grounds of mutual adultery which under Scots law is regarded as a case without precedent; by which is meant that each petition is judged at the discretion of the court on its own merits and the decree granted in favour of the less guilty party.'

'Have you been reading up on the law?'

'Of course I have,' said Gillies. 'Do you think I haven't thought about marrying you before now, Innis? There have been times when I've thought of little else. I've scoured the law books to find a loophole that would allow us to be man and wife. Under the law there's no impediment whatsoever, for the Matrimonial Clauses Act is clear and concise on the validity of marriage and offences against it.'

'I cannot undertake divorce proceedings,' said Innis. 'It would be an injury to the Covenant of Salvation and would put me in a situation of permanent adultery, even if I did not condone it.'

'Yes, yes.'

Gillies was maddeningly calm, she thought, maddeningly pedantic.

He had not been much surprised to learn that Michael had returned to Mull. He had asked not one single question concerning Fay. With his customary acuity he had moved straight to the core of her concern.

'Yes, yes,' he went on. 'If Michael has been in correspondence with Becky, even indirectly, then he must be aware that you aren't going to renounce your religion just to satisfy his desire to get spliced. Where is he now? Is he still at Fetternish with Biddy?'

'No, much to Becky's disappointment he returned to Tobermory,' said Innis. 'He has given Fay until Friday morning to decide what to do.'

'Does Fay *want* to go back to her husband, by any chance?'

'I will not let her.'

'What does it have to do with you, Innis?'

'Everything.' She paused, then capitulated. 'Nothing.'

'How did you find him, Michael, I mean?'

'He has grown fat.'

'Is that your only observation?' Gillies said.

'He did not even remind me of himself.'

'Are you frightened of him?'

'No, I am only frightened for the harm he may cause to you.'

'No doubt that's exactly what Michael intended,' Gillies said. 'Do you really think he came here to repair Gavin's marriage? Of course he didn't. He seized an opportunity to get what *he* wants, namely a legal right to marry again. Fay would be daft to go with him.'

'I am relieved to hear you say it.'

'There would be no point,' Gillies said. 'Michael's made his bid. I suspect he knew all along that it would come to nothing. Perhaps he made rash promises to this woman he lives with. Who's to say what goes on in his devious mind. However, the result is very clear: he has failed on both counts. He has failed to retrieve Gavin's wife on Gavin's behalf, and he has failed to frighten you into agreeing to an amicable divorce.'

'Do you not think, dearest, that if I had been able to separate myself from Michael and marry you that I would not have done so long before now?'

'Aren't you being a bit presumptuous in assuming that I'd want to marry you if you were a free woman?'

'I am not in the mood for your jokes.'

'No, and a joke it is,' Gillies said. 'God, how much easier

everything would have been for us if you hadn't . . .' He shrugged. 'I'm not complaining. I'd rather have your friendship than be married to anyone else.'

'I do not take you for granted, Gillies.'

'If you did you wouldn't be here now, warning me.'

'If Michael does seek a bill of divorcement and brings your name forward as a co-respondent then the School Board will sack you, will they not?'

'Guilty or not, indeed they will,' Gillies said. 'Or perhaps to save face they would request my resignation which, of course, they would get.'

'Would you not fight it?'

'There would be nothing to fight,' Gillies said. 'However, it isn't going to come to that. Michael has made his bid and it hasn't succeeded. The girl – Fay – will stay put with you in Pennymain and have her baby in peace. Michael will trail back to his Border wife and spin some tale to placate her and that will be an end of it.'

'And Gavin?'

'Ah, yes,' Gillies said. 'Gavin. It would not do to forget about Gavin.'

'No, I do not think that it would,' said Innis.

Quig was surprised, and rather alarmed, when Agnes Mac-Niven unfurled a great red rubber tube and advanced upon her patient.

He was used to applied science in relation to sheep but had expected something a little more discreet in dealing with a human being.

Agnes had taken off her coat and rolled up her sleeves. Her arms were no less muscular than her calves and she had rubbed them down with a watery oil that smelled a good deal less fragrant than perfume. In spite of a long day upon the road she was as brusque as ever, and when she spun round from the bed, the rubber tubing wrapped about her forearm like a python, Quig wilted.

'Where is Innis? I thought that Innis would be here?' Agnes said.

'She had to go out,' Fay said, unperturbed at the prospect of being examined. 'Becky will be home soon if you require assistance.'

'I am only going to take a look at you, young lady. I am not going to deliver the infant on the spot. I do not, therefore, require assistance,' Agnes MacNiven declared. 'Nor do I require you, Robert, to be standing gawking in the doorway.'

'I don't mind if Quig stays.'

'No, but I do,' said Agnes.

'I will be just outside in the kitchen if you need me,' Quig said.

'Thank you,' Agnes said, 'I will bear that in mind,' and with the back of her muscular elbow closed the bedroom door in his face.

CHAPTER FOURTEEN

Distant Voices

It had been many months since Biddy had last visited Pennymain. Her relations with her sister had never been good. Except for a spell of eight or nine years after her marriage to Quig she had seldom been free of envy of Innis and guilt that she, Biddy, had let Michael Tarrant lure her into adultery. Time had failed to heal old wounds and adolescent rivalries and she, in the confusions of middle age, blamed Innis for all her disappointments.

She had been shocked to discover Michael on her doorstep, even more shocked by the changes in him, changes that had driven her to conclude that memories of an undimmed love were no more than figments of her imagination.

Michael Tarrant now was nothing but a vulgar little bumpkin. She could hardly believe that she had once been deceived into thinking that his dour, egotistical persistence reflected true love. The realisation that she might have married Michael Tarrant if he had not been married to Innis filled her now with disgust.

Biddy came upon Innis in the garden in front of Pennymain. She was spraying the rose bushes with soapy water.

'Biddy!' Innis smiled the gracious little smile that Biddy had always detested, so calm, so patient, so pious. 'How nice it is to see you. Will you be coming inside? I will put the kettle—'

'I won't be coming inside,' Biddy interrupted. 'Is Michael here?'

'I thought that he was staying with you, at Fetternish.'

Innis shouldered the brass syringe and continued to smile that benign, infuriating smile, as if her husband's sudden reappearance carried no threat. For an instant Biddy even began to wonder if he had talked himself back into her sister's bed; she put that ridiculous notion swiftly behind her.

'What did he have to say for himself?' Biddy asked.

'Did Becky not tell you?'

'Becky! Huh, I can wring no sense out of Becky this morning. She's up there snivelling into the sink or running off to hide in the lavatory, bubbling away as if her heart were broken. Did Michael say something to offend her?'

'I think she knows she made a serious mistake in writing to Gavin.'

'Why in God's name did she do it then?' said Biddy.

'To pay me back for taking in a stranger, perhaps.'

'Is the Ludlow girl returning to Derbyshire, to Gavin?'

'No.'

'Is she ailing?' said Biddy. 'I heard that Agnes MacNiven called in here last evening.'

'Fay will need a midwife when the time comes. Meanwhile she is perfectly healthy,' Innis said. 'The baby is well positioned and Agnes anticipates that it will arrive before the end of August.' She hesitated then went on, 'If Michael is not staying with you at Fetternish he must have gone back to the Mishnish. Did Quig drive him to Tobermory?'

Biddy shook her head. 'Michael obviously realised he wasn't welcome in either my house or yours. Did he beg you to give him a divorce?'

'He did.'

'He wants to marry the widow he's living with, probably to get his hands on her money. What do you know about her?'

'Very little,' said Innis. 'Nothing at all, in fact. He is leaving tomorrow morning on the *Claymore*. He told Fay to be at the pier with her bag packed, though I am sure he knows she won't be there.'

'Tomorrow morning? God, he's not showing much persistence, is he, not like the Michael Tarrant of old?'

'It is my belief,' said Innis, 'that he came only to placate the woman.'

'The widow?'

'Yes, the widow. Michael wants no more to do with us than we do with him.'

'Are you over him at last?' said Biddy.

'I am,' said Innis; she paused. 'Are you?'

Biddy's cheeks glowed. 'What do you mean by . . .'

'*Are* you, Biddy?'

'Of course I am,' said Biddy. 'Over him long ago.'

'Why do you want me to talk to her?' Quig said. 'Why can't Willy do it? She has more respect for Willy than she has for me.'

'Willy has taken Aileen to ambush Hermann,' Maggie said, 'and I am not inclined to go chasing up the drive after him; nor am I inclined to put up with that girl's wailing for the rest of the morning. There is work to be done.'

'The work can wait,' said Quig. 'Where is Becky?'

'Out in the yard, sobbing.'

'Very well. I will have a word with her.'

It took him the best part of ten minutes to find Becky on the slope below the terrace. The lawns had been cut but warm, moist weather had brought grass up swiftly and clover, daisies and buttercups sprinkled the faded folds of hay. Quig surveyed the ill-kempt lawns and thought what a scandalous amount of time, effort and money had been squandered in trying to make the land yield more than its due. Then he spotted Becky almost hidden by one of the ornamental stone bollards that fronted the flagged terrace. Her knees were drawn up, hands in front of her eyes. He glimpsed the child in her, the unformed woman. Becky was stubborn, intolerant and argumentative: for all that, he felt sorry for her.

He hastened down the slope.

'What is it, Becky? Tell me what's wrong?' He sat beside her on the grass. 'Was your father such a disappointment?'

'I should never have written. I should have let well alone.'

'You should,' Quig told her. 'What did you hope to gain by it?'

'I missed him. At least I did when I was younger. I know that Mam loves me and wouldn't do anything to hurt me, but when Fay Ludlow came and I heard about my brother . . .' She looked up at him, her eyes magnified by tears. 'I wanted to find out who I really am and what sort of a man my father really is. I thought he would help me make up my mind about − things.'

Quig said, 'Did Rachel put you up to it?'

'Rachel has always known what she wanted.'

'But you don't.'

'No, I don't.'

'Biddy would have paid for you to go to college on the mainland, you know, but you did not ask it of her.'

'I didn't want to leave Fetternish, leave Mam.'

'Have you changed your mind?' Quig enquired.

'There is nothing here for me,' Becky said. 'I thought meeting with my father might solve my problems for me.'

'But you wrote to Gavin, not your father? That was your mistake.'

'You are right as usual, Quig. Why do you always have to be right?'

She wiped her eyelids with her fingertip. She was not a pretty girl but her bold intelligence would stand her in good stead on the mainland. Quig wished that he could bring himself to like her and regretted that he had not done more for Innis's girls while they were growing up.

'You're afraid, are you not?' he said. 'You are afraid of what you will have to face when you leave Mull.'

'I've seen how people change after they leave, how Donnie changed, and Tricia, even Rachel. They become other people, strangers even to themselves.' She rubbed a knuckle under her nose, and stared at the sea. 'Dada couldn't even remember my name,' she said, more puzzled than sad. 'He had no interest in me. He was only interested in getting what he wanted for himself.'

'Most folk are,' said Quig.

'But your own father – my father . . .' She jerked her head and scowled at him. 'I have to decide for myself, don't I, Quig?'

'Yes, you do,' Quig said. 'Decide soon, though, for it might be as well if you were not here when Gavin comes back.'

'I see now that I made a dreadful mistake. If Mam wants Fay to stay here, if it makes Mam happy . . .' She lifted her shoulders, let them sink. 'I'm a trouble-maker, aren't I? I always thought I believed in justice and fair play, but all I really wanted was an excuse to stay put and not have to face up to anything.' She shrugged again. 'I could be a nurse, you know. I could be a nurse if I want to be.'

'It's a very hard life, so I am told.'

'Hah!' Becky exclaimed, sounding less like her mother than her aunt. 'It can't be any harder than working under Maggie Naismith. If Rachel can tolerate it so can I.' She glanced at him quickly. 'Are you trying to trap me into making a decision?'

'No, I am only trying to trap you into making lunch.'

'You're a devil, Quig, do you know that?'

'Oh, I know that well enough,' Quig said. 'Will you be thinking about it, though – not about lunch, about the other thing.'

'I won't be thinking about much else.' Becky thrust herself upright and swept back the wisps of hair that had strayed across her brow. 'I'm beginning to understand what she sees in you.' She leaned down and smiled into his face. 'Little Miss Innocent, I mean. Better be careful, Uncle Quig, or I might not be the only one packing my bags and setting out for the mainland. Now, if you'll excuse me, I'm going off to serve lunch.'

'Becky, wait . . .'

But she had already gone racing up the lawn through the buttercups and clover heads.

Unmoving, Quig watched her go then with a little groan of submission, leaned his head back against the lichen and stared bleakly out at the sea.

It gave Biddy quite a turn when the girl rose out of the bracken, though she was far too solid to be one of Aileen's fairy sprites.

Biddy sensed that this was no chance meeting.

'Are you measuring out your ground, Mrs Quigley?' the girl asked.

'No, I am not measuring out my ground,' Biddy answered sourly.

'Are you looking for Mr Quigley then?'

'What business is it of yours what I'm doing?'

In fact she had been doing nothing but walking.

She had been restless since Patrick had left, her anxiety and guilt increased tenfold by the knowledge that Michael was presently in Tobermory. She was also upset because Christina and Robbie were soon due to return from school. Patrick gone, the children imminent: small wonder that her headache had come back. Depressed and apprehensive, she had headed out along the narrow track that led from the big house to the sandy hollows on the back side of Olaf's Hill. Here she was sheltered from sight of the house and the tract of land that would be hers no longer if she gave in to Patrick Rattenbury.

Fay, of course, had spotted her from the hill – nothing mystical about it – had lumbered down and hidden in the high bracken to pounce on her as she came by.

The drone of insects was abnormally loud. They hung in a cloud about Fay, dense and disgusting, as if she were a dead thing or a thing about to die. Biddy shivered, then, gathering her reserves, drew back her shoulders and looked down her nose at the great swollen lump of a belly that would soon spawn another Campbell, another link in the chain of perdition.

'Have you been following me?'

'Yes, Mrs Quigley, I have.'

They faced each other in the sump of the track, hemmed in by head-high ferns. Nervous and over-sensitive, Biddy experienced a sudden dread of Fay Ludlow, a shrivelling sense of foreboding.

'Why?' Biddy said.

'Are you going to see him?'

'I'm going nowhere,' Biddy said. 'Nowhere that concerns you.'

'Are you going to tell him the truth?'

Mouth dry, Biddy said, 'I've no idea what you're talking about.'

'Mr Tarrant; Michael Tarrant. Are you going to see him?'

'You have more reason to see him than I have.'

'He's Gavin's brother, isn't he?' Fay Ludlow said.

'He is Gavin's father, his *father*, for God's sake! How can he be—'

'They aren't cousins,' Fay said. 'I know they aren't cousins. I knew when I saw Robbie for the first time that he was more than a cousin to Gavin.'

Biddy felt a rush of watery fluid, acid as vinegar, rise into her throat.

'That's too far-fetched to be credible.'

Fay wafted a hand to ward off the black flies. There were more flies now, Biddy saw, a swarm, a cloud, hanging over the ferns.

Fay said, 'It were none of Quig's doing, was it? I mean, he didn't father Robbie. He might love him like a father but they ain't of the same blood.' She swatted with her hand again. 'I'm not after taking anything from you, Mrs Quigley. I just want you to think on what you've done before you condemn me.'

'Condemn you?'

'I never saw much of life when I was at Fream — but I saw enough,' Fay went on. 'I never saw a man naked till Gavin took me home on our wedding night. I never saw a man naked save for him. Just because I'm come up out of the orphan camp don't mean that I don't understand things, though. I understand that you done what you had to do for the sake of your baby, and that makes you and me the same.'

'Is that why you followed me, to pester me with foolish nonsense about my son? If you think you're going to wring one penny piece . . .'

'It's you that don't understand,' Fay said. 'He's down there in the town awaiting for me to go back with him. I ain't going. He'll send Gavin next. I'll have nobody to protect me if you don't stand behind me. I see as how your word will be better than mine, how nobody will ever believe what I've got to say even when they see how Gavin looks. You might think I've got it wrong about how Robbie and Gavin are two peas in a pod, but that's how it is. It ain't no coincidence; it's blood coming out.'

'What does my husband have to say about this story of yours?'

'I wouldn't dream of telling Quig. I won't go telling anyone, 'cause they won't believe me, even when they have the evidence before their eyes. If Mr Tarrant hadn't come here then I would have kept it to myself. If I'm wrong – and I know I'm not – then you'll just have to go hating me even more than you do now, even more than you will if things turn out bad.'

'If Gavin comes for you, do you mean?'

'He will.'

'What if he doesn't?' Biddy said.

'Mr Tarrant will send him.'

'Michael? Why would he do that?'

'To pay you back.'

'Me?' said Biddy.

'All of you.'

If it was guesswork on Fay Ludlow's part, she had none the less struck the nail square on the head. If it was more than guesswork then Biddy knew that Michael must be behind it. She gave the girl no credit for acuity, saw her only as a dunderhead without the wit or gall to be an opportunist.

'I'm not afraid of Gavin Tarrant,' Biddy said.

That, oddly, was the truth. She had always loathed the pug-faced boy with his brush of dark hair and snarling eyes. Had taken malicious satisfaction in the fact that nature had wished such a child upon Innis. Somehow she had blinded herself to the fact that Gavin Tarrant and Robbie, her Robbie, might be half-brothers.

She had never been sure who Robbie's father really was: Michael or Quig. She had lain with Michael only days before her wedding to Quig and had thanked her lucky stars that she had found a husband just when she did, a good husband, a quiet, biddable, unquestioning husband.

'If Gavin arrives here looking for trouble,' Biddy went on, 'Quig will take care of him.'

'Aye,' Fay said, 'but will Quig take care of me, me and my baby?'

'You . . .' Biddy hesitated. 'You aren't one of us, never will be.'

'But my baby is, my baby will be.'

Biddy was suddenly angry. She wanted only to be shot of the sweating girl with her vast, solid stomach. She remembered her own second pregnancy, the hell that Christina had put her through in the heat of the summer months: sickness, cramps, looseness of bladder and bowel, as if nature had sent Christina to punish her for the ease with which she had borne Robbie.

'I'm not going to be blackmailed over something that you cannot prove.'

'So it is true,' Fay said. 'I knew it was.'

'It's not true, not true at all,' said Biddy, with all the authority she could muster. 'Robbie is my son, Quig's son. He was born well within wedlock. I don't care how much resemblance there is between Gavin Tarrant and Robbie. It's a quirk of nature, that's all, one of those things that happens in some families.'

'Quig accepts it, does he?' Fay said.

'Oh, I have had enough of this,' Biddy said. 'I knew from the moment I saw you that you would cause trouble. But if you think you can intimidate me with your cock-and-bull stories then you had better think again. I'll not fall for your slurs and innuendoes. They cut no ice with me, Fay Ludlow, and they'll cut no ice with anyone in my family, least of all with Quig.'

'When Gavin comes he'll find out the truth.'

'No,' Biddy snapped. 'When Gavin comes—'

An iron fist suddenly gripped her brow. Shooting pains ran down the side of her face. She let out a little yelp, cupped a hand over her eye, felt the pain contract within her forehead. All thoughts of Gavin, of Robbie, of Quig vanished. An aneurysm had felled her mother and crippled her for the latter part of her life.

How old had Vassie been when disaster struck? Older than she, Biddy, was now – but not much.

She sucked in a mouthful of the hot, salty air.

'What is it?' Fay said. 'What's wrong?'

'Nothing. Nothing is wrong.'

'Are you in pain?' Fay said. 'Will I fetch Quig?'

No blurred vision, no dizziness, no nausea, no loss of motor power. She remembered all the signs and symptoms. Distant voices called out to Biddy, whispering news of her own mortality. She sucked in another breath, rubbed her brow to massage away the memory. Pain had surely been a distraction, a side-show to divert her from her other worries, not least of which was the girl. She wanted Patrick, desperately wanted Patrick. She needed a man to lean on, to love.

'I won't be telling anyone, you know,' Fay said. 'It was never in my head to tell anyone. I just wanted you to know that we're not so far apart as all that, Mrs Quigley, and you should not be thinking bad of me just because I'm young and a stranger here.'

'Very well,' Biddy heard herself say. 'Now, if you've said your piece, I would like to continue with my walk.'

'I'll walk with you a bit,' Fay Ludlow said.

'No, you will not,' Biddy snapped and, turning on her heel, set off up the sandy track, back by the way she had come.

Michael was alone in the dining-room when Biddy arrived at the Mishnish.

She had despatched Maggie to Crove to fetch the pony-trap and had driven herself to Tobermory soon after supper. Though it was still high summer light had been leeched from the mountains, and the sea lay dark under cloud. There might be rain in the air, or thunder, but Biddy reckoned that when night came the sky would clear and rain would remain no more than a distant threat.

The town had an oily smell to it, more mechanical than fishy.

The pier was all but deserted. Out in the bay, nestling behind Calf Isle, three trim yachts were anchored. On what passed for a promenade the day's quota of sightseers strolled aimlessly.

She hitched the pony to the rail by the old pier head, walked along the pavement to the front of the hotel and through the window saw him alone within the dining-room. He was sipping alternately from a cup and a brandy glass, his head wreathed in cigar smoke.

There was no one in the hotel foyer. A clatter of dishes came from the kitchen passageway and the tinkle of an untuned piano and halting singing drifted from the back parlour.

Biddy went directly into the dining-room and seated herself at Michael's table. She did it gracefully, sweeping the skirts of her muslin dress under her knees.

She wore a little cape in ruby-red boxcloth with a collar of Japanese fox, and a hat with a dove's wing stitched above the brim, smart and fashionable but not too ostentatious. Dressing for the outing had absorbed the best part of the afternoon and relieved her mind from dwelling on her woes.

Her headache had gone now.

319

'I thought you would come,' Michael said. 'I thought you wouldn't be able to resist.'

'Do not flatter yourself,' said Biddy.

'Will you be taking a drink with me?'

'What's in your glass?'

'Brandy and soda.'

'I would prefer a liqueur,' said Biddy. 'Drambuie.'

'Drambuie it is.' Michael did not rise from his chair. He called out in a loud voice, 'Tam, Tam, a Drambuie for the lady, please, and another of the same for me.'

It did not occur to him that he would not be heard or that his order would not be attended to immediately.

He scanned Biddy critically, eyelids heavy, and smoked his cigar very slowly, inhaling and exhaling with languorous satisfaction. He said nothing, she said nothing until the glasses materialised on a tin tray. Tam, the landlord, went away again, leaving the couple alone among the tablecloths, cups and cruets. Michael sipped from the fresh glass.

'Did Innis send you to plead her case?' he asked.

'Innis is not the pleading sort, as well you know.'

'She hasn't changed much then.'

'Hardly at all,' Biddy said. 'What did you say to her?'

He shrugged, sipped, puffed the cigar. 'There was little enough between us. Funny – peculiar, I mean – how little we had to talk about. There was never as much between Innis and me as there was between me and you, Biddy.'

'Except three children and a marriage.'

'You didn't come here to talk about Innis, did you?' he said. 'You're no more concerned about your sister's welfare than I am. What brings you to Tobermory at this time of the evening? Couldn't you let me leave in peace?' He leaned forward, his stomach creasing his vest. 'Couldn't you bear to let me go without saying a proper goodbye?'

'It's gone, hasn't it, Michael?'

'Aye,' he said blandly. 'Aye, Biddy, it's gone.'

'Tell me about this widow you wish to marry.'

'Ada? Oh, Ada is just fine for me at my age. She gives me what I want, I return the favour, and we rub along very well together.'

'And her daughters?'

'They approve.'

'Approve? What an odd word to use,' said Biddy. 'Do they approve of you sharing a bed with their mother?'

'As long as she's happy they don't care what we do.'

'Have you promised to marry her?'

'Ada understands the situation.' Michael paused. 'I warned her that Innis would be difficult. The endeavour will be enough for Ada, at least for the time being.'

'So you don't care about Gavin, or his wife?'

He tapped a nub of cigar ash into a saucer and refrained from meeting Biddy's eye. 'He's a wicked one, is Gavin. No use blinking the fact. You know it and I know it and for your information, Biddy, he did not grow up straight. He's the same now as he always was. I was forced to chase him out of the Ettrick Pen, get him away from Coraldene, before he ruined everything for me.'

'Coraldene?'

'Ada's place, Ada's farm.' Michael dabbed ash once more. 'It was the girls, you see, the daughters. He was after the daughters like a fox goes after hens. He would have torn them apart if I hadn't a-been around to drag him off. There were a few close-run things, more than a few. Bad for the nerves it was. Very bad for the nerves.' He let out a dry chuckle. 'He was – he is – a Campbell through and through, you see.'

'Just what do you mean by that?'

'Mad as a bloody hatter.'

She felt blood rise to her cheeks, temper bubble within her.

She could not in honesty defend her family's reputation, however, not to this man. She salved herself with irony, with the knowledge that he, Michael Tarrant, had perhaps fathered not one but two Campbell men, each as different from the other as chalk is from cheese.

'How can you say that about your own son?' Biddy asked.

'Because it's the truth.'

'And yet you'd take that poor girl, Fay, back to him?'

He chuckled again, mirthlessly. 'What do you do with folk like Gavin? Same as you did with your dada, old Ronan, same as you do with that loony sister of yours. You appease them. By God, yes, you appease them.'

'Have you no other children, no other sons?'

'Eh?'

'I mean,' said Biddy, cautiously, 'children to Ada Reese?'

'Ada's past all that, thank God.'

Biddy lifted the fluted glass and sipped liqueur. It lay on her lips and tongue, sweet and mellow at first then warming. She swallowed and took in a little more. The heat in her throat and chest helped melt her anger. Michael had mellowed in spite of himself; his arrogance now was no more than the vanity of a male whose feathers had wilted, whose fur had lost its sheen.

Biddy said, 'You haven't asked about my circumstances, or my children.'

'I'm a-waiting for you to tell me.'

'When you turned up last night I thought you'd come to make an offer for Fetternish,' Biddy said. 'Isn't that a laugh?'

'Times are hard for you then, Biddy? I guessed as much.'

'I am selling a part of the estate.'

'Not to me, you're not,' Michael said. 'We've been through that a'ready.'

'It's the only way I can be sure of keeping the house and enough of the land to hand on to my – to Robbie.'

'Is it really worth hanging on to?'

'You used to think it was. You used to covet it.'

'Not no more,' said Michael. 'I got all – most – o' what I want. I wouldn't take on a white elephant like Fetternish even if you were to give it me for nothing. Wrong there, Biddy. I didn't come back to Mull to size up your land, or you, or anything here. I want a clean break with all that, to be rid of it once and for all.'

He ground the cigar out, screwing it into the saucer. There was anger in the gesture, a hint of the old embittered frustration. He had not been telling her the truth, not the whole truth. However much Michael might profess to be content with his lot, Biddy knew that it was not so. Suddenly she felt better, clearer in her head. Somehow she had made a decision or, rather, a string of small decisions, one of which was that she would say nothing about Robbie to Michael, would keep that particular secret to herself.

Michael sat back, arms folded.

Acrid cigar smoke wafted up from the butt in the saucer.

'I've got a lot to crow about,' Michael said. 'You never gave me my proper place, none o' you: not your mother, not your sister, not you, Biddy Baverstock. You wouldn't let me in, not properly. Well, that was your fault not mine. I could have saved you from ruin, better than Quigley has done. You wouldn't have been a-selling off Fetternish now if you'd given me my place.'

He grinned fatuously.

He had no curiosity about her children or her circumstances, no more interest in her than he had in his daughters; she realised now why Becky had spent the morning in tears.

'I found my place, Biddy. I'm not so modest as all that and I'm worshipped down there in the Pen. It's not too strong a word, believe me. I got respect on Coraldene. I'm a king to Ada and her girls. Just how it should be, considering all the good I've done them.' He fixed her with his watery gaze, 'I could've done it all for you, you know.'

'For Innis, you mean.'

'Innis! No, for you. It might be dead and done between us, Biddy, but I ha'n't forgotten how it once was, have you?'

She could not deny him a truthful answer. She was not so lost, so forsaken and soured as all that. Perhaps there had been more love in him than she'd imagined, more romance. He had excited her as few other men had ever done.

She shook her head. 'No, Michael. I haven't forgotten.'

'I had to go home to the Pen, though, to find the richest pickings, but . . .'

'But?' said Biddy.

'You're still a fine-looking woman, Biddy.'

'Thank you.'

'I got a room upstairs.' He did not look away. 'I won't be back here. I won't bother you no more. I knew Innis'd never give me what I wanted, and I doubt if she'll give up the girl. That's something I'll deal with when I get home. But right now – I can guess why you came tonight, Biddy. You can't hide anything from me.'

'Hide . . .'

'Nobody will see us, nobody will know.'

She let out a gasp of astonishment. The anger in her turned to laughter.

The fat little remnant of the lean and hungry lover that he had once been was seducing her all over again: not seducing but assuming, yes, *assuming* that she would succumb to mere opportunity and fall back into his arms as if nothing at all had changed.

'Auld Lang Syne?' he murmured, and raised one gritty, grey eyebrow. 'Auld Lang Syne, Biddy. What do you say?'

Laughter exploded from deep within her chest.

It had been months, years, since she had laughed without inhibition. She was powerless to stem her laughter. Tears started into her eyes. Her diaphragm and ribs expanded. She felt open, released, as the laughter fed on itself, and Michael, rigid with amazement then with fury, clung to the dining-room chair as if her laughter, like a tornado, might sweep him up and swirl him.

'I take it,' Michael said through clenched teeth, 'that means no?'

Biddy was on her feet. She had spilled liquid from the glass in her haste and the stain stretched across the tablecloth like a honey trap. Her hat had slipped back on her head and her cape was flung wide open. She clasped her sides which ached with laughter at the outrageous gall of the shepherd and the crass male vanity that made him think he was still the man he had once been.

She shook her head, could not speak.

In the back parlour the piano tinkled into silence.

In the kitchen corridor there was silence too as Biddy, carried away, wept and laughed, laughed and wept and in that helpless state staggered out of the Mishnish on to the pavement, leaving Mr Michael Tarrant clinging with clenched fists to his chair, like a felon who had just been electrocuted.

She had not ridden far out of Tobermory before the laughter died within her and she was left with the tears. She could not be sure now that her laughter had not been hysterical or that Michael's ludicrous proposition had not struck a tender spot in her heart. She had been in his company less than ten minutes and yet had managed to humiliate him and, in turn, had been thrown back into a state of confusion.

When she reached the crossroads she steered the pony on to the fork that led to the stables. It was almost full dark when she reached Patrick's door. She climbed out of the trap, hitched the pony and went into the kitchen. She groped to the dresser and found a lamp and a match-box on the little shelf above it, lit the lamp and looked around.

She was no longer tearful. She felt daring, not guilty. It was, she reminded herself, her property. She was entitled to inspect it at any time of choosing. Oddly, the kitchen did not smell of Patrick. It smelled of the horsemen, the Bells, who had occupied it for so many years. Disappointed but undeterred, she knelt on the stone floor and systematically began to open the dresser drawers, most of which were empty or contained nothing more interesting than kitchen utensils.

Holding the lamp high she went upstairs.

He had chosen the smallest of the four bedrooms to sleep in: a narrow room just above the staircase. The bed was neatly made with a patchwork quilt and clean sheets. In the tiny square-paned window Biddy caught sight of her reflection. She appeared pale and enigmatic, phantom-like in the darkened room. She had no sense of betrayal and thrilled less at her daring than her determination.

She knelt on the floorboards and scooped an arm under the bed. She brought out a flowered china chamber-pot that the Bells had left behind. Leaning closer to the floor she fished again.

The document case was fashioned from hard-tanned leather, oblong in shape, not deep. It had a single brass lock and two catches.

She thumbed open the catches and, holding her breath, pressed on the lock which sprang open sharply. Biddy hesitated, apprehensive at what she might find – then she opened the case.

It was stuffed with letters, bills and receipts, neatly held together in clumps and clusters not by rubber bands but by faded scarlet ribbons of the sort that lawyers use. Commerce, she thought, not romance. She adjusted the position of the lamp and calmly and methodically began to empty the case, her head as clear as a May morning, her eyes so wide open that she could feel cool air wash under the lids.

She lifted out the bundles one by one and held each to her nose, as if to sniff out malice or deception before she untied it.

There were letters from dukes and letters from earls, a sheaf of printed accounts from a plantation somewhere in Perthshire; a receipted bill from the instrument-maker who had fashioned the wind device that whirred away on the moor; letters and little notes from several different women – Amy, Peggy, Lynette, Jane – professing affection, asking after his health, declaring love, sharing fond memories, berating him for indifference. Biddy was tempted to read them but was too single-minded to risk being distracted by jealousy.

Then there it was: a slim unfolded sheaf of letters written in a rather childish hand on heavy cream-laid paper.

The embossed blind stamp leaped out at her: *The Ards*.

She placed those letters on the bed, untied the ribbon, separated one and began to read. Three stunning pages later she encountered the signature: *Dorothea Lafferty*.

Biddy put the letter carefully to one side, picked up the next and read it too then another and another until she had read all six in the sequence that Frances Hollander's mother-in-law had penned them to her land agent, and understood precisely what was going on if not – not yet – the reason for it.

Quig had brought the pony-trap down to Pennymain in the early hours of the morning and had left it ready and waiting at the garden gate. He did not waken Innis or the girls, nor offer to accompany Innis to Tobermory.

How Quig knew that she would deliver the message to Michael, face to face, did not concern Innis. Quig had always understood her – better even than Gillies – for they were kindred spirits, he and she, and had once shared a rapport that had been almost too close to be comfortable.

Innis rode out early, and alone.

The night wind had cleared the low-lying cloud and the morning, though not sunny, had a promising aspect to it.

In Tobermory Bay the yachts had run up sail and were dipping off down the Sound of Mull, seeking a breeze. Line-fishers, the remnant of Tobermory's once mighty fleet, were nosing lazily out from the harbour and puttering away towards the inshore fishing grounds off Canna and the Point of Sleat. Along the harbour walls by the old pier there was much activity, for the *Claymore* was already making steam and the tourists were already displaying the subdued panic that preceded a departure at the height of the summer season.

The *Claymore* was making smoke as well as steam, its funnels pouring out the dark and stinky stuff. The piermaster, Harry Horseburgh, directed operations with a scarf bound about his nose and yelled instructions in a mixture of English and Gaelic that made him sound more like a highwayman than an employee of MacBrayne's shipping company. A parcel of lambs were being run up the gangway and a fretful young colt from the stud at Ardmore was being coaxed out of one gated box and into another on the foredeck.

Innis left the trap outside the Mishnish and walked to the pier.

Even among the tourists Michael stood out. He looked prosperous, and proud of it. Bowler tipped back from his shock of grey hair, thumbs stuck into his waistcoat pockets and a cigar in his mouth, he would have been perfectly at home shouting the odds at Ayr racecourse or, more like the thing, supervising a beer delivery to a better class of public house. He had several bags at his feet and two or three brown-paper parcels were tied to the handles of his valise. He watched Innis walk towards him but for all the greeting he gave her she might have been a stranger rather than his wife.

'Where's the girl then?' he said.

'Fay is staying here with me.'

'Then it will be Gavin you will have to deal with.'

'I am prepared to deal with Gavin,' Innis said.

'What else do you have to say to me?'

'Nothing,' Innis said. 'I just came to be sure that you got on the boat.'

'I will not be back, Innis. I have had my fill of Mull.'

'Will we not be meeting – with our lawyers – in court?'

'That remains to be seen.'

'By whom?' said Innis.

He took the cigar from his mouth and contemplated the coal on its tip. Smoke from the cigar and smoke from the *Claymore* mingled in the air over the lax waters beyond the wall and four large yellow-beaked gulls rose disdainfully from the mooring posts and glided silently away.

Michael dropped the cigar to the cobbles and ground it out. 'I'll make that decision when it suits me.'

'I take it you will be letting me know when you do?'

Heavy features, sagging paunch, the fine vulgarity of his apparel could not disguise his annoyance. He had played his hand in lacklustre fashion, utterly unlike the Michael Tarrant who had first come to Pennypol, who had pursued Biddy, who had married her, Innis, and had abandoned them all when it became clear that he wouldn't get what he wanted. Rage had become pique, passion a pipsqueak need to strut and be admired; reduced now to a state of bloodless affront he pouted like a parody of the angry, flinty fellow that he had once been.

He would not threaten her now, would not bring up the subject of law and lawyers, of writs and court proceedings again. Innis had known that he would retreat; he had always retreated from situations that he could not master. He had no character, no deviousness left in him. She regretted that a man she had once loved had turned out so hollow in the end.

'Had you not better be getting on board?' Innis said.

'Are you anxious to get rid of me?'

'I do not have to get rid of you, Michael,' Innis said. 'You are still there, still down there in the Pen where you are admired and respected. Is that not where your heart is, with your friend, the widow lady?'

He smiled, the muscles of his jaw lost in fat. 'Aye, you were always the smart one, Innis Campbell. If you and Biddy had been put together you could have been the Queen of Scotland with any man and all men falling at your feet.'

'That was never my need, Michael, nor my wish.'

'Vassie Campbell's daughters.' He shook his head ruefully. 'If there was a way of destroying a man the pair of you together would find it out. God, but I wish I had never met either of you.'

'And I thought you were paying us a compliment.'

'The only compliment you'll get from me, Innis, is seeing me leave without getting what I came for.' He glanced around, spotted a boy loitering by the wall of the harbour-master's office and snapped his fingers. 'I'll be going now. You do not need to see me off.'

'I am thinking that I will, though,' Innis said. 'Just to be certain.'

'Suit yourself,' he said gruffly.

Preceded by the boy with the baggage, he walked to the gangway and pulled himself up it. Once on board, he retired immediately to the passenger lounge and did not come out again. He did not emerge even when the paddles thrashed and ropes were cast off and the *Claymore* backed away from the pier, or when the wake broadened and gulls floated into line behind the steamer and flags a-mast found the wind and snapped out as if the voyage would be long and arduous and the destination more uncertain than Oban.

'Goodbye, Michael,' Innis murmured and turned away, relieved.

It was a little after noon and the sun had come out when Quig grounded the long boat on the beach at Foss. He had borrowed the boat from the salmon-fishers at Ardfinn and had sailed it round to the jetty at Pennypol where Fay waited.

He hadn't handled one of the cumbersome craft in years but the skills soon came back to him as he tacked along the coast with the sail slapping in the stiff little breeze out of the west and the rudder-bar strong and lively in his fist. He had forgotten how much fun sailing could be, how it stirred him. He was full of confidence and enthusiasm when he helped Fay down the steps at the Pennypol jetty and settled her beside him in the stern.

If the girl was nervous at being on the water she gave no sign of it.

She trusted him implicitly and snuggled into him. He put his arm about her.

The sea was crisp but there was no strong swell beneath. He had negotiated the path through the islands often enough to keep the bow up to prevent the boat from being slapped and guddled by cross-currents.

Fay was entranced by the muscular movements of the sea as the boat bowled over the blue-green water. She had never before seen seals basking on rocks or a whiskery face bobbing up to frown at her from the waves. Within her, so she imagined, the baby slopped happily in a similar fluid, capped and cloaked in an ocean of its own while together they sailed through channels and tideways between the little isles south-west of Mull and, in due course, came within sight of Foss.

Quig had told her a little about Foss. He had warned her not to expect too much of it now, though, for weather was a great destroyer and time and tides and seasonal storms would surely have pulled down the house where he had lived with Mairi and Aileen and Donnie under Evander McIver's protection.

The house was still there, however, a wooden bungalow, longer than it was broad. From a quarter-mile off, it looked quite solid and intact, but as they came closer Fay saw that the place was no more than a ruin and heard Quig utter little groans and *tuts* at the extent of the damage that weather had wrought.

He steered in bow foremost, dropped and reefed the sail, hopped over the side and dragged the craft half out of the water so that Fay might step down dry-shod. He was gentle with her, taking her weight on his arm. It wasn't until she was safe on the sand that he turned and hauled the boat further up the beach and moored it to a rusted iron stake just above the high-tide line.

Sweating with the effort, Quig peeled off his jacket and as if he were driven to begin work at once, rolled up his shirt sleeves. The sea breeze had licked his hair and reddened his cheeks and when he stood with his hands on his hips and surveyed the damage Fay thought that he looked more like an explorer than a farmer.

He helped her up the short steep slope from the beach and on to the sward of grass that fronted the verandah.

The roof had not collapsed inward but had shifted from its

beams as if a gigantic hand had shoved it, leaving only the chimney-breast intact. The room beneath was painted grey-green and white with lichen and bird-lime.

'Evander wanted a timber house,' Quig said. 'He imported all the materials by raft from the mainland. Built the place himself. Took him four or five years, I believe, though I was too young then to remember him doing it and too small to be of help. He had labour a-plenty, so my mother tells me, had all the women sawing and hammering away at the house as well as attending to the cattle that he had bought and brought in.'

'Is that what he did?' Fay said. 'Bred cattle?'

'Aye,' Quig told her. 'He was a cattle-dealer and cattle-breeder. He built up one of the finest herds of stud bulls in Scotland and made a great deal of money doing it. Before he retired to Foss he was a sportsman, a gambler, and the stories about him were legion, stories that are lost now, most of them, for his generation has died out and places like Foss and men like Evander McIver are best forgotten.'

'The house,' Fay said, 'couldn't it be repaired?'

'I expect it could,' Quig said.

'Could you repair it?'

'Yes,' Quig said, 'if I felt the need.'

The wooden steps that led to the verandah were still solid and intact, weathered to stone-grey, though, and shrouded in weeds. Quig took Fay's hand, led her up on to the sagging planks and guided her to the doorway.

The door had been blown half off its hinges and shells and strands of dried seaweed scattered the threshold like offerings and, after Quig shouldered the door, she saw that the great long parlour with its stone-built fireplace had become a refuge for rats and sea birds. The floor was littered with debris and droppings, and carpeted with dust and sea-slime.

She clung tightly to Quig's arm while he tested the boards and, finding them solid, led her forward again. Out of the corner of her eye she saw a rat scuttle away and, glancing up, saw another crouched on the main beam overhead, alert bright eyes peering down at her. She was not afraid of vermin and did not flinch when they shot like brown arrows across the floor and vanished out of the door.

'What do they live on?' she asked.

'Gulls' eggs mostly, roots and field-mice,' Quig said. 'God knows, there's nothing else for them. Looking at it now, it is a bleak place, is it not?'

'I don't think it's bleak,' said Fay. 'I think it's lovely.'

'Lovely?'

'It is a proper island house. If it was properly repaired and painted then it would still be a fine place to live, wouldn't it?'

'It was once, certainly,' said Quig, sighing. 'Aye, certainly it was once.'

He took her outside, fetched a canvas bag from the boat and walked slowly with her across the edge of the sward and slowly up the side of the little hill to higher ground. From there they looked out over the dancing waves to the place where the sea was darker than the sky and the waves planed out into a slender line upon which the sun glinted silver and the clouds, if clouds they were, hung low on the horizon, like islands almost invisible.

'That used to be the big pasture.' Quig pointed. 'Look at the weeds on it now.'

'Why does nobody keep cattle here?'

'Cattle, sheep – pah! It would not be worth the effort of visiting them three or four times in the year. They would run to seed, like the deer on the small isles. They would breed out in ten years or so or, worse, become sick with neglect. It is a town-dweller's mistake to think that animals thrive without intervention. If I came here, say, in the spring for the first calving I would find the beasts lean and ailing. If I cultivated a crop of hay or oats or ferried in feed then I would have to live here, or spend much money, and there would be no point. It is all money these days, Fay, all costs and tally. There can be no going back to what it was.'

'Is there water?'

'Hmm?' Quig was lost in thought. 'Yes.' He swung from the waist, looking this way and that as if, just for a moment, he had lost his bearings entirely. 'There.' He pointed. 'There is a rainwater lake in the bowl below the hill where the cattle drink. And there is a spring that comes up hard by the back of the house. Evander never did know why that spring was there or why it never ran dry. It was the sole reason he chose Foss for his home place and not one of the Treshnish Isles. We had rainwater butts too, of course, and catchments here and there, but Evander fretted that one day the spring would dry up and the goodness would go out of the ground and there would be no choice but to leave and go away.'

'Is it still there, the spring?' Fay asked.

She was not looking out to sea now or down at the emerald grassland or at the stoop of stunted little trees behind the house.

She was looking straight at him.

'Even if it is . . .' he said.

'We'll see, shall we? We'll go down there and see for ourselves.'

He knew it would still be there, that the water that had blessed the turf-covered speck of rock that Evander had chosen for his paradise would still be bubbling up between the four flat stones, that it would not have dried up like everything else but would be flowing still, oblivious to the passing of the men and women who had called the tiny island home.

Weeds flourished around the water-source; irises, willow-herb, the muted greenery of watered growth, and great clumps of buttercups, yellow as the sun, followed the streamlet seawards and petered out only where the water sifted into the sand.

Fay knelt with difficulty. Quig held her arm, her hand.

She knelt by the stones among the buttercups and scooped up water from the trout-brown pool, put her tongue to it, tasted it, cupped it in her hand and drank.

'Still here.' Fay smiled up at him. 'See, Quig, the water's still here.'

'Yes,' he said, 'I knew it would be.'

Leaning down, he kissed her softly on the lips.

They did not stay long after that. Quig was afraid of what might happen next. He did not take her out to the headland where the graves lay, those graves mysterious and friendly where Evander and his wives were buried, lost generations of men who had lived here long, long ago, seafarers and scavengers and warriors come to rest. He did know who they were and he was half afraid of what they represented, half in love with it too, drawn to the cycle of romance and survival and a history that was as hazy and insubstantial as a cloud.

They ate on the steps of the verandah, the house, the spring and the wild Atlantic shore behind them.

They ate casually, as if the day meant nothing.

They chatted and ate bread and cooked meat and slivers of smoked fish and drank cold tea from a bottle the way shepherds did when they were out on the pasture or like the drovers in the summer camps that were no more.

Fay ate hungrily, happily, humming to herself, now and then patting her stomach as if to comfort the foetus, or tease it.

It was still here, all still here: the bones of the fine old house, the spring, lush pasture, fertile soil, the graves of his kindred out there on the point. All it required to bring it back to life was the life Fay carried within her and the lives that lay beyond that.

Longing grew warm within him, as warm as the sun on his back.

'Quig?' Fay said, quite casually. 'Will we ever come back here again?'

And Quig, not smiling, answered her: 'We might.'

CHAPTER FIFTEEN

The Lion and the Lamb

Biddy arrived at The Ards uninvited but not unannounced. She had sent Maggie into Crove with a letter which Angus Bell then took round and delivered directly into Frances Hollander's dainty little hand. She, Biddy, would have despatched Maggie directly to the house across the loch except that she was no longer sure where Maggie's loyalties lay and had no wish, as it were, to tip her hand.

Quite what her hand consisted of Biddy was unsure but her desire to control the situation in which she found herself had become overwhelming in the wake of her discovery at the stables. It did not occur to her that she had done anything wrong by invading Patrick's privacy and she felt quite cocky in pushing forward without his knowledge or permission.

Check of her account books and the receipt of a summary of her balances from her legal adviser in Edinburgh presented a gloomy picture of Fetternish's finances. The big house itself was in fairly good repair and the stables, as Patrick had proved, were perfectly habitable but her other properties were running to rack and ruin and all too soon she would be obliged either to let them go or spend money on shoring them up.

The drain on the estate's resources was not entirely down to wind, weather and shifting markets, however. Biddy's drawing against the estate's accounts included the exorbitant fees that went out each quarter to educate her son and daughter and much of her concern over money was centred around her children's future, which she saw in a different light from her husband. Sale of ground would bring in a fat lump sum which, if prudently invested, would provide security for many years to come. She would no longer have to depend on Quig to keep the estate together or on the paltry earnings from sheep sales, would become once again a woman of independent means.

But why a woman whom she had never met and who to her knowledge had never set foot on Fetternish was so doggedly determined to wrest her house from her remained a complete mystery, a mystery that must be solved before she signed away a single acre.

She stepped down from the trap more or less into Frances Hollander's lap.

'What are you doing here?' the young woman demanded. 'What business do you have with us that cannot wait until Patrick gets back?'

'I have no business with you, Frances,' Biddy said. 'I am here to speak with Mrs Lafferty who is, I believe, your mother-in-law. I assume that she is at home?'

'She is always at home, as I expect you know,' Frances said. 'My mother-in-law is not a well woman and cannot leave her room.'

'In that case I will talk with her in her room.'

'What is wrong with you, Mrs Quigley? For weeks, for months you have refused all our overtures . . .'

'Patrick's overtures,' Biddy said.

'Patrick is our agent.'

'So I have learned.'

'Did he tell you everything?'

'No,' Biddy said. 'He told me little or nothing, which is why I'm here today, to find out the truth about your plans and intentions.'

'I suppose you had better come in,' said Frances.

'Thank you,' Biddy said and, handing the reins of the pony-trap to a young female servant, followed Frances into the house.

The woman was old. The woman was huge. She was seated in the downstairs drawing-room in a massive throne-like chair, propped up by stiff cushions, one foot resting on a stool. She had a stick in her hands, a wicked-looking ash-wood stick as stout and threatening as a knobkerrie that sat ill with the modern, pastel-hued furnishings.

Biddy was barely aware of the décor, however, for Dorothea Lafferty was so imposing that she could not help but stare at her. The woman's swollen fingers were heavy with rings, her wrists with bracelets, throat and chest with necklaces, all gold and glinting in the sunlight. She had had only two or three hours' warning of her arrival, Biddy reckoned, but if the effort of hasty dressing had tired her she gave no sign of it. Her head was held high, her eyes glittered; the only evidence of pain or discomfort lay in the manner in which she gripped the stick, her knuckles not white but scarlet.

Behind the chair was another female servant, no less pretty than the first. Small and dainty, like Frances, she hardly came up to the old woman's shoulder.

'It is too early for luncheon,' Dorothea Lafferty said. 'Will you take tea, Mrs Quigley?'

'No, thank you.'

'Valerie, that will be all,' the old woman said.

The servant glided from the room and closed the white-painted door.

Frances had already seated herself on a Regency divan. She seemed perfectly matched to the style and the silky, striped fabric suited her to a tee.

She, Frances, arranged her dress and sat up primly, hands folded in her lap.

'Do you wish me to remain standing?' Biddy asked.

'Stand or sit, Mrs Baverstock, it is all the same to me.'

'My name is Quigley. Why do you call me Baverstock?'

'A slip of the tongue,' the old woman replied. 'Take a pew: that one.'

Biddy seated herself cautiously on the edge of a fragile-looking chair. She was no lightweight these days but she felt dwarfed by the widow. The chair, she realised, had been cleverly placed to put her at a disadvantage. She could not quite see Frances without turning her head. She was aware of the younger woman, however, of her uncharacteristic stillness and silence; of the older woman, Dorothea, she could not help but be aware, for she had been positioned directly before her, eye almost to eye.

Her confidence dented only a little, Biddy seized the initiative.

'I believe you wish to purchase a portion of my estate?'

'No, I wish to purchase all of it,' said Dorothea Lafferty.

'May I ask why?'

'May *I* ask,' said Dorothea, 'why it's taken you so long to find me?'

'Possibly because I did not know that you were an interested party.'

'Rattenbury tell you?'

'Patrick did not tell me.'

'What he told me was that you won't part with a single acre until you know who's behind the offer. I reckoned I'd have to give in sooner or later.'

'Give in?' said Biddy. 'What is there to "give in" to, Mrs Lafferty?'

'Questions, questions,' Dorothea said.

'Answer, answers, that's the point we've reached,' Frances put in. 'Mama, Mama, don't you see you've been rumbled? Tell her what she wants to know or you'll never have your damned house and we'll be stuck here for ever.'

Biddy said, 'In case you suppose that Patrick betrayed a professional confidence, I assure you that he didn't. He doesn't know we're meeting today or even that I know who you are.'

'Who am I then?' said Dorothea.

Biddy said, 'I believe that you're a friend of an old acquaintance of mine and that you may – may – be acting on his behalf.'

'I'm acting on nobody's behalf.'

'Isn't Iain Carbery lurking somewhere in the wings?' said Biddy.

'Angel wings,' said Frances.

'Enough out of you, missy.' Dorothea gripped the ash-wood stick and eased her body forward. 'Iain's dead, that's what she means.'

'Oh!' said Biddy, blinking. 'Ah!'

'Been gone from us for the best part of five years,' Dorothea went on.

'I didn't – I mean – nobody thought to inform me,' said Biddy.

She was shaken by the news. Somehow she had always believed that Iain Carbery was out there in the world and that one day he would return to Mull, not to impose upon her, not to *assume*, but merely to remind her how much fun they had had together and how much he still adored her.

Iain dead! She could hardly believe it.

His name had cropped up in just one of Dorothea's letters and, intrigued, Biddy had woven a theory out of the reference: that Dorothea Lafferty was behind Patrick, and Iain behind Dorothea Lafferty. She could not imagine by what route fate had brought Iain into her life again but she had been comforted by the fact that he might become the owner of Fetternish. It would have been quite fitting, if a little ironic, for Iain to get the better of her.

Now she'd learned that Iain was dead and that part of her past had gone with him; her mouth went dry and her eyes became moist.

She blinked once more.

'You ain't gonna cry, are you?' Dorothea Lafferty said.

'It is – I admit, it is a shock.'

'He shot himself,' said Frances.

'He did what?'

'Stuck a gun in his mouth in a hotel room south of Chicago and blew his brains all over the wallpaper,' Dorothea said. 'I found the body.'

'But why, why did he do it?' Biddy said. 'Was he bankrupt?'

'Iain was rolling in money,' said Frances, far too lightly. 'Rich as Creosote was our Mr Carbery. He did it for love. That's what it's all about, Mrs Q all about love. Ask her and she'll tell you. She hasn't much option, after all.'

'Is it true?' said Biddy.

The old woman nodded. She inched forward, pressing her knees together as if to erase the painful memory by one more immediate and demanding.

'It's true,' she said.

'I almost married Iain,' Biddy said. 'If he had not been so—'

Biddy had sense enough to cut off the explanation. How could she possibly explain that Iain had been an agent of the Baverstock-Pauls, that he had fallen in love with her and had sacrificed himself and his profits for her sake. How could she tell this stranger that Iain would have married her if she'd shown just an ounce of forgiveness. She cleared her throat. 'Why did he do it?'

'I told you,' said Frances. 'Out of love.'

'Iain loved me,' said Dorothea Lafferty. 'He was my last love, my one and only, last true love.'

'Balderdash!' said Frances.

There was nothing lugubrious or lubricious in the old woman's voice when she spoke of love; her eyes glinted like mica schist.

Biddy could not imagine Dorothea Lafferty clasped in Iain Carbery's arms. She was willing to accept that the Lafferty woman may once have been attractive, however, and that what she saw now were the ravages of a life lived to the full, a life not wasted but wilfully, passionately squandered.

'Yes,' said Frances, 'it was just unfortunate that you happened to be married to Macklin at the time, Mama.' She moved from the divan, a quick darting little motion that carried her into Biddy's line of sight. 'Ain't it odd, Mama, that all the men in your long, long history seem to pop off at just the right time. No, no, I'm not suggesting that you helped them across the Great Divide, just that they wearied of you rather too quickly, wearied, perhaps, of never having you all to themselves. They just sort of slipped away. Obligingly. At least poor old Carbery was man enough to go out in style.'

'Frances, shut your goddamned mouth.'

Frances would not be deterred. When the woman took a swipe at her with the stick she side-stepped neatly and hid behind the chair.

Breathing heavily, Dorothea Lafferty rested her forearms on her thighs; deflated, Biddy thought, but not defeated.

She said, 'Did you say that Iain was wealthy?'

'Yes,' said Dorothea. 'So it wasn't my money he was after.'

'He couldn't hold a candle to you when the change was counted up, could he, Mama? I mean to say,' said Frances, 'few folk can. First you soaked up Larry's dada's fortune then you inherited another shovelful from Macklin. And Iain's portion too, in the long run.'

'I didn't want Iain's portion; the last thing I wanted was Iain's portion.'

'You just want Iain. Awwww, how sweet!'

'Frances, please, this is no occasion for sarcasm.'

Biddy said, 'How did he make his money? Iain, I mean? He was never very practical, more at home with a gun than an account book.'

'The gold-fields,' said Frances. 'Larry and Iain fought together in Natal. When the war ended Larry borrowed money from his father – who was on his last legs anyway by that time – and invested it in a company that was opening a new field somewhere in Mashonaland. Larry took Iain in with him. They were friends,

you see, chums. Shoulder to shoulder and all that. I think Larry
looked on Mr Carbery as sort of surrogate father.'

'Where is Larry – your husband – now?'

'Lord knows!' said Frances. 'Sailing over the bounding main, I
expect. I don't know, and she doesn't know, and the truth is that
neither of us care. Or, rather, we care too much and can't do
anything about it except pretend that Larry *will* come back to us
one fine day.'

'He will. He promised he would,' Dorothea said.

'Larry seldom keeps his promises.'

'And what about your promises?' Dorothea said.

'I continue to honour and obey him – whenever he's around.'

'Aye, but you won't love him, will you?' Dorothea said.

Biddy intervened. 'Where did you meet Iain?'

'In Cape Town,' said Dorothea.

'Love at first sight,' said Frances. 'But oh no, you wouldn't let
your heart rule your head, would you, Mama? Larry would have
been only too pleased if you'd married Iain Carbery. Instead you
hitched yourself to Macklin Lafferty, *wealthy* Macklin Lafferty.'

'Iain loved me.'

'Wealthy *old* Macklin Lafferty,' Frances added. She leaned on
the back of her mother-in-law's chair and propped her chin in
her hands. 'Iain and Larry sold out their interest in the gold-field
at a fat profit and returned to the United States. Montana first of
all and then Chicago. It was not the place for Larry, or for Iain,
but you wouldn't let him go, would you, Mama, wouldn't leave
him in peace?'

'He loved me. He did love me.'

'Not nearly as much as you loved him,' said Frances. 'Not
nearly as much as he loved this woman here: I mean you, Mrs
Baverstock. *That's* why we're here on Mull and why we stay.'

'Is it?' said Biddy. 'Because of Iain? I don't understand why . . .'

'He never stopped talking about Fetternish as if it were a
paradise on earth. God, some paradise! I've seen Chippewa
villages more civilised. But that was his dream, wasn't it, Mama?

That was the promise you made him, that when Macklin finally popped Iain and you would come back to Mull together, buy an estate, buy the whole blessed island and stroll into the sunset hand in hand. Hah!'

Biddy said, 'Do you really blame me for Iain's suicide?'

'Do not,' said Frances, 'flatter yourself. He didn't kill himself because of you *or* because of her. He was a sick man. Wasting away, rotting from some inherited disease or other. He knew his number was up, that he would never see Scotland let alone Mull again. He took the easy way out. Did the honourable thing.'

'To save me from suffering,' said Dorothea.

'Oh, yes, fine, yes,' said Frances. 'The eternal flame, and all that.'

'What happened to his – to his holdings?' said Biddy.

'Good God!' Frances exclaimed. 'The light of poor Iain Carbery's life turns out to be just as mercenary as the rest of us. She got it. Mama here. She gets everything in the end.'

Biddy got to her feet. Naturally she had assumed that Fetternish was being pursued for its worth and could not possibly have guessed that it was intended as a memorial. She studied Dorothea Lafferty, saw in her the imprint of imminent death, the shadow at her shoulder. There would be no cheating the reaper, no bullet in the brain for her, however: Dorothea Lafferty would exit stage left railing against the darkness, and fighting tooth and claw to the last.

Biddy said, 'If I understand correctly, you want to own Fetternish simply to fulfil a promise to Iain Carbery?'

'To put him to rest,' said Frances. 'Finally, for ever, to have him all to herself.'

'Where is he buried?' said Biddy.

'Buried? He isn't buried,' said Frances. 'He's here, right here.'

'What? I'm sorry. I don't follow your meaning,' Biddy said.

The young woman moved across the drawing-room and reaching up to the mantelshelf brought down an electro-silver-plated urn the size and shape of a large coffee pot. She grasped it firmly, without respect, in both dainty hands.

'Iain,' she declared. 'His mortal remains.'

'Please,' Dorothea said, 'be careful.'

'We had him cremated, didn't we, Mama? Had Iain reduced to manageable size so that we could fetch him back to dear old Fetternish.' She gave the urn a little shake. 'Ashes to ashes, Iain, hmm? Well, here she is, *your* one true love, old chap, come to pay homage at last.'

'Don't be disgusting,' Dorothea said.

There was, it seemed, a limit to how far Frances would push her mother-in-law. She turned and replaced the urn carefully on the shelf above the fireplace, turned again, smiling.

'Now you know all, Mrs Bav— Mrs Quigley. What do you say? Do we get the house or do we not?'

'If you wish to scatter Iain's ashes on . . .' Biddy began.

'No, no. No, no, no,' said Frances. 'Scatter Iain to the four winds? Never! He will rest only in Fetternish House where Mama can talk to him every day.'

'My house is not for sale,' Biddy said.

'Everything is for sale,' said Frances.

'You can't force me out,' said Biddy.

'I thought you wanted rid of the place?' Dorothea said.

'Land, yes, but not my home.'

'What will you do when it's ringed with trees?' Dorothea said. 'Because in a year or two it will be. If you imagine that you'll find another bidder for your scraps of land, let me tell you that you won't. Nobody will make you an offer that approaches mine. Perhaps I can't force you out or buy you out but I can starve you out, Biddy Baverstock, or whatever you call yourself. One day in the not too dim and distant future I intend to live in Fetternish House.' She tapped her stick on the floor. 'I'm patient. I can be *very* patient when necessary. If you won't sell me the house right now I'm sure you will sell me some of the land. You can hardly refuse an offer like the one Patrick will make you when he comes back. Then you can sit in your castle, financially secure, and watch the trees growing all around you and be goddamned sure that one day I'll consume you just as they will.'

'It's not what Iain would have wanted,' Biddy said.

'Perhaps not,' said Dorothea, 'but it's what I want, and what I will have.'

'If you live long enough, Mama.'

'Have no fear about that, honey,' the old woman said. 'I'll outlive you if I have to.' She raised her head and smiled at Biddy. 'You won't be able to pay off all your debts, Biddy Baverstock, for there ain't no way you can pay what you owe Iain Carbery. You broke a man's heart and my heart too and I'll not rest, nor will I die, until I make you pay for it.'

'By offering me a fortune for An Fhearann Cáirdeil?'

'That's only the beginning,' Dorothea Lafferty said.

Biddy drew in a deep breath and glanced at the urn on the shelf above the fireplace. It looked well in this room: functional shape, fluted handles, roundness reflecting the picture windows. She could not visualise the object in Fetternish House, lost in the vast hallway, out of place in the gloomy drawing-room. The best place for Iain Carbery's ashes was really the moor. Scattered over the heather, he would be happy and free then, if the dead needed freedom at all.

'I suppose you'll go off in the sulks?' Dorothea said. 'Bite your nail and keeping me waiting for another half-year or so?'

'No,' Biddy said. 'I think I'm inclined to accept your offer – in principle.'

'Sell me Fetternish?' the old woman said, surprised.

'A modest part of it,' said Biddy. 'For Iain's sake, not yours.'

'A modest part of it,' said Dorothea Lafferty, 'will do for a start.'

'I can be patient too, you know,' said Biddy. 'You'll never get the house.'

'Won't I?' Madam Lafferty said. 'Well, we'll just have to wait and see.'

'When will Patrick present your offer?'

'As soon as he returns from Perthshire.'

'And when will that be?'

'Soon.'

'Not soon enough, Biddy, hmm?' Frances said. 'Not soon enough for you.'

She drove slowly back from The Ards in early afternoon sunshine. Now that the school had closed for the holidays there were children in the fields helping with early harvest, gathering the patches of oats and barley that had ripened already or hay that had been left late. She saw them from afar, miniaturised against the broad expanse of the hillside or – Barrett's lot – spread along the foreshore by the whitewashed cottage that was briefly visible through the tall, uncultivated trees.

She felt strangely satisfied with her meeting with Dorothea Lafferty. With Michael gone, and Iain too, she experienced a curious sense of peace. It was as if she had deliberately set out to exorcise the ghosts of men who had meant so much to her and was left, centred at last, with Willy and Quig and, God willing, Patrick Rattenbury to inaugurate another new phase in her life.

She refused to be intimidated by the lovelorn old imposter who would probably not last long in any case. She felt sure that Frances Hollander, with or without her errant husband, would not stay on Mull one minute longer than was necessary after Dorothea passed away. She was confident that she would be the winner in the long run, and that Iain – or his mortal remains – would never squat glumly on the shelf above the hearth in Fetternish or claim pride of place on top of the piano in the drawing-room. There would be something comical about that, something farcical and sad, quite in keeping with the man she remembered.

She would tell Willy what had happened – but not Quig. She was out of kilter with Quig at the moment. She resented the time he was spending on Fay Ludlow. Instead she'd talk it over with Willy, swear him to secrecy. He would be amused to learn what had become of Carbery. He would also be scornful of the Lafferty woman's motives for setting up camp on Mull. She had neglected Willy Naismith for far too long, for he, more than anyone, understood her.

She drove the pony-trap into the yard and got out.

She went directly into the kitchen where she found Maggie cutting up beef for a stew. Becky was upstairs, airing beds. A broth pot simmered on the stove and an egg dish was baking in the oven, ready for late lunch. She would not eat in the kitchen. She would have her lunch served in the dining-room and would invite Willy to sup with her so that she might have him all to herself.

'Where is my husband?' she asked.

'Out in the fields, I expect,' Maggie answered.

'And Willy?'

'Where he always is,' said Maggie. 'In the garden with Aileen, waiting for me to shout them in for their lunch.'

'I wish to talk with him.'

'Talk with him then,' said Maggie, with a busy shrug. 'Will you be needing the pony-trap this afternoon?'

'No.'

'Then I'll take it back to Angus and walk home again.'

'Good,' said Biddy and, still buoyant, went out into the yard and across it to the little gate in the garden wall to find her confidant.

They were seated together on the rustic bench in the patch of sunlight that fell between the tower and gable wall: Aileen's patch, Aileen's place. Her sister had on an old straw bonnet and her jacket was worn about her shoulders like a cloak: her customary tinkerish look, not dishevelled so much as shabby. Her head was tilted back and her eyes were closed, though Biddy knew that she was not asleep. She held Willy's right hand with her left.

Willy was asleep, however, the scant tuft of hair above his left ear resting gently on Aileen's shoulder.

'Willy,' Biddy whispered. 'Willy, waken up. Lunch is ready.'

Aileen opened her eyes.

Biddy stepped back in alarm then stepped forward again and, with Aileen watching her, shook Willy's arm.

His head slid loose and sluggish, his ear trailing against Aileen's breast. He hung there limply until Biddy shook him again, then, just as he began to fall forward, Aileen caught him. She looked at the face close up to her own and smiled. Then she looked up at Biddy and in her sister's impenetrable gaze, Biddy recognised the truth.

'Oh, God!' she exclaimed. 'Oh, God!' and lifting her face to the sky let out a great long mournful wail while Aileen, still smiling, patted Willy Naismith's lifeless cheek and crooned, 'There, there. There, there.'

SIXTEEN

A Moment of Madness

They sat cross-legged on the grass at the edge of the plots and studied her without embarrassment. They were not small boys, however, and had been raised in a vigorous rural tradition that had endowed them early with a knowledge of the more demeaning facts of life.

'Is it sore?' Billy enquired.

'No, not sore,' Fay answered, 'but it's not awfully comfortable.'

'My mother was sick all the time with our Marion,' Billy said.

'I've hardly been sick at all.'

'Apparently, the baby presses on the stomach as it grows,' said Robbie, 'and on the bladder. The internal organs have to yield to accommodate . . . Sorry, I shouldn't discuss such things in female company.'

'Is this what they are teaching in school these days?' said Fay.

'My father told me all about it years ago.'

'At the lambing it was,' said Billy. 'I was there too, remember.'

'Why is your husband not with you, Fay?' Robbie said.

'She ran away.' Billy clapped a hand to his mouth. 'Sorry.'

'It's true,' Fay said. 'I did run away.'

'Why, if I might be so bold?' said Robbie.

'Because he was a cruel man and I was frightened for the baby.'

'Gavin's my cousin, you know, but we've never met and in the light of what I've learned about him I have absolutely no desire to get to know him now.'

'Who told you about him?' Fay asked. 'Your daddy?'

'I got the information from my other cousin, Donnie, when he came over for Willy's funeral.'

'Donnie did not stay long this visit, did he?' said Billy.

'No, he left Tricia and the family in Glasgow. He said that they'd had enough of Mull for a while and preferred to take a holiday closer to home. My mother was most put out.' Robbie hesitated. 'Will you be the same after the baby's born, Fay?'

'Of course,' Fay said, then frowned. 'Well, perhaps not quite the same. I'll be a mother, and mothers are not quite the same as other women.'

'I mean your — your shape?'

'Nature sees to that,' said Fay. 'I'll be just the same as before, yes.'

'Good!' said Robbie. 'I'm glad.'

'Are you? Why?'

'I wouldn't like you to change.'

'I'm flattered.'

'I like you too, Fay,' said Billy, not to be outdone. 'I am not even minding very much that you are all swollen up.'

'Thank you, Billy, that's very nice of you,' Fay told him.

The boys had come down to Pennypol to help lift the potatoes. They had worked hard and the job had been completed quickly. But Fay was disappointed in the volume of the crop and had begun to realise that expertise and enthusiasm would never compensate for acreage and extra hands.

Quig had helped her take up lettuce and carrots and extract most of the leeks. He had boxed the vegetables and carted them off to market in Oban — or so he claimed. Fay did not believe him. When he informed her that he had turned a little profit on his investment she knew that he was lying just to appease her. Potatoes were stored everywhere at Fetternish House, carrots and lettuce too. And on the afternoon of Willy Naismith's funeral, Becky informed her, the mourners had been treated to a feast of cooked vegetables, more than anyone could possibly consume.

It was tempting to let the garden go, allow the fence to sag, weeds sprout in the rows and the strawberry plants wither for lack of water. But Fay was a gardener by vocation and had learned valuable lessons from her first brush with commerce.

'When are you off to Oban, Billy?'

'At the weekend.'

'And you, Robbie?' Fay asked. 'When do you return to school?'

'Oh, I'm going back early to Edinburgh to set up with a crammer for a week or two. This is my final year and then I hope to obtain entry to a university, possibly Cambridge, depending on the current state of finances. I'm off in a couple of days, in fact.'

'Come to think of it, I haven't seen much of your sister,' Billy said.

'Christina only stayed for a day or two then set her course for Haddington,' said Robbie. 'She's gone to spend the rest of the holiday with a school-friend there. Christina is much happier hobnobbing with lords and ladies than with mere nymphs and shepherds.'

'Nymphs?' said Billy.

'Figure of speech, old chap, figure of speech.'

In two or three years, five at most, Mull would be a fading memory for the shepherd's son, Fay thought, and for Robbie too if the rumours that Biddy was planning to sell Fetternish proved true.

She looked at the young men seated cross-legged on the grass: dirty hands, grubby boots, shirt sleeves rolled up. Soon they would grow tall, fill out, tower over her. She would seem to become younger as they grew older, until there came a time when they would all be equal, when age levelled them out again.

Robbie got to his feet. He slapped his hands on his thighs and rubbed them up and down. 'Well, I must be toddling, I'm afraid. I'm obliged to pay calls on Gillies Brown and the Ewings before I go. Angus is bringing the trap out at three o'clock.' He paused, awkwardly. 'I'll be saying goodbye, Fay, and wishing you – what do I wish you? What is the polite thing?'

'Well,' said Fay. 'Well is better than good luck.'

Robbie laughed. 'I wish you well then. Thank you.'

Billy scrambled to his feet. 'If we are done here,' he said, 'I will be walking with you as far as the hill, Robbie.'

Fay sensed that they were moving on, that their maleness somehow excluded her, not intentionally but with the carelessness of young men.

'Will you be able to walk back to Pennymain on your own?' Billy asked.

'Of course I will.'

'I expect that the spuds will be snug enough in the cottage until my father sends a cart to collect them,' said Robbie.

'I'm sure they will,' said Fay. 'Go on. I know you both have things to do.'

They nodded, cocked their heads, then they went off together, walking side by side along the line of the drystone wall, up through the weed-strewn park and up again to the edge of the bracken that surged off the ridge.

Wistfully, Fay watched them shake hands and part and go their separate ways. And then, quite wearily, she sat down again to wait for Quig.

Since the day of Willy's funeral in the graveyard behind the kirk Biddy had gone into retreat. She had been more affected by the old man's passing than Maggie whose practicality amounted almost to callousness. Willy had been a good husband, Maggie declared, but he was better away quick since he had outlived his usefulness.

The week of the funeral had been hectic. Fetternish House

had been full to overflowing. Muriel Barrett and her eldest daughter had been conscripted to help in the kitchens. Becky had been promoted to chief cook for the course of the day Maggie devoted to mourning. Donnie had whisked in, cool and haughty. Two sons and three of Willy's daughters had also made the crossing. They were fine men and women, not young themselves, but they seemed to have inherited the old man's dry sense of humour so that the visit was spoiled for Biddy by a degree of hilarity that she considered almost sacrilegious.

Christina had been lofty and impatient, Robbie suitably solemn. Rachel had been unable to free herself from hospital duty but had despatched by carrier not a wreath or flowers but a huge bottle of whisky for the mourners to toast the old man's memory, a gesture of which Willy would surely have approved. Innis had the imminent arrival of a grandchild to distract her and, curiously, only Becky had had to be led away from the graveyard in floods of tears.

By noon on Friday all the guests had departed, Maggie was back in harness and household routines closed swiftly over Willy's memory. Even Aileen displayed no bewilderment at his absence but took to following Maggie about, crooning and chirping as she had always done.

Then there was nothing left to do but await delivery of the marble headstone that Biddy had ordered by letter from the mason's yard in Oban.

Maggie went back to her pots and saucepans.

Innis went back to Pennymain to look after Fay.

And Biddy went into the library with six or eight boxes of letters and papers that she collected from office and attics and, with all the facts and figures gathered around her, remained there, more or less undisturbed, for the best part of a week.

'She wants to talk to you privately,' Quig said.

'What on earth for?' said Robbie. 'She saw me at dinner and hardly said a word. In fact, Dad, she has hardly said a word to me all holiday. Christina was wise to leave when she did and I must confess that I won't be entirely sorry to get back to school a little in advance of term.'

'What about the Fair Maid of Pennypol, won't you be sorry to leave her?'

'Dad!' Robbie sighed. 'The woman is eight months gone.'

'Yes, I am sorry, son. It was a stupid thing to say.'

Robbie rolled over on the sofa in the great hall and peered at the closed door of the library. 'Does Mama really want to talk to me?'

'I am afraid she does.'

'What's wrong with her? It can't be Willy's death that's thrown her into this terrible mood. I mean, after all, he was an old man and had to go some time.'

'Your mother loved Willy.'

'Really!'

'She depended upon him.'

'I thought she depended on you.'

'It has not been an easy time for us lately.'

'I'm not a child, Dad,' Robbie said. 'I know how difficult Mother's been these past few years.'

'She has much on her mind.'

'And will not allow you to share her worries. I find that awfully odd, you know, considering that you're her husband.'

'Well,' Quig said, 'she does not go trusting me to do what she wants all the time. Her streak of Campbell stubbornness comes out when she is crossed.'

'Crossed about what? About money?' Robbie tossed aside the copy of *The Times* that Hermann, without intervention, had delivered straight to the front door. He stretched, and glanced once more at the library. 'Why do I have the feeling that Mother is going to put me on the spot?'

'Because she probably is,' said Quig.

* * *

Boxes were piled beneath the bookcases and Biddy was seated behind a scarred Jacobean table that her first husband had bought from an unscrupulous dealer in Dundee. Placed on the table were an ink-stand, a pewter drinking mug containing pens and pencils, a large portfolio fastened with ribbon, and a tidy little sheaf of foolscap paper.

Biddy had her back to the window and seemed to her son as still and grey as the cloud that pressed down on the sea. She was wearing her 'middling-best' dress, a long-sleeved satin thing with very little trimming; no jewellery at all except a cameo brooch at her breast.

Robbie entered jauntily in the hope of lightening the mood, which was, he quickly realised, a mistake.

'Be seated, Robbie, if you please.' His mother indicated a chair.

Robbie hitched up his trousers, seated himself four-square.

'I believe you wanted a word with me.'

'You're leaving tomorrow, aren't you?'

'I am,' he said. 'Dad thinks an uninterrupted period of cramming will do me no end of good come end of term. Finals, you know.'

'Are you packed?'

'Yes, Maggie helped me.'

'I've been much occupied – as you may have noticed – with other matters,' Biddy said. 'I've decided to sell a portion of the estate to Louden, Lafferty and Spruell, and have been busy calculating the value of the land together with the properties that the company will require to house foresters.'

'So it is to be trees then. What does Dad have to say about that?'

'I'll discuss it with your father when the time is ripe,' Biddy said. 'I felt it only proper to tell you first. Fetternish is, after all, your birthright.'

'What about the house? Are you going to sell the house too?'

'The house?' His mother seemed startled. 'What have you heard . . .'

'Nothing,' said Robbie. 'I just thought you might decide to make a perfectly clean break and put the house into the pot with the rest of it.'

'The house is ours. It will remain ours, no matter who tries to wrest it away from us. In due course it will be yours, Robbie, then it will be up to you to decide what to do with it.'

'I'll keep it in the family,' said Robbie. 'Isn't that what you want me to do? Does Dad have no say in the matter?'

'You are my son, Robbie, and this is my house. Your father will, of course, be informed.'

'Informed? You make it sound as if you and Dad are at loggerheads.'

'No, that's not so.'

Robbie had never been in awe of his mother. He loved her in a manner beyond defining – but he did not like her very much. He was faintly aware that eventually he might have to take her under his wing and look after her and for that reason he did not feel inclined to challenge her authority; nor did he feel up to telling her that he was more interested in how much the family would make from the sale than in the fate of the estate at some nebulous point in the future.

'Whatever you decide to do I will stand by you,' Robbie said.

It sounded suitably mature and sincere; he was proud of his diplomacy.

'Do you mean that, Robbie?'

'Of course I do.'

She looked at him without rancour, seeing in him perhaps the shadow of his natural father, Michael Tarrant. Although she loved him deeply she was glad that he was leaving early, for she did not wish either of her children to be present when she did what she had to do.

Robbie said, 'As a matter of interest, what sort of sum are we talking about here, apropos the sale?'

'There are close to nine hundred acres at An Fhearann Cáirdeil,' Biddy said. 'Three thousand pounds would be a reasonable offer but I will ask for more if the standing properties are included.'

'By properties I assume you mean the stables and the vacant cottages?'

'Yes.'

'Will Mr Rattenbury stay on to manage the plantation?'

'Why do you ask?' said Biddy.

'If he's employed to manage the plantation perhaps he'll rent the stables for himself?'

Biddy brushed a coil of hair from her cheek, paused, then said, 'I have no information on when or how the company intend to begin fencing and draining, or even if Patrick – if Mr Rattenbury will be put in charge. Do you approve of me selling off a piece of Fetternish?'

'If it makes you happy, Mother, of course I do. If it solves our financial problems and stops you worrying about money then I'm all for it.' He looked round, turning from the waist with a litheness than Biddy envied. 'Is Dad against it? Is that why you and he are at loggerheads?'

'Fetternish is registered in my name, not his.'

Robbie nodded, then said, 'It's a pity Willy died just when he did, isn't it?'

'Willy?' Biddy sat up. 'What does Willy have to do with it?'

'You'd have listened to Willy, wouldn't you?' Robbie said. 'I mean, it would have been useful to have Willy's guidance and advice. You always relied on the old boy, Mother, don't deny it.'

'If I did – well, it hardly matters now. Willy's no longer here.'

'Be none of us here soon,' Robbie said. 'None of the old crowd.'

'What do you mean by "the old crowd"? I hope you don't mean me?'

'The older generation,' said Robbie. 'Grandmother's generation.'

He was anxious to leave, to get out of the gloomy library and into the great hall again. Something about his mother dismayed him: intensity or vagueness, he could not decide which. He could not imagine what more she wanted from him. It could hardly be approval; he had already given that. He stirred restlessly on the chair, hoping that she would end the interview soon and release him.

He cleared his throat.

'I do have some packing to finish, Mama, if you've no more to tell me.'

'You don't care, Robbie, do you? About Fetternish, about me?'

'Oh, Mama, that's dreadfully unfair. Of course I care about you.'

'I love you, Robbie,' Biddy said. 'I want you to remember that. I love you and always will, no matter what.' She waved her hand dismissively. 'Go on with you. Go and finish your packing. I'll see you at breakfast.'

'Do you want me to send Dad in?'

'No,' Biddy said. 'That I do not.'

He was waiting in the hall, seated on the sofa, leaning forward, hands between his knees. He swivelled when Robbie emerged from the drawing-room and peered at his son. 'What did she want with you?'

'She's selling Fetternish,' Robbie said. 'A large part of it at least.'

'I thought she would,' said Quig and, without another word, got to his feet and went out by the front door into the falling darkness.

It had been silly of her to struggle across the hill to Pennypol. She had fed the poultry, washed up the breakfast dishes and tidied the garden in front of the cottage before she had set out for the plots.

It was hot for late August. Talk of an Indian summer meant that she might need to water the crops still in the ground and when her time came would have to depend on Quig to see to it that the plants did not shrivel. There might be no Indian summer, of course. Weather was notoriously fickle – Mr Musson had told her to set no store by rumour or traditional methods of prediction – and all she could say for sure was that the day was sticky and sultry and that the clouds over the mountains had a leaden heaviness that mimicked her own lethargy.

Rabbits were nibbling at the weeds along the line of fence and she walked around the fence kicking in the mounds that the rabbits had scraped up and packing them down again. She was hot, very hot, boiling up in fact. She looked longingly at the sea and the isles that lay offshore, the little green shell shapes that seemed so cool and grassy out where the waves broke and the sea rippled blue and dark under a soft offshore breeze.

She could hardly catch her breath in the clammy air. Her stomach seemed to have risen up and be pressing on her lungs. Mrs MacNiven had advised her to rest in these last days but she had plots to attend to and plants to water and did not want to appear lazy, not to Innis, not to Quig.

She fished out the watering-can and limped up the path to the burn. There, on her knees, she dipped the can deep and hauled it, dripping, from the pool.

The pool had diminished, sinking under arches of turf. She could see the bottom plainly and she wondered what would happen if the stream dried up. She had heard stories of the great drought of '83 when water had had to be purchased from the Duke of Argyll and carted in barrels overland to keep stock alive, and how, that year, the corn crops and barley had burned up and many families had fallen into debt.

August now, August almost out: the rains would surely come

soon, the frequent, familiar rains that drenched the north quarter, pulled down by the high hills. She glanced towards Ben Talla and Ben More, hidden behind the hunch of the headland. She knew where the big hills lay, for she had developed a sense of the place. She watched the clouds drift in soft, thick, sluggish layers for a moment and then reached for the watering-can, grabbing at the wet handle as it slid away from her – and felt the first stab of pain.

She drew back, crouched, as pain radiated down into her thighs. When she tried to stand upright it seized her across the small of the back like a vice.

She was startled by the abruptness of it all, frightened by the emptiness around her.

She crawled backward from the pool on to the shoulder of the burn.

She had learned from Mrs MacNiven the rota of labour but had anticipated that her contractions would be gradual, not sudden and insistent. She tried to stand up again and as she did so felt a little fluid deluge map a course on her thighs. She stared down her lap and saw staining on her thin cotton skirt.

She cried out, leaned forward, breathed in smudged little hoots as if trying to blow out a candle. She was beginning to suspect that she had ignored the premonitory signs and was well into what Mrs MacNiven called 'the second stage'. When the pain dwindled slightly she relaxed, got her knees under her and lofted herself upright.

Her lame leg hurt more than her back or her stomach. She clenched her teeth and forced herself down the path towards the cottage. It did not occur to her that the Barretts' cottage was closer than Pennymain. She was focused only on Pennymain, on Innis, on Quig. She wanted them to be with her when her baby came, Quig, Innis and the midwife – no one else.

She wrapped her forearms under her stomach and walked with tiny mincing steps, pressing her thighs together, feeling them rub and slide in a weirdly comforting rhythm. The contractions – if contractions they were – had eased with 'the show'. Yes, she remembered: no expulsion unless she willed it. I'm all right, she told herself. It's all natural and right. I'll walk home to Innis and she will make it all right. Quig will send for Mrs MacNiven and she will make it all come right.

She passed the ruined cottage and followed the line of grass above the fence to the drystone wall. Pain came creeping up again. She tried to pretend that it wasn't pain at all, just the strain of walking upright.

She squeezed her fists into her abdomen and kept on walking, kept putting one foot in front of the other, bracing the weak knee before she put her weight on it. The pain did not diminish. It was not knife-like, not sharp but dull and resonating like being struck repeatedly by a mallet.

Dripping with sweat, she removed one hand from her stomach to wipe her brow and, leaving the shelter of the wall, set off along the track to round the hill by the back way. Then she stopped, bowed forward, hands on her thighs as another crab-claw of pain gripped her low down. She breathed and gasped, saw sweat drip on to the grass beyond the swell of her belly.

'Billy,' she cried, though she knew that Billy had gone to Oban. 'Bill-eeeee.'

There wasn't a soul in sight on the moor.

She was dimly aware of cattle bellowing on the foreshore.

She cried out again, urgently this time, 'Quig, Quig, Quig, Quig,' then, desperate and foolish, stumbled off the footpath and up into the bracken that coated the shoulder of Olaf's Hill.

'What is it that is wrong with that damned dog?' Quig said. 'I have never seen him so agitated.'

'Fay spoils him.' Innis's reply was muffled by a wooden clothes-peg in her mouth. She was hanging out smallware, towelling strips and minute woollen garments that she had knitted for the baby. 'Fay plays with him when he should be having training.'

'He is the daftest dog I have ever seen,' said Quig.

He followed Innis around the washing-line holding the clothes basket. If Barrett had come striding over the hill, he would have dropped it immediately, for laundry was menial work, women's work. Maggie Naismith would have thought him mad if he had laid a hand on a laundry basket, let alone peg clothes on the drying ropes. Innis did not think less of him for helping out. She had Gillies Brown well trained in domestic chores; or perhaps the trainer had been Janetta which, now that Quig thought of it, seemed much more likely.

'Kilty, will you kindly stop whining,' Quig said, not harshly.

The spaniel ignored him. He squatted on the path ten or twelve feet from the gate, his eyes fixed on the hillside on the far side of the pasture. He whined in his throat and, now and then, growled as if he had caught wind of an intruder.

'What is it you hear?' Innis said. 'Is it a fox up there?'

'There are no foxes in this part of the quarter,' Quig said. 'He is just intent on making a fool of himself.'

Then, suddenly, the spaniel leaped forward, balanced his forepaws on the wicket and set up an unholy barking.

Quig dropped the basket to the grass and advanced upon the dog.

'Kilty, what do you hear out there? What is it, boy?'

Quig cocked his head, listening, heard nothing but the barking dog and a long, low, purr of thunder, too indistinct to be threatening.

'Is it not time that Fay was back?' Quig said.

Innis took the peg from her mouth and, with one little garment left hanging by a sleeve, studied the hillside too.

'Are you thinking it is Fay he hears?'

'I am thinking it might be,' Quig said.

The dog stopped barking. He seemed to weigh up his capabilities, then with a hop that was both supple and incredibly dainty, he leaped clean over the top of the gate and shot off in a beeline for the hill.

It was mid-afternoon when Biddy arrived at the stables.

Maggie had told her that Patrick was back on Mull. Maggie had received the news from her brother, Angus Bell, who had been down in Tobermory that morning and had seen Patrick Rattenbury walking in the direction of Ardmore, probably to pick up his horse from the livery.

Biddy had received the information about half past noon and had gone upstairs to bathe and change: nothing too floral, her newest tweed skirt, the blouse with the mutton sleeves and tightly buttoned cuffs. She had applied no cosmetics but had spent a considerable time on her hair, brushing and twisting it into shapes that were neither too decorative nor too severe. She settled at last for a broad blood-red ribbon and two pins, then, in riding boots not shoes, set off for a confrontation with Madam Lafferty's lackey.

She had no fear of meeting her husband: Quig was down at Pennymain again, fussing over Fay as if he were her father, or the father of her child.

The stallion was stalled in the stable yard, groomed and glossy and as bad-tempered as ever. He stamped and screamed at her as she crossed the cobbles.

The racket brought Patrick to the door.

He was dressed in a clean striped shirt without collar and a pair of smart new trousers held up by braces. He had obviously been shaving. Flecks of soap, like snowflakes, clung to his earlobes. He held a towel in one hand and peered out at her, scowling. 'I didn't think you'd have the gall to show your face here, Biddy,' he said. 'At least not so soon.'

'Aren't you going to let me in?'

'For what? To rifle through my papers and poke about in the drawers?' he said. 'In any case, I have a previous engagement.'

'Oh, do you?' Biddy said. 'With your mistress, no doubt.'

'My mistress?'

'The Lafferty woman, the widow Lafferty who you were so very careful to say nothing about.'

'No,' Patrick said, 'not with the Lafferty woman.'

'She informed you, of course, that she and I have had words?'

'You'd better come in,' Patrick said.

He stood back from the door and allowed her to enter. There was luggage on the floor, an oblong hamper, a valise, a fishing-rod cased in oilcloth. His coat was draped on a chair-back and his collar, tie and studs were on the kitchen table along with a bowl of shaving water, a brush and a cut-throat razor.

The clutter made the kitchen seem more homely, more permanent.

Patrick wiped his face, tossed the towel on to the table.

'Do you always perform your toilet in the kitchen?' Biddy asked.

'Where I perform my toilet is no business of yours.'

'It's my house. You are my tenant.'

'Not for much longer, perhaps.'

'Not for much longer?' She brought herself up and looked at him directly. 'Are you moving out, Patrick, or moving in?'

'Moving in.'

'To be at Madam Lafferty's beck and call, no doubt.'

'I don't want to quarrel with you, Biddy,' he said. 'We'll have to do business together and it is better if it's done amicably. I must say, though, I'm disappointed in you. Didn't you trust me to deal fairly with you?'

'I doubt if you know what that means, Patrick. Why didn't you tell me about the Lafferty woman – and Iain Carbery?'

'I felt it advisable to let that particular dog sleep.'

'Did you, indeed? That was not for you to decide.'

'What was this chap to you?'

Biddy pursed her lips and pushed the words at him like soap bubbles. 'My lover. Iain was my lover. There! Does that shock you?'

'Not in the slightest.'

'At least Iain didn't try to seduce me into selling my house to a mad woman.'

'Ah! So that's what you think, is it?' Patrick leaned against the edge of the table, legs crossed at the ankle. His feet were bare, Biddy noticed, elegant feet, white as marble, with just a little grey dust on each sole. 'I did not deceive you; and I most certainly did not seduce you.'

'No? What about that escapade at An Fhearann Cáirdeil? What did that amount to if it wasn't seduction?'

'It had nothing whatsoever to do with Madam Lafferty.'

'I don't believe you.'

'What will it take to make you . . .'

He came forward suddenly, caught her in his arms and tugged her to him.

'This?' he said thickly. 'Or this?'

He kissed her hard on the lips.

She opened her mouth instantly and let his tongue enter.

He held her, kissing her, probing her, then drew back.

'Or this?' he said.

He thrust his hand upward against her stomach, fingers spread. He pressed against the rounded flesh of her belly and laid his thumb into the vee that her skirt and underclothes made between her thighs.

'If I had wanted to . . .'

'What?' Biddy said. 'If you had wanted to, what would you have done?'

He turned her against him, mouth against mouth, tongue wet against tongue. She yielded, heavy, angry and filled with need. She could no more resist what he offered her than she could fly.

He unbuttoned her blouse, pushed it down across her shoulders, kissed her shoulders, slipped his fingers under the scalloped edge of her bodice and sought her breast. Below, she felt his hand nuzzle and burrow into her thighs. He was not calculating now, was not the widow's lackey doing the widow's business. He was her lover, her redeemer. He wanted her because she was irresistible.

He lifted her clothes so that he could stroke the bare flesh of her thighs: too much, too much clutter, too many folds and fabrics. She wanted him to take all her clothes off, to be raw and rough with her, to reduce her to the state of heedless wickedness that she had known when she was young.

'Not – not here,' she said, gasping. 'We might . . .'

He angled her round once more, edging her hips against the table's edge. He put his hands down and pushed her knees apart.

She tilted awkwardly against him, then, in a rush of impatience, reached out and clasped him by the small of the back, snared him and pulled him into her. She felt him nuzzle against the silks, rub and chafe and then, like a small, shockingly hot splash of oil against her skin, the sensation of his nakedness, not pliant but demanding. He rocked against her carefully, teasingly, touching himself to her then drawing back, touching again and then, at last, forcing himself into and around the silken folds of her underclothing.

He continued to cup her breast, his thumb moving almost casually over her nipple. He kissed her on the side of the neck, whispered into her ear, not sweet nothings but a question, a single, simple question to which Biddy unhesitatingly answered, 'Yes.'

The ruler was a yard long, a work of art in jet-black ebony inset with slivers of ivory that measured distance down to the sixty-fourth part. It was capped with brass ferrules and reposed in a case of dark-green morocco, lined in leaf-green velvet.

Patrick had presented it to her in the classroom and she had laid the case open on her desk for the children to look at and admire.

He had ridden up on the stallion about an hour after bell-time, had knocked and entered the classroom and with not too serious solemnity had presented his gift to the schoolmistress in full view of sixteen gawking infants who, rather to Netta's surprise, had had the wit to cheer when she had opened the case and held it up to view, while Mr Rattenbury had bowed and declared that it was his pleasure to be a benefactor to the school and to the schoolteacher and that yes, he would be delighted to return some other afternoon and demonstrate how the ruler could be used to calculate vast distances.

As demure and schoolmarmish as it was possible to be under the circumstances, Janetta had accompanied Mr Rattenbury to the door.

'I am most grateful,' she'd said. 'Your generosity is overwhelming.'

'It's your gift, Janetta,' he'd said. 'Not school property, remember.'

'Will you come for supper tonight?'

'I'd be delighted,' Patrick Rattenbury had said.

The ruler, still cased, was displayed on the supper-table among the best china and the vase of cut flowers that Janetta had scrounged from the manse garden. The apartment above the school was filled with the aroma of cock-a-leekie soup, beef olives and a cream pancake mixture that was standing to cool by the window.

Janetta primped her hair and nervously tugged at the bow of her apron.

'What time is it, Daddy?'

'Half after six,' Gillies told her.

'Patrick's late.'

'Give the poor man a chance, dearest,' Gillies said. 'He's just back from the mainland and will have much catching up to do.'

'Catching up? What do you mean?'

'No doubt he'll have had to report in to the Hollander woman and she'll have kept him late with her chattering.'

'He told me he was going home.'

'Home? To the stables, you mean? Yes, well . . .' Gillies put down his newspaper and stared out of the window at the hillside. 'I do rather wish he would get his skates on, though: I'm famished.'

Ten minutes passed, then twenty.

Janetta moved the soup pot away from the lid of the stove and ventilated the casserole. She knelt before the oven, knees pressed together, hands wrapped in the folds of the apron.

'Where is he? Oh, where is he?' she murmured and then, getting up, she went into the parlour again. 'Patrick will come, Daddy, won't he?'

'Of course he will,' said Gillies.

'Perhaps I should walk out and see what's become of him.'

'No.' Gillies answered more out of instinct than common sense. 'No, dear, somehow I do not think that would be wise.'

When he had put her on the bed she had been both fierce and frightened but his love-making had been so prolonged that if she had not been in love with him before, she was certainly in love with him now.

She lay back against the bolster and looked up at the small, square window. She could see nothing of the landscape, no inch of Fetternish, only the sky above it and a little bit of banded cloud.

Propped on an elbow, Patrick touched her brow with his fingertip, brushing back a strand of her hair. His chest was broad, the hair that downed his body licked with sweat, for it had been hot in the upstairs room in the glare of the afternoon sun, hot under the bedsheets, and on top of them too.

Biddy lay quite still, quite sated, and allowed him to play with her hair.

Then she said, 'If you were me, Patrick, what would you do?'

'What do you mean?'

'Would you keep me close by?'

He paused, lifting away his fingers, letting his hand hover.

'If I could, yes. Probably.'

She sat up a little. 'Probably?'

'I'm not you,' he said. 'I can't tell you what to do, Biddy.'

'I'm in debt, Patrick. I'm sliding deeper into debt with each quarter. I've secured a loan against the wool crop but the crop will hardly be enough to pay off the interest let alone the capital.'

'This is hardly fitting talk for—'

'No, listen. Listen to me, please.'

'Very well,' Patrick said.

He lay back, an arm over his chest and tried not to let his irritation show. Biddy drew herself closer, brushing his shoulder with her breasts. She was above him now, looking down on him.

'Whatever happens, I won't sell the house, Patrick. I want you to make that absolutely clear to the Lafferty woman. I will not sell the house or the ground around Pennymain.'

'What about Pennypol?'

'Possibly.'

'I thought you were opposed to selling off the shore land?'

'She wants me out. She wants me far away. She wants to transform Fetternish into a shrine for Iain Carbery, which strikes me as bizarre and very unwholesome. I cannot understand it. I mean, yes, for all his faults Iain was a decent enough fellow but he was no Lancelot, no Lochinvar. She has a mad, obsessive streak in her, that woman, don't you agree?'

'I think,' Patrick said, 'that I don't know enough about her, or about Carbery, to offer an opinion.'

'Can't you persuade her to take An Fhearann Cáirdeil off my hands without entailing the house or the acreage at Pennymain?'

'There are legal difficulties about Pennymain.'

'I know. I'm not sure what's involved but it would be better, probably, to leave my sister right where she is. Can you do it, can you persuade her?'

'I don't have to persuade her. Madam Lafferty has already decided to make you an offer for the headland, which is ideal for our purposes.'

'*Our* purposes?'

'For growing timber.'

'Are you in on this with her, Patrick?'

'Only insofar as I will oversee the scheme for the first three years.'

'And stay here? Stay here on Mull?'

'Yes, that's the plan. After that – my parents are growing old and may need more of my attention. But three years, yes, that should see me through.'

'Good!' Biddy said.

She patted the bolster and lay back, hands above her head. She had hardly settled before he stirred. The movement was so abrupt, almost violent, that it startled her. Patrick flung himself from the bed and, casting off the trailing sheet, padded naked across the floorboards to a little chest of drawers. He did not have to open any of the drawers, for the card-backed brown paper envelope was propped against the ewer, hidden behind the water basin.

Biddy watched him, admiring him without desire. He was leaner than he appeared to be when clothed, his back and buttocks shapely, curving in and then out again, down into slender, hair-downed thighs. Some men looked comical in their nakedness; Patrick was not one of them.

He returned with the envelope to the foot of the bed.

'In case,' he said, 'just in case you think that what happened between us has anything to do with Dorothea Lafferty or my employment by her, here, Biddy, is our official offer for eight hundred and eighty acres of land on the peninsula at An Fhearann Cáirdeil. The document is legal, a final contract not a draft. Appended are offers for the purchase of three properties and the lease of three more. You won't find too much to quibble about, I think.'

'Well!' Sitting up, Biddy covered herself with the bedsheet. 'Well, this is a surprise. I thought that you were putting me off.'

She turned the envelope in her hands and applied her thumb to the sealing.

'No,' Patrick said, sharply. 'Don't open it now, Biddy. Please, not right now.'

She gave a little laugh, raised her eyebrows. 'Why ever not?'

'Take it away with you. Talk it over with your husband and your lawyer before you reach a final decision. Consider it carefully before you sign because once you do there can be no going back on it.'

'I don't want to go back.' Biddy tapped her lips with a corner of the envelope. 'I want to go forward. Don't you, darling?'

'Hmmm,' he answered and then, turning from the bed, poured water from the ewer into the basin and with a thoroughness that Biddy found oddly disturbing, set about washing his hands.

For an hour or two Quig had thought that he might have to deliver Fay's child himself. He would not have balked from doing so if it had become necessary; God knows, he had delivered enough lambs in his time. Fortunately Barrett had located Agnes MacNiven on the road from Dervaig and had despatched her to Pennymain as fast as her stout legs would carry her.

Fay had been in a poor state when Quig and Innis had discovered her on the hill. She had been close to panic, crying out and weeping loudly. If there had been less to do, less urgency, Kilty would have been the hero of the hour. As it was it took Innis and Quig a good forty minutes to help Fay back to Pennymain and put her on the bed in the back room. She was calmer by then and with Innis holding her hand and talking soothingly, began to breathe more regularly until the contractions eased into a rhythmic pattern that indicated that while labour had definitely begun the baby's arrival was not imminent.

Quig set out to find Barrett. Barrett in turn tracked down his sister-in-law and by the time Becky arrived home at a quarter past seven that evening events in the back bedroom were moving towards their conclusion under the experienced hands of the midwife. Becky was more put out than she had anticipated she would be. She tried to close her ears to Fay's shrieks and busied herself making a supper of sorts which neither Quig nor her mother seemed interested in eating.

They sat, all three, around the kitchen table, drinking tea, until about ten when Agnes opened the bedroom door and summoned Innis in to help.

Quig shot to his feet. 'Is she all right? Is she . . .'

'Calm down, Robert. The baby will be with us soon.'

'And Fay? How is . . .'

'She's giving birth, you stupid man,' Agnes snapped. 'How do you think she is?' and stepped back into the bedroom and closed the door.

Around eleven Fay's shrieks changed to a series of long, grunting cries and then, with Quig and Becky pacing the confines of the kitchen, there was another cry, a mewling little wail that stammered, started, stopped and then, after a heart-stopping pause, commenced again, stronger and more persistent than before.

'It's a baby,' Becky said, round-eyed. 'Is it not?'

'It sounds like one to me,' Quig said and, weakened by hours of tension, slumped on the chair by the fire and covered his face with his hand.

'Dear God, Quig, are you crying?' Becky said.

'Of course I am not crying,' Quig said, but did not, she noted, take his hand away from his eyes.

A quarter of an hour later Innis brought the infant, wrapped in clean linens and a huge soft white wool shawl, into the kitchen.

Quig got to his feet and Becky, on tiptoe, craned her neck to look down at the tiny, red-faced creature who lay, passively enough, in her grandmother's arms.

'It is by way of being a girl,' Innis said. 'A fine healthy wee girl.'

'Thank God for that!' Quig exclaimed and then, still with

tears in his eyes, gathered at Innis's side to inspect the brand-new-arrival.

She had, he thought, Fay's features but was dark-haired like her father, her little pink skull licked by damp feathery curls. Her eyes were squeezed shut and her fists – perfect little fists with perfect pearly little nails – were pressed to her cheeks. Quig could not resist making a first gesture of communication, a reassuring contact. He put out his pinkie and touched her hand, saw to his wonderment the tiny fist unfold, stretch, curl and grasp at the air, at the softness of the shawl and then, like a fern seeking sunlight, rotate in search of his finger.

He touched her, feather-light.

The infant opened her eyes.

And wailed.

'Can I hold her?' Becky said. 'Let me hold her, Mam. Please let me hold her.'

'In a while, dear.' It was clear that Innis would not give up the bundle to anyone. 'I will be taking her back to her mother as soon as Agnes is finished.'

Quig shook himself, a long, dog-like shudder. 'Fay? Is she all right?'

'She is fine, just fine,' said Innis. 'She will be resting, though, for it is hard work giving birth to a daughter.'

'I'll hold the baby,' Becky said. 'Go on, Mam, let me . . .'

Quig stepped past the women and went to the bedroom door. Two laundry buckets, scalded, scrubbed and filled with warm water, stood on the floor by the bed close to a bundle of stained towels. The odour of sweat mingled with soap as Agnes, leaning over the bed, washed Fay with a yellow sponge and dried her with a fresh towel. The girl was drowsy and bedraggled but the cleansing seemed to revive her and she looked past the bulky figure of the midwife at Quig and raised a limp hand in greeting.

'Have you seen her?' Fay whispered.

'I have seen her.'

'Isn't she lovely?'

'Quite lovely,' Quig said. 'She is like her mother in that respect.'

'That will be enough out of you, Robert Quigley,' Agnes MacNiven told him.

'We will have to give her a name,' Fay said.

She tried to sit up but Agnes, with the sponge, pushed her down again. From the pocket of her apron the midwife produced a comb.

'Here,' she said, 'if you are going to flirt with married men then at least you can make yourself presentable.'

Fay took the comb and, sitting up a little, began to draw it through her fair, tuggy hair. She was weak, though, and only her pleasure, her joy, kept her upright.

'We will think of a name, never fear,' Quig said.

He wanted to touch her, to kiss her, to hold her in his arms and tell her how proud he was of her, to assure her that he would take care of her and the little pink morsel in the shawl.

'We'll call her Vanessa,' Fay said. 'Do you think Innis will object if we called her Vanessa?'

'You will have to ask Innis about that,' Quig said, 'when you are feeling a little stronger.'

He was not at all sure that the girl's choice of a name would sit well with Innis or that a Campbell child should be burdened with a Campbell name. And then he thought, No, it is not a Campbell name: it is a McIver name, for Vassie was once a tiny child too, a girl too. Before she met and married Ronan Campbell, she had been Evander McIver's beloved daughter. Vanessa, Quig thought, will do very well, if Innis agreed. There would be no 'Vassie', though, for Fay Ludlow's daughter. He would make sure that she was called Vanessa, always Vanessa, with that round, soft sibilant sound that the island tongue made of the name, giving it strength and dignity.

Agnes wrung out the sponge, rolled down her sleeves and buttoned up the collar of her shirt. She too was sweating, for the night was sultry and thunder still puttered away over the mountains. Quig could hear it, just, over the hiss of the lamp and the hungry whimpering cries of the baby.

'Will you bring her to me, Quig?' Fay said. 'Will you put her by me?'

'Is that permitted, Agnes?'

The midwife shook her head, ruefully. 'Of course it is permitted. Damn it all, Robert, the girl is the baby's mother, is she not? Bring the child in and put her down and let them be together. Then I can be off home.'

'Will you not be taking a drink with us first?' Quig said.

'No, I will not be taking a – well, a small one, if you have whisky.'

'I have whisky,' said Quig. 'Water with it?'

'Huh!' said Agnes MacNiven, as if he'd insulted her.

Ten minutes later he carried the midwife's bag out into the garden and watched her strap it on the pannier, watched her fiddle with and light the big carbide lamp that was clamped to the spar above the front-wheel fork. He offered her his arm to help her mount but she ignored him and, perched on the saddle, steered down the front path to the gate that Quig opened for her.

She leaned a hand on his shoulder, one foot on the ground.

'She is a fine girl, the baby and the mother,' Agnes said, without, for once, any trace of cynicism. 'Will it be necessary for you to inform the father or will you register the birth in the town hall with your name upon it as ward?'

'Can I do that?' said Quig, surprised.

'You can do anything you wish,' said Agnes MacNiven. 'Anything that will not damage the child.' She gave him an amiable little pat on the shoulder that changed into a cuff to the side of the head. 'Or damage the mother either, Quigley. Bear that in mind. I will call tomorrow evening just to see that all is as it should be. And I will be keeping my eye on you as well, do not forget.'

'And the bill?' Quig said.

'Will arrive in due course,' said Agnes. 'Goodnight.'

'Goodnight, Agnes,' Quig said. 'And thanks.'

She went away from him, pedalling strenuously to work up speed for the hill. He could see grass stems vividly outlined in the flickering light of the carbide, a thistle stalk magnified, the stones that lined the track raised in sharp relief. He stood by the gate watching the light bob and dwindle and fade out of sight into the high, rough breast of the moor. Then he returned to the cottage where Innis and Becky were seated by the side of Fay's bed.

Innis had the baby still, cradled in the shawl in her arms.

He watched them from the doorway, Fay and Innis with the tiny girl child caught in the light of the lamp.

And in that moment fell in love, all over again.

She was exhausted, utterly exhausted, and only a kind of euphoria sustained her throughout a solitary dinner and enabled her to be pleasant not only to Maggie Naismith but even to Aileen who came into the library to stare at her for two or three wordless minutes before taking herself upstairs to bed.

Aileen offended her: Aileen had always offended her.

She regretted the charitable impulse that had induced her to offer her sister a permanent home. Now that Willy was gone, Aileen might be better off at Pennymain, closer to the sea and the shore. Closer to Pennypol which – Biddy had convinced herself – was where her sister was happiest. She did not discuss the matter with Aileen, for that would have been a pointless waste of breath. Aileen had no opinions about anything. She was like a goose that attaches itself to anything that moved. What she thought about, what notions filled her vacant head when she stared at nothing out of those chilling blue eyes, Biddy could not imagine.

She sat in the old chair in the library, one lamp lighted.

Maggie came in to clear away the dinner tray.

'What time is it?' Biddy asked.

'Going on eleven.'

She did not ask the question; she knew that Quig had not come home.

Maggie said, 'Will I be closing up now, if you are done with me?'

'Yes.'

The housekeeper had assumed the duties that Willy had once jealously guarded. She would close but not lock the big outer door, close but not lock the inner door. She would rake the fire in the grate in the hall, and check each of the ground-floor rooms before going downstairs to bank the stove for the morning and seal it up with just a suck of air in the vent to keep it smouldering. She would go into the room that she had shared with Willy, undress and climb into the empty bed with, Biddy felt sure, some relief now that the big, awkward, arthritic shape of her husband was no longer there; or perhaps, Biddy corrected herself, that was when Maggie Bell remembered that she was Widow Naismith and would let dour tears fall into her pillow in memory of the man and the days that were gone.

Biddy lay back in the chair. She had not closed the curtains and could feel oppressive air pressing against the glass and the windless silence of the night outside, even the throb of the sea on the black rocks at the base of the cliffs that lifted above the headland of An Fhearann Cáirdeil.

She lay back against an embroidered cushion and stretched out her legs, easing her fatigue, stretching her stomach and her hips and feeling the soft, pleasant, tender ache where Patrick had proved himself again and again: an ache that was like longing, a weary sort of longing, like the memory of an ancient tune to which she could not put a name.

The envelope lay unopened on the library table.

No doubt Patrick expected her to rip it open, to scan the last page schedules, the per-acre figure and the property prices; the final sum that would accrue if she agreed to the terms and signed on the dotted line. How surprised Patrick would be to learn that she did not care much about the offer, that she cared more about him than her debts.

She would sell An Fhearann Cáirdeil, of course, sell the empty cottages, the stables, perhaps even the ground at Pennypol if the offer was substanial enough: sell it all, all except the house, without compunction in exchange for a last, loyal lover who, if she played her cards right, would never leave Fetternish again.

CHAPTER SEVENTEEN

Rough Pasture

The letters from Hermann's sack were delivered to Becky at the big house. With Willy gone and Quig preoccupied there was no one to remark upon them and Becky read the missives undisturbed. Thereafter she performed her tasks in a little cocoon of silence that Maggie mistook for sulk, and with the letters tucked into the waistband of her skirt, set out for Pennymain before Biddy announced to Maggie that she, Biddy, would be leaving for Edinburgh first thing in the morning.

Quig was at Pennymain when Becky arrived. He had been over at The Ards with Barrett cutting out fat lambs to ship to market at Dalmally and had dropped in for a bite to eat and to play with Miss Vanessa Tarrant on his way home. She was a quiet, smiling wee thing who slept a great deal and suckled without much persuasion. Agnes MacNiven had pronounced her sound in wind and limb and with a scale more suited to the kitchen than the nursery had been weighing her regularly just to make sure that she was gaining, which, happily, she was.

The cottage smelled of baby now, a soft, sweetish odour of towels, powder and bath water, but Becky was no longer resentful of the little intruder. Preoccupied with her daughter, Fay did not appear to be particularly anxious to return to the plots at Pennypol and had left it to Quig to clear the spent crops, dig the vacant ground, and plant out the strawberry runners for next summer's fruiting.

It was only after Quig had finally left for Fetternish and Fay had gone into the back bedroom to feed her baby that Becky broke the news to her mother.

'I have been expecting it,' Innis said. 'I know that you have not been happy since Fay came.'

'It isn't Fay or the baby,' Becky said. 'I can't stay here for ever, Mam. I have to go outside to find out what life is really like. It's been on my mind ever since Rachel left.'

'Well, you will not be lonely in Glasgow, dear,' said Innis. 'You have more relatives there than you have here now. I gather Rachel has arranged it for you and that you will have her experience to guide you.'

'I'll stay with Donnie until I pass the test to train as a nurse then I'll move into the nurses' home at the Infirmary with Rachel. I received my letter of acceptance from the Board of Governors today.' Innis nodded. 'I'll be needing a little money, Mam,' Becky went on. 'I've a bit saved but not quite enough.'

'I will see that you have what you need,' Innis said. 'There will be clothes to buy and you must offer Donnie rent money. He may not accept it but you must offer it none the less.'

'Independence,' Becky said. 'I understand.'

Her mother had barely glanced at the letter from the Assistant Secretary of the Board of Governors of the Victoria Infirmary that Becky had put on the table. Leaving home was a major event in her life, Becky thought, but for her mother the arrival of a granddaughter was more important. Innis had already lost so many folk to the mainland that one more would make no difference.

'What is the test that you will have to pass?' Innis asked.

'Rachel tells me it is a simple matter of proving my reading and writing ability, and that I can count in fractions.'

'Aye, you can do all of that, thanks to Gillies. Have you told Biddy yet?'

'I'll tell her first thing tomorrow.' Becky got up. 'I take it you've heard the rumour that Aunt Biddy is trying to sell part of Fetternish?'

Innis nodded. 'I have.'

'Did Aunt Biddy tell you so herself?' Becky asked.

'She has told no one of her real plans, not even Quig.'

'Why not?'

'Perhaps she is afraid that he will try to prevent her.'

'How could he do that?' said Becky. 'I mean, no one has ever been able to prevent Aunt Biddy doing exactly what she wants, have they?'

Innis did not answer. Suddenly there were tears in her eyes and she reached up and caught Becky's hand.

Becky had seldom seen her mother weep. She found something rather demeaning in it; tears seemed to negate her mother's belief that all life's trials and tribulations, all joys and pleasures too, came from God. Perhaps it was change, the bleak inevitability of change, that Mam could not accept.

Becky felt tears dampen her eyes too but also the first hard, selfish flush of excitement. Soon, very soon, she would not be feeding hens, cooking breakfasts, skinning rabbits or peeling onions. She would no longer be forced to listen to Maggie Naismith's endless chatter about matters so inconsequential that they had no bearing upon reality. But she wept in acknowledgement of the fact that she had changed already; that when she had seated herself under the lamp in the back room and penned the first letter to her brother she had been true not to her family but to her generation and that the blood of the Campbells was running thin at last.

As soon as she stepped off the *Claymore* and headed for the railway station she would be herself no more, would discover things about herself that she had never suspected were there, weaknesses and strengths that had been hidden while she remained on Mull.

She hugged her mother, rejoiced in her mother's tears and in the new-forged bond of sentiment that was not quite genuine or stable but that she, like Rachel before her, would soon learn to substitute for love.

When the baby wakened Becky wakened too. She had been dreaming, travelling, travelling out of the warm sleep-smelling, baby-smelling bed in the room she shared with Fay, half listening for little Vanessa's hungry cry and the stirring of the girl beside her. Awake now she listened, reconciled, to Fay's whispers and the sound of the baby's suckling. In the almost-darkness of the room in which she had slept since childhood she was unable to relate the tender, pink-skinned little creature who lay in the wicker cradle under a pure white shawl to the tiny, gluttonous beast that sucked on Fay's breast, demanding with cries and whimpers to have a teat in her mouth and milk in her belly whatever the hour of day or night. It's instinct, Becky told herself, a selfish instinct for survival and the appeasement of appetite.

She waited until Vanessa had satisfied herself and Fay had begun to pad up and down the carpeted strip, patting and pampering the child, before she sat up.

'Fay?' Becky hissed. 'Fay?'

'Did I wake you? Sorry. I'll take her into the kitchen.'

'Wait,' Becky said. 'I've something to tell you. I'm going off to Glasgow to train as a nurse.'

'Oh!' Fay managed to whisper her surprise. 'Are you? When?'

'I leave on Saturday week.'

'I'm sorry.'

'What do you have to be sorry for?'

It was chilly in the bedroom in the wee small hours. Stone walls that held summer-night warmth cooled in the autumn rains and when the temperature dropped in the hour before dawn an age-old dampness came creeping out of them like the stealthy seepage of vapours on the coastal plain.

'I'm sorry,' Fay said, 'if I've driven you away.'

'You?' said Becky. 'You haven't driven me away. I'd have gone sooner or later. You've only made it easier for me.'

The girl was close to the bed. Becky could discern her shape in a faint effusion of light from the kitchen. The white shawl seemed to float in mid-air as if little Vanessa were suspended like a gull on an air current.

Becky said, 'You'll look after her, won't you?'

'Vanessa, of course I—'

'My mother I mean.'

'She looks after me,' Fay said.

'Answer me: will you look after her?'

'She has Gillies Brown to do that.'

'Gillies is only her friend. He may be a good friend, an old friend,' Becky said, 'but he can be no more to her than that. You know perfectly well what I mean, Fay. Why won't you give me a straight answer?'

'I'll look out for her, never fear.'

'Do you mean it?'

'Cross my heart,' Fay said. 'I'll look out for her.'

'And stand by her?'

A laugh, slight and unconvincing, came from the shape at the side of the bed.

Becky was tempted to reach out and grab her wrist but the presence of the baby prevented roughness and their little quarrel was conducted quietly, almost furtively, in the presence of the child.

At first she had been thrilled to hold her niece in her arms and respond to smallness and new life but gradually she had become aware of the paradox, that Vanessa Tarrant was her brother's daughter, the daughter of a man who was as shapeless in her imagination as a tree stump or a boulder.

'Yes, yes, Becky,' Fay Ludlow answered. 'I'll stand by her.'

'You owe her that much.'

'Do I?' Fay said then, before Becky could question her further, added slyly, 'Of course I do,' and padded out into the kitchen to walk her baby to sleep.

It had been early, not much past nine o'clock, when Quig had returned from Pennymain. He had poked his head into the library expecting to find Biddy seated in the ancient old chair with a book open on her lap. The library had been in darkness, however, and the drawing-room too. The house seemed like a vast mausoleum, empty and echoing, and Quig had been smitten by a sudden bout of guilt at what he was about to do.

He had crept upstairs, peeped into the bedroom, found Biddy in bed with the lamp turned out. He had gone along the corridor to check on Aileen who lay on her back, arms akimbo, snoring like a horse. He had pulled the quilt over her, had snuffed out the candle and had gone downstairs again, down to the kitchens, all spick and span – and empty. He hadn't had the heart to rouse Maggie and had settled himself on the sofa in the hall to eat a supper of cheese and biscuits washed down with whisky and soda.

He had wondered what he was doing there and why, this past half year or so, Biddy had cut him off and dropped him from her life.

He did not have long to wait to find out.

She was at breakfast in the dining-room by half past six o'clock.

She was dressed in her best tweed travelling outfit and wore a broad-brimmed hat with a goosefoot feather nodding over the crown.

Two cases and a hat-box were set out in the hall.

Maggie, grumbling, had been despatched to Crove to fetch the pony-trap.

'What is this?' Quig said. 'What is going on, Biddy?'

'I'm going to Edinburgh.'

'For how long?'

'Three or four days, possibly as long as a week.'

'Why did you not tell me this yesterday?' Quig said.

'What difference would it have made?'

He was tempted to give her the answer she sought, to say, 'None, damn it,' but habit rescued him. He answered meekly, 'I would have fetched up the trap myself to save Maggie the trek.'

Biddy cut toast into oblongs, dabbed up the last of her poached eggs.

She popped the toast into her mouth and chewed vigorously. The clock under the staircase chimed the half-hour.

It was, Quig realised, an incredibly early hour for his wife to be on the move.

He said, 'What do you intend to do in Edinburgh, dearest?'

'I'll take Christina out for afternoon tea. I believe the school permits it now and then and, after all, it's not as if I've visited her very often.'

'Hardly at all.' Quig seated himself at the table. 'Does Christina know that you are going to be in Edinburgh?'

'I'll send her a note from the hotel as soon as I arrive.'

'Where will you be staying?'

'I'll try for the Wellington, as usual.'

Quig nodded. It had been years since Biddy had last stayed at the Wellington, one of the capital's most expensive hotels. He said nothing about the need for economy. He was too dismayed to criticise, let alone resist. He knew perfectly well why she was going to Edinburgh, not to see Christina but to meet with her lawyers. He was hurt that she had not consulted him. Hurt stiffened his resolve not to coax and cajole and give in to female autocracy.

He watched her consume a third slice of buttered toast and swallow a second cup of tea, her appetite apparently unaffected by the quarter's bills.

'I'll be going to Dalmally with Barrett on Tuesday,' he said.

'How many lambs are we selling?'

'Sixty.'

'Are you selling for the Hollander woman too?'

'Yes,' Quig said.

'How many?'

'A dozen or so.'

'Will she make a price?' Biddy said.

'I doubt it. I doubt if any of us will make a price this year.'

Biddy wiped her hands on a napkin and threw it on to her plate.

Every gesture was rapid and forceful. He had not seen her so exhilarated for many, many months. He felt no sense of relief or gratitude that she had emerged from her doleful mood. She had restored herself at his expense and had drawn confidence only from Patrick Rattenbury and the offer that the agent had or was about to make for all or part of Fetternish.

She had used him and Quig saw it now and wanted no part of it.

He said, 'What sort of a price are you hoping to get for Fetternish?'

Biddy said, 'Oh, I didn't think I'd be able to keep it from you.'

'Why would you want to keep it from me?'

'You'll only fly into a rage.'

'I never fly into rages, Biddy; you know that.'

'Sulk then, or spend even more time at Pennymain with your—'

'This has nothing to do with Fay or her daughter.'

'Vanessa! Huh! Don't you see how sly she is, currying favour with the family with that name. Vassie . . .'

'Vanessa,' Quig said, more sharply than he had intended. 'She will be called Vanessa, not Vassie.'

'She'll be called whatever Fay Ludlow elects to call her. And you will agree to it. She has you twisted around her little finger, Quig, but you're too stupid to—'

'I am not too stupid to recognise evasion,' Quig said. 'How much has Rattenbury offered you for the ground at An Fhearann Cáirdeil?'

She paused, wiped her lips carefully with the napkin, threw it down on her plate again. It wasn't temper that moved her, of that he was sure. She was wild with exhilaration, an aggressive kind of arrogance that he found insufferable.

'Twelve thousand pounds,' Biddy said.

'You mean twelve hundred, surely?'

'I mean twelve *thousand*, dearest. Twelve thousand pounds; think of that.'

'For the whole estate, the house included?'

'The house is not for sale,' Biddy told him. 'The offer is for eight hundred and eighty acres on the headland, four derelict cottages and the stables.'

'It is hardly worth the half of that,' Quig said.

'That depends on who's buying,' said Biddy. 'In any case, it will be off my hands in the matter of a week.'

'I take it you have accepted?'

'I will accept, of course. I'm having Mr Sneddon check over the small print in the contract and settle some of the more obscure points in the deeds.'

'Twelve thousand.' Quig was impressed in spite of himself. 'That will settle everything for us — but what will we have left, Biddy?'

'More than enough for my needs.'

'And if we haven't will you sell him more ground?'

'I might. I may.'

'Until there is nothing left.'

'Pennymain will be left. I have stipulated that much. Pennymain and the house. Robert, you are getting ahead of yourself. I haven't sold off anything that is valuable, only some wasted ground on the headland.'

'If it is wasted ground why is it that Rattenbury has been empowered to offer so much for it?'

'It's wanted. It's required.'

'For tree-planting?'

'There's a great deal more to be made in tree-planting than

you or I know about. It's the thing of the future, an investment,' Biddy said. 'Ask Frances Hollander if you choose not to believe me.'

'It is the Hollander woman who has bought An Fhearann Cáirdeil, is it not?'

'She is a shareholder in the company, I believe.'

He was weary of it, of the game that Biddy was playing. It was not that he was too ignorant or provincial to grasp the salient points of land sale or entirely opposed to new uses being found for dormant ground. He was progressive only by proxy, however. In his heart he yearned for the simplicity of the old days when a man had only to husband his resources and manage his cattle, and money was counted in coins and banknotes not in deeds of ownership and complicated conveyances.

'Biddy, for God's sake, why did you not tell me what you were doing?'

'Because it is none of your concern.'

'None of my concern? I have put half my life into this estate; is that not enough to make it my concern?'

'There's no agreement between us.'

'I never thought to ask for one or that one would be necessary. I married you, Biddy, because I loved you and because you needed me – or so I thought.'

'Needed you?' said Biddy. 'For what?'

'To – well, to run Fetternish for you.'

'I gave you everything, Robert. You brought nothing into our marriage and you have been dependent upon me for everything ever since.'

'Dear God, Biddy!' His patience and resignation all but dried up, he was close to explosion. 'Do you blame *me* for the downturn in market prices and the loss of the Baverstock-Paul contracts? I did my best for you and for this estate; aye, and for the marriage you wanted so desperately.'

'Is that what you think?' She laughed, coughed. 'I needed you only to father my child – my children. For the rest of it, I could have employed someone to do what you've done, and they'd probably have made a better job of it.' She pushed herself up from the table, adjusting the tilt of her hat. 'All of this is rather beyond you, Quig, is it not? I mean, you have no idea what I had to do to rescue Fetternish from the predicament into which you—'

'I think I do know,' Quig said. 'I know more than you might imagine.'

That stopped her: her confidence flickered for an instant.

She froze, one hand on her hat and the other placed over her breast as if she were about to swear an oath of fealty. Swollen with tension, she waited for him to throw Patrick back at her to justify his own capricious indiscretions, his weakness for lame ducks, and declare that he knew of her adultery and that she was in cahoots with Patrick Rattenbury and intended to remain that way.

Quig drew in breath through his nostrils.

'Robbie is my son,' he said. 'I am aware, Biddy, that you have your doubts but he is *my* son, not Michael Tarrant's. Anything you may say now will come as no surprise, nor will it make me doubt.'

She perched herself side-saddle on the chair, her heart racing. The excitement that had buoyed her up turned into a sickness that made her cheeks burn and her brow sweat.

'Who – who told you? Was it Michael?'

Quig tutted, shook his head. 'Nobody had to tell me, Biddy. I have known since the day of our marriage that there were others, lots of others, Michael Tarrant among them. I did not care then and I do not care now. The boy is mine. Robbie is my flesh and blood. He has as much of me in him as he has of you. I can count, Biddy. I can add, subtract and multiply with the best of them. Do you think I do not know how to calculate the cycles of nature?'

'I – I do not know what . . . why did you say nothing until now?'

'Because I knew you were afraid to tell me.'

'It's all your fault, you know,' Biddy said. 'You could have saved me a great deal of worry and concern if you'd—'

'He is my son, Biddy, is he not?'

She had the sense, the decency not to hesitate.

'Yes, of course he is.'

Quig jerked his head, a stiff, sudden gesture. He got up from the table. He made no attempt to touch her, to comfort her or apologise for the manner in which he had exposed her weakness. If ever she had been vulnerable she was not vulnerable now: he saw that all too clearly.

'Will Rattenbury be with you in Edinburgh?'

'Patrick? No, why?'

'I just wondered, that is all,' Quig said. 'I thought that his signature might be necessary to execute the conveyance.'

'That isn't how it's done, not exactly.'

He sighed, raised his hand over his head and brought it down again, scything it down as if to signal the start of a race.

'To hell with how it is done, Biddy. To hell with you and with Fetternish. You may sell it all as far as I am concerned. I have had enough of all this duplicity, all your moods and cravings and excuses. It is not how it is with women of your age: that is what you would have me believe, is it not, that you are powerless to help yourself and that nature has taken you over and is playing you false? No, Biddy! It is *you*, just you and your damned arrogance that makes you suppose that everyone is here to provide for you.'

'I made money, Robert. I made twelve thousand pounds and got us out of debt. I didn't run Fetternish into the ground through *my* laziness.'

'God!' He shouted at last. 'God! Do what you will, Biddy, make up your own laws of loyalty and decency – but let someone else suffer . . .'

'Suffer?'

He let out a roaring sigh, the last.

She had taken her hand from her hat and folded her arms. Aye, Quig thought, that was it: the pose, the image of an indomitable woman, a woman who would not be conquered, who would rise up and triumph against all the odds. A sham, a fantasy: Biddy was as she had always been, utterly selfish, utterly dedicated to getting what she wanted. And he had been fool enough to fall for it.

For a fleeting moment it was on the tip of his tongue to tell her what he thought of her and what he intended to do. But he had acquired some suavity, some accursed female wiles during the years of his marriage. He let himself sag, let himself ease down until rage and impetuosity drained away.

'Tell Christina I was asking for her,' he said. 'Oh, and have a good trip, Biddy, and come home wealthy.'

'Are you being sarcastic?'

'I mean every word of it,' said Quig and, dutiful to the bitter end, went out into the hall to carry her bags to the trap.

His tact was irresistible. He did not attempt a reconciliation face to face. First of all he sent a letter which Janetta read coldly at first then with relief. He had let her down, had been ill-mannered, Patrick confessed, but he had not done so intentionally. He had been, he wrote, unavoidably delayed because the horse had gone lame and he had been obliged to send for the surgeon from Ardmore to come and take a look at him. The lameness had been temporary, a strain no more, and the surgeon had ridden back to Ardmore cursing under his breath but three guineas richer for his pains. Then, Patrick went on, he had received a visit from Biddy Quigley which, given the circumstances and the nature of their relationship, had proved difficult to terminate without offending the lady. He had given in, not for the first time, and put loyalty to his employer first over all. In a word, he wrote, he had foolishly placed duty above love.

The word blared out triumphantly: *love!*

All that had gone before, all that would come after was lost on Netta Brown. She was swirled around, sucked down and lost in that word – *love* – like debris in a whirlpool: no man had ever declared himself in love with her before, not in script or off the tongue, no man except her father, and fathers didn't count.

She pressed the letter to her bosom in the shelter of the kitchen door and heard the little *coo-ing* sounds that emerged from her throat as if they had nothing to do with her whatsoever.

'Netta? Are you all right?'

'Never better, Daddy. Never better.'

She replied at once, sealed the letter and sent it not by post but by the hand of one of Angus Bell's apprentices out to the Fetternish stables.

By the same route she received a little note thanking her for her forgiveness and understanding.

Two days later, burning with hope, Netta wrote again and invited Patrick to dine – supper had apparently gone by the board – to dine at the schoolhouse at half past six o'clock on Wednesday.

Mr Rattenbury, it appeared, could not wait that long.

He returned with the stable-hand in Angus Bell's gig, walked up the lane and across the yard and, it being evening, ascended the staircase unseen, knocked upon the door at the top of the stairs and when Netta opened it, held out a letter and said, 'Special delivery, Miss Brown, a very special delivery indeed.'

In the parlour Gillies stared at the wall for an instant and then, leaping up, grabbed his jacket and his hat and, all smiles, hurried through the tiny hallway, saying in a loud voice, 'Must be off now, Netta. Just off to supper with the Ewings,' and feigning surprise, reared up in front of Patrick. 'Well, now, if it isn't our errant knight come riding out of the gloaming. Will you not be coming in, sir, or do you have other more pressing business across the river?'

'No business at all, Mr Brown, and certainly nothing nearly as important as making my peace with Janetta.' Patrick leaned a hand against the doorpost. 'I had hoped that I might have a word with you too as it happens?'

'About the ruler lesson?'

'Ruler lesson?' said Patrick. 'Oh, that! No, no, on a matter much more fundamental than the mere measurement of space and distance.'

'What could be more fundamental than that, I wonder?' Gillies said.

'May I come in?' Patrick said. 'I'll not detain you long, Mr Brown.'

'Gillies.'

'Gillies, I would like permission to ask for your daughter's hand.'

'Her what?' Gillies said.

He glanced at Netta who had not swooned away, not entirely, but had sagged one bony shoulder against the doorpost and looked, he thought, as if she had just been visited by the Grim Reaper not a potential bridegroom.

'Hand,' said Patrick, 'in marriage.'

'But there hasn't been – I mean, no courtship. You hardly know each other. I'm not certain that my daughter's the one for you, Mr . . .'

'Patrick.'

'Patrick then. Look, you'd better step inside.'

'Yes,' Janetta said. 'Step inside. Please step inside.'

'Yes, step inside a minute, do,' Gillies said.

'No,' said Janetta. 'Yes, you may have my hand in marriage, Patrick.'

'Now, now, now, hold on a wee bit, Netta,' Gillies heard himself say, much more sternly than he had intended. 'You don't know this man from Adam – well, hardly. He might not be suitable. Are you playing fast and loose with my daughter's affections, sir?'

'I would be honoured to become engaged to marry your daughter,' Patrick said, 'if Janetta will agree, that is, and if you feel up to putting your objections aside. As to the speed with which I've reached this decision, well, I may as well tell you that a certain amount of it is down to Mrs Quigley.'

'Biddy? What does she . . .?' Janetta began.

But her father grunted, 'Uh-*huh*, uh-*huh*!', removed his hat again and, with a cocked thumb, indicated to Patrick that their conversation would be better conducted in the parlour with all doors closed.

'She must have been astonished,' Frances said. 'Did you have to pick her up off the carpet to have her answer?'

'She took it very well, in fact,' Patrick said. 'She agreed without quibble to a long engagement.'

'How long? Ten years?' said Frances.

'Until I have the stables renovated and in habitable order.'

'Habitable order? Hold on, surely you don't intend to plough on as far as a wedding?' Frances said. 'I mean, announcing your engagement to Netta Brown and sticking by it for a while will be quite enough for Mama.'

'Ah, but I'm not doing it for your mama,' Patrick said.

'You mean, you actually mean that you'll go through with it?'

'Probably. Almost certainly.'

'Great God in heaven!' Frances exclaimed. 'Wait until Mama hears *this*.'

'If you think I'd deceive a gentle soul like Janetta Brown just because your mother-in-law suggested it then you've seriously misjudged me.'

'Oh, come now, you can't possibly be in love with Netta Brown?'

'Why not? You were.'

'Not the point, not the issue,' said Frances, flushing slightly. 'You have your pick of the ladies, Patrick. You could marry some ducal daughter with a snap of your fingers. Why settle for a dowdy schoolteacher in a dirty little town like Crove?'

'Janetta isn't dowdy,' Patrick said.

'Oh, dear God! So you are in love with her?'

'No, I'm not – not yet. On the other hand, Frances, I've had my fill of grasping women and if I'm committed to a life on Mull then Netta Brown will make me an excellent wife under the circumstances.'

'Suddenly you've become a romantic. Patrick, I'm amazed.'

'I've always been a romantic.'

'But not romantic enough to announce your betrothal before Biddy Baverstock Quigley signs on the dotted line?'

'Not quite that romantic, no.'

'Did you tell Janetta about Biddy?' Frances said.

'About . . .'

'That Fetternish is to be sold?'

'Yes,' Patrick said warily. 'I also told her that Biddy Quigley was dangerous and should be treated with caution. And, do you know, Janetta agreed with me?'

'What about her papa?'

'He wants his daughter off his hands.'

'Who can blame him?' Frances cocked her head and blew a little bubbly kiss at the window. 'I'd have taken her on, you know.'

'Oh, I know,' said Patrick. 'But you frightened her, you and what you are.'

'What am I, Patrick? What do you think I am?'

'I'm not one for the labelling game,' Patrick said. 'Besides, even although you're not the one who holds the purse-strings I prefer to keep on your right side.'

'Until Larry comes to fetch me?'

'Will he ever come, do you think?'

'Some day,' said Frances. 'Some day when least expected.'

'Or when Madam Lafferty dies?'

'Bite your tongue,' said Frances. 'Mama has no intention of dying.'

'Is she napping, by the way?'

'She is.'

'In that case I'll leave it to you to convey the glad tidings.'

'That it's all up with Biddy Baverstock?' Frances said. 'Hee-hee-hee!'

Onions were roped in the old cottage and in a dry corner the last of the carrots had been stored in sand. Quig's trenching had been completed; the dark earth in the top strips had been exposed ready for the winter rains.

Fay had tended the strawberry bed herself, picking off the dusty foliage and turning the soil around the runners which Quig had planted out. In the wicker cradle, to which Quig had fixed two leather handles, Vanessa lay awake. She was sighted now, the swimming blue eyes in focus, and she had begun to respond not only to touch but to voices and familiar faces.

What Vanessa saw and how she interpreted it were mysteries long lost to Fay and Robert Quigley. They had forgotten that an innocent remaking of the world is the right of every child.

Quig walked her by the sea and under the shadow of the hill. He held her against his chest, his brown hand cradling her skull, and as she bobbed in Quigley's arms or lay on her back in the basket she stared and stared, smiling or frowning, and now and then let out a whimpering cry as if she'd glimpsed the indifference of the great vast landscape into which chance had dropped her.

They walked side by side, Fay and Quig, with the cradle between them.

There had been rain and the sea was pricked by little waves in the wake of the wind that brought clouds skirting along the coast. On the foreshore the last of Biddy's cattle roved and the waves skittered on the sands quite willy-nilly and the noise they made was like a thousand little flags fluttering in the breeze.

'Quig,' Fay said. 'The garden hasn't been profitable, has it?'

'Oh, we have cleared our feet,' Quig answered.

'You ain't telling me the truth. I know what a large crop looks like and there wasn't enough came off Pennypol. Even the potatoes . . .'

'There was enough.' Quig glanced down at the baby, round-eyed and content, lulled by the rocking. 'Was there not now, Vanessa?'

'Would there have been enough for us?' Fay said.

'Us?'

'To feed us, just you and me and her, nobody else? Would what we've taken from the ground be enough to feed us for a winter, say?'

'With flour, fish, eggs and fresh milk what you've coaxed out of Pennypol would keep any crofting family alive and thriving,' Quig said. 'When I lived on Foss with Evander there were a dozen of us and we never went hungry, not even when storms cut us off from the big island for weeks. It was a matter of good housekeeping, Evander claimed. He and my mother were cautious to a fault. There was always enough oatmeal and the sheds were always stacked high with potatoes.'

'Would you have those days back?'

'I would,' Quig said. 'They were hard but they were satisfying, satisfying in a way that I have not experienced since.'

Fay walked on, one foot in front of the other, leaning against the weight of the cradle. At length, she said, 'Why has he not come for me yet?'

'Gavin, do you mean?'

'Yes. Gavin. Nine weeks since Mr Tarrant went away and – nothing. I'm tired of waiting for him.'

'Do you want him to come for you?'

'I want him to come so that I can be rid of the fear of him.'

Quig said, 'Perhaps he has found another woman.'

'That's not Gavin's way.'

'Well, perhaps Michael Tarrant said nothing to Gavin or – though I doubt that this is the case – perhaps he persuaded him to leave you in peace.'

'Peace,' Fay said. 'Yes.' She stopped, made Quig stop too. 'Will you take me to Foss?'

'It will soon be the time for the autumn gales,' said Quig, 'and I am having to be going to Dalmally soon to sell sheep. If it stays fine after that I will borrow the boat again and we will take Vanessa over with us to see what she makes of it.'

'And not come back?' said Fay.

'I – I cannot be leaving you there on your own.'

'I know.'

'Fay, there is the matter of my wife.'

'You are not in love with her,' the girl stated.

'None the less she is my wife.'

'Then we'll pretend,' Fay said, 'we'll pretend that your wife has gone away or that you are not her husband, and I'll ask you what we'd need to make a farm on Foss. What would we need if we were setting up, just you and me and the baby? We would need a boat, wouldn't we?'

'Aye,' Quig said uneasily. 'We'd be needing a boat and a pony and a plough. Poultry, some of the hardy hens that Innis has, and a cock to serve them.'

'And a cow for milk.'

'Bull calves,' Quig said; he swallowed. 'Aye, bull calves.'

'To breed and sell,' said Fay. 'And a garden for me to tend.'

'Oats and a bit of a barley field for winter feed,' said Quig. 'And a house to live in, of course, and – oh, I do not know how it would be now, with all the things that we would be needing.'

'How much?'

'In cash? Two hundred pounds would just about do it.'

'Gavin would never find me out on Foss,' Fay said.

'So it is a safe haven that you are after?' Quig said. 'There is no reason for you to go chasing off the edge of the sky just to avoid him. He has not come yet. It may be that he will never come at all.'

'It ain't Gavin,' Fay said. 'It's you, Quig.'

'Me?' He looked down at the infant as if her innocence might remind him that his morality was not as primitive as all that. 'Would you be stealing me away from Biddy, Fay?'

'I would do anything to have you for mine,' Fay said.

'It – it would not be right.'

'Who's to say what's right?' Fay told him. 'I would go anywhere with you, Quig. I'll go back in time with you if that's what you want.' She put up her free hand and tugged at her fair hair, swept it away from her brow. 'It was a fine house once, the house on Foss – you told me so yourself – and you were happy there. The house could be repaired, couldn't it? You could relay the floor and batten the roof again and we could sleep in a dry corner by the fire at first.'

'There is no fuel on Foss. The peat is too shallow to cut.'

'What did your father do for fuel?'

'He brought in logs and a load of coal.'

'Well?'

'Fay, Fay,' Quig said. 'It is no more than a dream of mine. It is not the sort of thing that we should even be thinking of.'

'You're lying to me again, Quig. You've thought of nothing else for weeks.'

He shook his head, grinning crookedly. 'What if I have now? Are grown men not entitled to be having a bit of a dream now and then?'

'I would love you,' Fay said. 'That wouldn't be a dream, would it?'

'No,' Quig said. 'No, that would not be a dream.'

'Will she not give you your share?'

'Biddy? I doubt it.'

'What will she give to keep you?'

'She will keep me only if she thinks she still needs me.'

'And your children?'

'They . . .' He could not bring himself to say it, not all at once. 'My children, they care for me,' Quig said, 'I think.'

'Do they *need* you, though?'

He listened to the gadding of the waves on the sand, confused by wind and current, and lifted his eyes to the horizon, to the place where the last of the little isles set its prow towards infinity. He had lived with the shape of the island hills, with headlands set against a patch of sky, with something unchanged and unchangeable, and had not known what held him, or why, in the dog days of his youth, he had sought change at all, sacrificing simplicity and cunning and courage for Biddy Baverstock's bed and the towers of Fetternish House. He had mistaken ambition for progress and progress for fulfilment.

Soon the character of the north quarter would change too, reshaped by tall, quick-growing spruces, larches, birches, ash and elm and cone-bearing pines, by high-fenced enclosures, metalled roads, bridges, by the maul and splutter of heavy machinery and the presence of men who were strangers to the island way of life.

'No, Fay,' he said. 'Robbie and Christina do not need me now.'

'Will you go then, will you take me with you?'

'Ah!' Quig breathed softly.

'Isn't that what you want, Quig?'

'It is,' he said. 'Oh, God! Yes, it is.'

On a blustery afternoon Biddy finally returned from Edinburgh. There had been no communication from her for over a week and Patrick learned the glad tidings not by letter but by a telegraph message which had had Hermann pedalling out to the stables at an ungodly early hour.

Patrick, in striped night-shirt, had received the message at the kitchen door, had given the dog a biscuit and Hermann sixpence before retiring inside to read what Biddy had to say for herself.

Her message was succinct: '*The Deed is Done. Biddy.*'

Patrick went back to bed.

He was up again, dressed and saddled by nine o'clock, however. He rode to the schoolhouse to pass word to Janetta before continuing on to The Ards to convey the news to Madam Lafferty.

Madam Lafferty was understandably elated. She despatched Patrick to Tobermory to send a telegram to her legal representatives in Perth instructing them to communicate with Biddy's lawyers in Edinburgh and confirm that her eight hundred and eighty-acre foothold on Fetternish was finally legally secure. Louden, Lafferty and Spruell's answer came over the wire that evening and Hermann and the dog had another long haul before dusk.

'Well, Mama, are you satisfied?' Frances and Dorothea were sipping champagne by lamplight in the upstairs apartment. 'Or do you still want more?'

'I still want more,' said Dorothea. 'A whole lot more.'

'Her head on a plate?' Frances suggested.

'Some other part of her would do just as well,' said Dorothea and, blowing into her champagne glass, laughed at her own vulgarity.

Two days later Biddy returned to Mull.

It had been a choppy crossing but she was a good sailor and had eaten a hearty second breakfast on the *Grenadier* while the handful of late-season tourists were hanging over the rails trying not to retch. A banker's draft for twelve thousand pounds was a fine nostrum against sea-sickness, of course, and against most of the ills that had affected her this past year or so.

By the time the Tobermory gig deposited her at the front door of Fetternish House Biddy was her old imperious self again. She had half a mind to drive straight to the stables and demand that Patrick help her celebrate her good fortune not in wine but in bed. Instead she had to make do with her husband. He was waiting at the end of the drive and when the gig rolled past walked after it and reached the front door in time to help unload Biddy's luggage, more luggage than she had gone off with.

'Been shopping, dear?' Quig said.

'I did buy one or two things in Edinburgh, yes.'

'I will be taking them up to your room.'

Biddy shot him a speculative glance. She had been thinking of

Patrick, of what Patrick would do to her and carried the desire over to her husband.

'What do you mean?'

'I mean,' Quig said, 'will I take your luggage upstairs?'

'Becky will do it.'

'Becky has left us.'

'What do you mean?' Biddy said again.

'Becky has left our employment.'

'How can she?' Biddy said, scowling. 'Where else will she find work?'

Quig said, 'She left on Saturday to train as a nurse in Glasgow.'

'A nurse! A nurse! God help her patients.' The information had disrupted Biddy's train of thought and her edgy desire to share pleasure with Patrick. 'Why did you let her go?'

'How could I stop her?' Quig lifted two hat-boxes and tucked them under his left arm and he had just stooped to take a grip on a new kid-skin valise when a thought seemed to occur to him. He placed the boxes on the table and leaned lightly upon them. 'Did you manage to see Christina on your travels?'

'I did. We had tea at Jenner's yesterday afternoon.'

'Is she well?'

'She is.'

'Did she ask after me?'

'Yes, I believe she did.'

'And Robbie? Did you meet with Robbie?'

'No, apparently he was busy at school.'

She removed her overcoat, tossed it across the sofa, placed her hat and gloves on the table. She glanced at the post that Quig had allowed to accumulate, hoping to find an unstamped letter from Patrick: none, of course. Silly of her to suppose that there would be. Patrick would be at the stables, eagerly waiting for her to drop in. She would keep him waiting a little longer, for as long as it took to change her clothes and drink a dish of tea – and get Quig out of the way.

'I suppose,' she said, 'I'll need to find a replacement.'

'A replacement?'

'For Becky? Your friend from Pennymain might care to fill the bill.'

'Fay is a gardener not a kitchen-maid.'

'There won't be much call for gardeners on the new Fetternish, I'm afraid,' Biddy said. 'Innis could look after the child while the girl worked here. Maggie would soon train her and it would give her something useful to do instead of scratching about on Pennypol. Besides, if she worked here I could keep an eye on her. I'm sure if you put it to her nicely, Quig, she would leap at the chance to work in my house.'

'I think Fay has other plans,' Quig said.

'Oh, is she leaving us too? Is she going home to her husband at last?' Quig sucked his underlip. Hat-boxes and luggage lay neglected. Biddy went on, 'I thought you might be down at Pennymain with your little friend and her baby. I mean, don't feel that you have to spend the evening with me. I can manage very well on my own, if you have better things to do.'

'Biddy, is it signed, sealed and delivered?'

'Yes, it is. I have the banker's draft right here.' She let her reticule swing out on its little strap and oscillate before him. 'Can you not smell it?'

'So you sold a large piece of Fetternish without once consulting me?'

'It isn't yours, it's mine,' Biddy reminded him.

'And is the profit yours too?'

'The profit will clear our debts and go back into the estate.'

'What's left of it,' said Quig.

'By the way,' Biddy said, 'how did you know to expect me today?'

'Patrick told me.'

'Patrick? Have you been talking to Patrick?'

'He has been talking to me,' said Quig.

Biddy could not help herself. She spun round to face him. 'And what, may I ask, did he have to talk to you about?'

'Sheep, Biddy, just sheep.'

Before she could probe into the meaning of the meeting between her husband and her lover the sound of wheels on the gravel drive drew her to the window.

She looked out, eagerly at first and then, stiffening, in dismay.

'Good God! It's that woman.'

Quig did not ask what woman. It seemed as if he had known that Frances Hollander and her mother-in-law would arrive at a crucial moment, almost as if he had planned it.

He lifted the hat-boxes and carried them upstairs.

'Quig. Quig. What will I do?' Biddy called out desperately.

'Let them in, I suppose,' Quig answered, and vanished along the gallery.

There were four females in the American buggy and two horses, not one, between the shafts. Frances was at the reins. The female servants sat one on either side of Madam Lafferty to bolster her from the shocks of the journey. Madam Lafferty was wrapped up as if for a sleigh-ride in a black fur hat and a mink muff and had such a swaddle of quilts and blankets about her that she seemed not merely large but elephantine.

After the buggy halted she was assiduously unpackaged and helped down the broad-stepped ladder that had been brought along for the purpose. She used the servants as crutches, arms about their shoulders, and for a moment or two it seemed that her limbs had failed her entirely and that she was being dragged unwillingly into the camp of her enemy.

Then, quite suddenly, she recovered her strength. She shook herself free of the servants and, waving for her sticks, balanced herself upon them, rigid as rock, stared up at the tower and pediments and then, smiling, at the half-open door.

'I've only just arrived home,' Biddy called out. 'I'm in no position to receive guests.'

'Guests?' Frances called back. 'Do you think my mama's a

guest? She owns more of Fetternish than you do, Biddy, close enough to make no matter.'

'Open the door,' Dorothea said. 'I'm not going away until I see what there is to see.'

'There's nothing to see,' Biddy said. 'Nothing that concerns you.'

The woman lumbered forward, negotiated the shallow step without assistance and as Biddy retreated before her, thrust one stick against the door and, leaning her weight into it, pushed the door wide open and entered the hall.

The servants followed her for a little then fell back and Biddy lost sight of them as Frances bounded into the hall and flounced about it, coo-ing: 'Oh, I say, Mama, isn't it marvellous? Isn't it grand? Have you ever seen any place so traditionally seigneurial?' She spread her arms and pirouetted under the gallery. 'We could have balls in this room, grand balls. Larry will love it, don't you think?'

Numb and tight-lipped, Biddy said, 'Do you require to be seated?'

Dorothea laughed. 'I ain't falling down on your carpet, honey. Oh, no. I got here under my own steam and I'll get out the same way.'

'Why – what – I mean, why are you here?'

'We came to welcome you home,' said Frances.

'Patrick told you, did he?' Biddy said.

'Someone told us,' said Frances. 'Can't recall who: perhaps it was Quig.'

Biddy snatched her overcoat away as the young woman threw herself down upon the old sofa and wriggled and bounced experimentally. Her animation was in stark contrast to Dorothea's stillness: so still and motionless was she that she seemed to be listening for the faint, sweet whisper of her beloved's voice lingering in the atmosphere, her head tilted so far back that the black fur hat stuck out horizontally behind her like the muzzle of a cannon. Then she turned her head, cranking it round on the

407

great, quivering pediment of her neck and signalled to the servant, Valerie, to bring in the electro-plated urn.

'Oh, God!' Biddy groaned. 'Oh, God! It's Carbery.'

'The essence of Iain,' said Frances, not quite giggling. 'Home at last.'

It was too much for Biddy. She waved a hand and cried out angrily, 'That's enough, quite enough. Get that – that *thing* out of here. And you, Dorothea, you, Frances, get out of my house. Do you hear me, clear out of my house at once.'

'Ain't very hospitable, is she, honey?' Dorothea said to her daughter-in-law.

'Or very grateful,' said Frances, on her feet again and prowling. 'I think I'll take a look at the upstairs. All right, Mama?'

'*No!*' Biddy shouted. '*No, you will not.*'

Valerie had positioned herself by her mistress's side and held the urn aloft as if it had a window in it from which the spirit could look out and breathe easy now that he – or it – had been returned to the site of so much happiness and suffering.

Farce, Biddy thought, a disgusting and degenerate farce – of which Iain would have thoroughly approved, no doubt. What galled her was the realisation that the gross-bodied woman and her flighty daughter-in-law had so much more knowledge of Iain than she had ever had, that their revenge, vulgar and lacking in dignity, was so opportune and appropriate. She was sorely tempted to snatch the urn from the servant and fling it into the empty hearth, to prise open the lid and spread Iain's dusty remains about the hall so that Maggie, with pan and brush, would sweep them up and cast them away along with the rest of the trash. Some last grim element of control stayed her, however.

She drew herself up, took three or four steps forward and placed herself directly before the old woman.

'You may do as you wish on An Fhearann Cáirdeil or on any of the cottages that I have sold to you,' she said. 'You may ride the trackways and access roads and I cannot prevent it but I can prevent you entering my house which is and will remain my property, my *private* property.'

'I think she wants us to leave, Mama,' Frances said. 'Have you seen enough?'

'I've seen enough,' Dorothea answered, 'for the time being.'

'You will not enter my house again without an invitation,' Biddy said.

Frances bowed. 'If that is your wish, so be it.'

The old woman bowed too, or seemed to. She swung herself forward so that her nose was no more than six inches from Biddy's. Her eyes glittered with a malice that was close to madness and in them, for an instant only, Biddy glimpsed the sexual nature of Dorothea's character, the allure of utter ruthlessness, pale now and dwindling but still apparent, still frightening.

'Perhaps you will ask us to supper along with Patrick,' Madam Lafferty said.

'Patrick,' said Frances, 'and his wife.'

'His . . .'

'Oh, haven't you heard?' said Frances. 'Oh, Mama, she hasn't heard.'

'Heard? Heard what?'

'Patrick is engaged,' said Frances. 'Our agent has chosen a wife.'

'A wife? Wh – wh – who? Not you, Frances?'

'God, no.'

'The schoolteacher.' Dorothea smiled, all her chins quivering. 'Miss Janetta Brown. They intend to marry, I believe, in the spring.'

Biddy retreated by inches, one slow inch at a time, rocking backward from the shoulders then the waist, withdrawing from the proximity of the foul-breathed old woman who told such foul and inventive lies without a qualm. She knew it was a lie, a fairy story designed to hurt, to tighten the screw. She would not fall for it, would not react, would not allow herself to believe that

Patrick preferred flat-chested Janetta Brown to her; Netta who had lodged in her cottage, taught her children and had been if not a friend at least a favoured acquaintance for almost as long as she could remember.

'*Hoh!*' Biddy grunted. '*Hoh!*' as the pain suddenly arrived.

It tore at the roots of her hairline and bored into the depths of her skull. It spread rapidly across her scalp into her ears and down into the veins that pumped blood to her brain. She felt not faint but inflamed, inflamed to the point of combustion. '*Hoh!*' she grunted again, then, clasping hands to her head, screamed aloud, screamed and screamed and screamed, while Dorothea and her entourage made their way outside and, laughing, boarded the buggy.

Lurking in the shadows of the gallery Quig looked down on his wife in her anguish – and did absolutely nothing at all.

'Is she better now, Robert?' Mairi Ewing said. 'I heard that you had to call in old Dr Kirkhope and that he was not happy with her condition.'

'She isn't ill, Mother,' Quig said.

'Is that what Dr Kirkhope told you?'

'He did not tell us anything that we did not already know.'

Mairi crossed her knees under the voluminous skirt that she wore for entertaining at home. She had not been intending to entertain anyone that afternoon, however, for the whole north quarter was lashed by autumnal rains and soon after Tom had gone out she had settled in the parlour with a glass of brandy and one of the small cheroots that Tom had bought her as an anniversary present. She had put on the colourful skirt and brocaded blouse and three or four bangles out of the trinket drawer because dressing up even in the privacy of the manse made her feel youthful and fiendishly unconventional again.

Tom had gone shuffling off to visit an ailing parishioner on a farm south of Crove and had said that he would carry on into

Dervaig to pick up an order of butcher-meat to see them through the weekend. She didn't like Tom being out in bad weather these days and she dreaded the approach of winter, a fear by no means uncommon in the tinker-gypsy clan out of which she had been plucked to become the chatelaine of Foss. That she had shared a bed with Evander McIver, Quig did not doubt. His mother was a hot-blooded woman, as fair and sonsy as any woman he had ever met and it occurred to him that she might have dolled herself up just for his benefit, except that she hadn't known that he would drop in that afternoon. Similarly it struck Mairi that Quig's long black oilcloth overcoat and rain-sodden brown felt hat were affectations, visual reminders that he was ageing faster than she was, and that though he was not yet fifty he had begun to acquire the hangdog shabbiness of a martyr to a marriage that had lost all purpose and heart.

She brought him into the parlour, gave him brandy and would have made him tea and warm scones if he had wished it.

He was here for a purpose, though, and would soon come around to it now that he'd had the good fortune to find her on her own.

'I do not think that you should be feeling too sorry for Biddy,' Quig said. 'She is suffering no more than other women suffer in that way.' Mairi chose not to argue the point and her son went on, 'I would not be going so far as to say that it is an excuse, her age, but it is not the factor that has turned her into herself.'

'Into herself?'

'It's the agent, the land agent, Patrick Rattenbury.'

'She thought that he loved her,' Mairi stated. 'I heard as much from Tom. Do you think, son, that she sold An Fhearann Cáirdeil to please him?'

'I cannot be saying that for sure.'

'Aye, but it would not be beyond Biddy to be doing such a thing.'

'You have never taken to Biddy, have you, Mam?'

'In all honesty, no, I can't say that I have,' Mairi admitted. 'She was dependent on Tom for so many years – he was in love with her once, you know – then she just cut him off, piece by piece, like she is cutting you off now.'

'I worry about the children.'

'They are old enough not to care too much.'

'I did not make them that way – uncaring,' Quig said.

'It's the way it is with many folk these days, especially folk like Biddy.'

Quig drank brandy from the glass. The liquid glowed in the light from the little coal fire and the room, though sparsely furnished, seemed cosy and welcoming. It was, he knew, a meagre existence, for a minister's stipend was small. Somehow, though, Tom and Mairi Ewing struggled along and managed to make the most of their creature comforts. His mother had certainly kept her bargain with the minister, had loved him, been loved by him, had supported him throughout many years of marriage. There was kindness in the manse, forgiveness, a mutual sharing that Biddy and he had never been able to capture.

Quig sat back in the wooden-armed rocking-chair. His collar was damp and his feet were wet, for it had been a long walk from Fetternish, the miles stretched by appalling weather. He felt damp within himself too and brandy helped only a little.

'Why would she not allow Tom to visit her?' Mairi asked.

'She said that he would only want her to pray.'

'I am thinking that there are worse things than prayer for Biddy to be clinging to at this time.'

'Like me?' said Quig.

'Has she really let you go?' Mairi asked softly.

'I have let myself go,' Quig answered.

'Do you blame me?'

'Blame you, Mam. For what?'

'For pushing you into Biddy's arms all those years ago?'

'No, no, Mam. I wanted her.' Quig put the glass on the carpet between his feet. 'I still want her, if you can believe it.'

'I believe it.'

'But . . .'

'Is it the Ludlow girl?' Mairi said.

'Aye, it is.'

'Have you . . . No, that would not have been possible?'

'It is not that at all,' Quig said. 'It's many things and that one is the least of it. I'm in love with her. I feel that her child is more mine that Gavin Tarrant's and that in Fay some of the old promise still stands a chance of being fulfilled.'

'You have a funny way of putting things, Robert.'

'Do you not know what I mean?'

'Aye, I do. It was the same with Evander then as it is with you now. You are more like him than any of the children he fathered, but he would not have been asking my permission to do what he felt was right.'

'Is that what I'm doing,' Quig said, 'asking your permission?'

'To take love over profit, yes?'

Quig gave a rueful snort. 'Aye, Mother, there has never been any pulling of the wool over your eyes. That is it in a nutshell: love over profit. Biddy has no need of me. She would have taken Rattenbury for amusement, not to love, mark you, but just for the fun of it. She believes that he is "good" enough for her; that is something I have never been.'

'You are making too much of it, Robert.'

'Or not enough?' Quig said. 'Do not think that Biddy is simple. The older she gets, Mam, the more complicated she becomes. The bald fact is that she sold land without consulting me, without even telling me. Did it for this Rattenbury man, not to get us out of debt. Oh, she thinks I am just a stupid male and too insensitive to understand what's going on but Biddy's the stupid one for not realising that I loved her for herself, not for what she had wrapped around her.'

'Take it, Robert,' Mairi said. 'Take it while it is offered. Tomorrow it will be too late for anything but regrets. Go with the girl if she will have you. We are all just bundles of selfish desires but it is the desires we share that make a woman and a man tolerable companions. Marriage vows and rings and parish registers have no more to do with it than candles lighted unto God.'

'I did not expect that from you, Mam.'

'Do you think I do not believe in God?'

'Tom does, that I know.'

'I am no hypocrite, Robert. I know there is a God in heaven, that He will be looking after me when I need Him and that one day it will be Him and only Him that I will have to answer to, not Tom or Evander McIver or the parish council.'

'Are you telling me it is no sin to do what I want for a change?'

'I am telling you just that.'

'What if it is just rashness, an impulse to do with getting older?'

'What if it is?' said Mairi. 'It isn't, though, is it, son?'

Quig paused, considering, then shook his head. 'No, it is not.'

'Does this girl, Fay, love you enough to go with you? It is no small undertaking to run off with a man twice your age and trust him not just with your future but your child's future too.'

'She will come with me, Vanessa and she.'

'And where will you go, Robert? To Glasgow?'

'No,' he said. 'To Foss.'

She was quiet then, the cheroot held in her fingers the way a man would hold it, knees spread under the wide and gaudy skirt. She stared at him expressionlessly for almost half a minute, and then she laughed.

'Well,' she said, shaking her head, 'there will be no time left for dancing if that is the life you are choosing for yourself. Foss! By God, son, it will be hard scrabble for a year or two to make Foss habitable again.'

'Hard scrabble on rough pasture,' Quig said.

'I do not envy you.' Mairi paused, cocked her head, then added, 'Och yes, I do. I do I envy you, Quig. I envy her as well, for she will have you to stand by her and look out for her when the big winds blow over the sea and the nights are cold and the cattle are off their feed. She will know what it is to live on the edge every single day of her life and it will all be fine and lovely because she will have a man who loves her and a man whom she can love.'

'What will Tom say to it?' Quig asked.

'He will mumble and he will mutter and he will pretend to disapprove.'

'He will not disapprove, though, will he?'

'Not him. He will bless you in the quiet time, and envy you too, no doubt.'

'That,' Quig said, getting to his feet again, 'is all I needed to know.'

'When will you take the girl and go?'

'As soon as I can,' said Quig, 'before the winter comes.'

'She will fight you – Biddy, I mean.'

'I am prepared for that,' said Quig.

'She will give you nothing.'

'I am prepared for that too.'

'And money to get started?' Mairi said.

'I know where to get money.'

'Honestly come by, I hope?'

'Aye, Mam. Quite honestly enough for me.'

'Let me see if I understand you correctly,' Dorothea said. 'You are offering me a thirty-year lease on one hundred and forty acres from the foot of Olaf's Hill to the stream south of the cottage at Pennypol. Will that include water rights?'

'It will.'

'And the foreshore, jetty and buildings?'

'I will retain access rights to the jetty,' Quig said. 'But the rest of it will be yours to do as you wish. Plant more trees, I expect.'

'Aren't there cattle on the shore and sheep on the moor?'

'There are,' said Quig. 'They will not be included in the transaction.'

'Thank God for that,' said Frances. 'I've had just about enough of sheep.'

'The stock belongs to your wife, I take it?' Dorothea said.

'It does,' said Quig. 'The beasts will be moved on to the moor behind fences, or will be sold off. That is not a decision for me to be making.'

Dorothea sat forward in the upright chair. Behind her the sky was thick with grey cloud and the window rivered with falling rain. Quig could see her plainly, however, distinct against the diminished light and she seemed less substantial than he remembered her, less gargantuan.

She had been eating grapes when he had been shown into the upstairs room and chewed on them while he put his proposal and, long after the pulp had gone, spat seeds into her palm and closed her swollen fingers on them as if she could not bear to part with them. Frances remained in attendance but the servant, Valerie, had been sent out of the room as soon as it became apparent that business was about to be transacted.

'Do you have a document to prove your ownership of Pennypol?'

'I do,' Quig said. 'I have it here in my pocket.'

The old woman frowned. 'Did Biddy send you to trade with me? Is it some sort of a trick?'

'It is no trick, Mrs Lafferty, I assure you,' Quig said. 'I am the sole owner of the ground at Pennypol. It was left to me by Evander McIver, who was my adopted father, and anything my wife may have led you to believe to the contrary should be disregarded.'

'Patrick hasn't done his job very thoroughly, has he, Mama?'

'Patrick isn't to blame. Biddy Baverstock is to blame for not making it clear from the beginning that . . . Well, no matter. I'll have my lawyers check the validity of your right of ownership, Quigley, then I will take counsel with Patrick Rattenbury on your proposal.'

'No,' Quig said. 'I must have your decision now.'

The woman eased back, stretched one huge arm across her bosom and rubbed her ear with pinched fingers. She had no doubt that he was telling the truth, Quig felt, yet she felt obliged to question his honesty.

At length she said, 'That's asking a lot.'

'It is not asking so much,' Quig said. 'Twenty-eight shillings per acre is a fair price considering what you paid for the headland. I will not be accounting the cottage or the jetty or the fact that you will have water rights, the best of the pasture and about the only patch of ground on Fetternish suitable for cultivation.'

'Seven shillings per acre per annum would be fair,' Dorothea said.

'I will take one sum, lump, against the lease and a nominal annual payment of, let us say, five pounds to be paid every spring quarter day.'

'I'd no idea that you were conversant with land deals, Quigley,' Dorothea said. 'It might have been better for all of us if your wife had let you handle the negotiations in the first place.'

'At least he wouldn't have scrambled into Rattenbury's bed,' said Frances, 'and had a hysterical breakdown when Patrick decided to marry someone else.'

Quig did not react. He blotted out Frances's remark and concentrated on his own immediate concerns. He felt cold and not himself, however. He stood stiffly, almost like a guardsman, before the dais in the window bay, looking up at Madam Lafferty. He heard the younger woman laugh, a brittle sound like a salt-spoon tapping on glass.

'That's enough out of you,' Madam Lafferty told her daughter-in-law, then, almost apologetically, said, 'I ain't so green as I look, Mr Quigley, though she took me in about some things, I'll admit. What is it you really want from me?'

'One hundred and ninety pounds, hard cash.'

'For what purpose?'

'To buy a small boat, a pony, some farm equipment and stock.'

'Good God, Mama!' Frances shrilled. 'He's leaving her.'

'Is that true?'

'I am going to farm on the island of Foss,' Quig said. 'If you do not know where Foss is then I suggest you look out to the west of the Treshnish Isles and you will have its general direction. It's too low-lying to be visible from the Mull shore, except on the point of Calgary.'

'It's where you come from, ain't it?' Dorothea said.

'It is,' said Quig. 'I will be giving you a week to have the validity of my claim to ownership checked, Mrs Lafferty, but no more than a week. If you are willing to trust me then I would like an answer from you now, this hour.'

'And the cash too, I suppose.'

'By the end of next week, certainly.'

'Two hundred pounds ain't gonna see you far.'

'Far enough for me,' Quig said.

'Do you own Foss too?'

'No, Innis Tarrant and her brother Neil are the co-owners. Foss is too small and too far offshore to be leased for winter grazing. I will strike an arrangement with Innis and Neil before I raft cattle over there.'

'And Innis Tarrant will charge you nothing?' said Frances. 'Ah, but you're the crafty one, Quigley. You're getting out Scot-free, by the skin of your teeth. Who are you taking with you, hmmm? That little girl from the south? Baby and all? It's a fair trade if you ask me, especially after my mama gets through with your wife.'

'I want no part in your revenge,' Quig said. 'It is not a thing that any decent man would want to be part of. I do not admire you or even understand you, Mrs Lafferty, but I believe that afforestation will be good for this community whether my wife thinks so or not. It will not be good for me, however.'

'Because you're a cattle rancher, Quig?' said Frances.

'I do not know what I am any more,' Quig said.

'You're betraying her,' Frances said. 'You're abandoning your wife for a younger woman and there's no blinking that fact. I had you marked down as loyal to the bitter end, a devoted, loyal husband. Just goes to show that even the best of men are flawed, don't it, Mama?'

The old woman had one arm along the arm of the chair and the other still folded across her breast. She seemed serious now, sad not smug. Quig wondered if she had discovered a conscience and if he was about to stumble over it. He looked up into the old woman's hazy, somnolent eyes, not bright now, no longer acquisitive, and wondered at the common bond that women shared, all women, enemies and rivals, sisters and friends alike: a distrust and condemnation of men. He had given Biddy what he thought she'd wanted, and she blamed him for it. He was handing the Lafferty woman everything she'd wanted yet she blamed him for the fact that she would accept his offer, that her sworn enemy had become a victim of one man's selfishness.

He thought of Fay, of little Vanessa, of the tiny green haven out there on the edge of the Atlantic, of the ruined house in which he had been raised and of the man who had raised him – and all doubt vanished.

'What is it to be, Mrs Lafferty? Do I get what I am asking for?'

'You do, Mr Quigley,' the old woman answered. 'Oh yes, indeed you do.'

She waited the best part of a week for him to call, to offer apology or even a retraction, to tell her that it was all a dreadful mistake and that he had no intention of marrying Janetta Brown after all. She knew, of course, that he would not retract. Far too many people were privy to the news. Indeed, the whole village was agog and Miss Fergusson's shop in the main street was busier than it had been for many a long day. Maggie was by no means as sympathetic towards Biddy's suffering as Biddy expected her to be. Not for the first time she missed Willy's wise counsel. He would have berated her for making a fool of herself, of course, but he would also have told her to stand upon the remnants of her dignity and not to go chasing after Patrick Rattenbury any more.

She went up to the moor to find the wind device in the hope that he would be there, taking readings. The instrument had gone, though; the crown of rock upon which it had stood was as bare as it had been for a thousand years. She followed one of the old sheep paths to the crest above the stables and, looking down, saw smoke whipping and billowing away from the chimney on the strong wind. He was still in residence in the house that no longer belonged to her. She searched for a sight of the black stallion but saw nothing of him and wondered if Patrick had gone riding off to visit his bride-to-be in Crove.

She knelt in the withering heather and watched for an hour or more until the headache – a different sort of headache – began, then, crawling backwards, she got to her feet and walked home through the falling rain.

The only man who could help her now was her husband, but she had cast him aside. She was tempted to try to rein him in again but knew it was too late. At night she lay by him rigid with the need to have him hold her and be caring and tender again, but she was too haughty and stubborn to offer an olive branch, to give him a sign that she was willing to forgive his fling with the Ludlow girl.

Only when the foresters began to move in did anxiety finally overcome arrogance. She received no word of their arrival – none, it seemed, was needed – and the speed with which the laying out and digging up of An Fhearann Cáirdeil got under way alarmed her.

'There are men in the McKinnon Arms, strange men,' Maggie said.

'What strange men?'

'Surveyors.'

'Who told you that?'

'Hermann.'

'How does he know that they are surveyors?'

'Because he has seen them surveying,' said Maggie.

'What are they surveying?'

'The ground you sold to Mrs Lafferty,' said Maggie.

That night in bed Biddy broke the silence long enough to put a question to her husband. 'Have you heard anything about surveyors measuring the ground on the headland?'

'No,' Quig said flatly.

'Have you not seen them?'

'I have seen nothing,' Quig said.

'So soon,' Biddy said. 'So soon. I thought it would be the spring before anything was done.' And Quig turned away from her, rolling on to his right shoulder and giving her no more to talk to than his back.

The following morning, soon after Quig had left, Biddy went down to the stables. Patrick was not alone. Four or five men were devouring breakfast in the kitchen and Patrick was out in the yard supervising the unloading of a three-horse wagon piled high with timber posts. He made it clear by his manner that he was not at all pleased to see her. He handed the manifest to a young moon-faced fellow and came over to Biddy, frowning.

She said, 'You haven't wasted much time, I see.'

'We were all triggered and ready to fire,' Patrick said. 'It was only a question of waiting for the contract to be ratified.'

'I thought you might have gone back to Perthshire.'

'Really? Why would I do that?'

'To introduce your bride-to-be to your parents.'

'There will be time enough for introductions at Christmas.'

Biddy glanced at the men through the open kitchen door. They were laughing, laughing at her perhaps? The wagon and three Clydesdale horses dwarfed the house, and timber posts, raw but evenly cut, were piled against the gable like shoring. Four men, all strangers, laboured on the unloading.

She would not come here again. She was not entitled to be here, wasn't welcome. Men, strangers, had taken over Fetternish. She felt threatened by their encroachment, the first tightening of the Lafferty knot.

She said, 'Why are you marrying Janetta Brown?'

'Because I'm attracted to her.'

'Attracted?'

'I am very fond of Janetta, Biddy, and I won't let you—'

'You don't love her, do you? You don't love her as you loved me?'

'I had hoped that you wouldn't make a scene.'

'I wonder what sort of scene Netta Brown would make if she knew what you had done to me.'

'I did nothing to you,' Patrick said.

'It *meant* nothing, you mean? I was – what? – a bit of diversion, convenient and willing. God, how you must have laughed up your sleeve, Patrick, when I gave in to you.'

'I am in need of a wife, Biddy, not a mistress.'

'I'm no man's mistress.'

'Oh, I'm well aware of that.'

'Why, why do you need a wife?'

'To protect me from women like you, Biddy.'

'Netta Brown won't give you what you want.'

'Janetta will give me everything I need, more perhaps than I deserve.'

'She's – she's a lump, a peasant. She isn't even an islander.'

'Ah!' Patrick said. 'And here I thought she was perfect.'

'God, but you're a heartless pig.'

'Am I?' Patrick said. 'Yes, I suppose I am.'

'If you expect help and co-operation from me . . .' She gestured agitatedly at the wagon. 'If you think I'm going to . . .'

'I don't need your help, Biddy, or your co-operation. I have everything well in hand, thank you.'

'Well, one thing is for sure,' Biddy said. 'If you and that revolting old woman have your beady eyes on Pennypol, think again. You will not lay hands on one more acre, not one more acre of my land, I promise you.'

'Really?' Patrick Rattenbury said.

And smiled.

Two days later, late in the evening, Quig broke the news.

'I am leaving, Biddy.'

'Yes.' Biddy put down her fork. 'You're going to Dalmally market to sell another parcel of lambs.'

'Barrett will be doing the selling on his own this time,' Quig said.

'Why, where are you going to be?' She looked down at her plate and pushed it away. She gave an uncertain laugh. 'Don't tell me you're taking up residence in Pennymain? Might as well, considering the amount of time you—'

'Not Pennymain.' Quig too pushed away his plate. 'Foss. I am going to have a shot at crofting on Foss.'

Biddy said, 'I won't let you. I won't allow it.'

'I am taking Fay with me, Fay and the baby.'

'Oh, are you indeed?' Biddy laughed again and to demonstrate her lack of concern dragged her plate towards her and spiked a piece of chop. Shaking her head, she put the fragment of lamb into her mouth. 'Oh no, you're not.'

'I am, you know. I'm going to farm on Foss.'

'Farm with what? You need starting capital to farm anywhere, Quig, and I'm certainly not going to provide you with money to go off and have a jolly time with your trollop.'

'It will not be a jolly time for either of us,' Quig said, 'but since you have seen fit to sell Fetternish from under my nose—'

'I have not sold Fetternish, not all of it.'

'The best of it,' Quig said. 'The rest will follow soon enough.'

'Oh, no, no, no. The rest will not follow.' Biddy chewed and swallowed and contemplated the last piece of meat on the plate. 'Are you serious about going away, Quig? I can't believe that you would leave me in the lurch?'

'It is not the lurch, Biddy,' he said. 'You have twelve thousand pounds and a fine big house and a piece of land – though not much – to give you something to do. You also have friends in the tree-planting fraternity and, knowing you as I do, you will soon make more. It is not for me, dearest. I'm leaving.'

'Do you want her that badly?'

'Yes,' Quig said. 'I do.'

She got up so clumsily that the table rocked with the force of it. She leaned on the table, hands spread among the plates.

'How dare you, Robert,' she snapped. 'How damned dare you sit there meek as milk and tell me that our marriage is over. After all I've done for you, after all I've given you, you have the gall to run off to some god-forsaken . . . Foss! Oh, yes, I see. You're retreating, that's it. You're running away, running back to . . . Not a penny: I said and I mean it. Not one brass farthing, Quig. If you want to farm on Foss then you'll have to starve.'

'I sold Pennypol.'

'What?'

'I did not dangle it in front of Mrs Lafferty like a carrot. I sold it, Biddy. I do not need your money to set myself up.'

'Pennypol wasn't yours to sell.'

'Aye, but it was,' Quig said. 'Think on, dearest, and you will remember how it came to me when the old man died and Vassie, your mother, endorsed it. I see now that Vassie left it to me because she wanted me to have something to call my own.'

'That is nonsense,' Biddy shouted. '*Nonsense!*'

'I will be paying Innis and Neil a little bit of a rent for Foss,' Quig said. 'The rest will go into stock. The ground is fertile and the house is not beyond repair.'

'Innis will not let you take the baby away.'

'Innis has urged us to go.'

'Oh! Oh! I see. You are all against me, are you? You've all got
together behind my back to ruin me.'

'Nobody is out to ruin you, Biddy. Whatever has come about
you brought on yourself. Innis is only sorry that—'

'That bitch, that cow of a sister. She's never forgiven me for
what happened with Michael,' Biddy ranted. 'She'll be happy
now, I suppose, delighted to have ruined my marriage just the
way she ruined her own.'

'What did happen with Michael?'

'None of your . . . It's – damn it – it's water under the bridge.'
Then her voice slid down the scale, lowered and melted into a
tone so pitiful that it seemed not like her voice at all but that of a
simpering little girl. 'Oh, please, Quig. Please, Robert. Do not be
doing this to me, not now. I need you. I still need you. I have told
lies, yes, and I have deceived you, yes, and I would do anything
not to have done so. But that's in the past and the future is all
that matters and I'll – look, I'll give you the money. I mean, I'll
share it with you. We'll restock the pasture with sheep or cattle,
whatever you wish. Please, don't do this to me.'

'There is no pasture left, not enough of it,' Quig said. 'Even if
there was, Biddy, it would not be for me to stock or me to tend. I
have been here for you for twenty years, aye, and loved you for
twenty years but . . .'

'And still love me. And still love me.'

'But I have my own life, what is left of it, and you have yours
and that will have to be enough for both of us.'

'Oh, God! First Willy, then Patrick . . .'

'Uh-huh!' Quig murmured under his breath. 'There is Patrick
to consider, though I am fearing that you have lost him too.'

'What did she give you for Pennypol?'

'Enough to get me started.'

'You and your tart, your English trollop. I knew from the
moment I clapped eyes on her that she spelled trouble. Very well,
if you must have her then I'll let you see her. I'll even let you
bring her here to live, Quig, but please don't leave me now.'

'I have to, Biddy,' Quig said. 'I am sorry but I have to.'

'What about our children?'

'You will see to them, as you mostly have in the past.'

'They'll hate you. They'll hate you for what you're doing to me.'

'I doubt it,' Quig said.

He had shown patience and the kind of honesty that she had failed to acknowledge in him before. She had thought him pliant when all the time he had been sly; had thought him meek when he had been bold, had thought that he would love her devotedly no matter how she treated him and that his penance for having been born poor was to love and cherish her and serve her until her dying day.

And she had been wrong.

He got up from the table, wiped his lips on the napkin, folded it and placed it very precisely by his empty plate.

'That is all, Biddy. I will not be staying.'

'Quig?'

'I will be going over to Foss tomorrow if the weather holds.'

'Quig?'

'There is much to be done there.'

'Quig? Oh, Quig?'

'Maggie will look after you, Biddy, and – and that is all I have to say.'

He walked out of the dining-room, out of the house while Biddy, lying across the table, cried and cried his name over and over as if mere repetition, like a spell, would wipe away all the bad memories and bring him running back to her just as he had done before.

EIGHTEEN

The Strawberry Season

'A wild night in the offing,' Gillies said. 'I would not be too tardy in leaving tonight, Patrick. Even that black Bucephalus of yours won't take too kindly to picking his way back to Fetternish in the teeth of a nor'wester.'

'If it gets too bad,' Janetta said, 'and you would not be too uncomfortable, I could make you a bed here in the parlour.'

'Thank you,' Patrick said, 'but I've five chaps billeted at the stables and if I'm not there to stir them out of bed first thing in the morning then nothing will be done, indoors or out.'

'How long will the crew be with you?'

'Ten days, a fortnight at most. We'll bring in a smaller team once the exterior fencing has been erected and the lines of the fire ditches laid down. The underwood will have to be grubbed up, of course, but given that we have the best part of nine hundred acres out there that won't be something that I can hurry. Winter is no bad time for that sort of work, though, and if we have a dryish spell we can move along with draining, road-making and bridging.'

'And the trees?' said Netta.

'They will be brought in as one-year transplants in the spring.'

'The strawberry season,' Gillies said.

'That's an odd way of putting it, Daddy.'

'It's what Fay Ludlow calls it. The spring: the strawberry season.'

'Not strictly accurate,' said Patrick.

'But I do know what she means,' said Janetta. 'Don't you?'

'Oh, I believe I do,' said Patrick. 'Talking of Fay Ludlow, is there any truth in the rumour that Robert Quigley is taking her off to some island farm?'

'It's true,' Gillies said.

'What does your friend feel about that?' Patrick said.

'Innis is all for it,' Gillies said.

'Is a small island cut off from civilisation quite the proper place for a very young child to be reared?'

'Quig was reared there, you know, and other babies too,' Janetta said.

'On a night like this, though . . .' Patrick glanced at the window, shrugging.

'On a night like this Foss will be no more cut off than anywhere else,' said Gillies. 'One of the curious things about town folk is how afraid they are of the unpredictable.'

Patrick nodded. 'I'd thought you might want to be with your friend at Pennymain if a storm's coming up.'

'Innis does not need me to weather storms,' Gillies said. 'Besides, she has Fay with her, and the baby. I'll go down there tomorrow after school just to make sure that everything is well.'

Patrick glanced at Janetta across the width of the hearth. She had taken off her apron now that the supper things had been cleared away and looked very appealing in the firelight. His parents would approve of his choice of a wife; his father certainly. He was less sure about his mother who had never reconciled herself to the fact that he was no longer a small boy who could be told what to do and what not to do. In a way he hoped that his mother would not approve of Janetta, for then he would have the pleasure of watching his schoolmistress woo the old lady and, as she surely would, win her round.

He caught Janetta's eye and winked.

Rather to his surprise, she winked back.

'I hope you're not taking me off to live in a ruined croft, Patrick?'

'I like my creature comforts far too much for that.' He was comfortable with this woman: the fact that he felt no physical desire for her did not much matter. 'I'm considering placing an offer for Dr Kirkhope's house in Tobermory. I've heard he intends to leave quite soon to live with his son in Dumfries.'

'It's a large house, you know,' said Janetta. 'Might it not be too big for us?'

'Plenty of room for a family, eh, Patrick?' said Gillies.

'Daddy,' Janetta said reproachfully. 'How long will you have to superintend the new plantation, Patrick?'

'Three years; longer if other local landowners decide to convert dormant acreage to forest. I'm not averse to staying on Mull, are you, Janetta?'

'I'm happy to go where business takes us, Patrick.'

Gillies stared into the fire, at the long lick of the flames, and listened to the roar of the wind in the chimney.

He thought of the strange inefficiency of fate and how it threw unlikely partners together to construct a future that no man, no matter how astute, could begin to predict: thought too, in passing, of Biddy Baverstock Quigley rattling around in the big empty house of Fetternish now that her husband had left her.

'Daddy?'

'Hmm?'

'Patrick is suggesting that a June wedding would best fit the school term?'

'It would fit perfectly, dearest,' said Gillies.

'June it is then,' Patrick said. 'Do you agree, Janetta?'

'Of course I agree,' said Netta.

*   *   *

Although she had felt quite well that day Dorothea had taken to her bed in the latter part of the afternoon and had dined from a tray in her room.

The room faced north-west and the tall lead-paned window collected the full force of the blast. She loved wild weather. She recalled a crossing of Lake Michigan with Macklin when it had seemed that the paddle-wheeler would tip over at any moment and the lashing waves consume them. Only Macklin and she had not been afraid and, with a great deal of bourbon inside them, had clung to the taffrail, soaked to the skin, and cheered each mighty wave as it swamped the lower deck and raised the wheel, thrashing, clear out of the water.

Nights like this stimulated her and the movement of blood in her veins carried the worst of the pain away. She ate a hearty dinner and as evening turned into night, had Frances bring up a bottle of champagne, two morphine pills and a box of marzipan dainties: rain, high winds, sweetness in her mouth, bubbles in her nose, the gentle sedative effect of the drug in her bloodstream, and Frances, of course, dainty little Frances, sweet as marzipan, to argue with and taunt: Frances who always gave as good as she got and who, if she had not been perverse, would have been a perfect mate for Larry and who, perverse or not, would surely bring him back to her like a bass to shiny bait.

She had Frances fetch the urn from the parlour.

Frances indulged her without a word of protest.

Dorothea knew, of course, that there was precious little left of Iain, that what dust remained had been shaken so many times that any essence of the man would be scant and, as it were, insensible. Even so it comforted her to have the urn propped on the window ledge so that Iain could look out through the rain to the wan glimmer of light in Fetternish House where Biddy Baverstock hunkered alone and unloved.

Frances, in taffeta, was reading a novel.

Cheeks stuffed with almond paste, Dorothea looked down on

her daughter-in-law indulgently. What tales they both could pen if the writing of history had not been so demanding a pastime. Better than any fiction, Dorothea thought. Better than being ravished by sheikhs or wooed by handsome strangers on the Orient Express. More incredibly risqué than any of the novels that Frances ordered from Truslove and Hanson's catalogues. But so tangled that sometimes she could hardly sort out one strand from another as if it were all one, a great rolling tapestry within which she would be preserved for ever, as Iain was preserved in his magnetic little urn.

'Have you written to Larry lately, love?' Dorothea asked.

Frances glanced up, eyes narrow with concentration, then, in theatrical mode, flaring wide open and becoming blue and sparkling in the light of the lamps.

'Love?' she said.

'Have you written to Larry?'

'Yes.'

'At what address?'

'The Egmont, in San Francisco.'

'He hasn't been there in months,' said Dorothea.

'Which is not to say that he won't turn up there again.'

'I wonder if he has found another companion yet.'

'I'm his companion,' Frances said. 'I am his life, his soul, his passion. Simply because we're seldom in the same hemisphere at the same time matters not a jot. Your boy and I are bound together for all eternity.'

'What rot! What balderdash!' Dorothea chuckled. 'Havers! That's what my dear old drunken mammy would have said to that. Havers!'

'Once he manages to sink the yacht, or the yacht manages to sink him,' Frances said, 'he'll come looking for us. He knows where we are. I mean, Mama, it isn't as if he's chasing along one line of latitude and we're travelling on another. Larry will find us just as soon as the money runs out.'

'You do love him, don't you?'

'Absolutely,' Frances said. 'As much as I ever loved any man.'

'And the schoolteacher?'

'Passing fancy.'

Dorothea sniffed and lifted herself from the pillows to look at the urn on the window ledge reflected against the glass.

'I'd love to fall in love again,' Dorothea said.

'Fat chance now, Mama!'

'Yes, I know.'

'Larry still loves you, however.'

'It isn't the same.'

'Perhaps we could pop Larry into an urn and carry him about with us.'

'That ain't funny.'

'No,' Frances agreed. 'You're right.'

Rain beat furiously upon the window and the reflections of the room were sharpened in the mirrored glass. It seemed to Dorothea that she could see her future there, that the heaven that Macklin had believed in was less tangible than the heaven that Iain had made out of this wet, God-blighted island. She too was a Scot, though; that much they had shared below the action of the blood, an unholy yearning for a homeland of heather and mists.

Frances closed the book and stared out into the night as if she too – English as a tea-rose – were finally beginning to share Dorothea's dream and to define the shapes and faces of a future that rolled in like sea-waves out of the great, wild, roaring darkness of the past.

'I wonder where he is now?' Frances said.

'Larry?'

'Iain.'

'Oh!' Dorothea chuckled again. 'On a night like this . . .'

'He's here, isn't he?' Frances plucked the plated urn from the window ledge and holding it against her like a doll, looked out without longing to the headland and the invisible isles beyond. 'I know it, Mama. He's been here with us all the time.'

THE STRAWBERRY SEASON

'Of course he has,' said Dorothea and, with a contented little
sigh, lay back against the pillows and placed another marzipan
on her tongue.

Whatever else he purchased with Madam Lafferty's money it
would not be the salmon-fishers' boat. It handled well enough in
the water but was the devil to drag ashore. He had barely
managed it that morning in spite of an incoming tide and had
kept an eye on it throughout the day, peeping from the shell of
the house now and then to make sure it had not floated off while
his back was turned.

He had unloaded all the gear that had been delivered from the
tent-maker in Greenock together with a huge patched tarpaulin
that he had picked up for a song from the piermaster at
Tobermory. He had also brought along bait and poison, for
the main purpose of the trip was to rid the house of rats.

They were curious creatures and not cunning; the generation
that plagued the ruins of the bungalow were eight or ten
generations removed from the handful that had survived Evander's traps. Now though they were legion, would gnaw and
devour anything and everything not lockered in metal, and hung
from the rafters and peeked from their holes and watched with
interest while he spread the tarpaulin on the floor and measured
it against the gaping aperture in the roof.

Casual inspection indicated that even the main beams were
rotted and would have to be replaced. He had already ordered a
load of planed timber and when it arrived on the puffer from
Croig he would have to raft it ashore and stack it for a week or
two to let it dry out before he could even begin to make the
living-room weatherproof. There was precious little time before
winter set in too, and his skills were rusty. He had ordered tools,
mallet, adze, saws, nails and hammers and knew that he would be
obliged to work from dawn until dusk, sleeping rough in the
cavernous old fireplace or in one of the tents. He couldn't even

433

begin to think of camping, however, until he had thinned out the rat population.

An hour or so after noon he went back to the boat and fetched the eight long corn loaves that Innis had baked for him, along with a packet of salted ham and four cod that he had cadged from the fishers, cod that had been so long in the basket that you could smell them all the way from Penny-main. He did not like what he had to do but he knew that it was necessary if he was to find any peace on the island and make Fay and Vanessa happy.

Biddy had never been to Foss. The little isle was free of all association with the auburn-haired woman whom he had chosen to marry. But neither did he hear Evander calling to him from the back of the hill or the bellow of cattle long gone to slaughter or Aileen mewing from the nettles, or any nostalgic echo to impinge on the unpleasant chore of setting bait.

It was a big, blustery autumn afternoon, not bright but not gloomy. When he paused and went outside for a breather he could smell the tang of the kelp beds heaving against the cliff below the graves of the wives and the faint, doughy odour of the marsh ground where reeds rustled in the sweep of the wind – and that helped him forget the rat smells and rot smells and the fishy smells of the splashes that the gulls had daubed all down the chimney-breast.

He marked where the holes were and the nests and thanked his stars that the rats were not spread out as they would have been if there had been crops or cattle. Later he would stop the holes with tar-paper and dig a pit or two, but today he would do nothing but lay bait.

He had rejected the latest Danish bacillus cultures and had chosen old-fashioned Ratlin which had a strychnine base.

He hated doing it. He hated breaking down the loaves and smearing them with aniseed and molasses, sprinkling on the lethal powder. He hated the way the rats came out to watch him do it, weaving and scuttling and eager, so eager that they would be upon the piece of bait almost before he had moved away. Part of him wanted to warn them, to chase them off, but he was gratified too to see how they gorged on the poison and fought among themselves for the ham and stinking fish.

He baited the house, the runs under the house and the nest holes under the fireplace. Finally, hoisting himself up, he put several fragments of corn loaf on the main beams; then went down to the sea's edge, stripped off his jacket and shirt and washed himself thoroughly, scrubbing his hands and forearms until the skin was red. He hid the Ratlin tin in the heather on top of the knoll and did not go near the house after that. In three or four days he would come back to shovel out the corpses and burn them before the gulls got to them and ingested the poison too. In ten days Foss would be wholesome enough to accommodate him and, in three weeks at most, he would bring Fay and Vanessa over to stay.

It was a good day's work – and a bad day's work; but it had to be done.

He would not stay to see them die. For a moment, an instant only, he resented Fay, the love she had for him and the love he had fostered in her, and the hardness of the life to which he had committed himself for her sake.

It was wearing on towards evening before he finished.

The wind had stiffened and there was rain in the air, big, blotting droplets that splashed into the sand and stained the shoulders of his jacket. To the north-west the cloud had solidified into a black band that stretched like mourning crape across the horizon.

He glanced back at the house where the rats were dying.

He looked at the reeds, the grassland, the spring and the hill. Beyond the hillock the ground swept down clean to the little cliffs above the Atlantic. He felt better, more confident now.

He went to the boat, gripped the keel with both hands and turned it six or eight inches at a time until the bow faced into the breaking waves.

The tide was at full ebb and the waves were jagged and rash as they forged around the corner of the bay. He was tired and he was hungry, his hands raw with man's work, but the killing part would soon be over and he would have Fay and the baby to comfort him. Every day the house would grow stouter, every night they would be warmed by driftwood fires, and the smell of cooking would come down on the wind again, and there would be cattle and sea traffic and a garden where Fay could cultivate vegetables and fruit. And soon it would be the strawberry season and all would be well again.

Quig pushed the boat down into the water.

He clambered over the stern and, poling with a single oar, rowed out into the little bay, steering for the Mull channels, just as the heavens opened and the rain came sweeping in.

It did not take Innis long after Becky's departure to find her feet again. She rose early to feed the hens and collect the eggs while Fay fed the baby. She no longer dallied over prayers but got on with making breakfast so that Fay and she might sit awhile before the business of the day claimed their attention.

Fair to say that Innis missed Becky less than Becky might have hoped. She was glad of the letters that Hermann delivered, however, and relieved to learn that her daughter was settling into life in the city. Her 'test' at the Victoria Infirmary had gone well, Becky wrote, and she expected to be accepted for training in October. There was news too of Donnie and Tricia, of Bobby Brown and Evie, even of Neil and his family, for Becky was a more conscientious correspondent than Rachel had ever been.

Innis replied to all the letters. She was careful not to make too much of Quig and Fay's decision to farm on Foss, though, or to stress that in a week or two she would be alone on Pennymain, for she knew that Becky would regard Fay's departure as a betrayal of sorts.

Adultery ran counter to all Innis's Christian beliefs; even so she could not find it in her heart to condemn the couple or grudge them their happiness. She steered clear of Fetternish House and made no attempt to offer Biddy sympathy; she reckoned that Biddy would think that she had encouraged Quig and Fay in their folly and would want nothing to do with her at this time. Vanessa was the centre of her life in those autumn days and she knew that she would suffer a dreadful sense of loss when Fay finally took the child away to live on Foss.

She had expected Gillies to drop in that afternoon. He still seemed to imagine that she needed protection against heavy rain and big winds, but Innis had never been intimidated by rough weather and Pennymain cottage was the snuggest dwelling in the whole north quarter. It lay against the lip of the gully at Na h-Vaignich which funnelled the wind away from the house. Oh, you could hear the gale whistling like a locomotive and feel the shake of it when the gusts tramped over the slates, and you could see the scrub alders at the top of the gully bend almost double and leaves whirling away like brown snowflakes and all the fallen debris of the summer, straw and twigs and parched bracken, swirling up into the sky. But there was no washing on the drying lines, the hens were snuggled into their stone roost, the coal bucket and water tubs were filled and Kilty lay under a chair by the hearth in the kitchen pretending to be asleep, and Vanessa, wide awake, was as entranced by the drone of the wind as if it were the music of a fair going by.

It would have all been fine and comfortable in Innis's kitchen if Quig had not made the trip to Foss that forenoon and, with dusk approaching, Fay hadn't begun to worry about him.

'He is no fool with a boat, our Quig,' Innis assured her. 'He will have stayed on Foss if he thought that a turn in the weather might catch him out.'

'He'll starve.'

'No, he'll not starve. He took a pack of food with him.'

'The rats . . .'

'Quig is used to this sort of thing, Fay. He will not consider it much of a hardship to spend a night alone, rats or no rats. If the sea is still running heavy tomorrow then he will stay on for another day or even two.'

Fay, kneeling by the baby's basket, looked up. 'I think I'll walk over to Pennypol just to see if he's back yet.'

'You will not be leaving the house tonight,' Innis said. 'If Quig thought that I had let you go out in this weather he would be having a fit.'

'What time is it, Mam?'

'There is the clock. See for yourself. It is half past six o'clock.'

'It's so dark out there.'

'It is dark because of the storm.'

'What if he drowns?'

'Stop it,' Innis said gently. 'He will not drown. He is not like the fishermen who go out in all weathers to secure a catch. He will be safe on Foss, believe me.'

The storm made Fay nervous. She hated the demented wailing of the gale that shook the walls and pushed gouts of smoke from the sides of the stove. She glanced at Kilty who had one eye open and one ear pricked; at Vanessa who was staring wide-eyed at the ceiling as if she could peer through the slates and see the moiling clouds and silvery rods of rain outside.

The plots would be ruined, Fay thought, the topsoil washed away, the fence flattened. There were bedding plants still to lift for transportation to Foss and a heap of seed potatoes stored in the cottage, and she suspected that the deluge would ruin them. She would feel safe only when Quig was with her again, Quig and baby and she all together.

'What's that?'

'Nothing. It is nothing,' Innis said. 'The door of the shed has sprung loose. I should have been changing the rope on it weeks ago.'

'Is it Quig? Is it Robert, do you think?'

'It is the shed door, that's all. Sit down, Fay, or you will frighten the baby.'

Vanessa's fingers opened and closed, kneading the air close to her ears. She was animated but not fractious, her little moods and fancies showing in changes of expression as faint as a cat's breath on milk.

Fay listened to the battering of the door against the wall of the shed. She longed for Quig to come home, to reassure her, to go into her bedroom and peel off his soaking clothes and put on the clean drawers and flannels and shirt that he kept there now that he had left Fetternish House for good.

'Damn it!' Fay snapped. 'I'm going out to rope that door before it comes flying in on us. Is it the water closet or the shed?'

'The shed.' Innis sighed. She lifted Vanessa from the cradle into her arms. 'Go and do it, dearest, if it will make you feel better.'

Fay unlatched the kitchen door and eased it open.

The wind came from behind the house and ripped at the water that poured from the eaves, carried it off in glossy sheets that smacked on the path and the lawn. The path ran like a flooded river. The rose bushes were stripped of their blooms. She heard the wicket gate chatter as she slung an overcoat over her head and scuttled out into the garden.

The shed loomed in the darkness, its door flapping loose, slapping violently against the woodwork. Fay groped for the hook and the tattered rope, drew the door shut and fumbled to knot the rope's end through the hook; then an arm fastened itself around her throat and a hand clamped over her mouth and above the babble of the wind a voice yelled into her ear: 'Hello, Fay, do you remember me?'

Biddy had elected to eat an early supper at the kitchen table with Maggie and Aileen and did not have the temerity to demand that Maggie set the table with a linen cloth.

They ate soup, and macaroni pudding, stewed apples and raisins for dessert. Biddy sipped the coarse blend of tea that

Maggie preferred and offered no complaint at plain fare. She had no urge to converse, no desire to trade gossip or allow Maggie an opportunity to slip in sly, insidious questions about Quig and Fay. She was certain that the housekeeper would broadcast her answers to acquaintances in Crove or, since Hermann and Maggie had become 'cosy', relay them via the postman to every nook, cranny and isolated steading in the north quarter.

It was already obvious to everyone that Biddy Baverstock Quigley had sold out to the tree-planters. Some folk praised her foresight, some condemned her greed.

In the matter of Quig, the English girl and her baby, however, there was still too much speculation for Biddy to give in to Maggie Naismith's probing. Biddy had no idea just how much Aileen understood, for she'd never been able to communicate with her troubled sister. Supper therefore was a silent affair. Biddy tactfully praised the pudding and, afterwards, helped Maggie wash up while Aileen sat on the end of the iron range humming and smiling to herself, as if the sight of her older sister plying a dish-towel amused her.

'Will you be staying down here with us?' Maggie asked when Biddy folded the drying-cloth and draped it on the rack above the stove. 'I have a good fire going in my parlour and you are welcome to sit in with us there if you are finding upstairs on the empty side.'

'Thank you, Maggie,' Biddy said. 'I've work to do in the library.'

'Work? Is there still work for you to be doing then?' said Maggie.

'Of course there is,' said Biddy. 'Just because . . . I have letters to write.'

'To the little ones, I suppose.'

It had been so many years since Robbie and Christina had been 'little' that Biddy suspected the housekeeper of sarcasm or the kind of irony that only Tom Ewing would appreciate.

She would not see much of Tom now, alas: the minister and his wife were on the side of the enemy and any dealings with them were bound to be awkward and embarrassing. She could not even bring herself to go to church services to face her former friends and her enemies and rivals. How could she possibly pretend – as Innis had done – that all was fine and dandy, that she didn't mind in the slightest that her husband had abandoned her for a younger woman?

Besides, Patrick would be sharing Gillies Brown's pew now, Janetta clinging to her man, and swanking; the impossible bride, the spinster bride, the virgin queen of the classroom, showing off her marvellous catch.

Soon there would be diggers, drainers and foresters filling the kirk. They would be sniffing after the village lassies and the village lassies would be sniffing after them and there would be lots of scandal to keep tongues wagging in the coming months and years. If she, Mrs Bridget Quigley, kept her head under the parapet and her nose clean she did not doubt that in due course of time the villagers would be unable to endure the fact that she could rub along quite merrily on her own and would coax her back into favour – and then she would show them what it meant to have money and power, by God she would.

She went into the library and stood before the windows, looking out. A tiny nagging headache, nothing really, ticked quietly above her left eye. She felt rather well, however, not lively but calm and almost drowsy, as if her body were telling her brain to rest. Resting would be the best way of getting through the winter months, the fallow season, until she felt able to take up cudgels once more. She might emerge before that, travel to Edinburgh for Christmas and New Year, say, have the children stay with her in the Wellington, make a proper party of it.

And then again she might not.

She watched rain solidify against the glass and listened to the wind hunting through the corridors and passageways. She felt the house around her, its massive emptiness bearing down, pressing her like a leaf between its pages. She carried the lamp to the table by her mother's chair and seated herself with her back to the window. She had no work to do, nothing worth doing, nothing left of the events of the summer but vague remnants of anger and desire.

She had only been asleep for a few minutes when Aileen came into the room.

Aileen wore a simple gingham dress that Maggie had picked out for her and looked as neat and plain as a schoolchild ready for her first class. She had a bonnet on, though, a poke bonnet that she'd unearthed from the chest in the dusty sewing-room high up at the base of the tower, a bonnet that hid her greying curls and made her features as sharp as a weasel's. She stood motionless in the doorway, firelight flickering on the panelling behind her.

Biddy let out a little groan and then – the new Biddy, prim and patient and emotionally organised – said, 'What is it, Aileen? What do you want?'

Aileen giggled.

'He's here again,' she said.

Frowning, Biddy sat upright. 'What? Who's here?'

But Aileen, still giggling, had already scampered away.

The scuffle alarmed her but when he came into the kitchen and she saw who it was her apprehension drained away.

'Gavin,' she said, and then, 'Gavin, is it really you?'

'Aye, Mam, it is.'

He held Fay by the arm, not the hand; held her, it seemed to Innis, gently, for she did not see the knife in his fist.

She glanced at the baby in the shawl in her arms, back up at her son.

He was exactly as she had imagined, a grown-up version of the boy he had been when she had seen him last, walking away from her up the track to the road. He was taller, broader, more muscular but his shock of dark hair reminded her of those wet winter days when he would sneak in from wherever he had been with his hair sticking up like a crown of thorns; how she would try to dry him and how he would wriggle from her and, scowling, snatch the towel from her grasp and go off into the space behind the stove to do for himself. He had had a child's body, hairless and slender, but even then she had known how much of a man he would become, smooth-muscled and compact and strong; handsome too, handsome the way her brother Donald had been before he drowned, as handsome as young Robbie Quigley who, Innis realised, might have been Gavin's twin.

For a moment she was caught off guard and thought angrily how wrong it was of Quig to separate her son from his wife; how, with his arm about her and his hand on her arm there was something so pleasing and natural in his treatment of his wife that there could be no place in the world better suited for Fay than with Gavin.

'Is it a boy?' he asked.

'No,' Innis said. 'It is a daughter you have. Did your father not tell you?'

'He tells me nothing,' Gavin said. 'Give her here.'

Fay wrenched free of him. She lashed out, swinging her arms.

The knife was suddenly visible in his fist, a shepherd's knife with a short, curved blade and a ram's horn handle. Gavin wore a shepherd's smock in the English style. It was draped over a shabby suit. Strapped to his back was one of the meal-packs that shepherds carry on to the high Dales. Fay had sketched the picture for her and Innis saw him there clear as a vision among the ewes and the larks in the clear morning air.

'Girl or not, I'll take her,' Gavin said.

'Wait,' Innis said, as if she hadn't seen the knife, as if the knife did not exist. 'Wait, son, you are wet through. Come and I will give you a towel and a dry shirt and something to eat and then you can have her to hold for a while.'

'I'll cut her.' Though his voice had deepened it was still flat and dead-toned, not a Highland voice, soft around the edges. 'I will, Mam, I'll cut her quick as wink if you don't give me the kiddie.'

Innis felt a sudden sough of horror, a shock of recognition.

He was not one of them, she realised, he was all of them: Ronan her father, Evander her grandfather, Michael too, her husband, his father. He was the dark part of Aileen and the stubborn part of Biddy and she knew that he was beyond all redemption, all prayer and pleading and that her piety would count for nothing in the face of the son she had lost.

Innis clasped Vanessa to her breast and stepped back.

Gavin drew the knife blade across Fay's forearm.

Fay did not cry out or flinch. She leaned into him, hugging him, then reached up and thrust her hand into his face with the tenacity of a mollusc seeking a hold on rock.

He lifted her and held her clear of the floor. She seemed to have no weight, no substance at all. He held her as he might have held a lambskin and then, just as effortlessly, threw her down. He rubbed the back of the knife hand across his cheek and examined the streaks of blood that her nails had torn from his flesh. Then he trod on her, digging into her shoulder with his hobnails.

Fay scrambled away from him just as the spaniel emerged from under the chair, growling. She caught up the little dog and flung him with all her might at her husband.

Innis stepped back, back again. Vanessa wailed. On the wall, above the cup, the statue of Our Lady was blue and cool. Innis bowed towards the statue, yearning for it. Gavin caught her by the shoulder and dragged her away from the bedroom. She could hear Kilty squealing and gasping, glimpsed his body on the floor, blood welling around his flanks. Gavin tugged at her skirt, caught her by the hips, dragged her backwards into the kitchen and punched her once on the brow. She felt rather than saw him snatch Vanessa. Heard Vanessa's infant wail rise to a high keening note, too strident for small lungs. She staggered, fell against the wall and slid slowly down it, her senses blurred.

She had lost him, had lost the child, had lost Vanessa.

Nothing could be saved. No redemption for her soul, his soul, none of the infinite mercy in which she had always believed. She felt hollowed out, scooped out, and sat on the stone floor, doll-like, with blood all around her.

'Where is he?' Gavin said. 'Where's Quig?'

Dimly, Innis heard Fay answer: 'You willn't have my baby, Gavin.'

'Is he at the shore? Is that where Quig's at?'

'Who told you I was here?' Fay sounded frosty and aloof as if she were in control of him. 'Was it your father?'

'Him! Christ!' Gavin shrugged the shawl against his shoulder and tucked it in about the baby. 'He told me you was gone for good. He told me you wasn't here. I knew you was here, Fay, knew you was here from the first. Knew you was carrying too. What you think, Fay, think I let you go off and tell the world about me?'

'Josh ain't the one.'

'Josh ain't the one.' Gavin did not mock or mimic. 'Josh ain't anyone now. He dead. He dead and buried on the limestone and they won't find no bones, cause the birds got his bones.'

Kilty had fallen silent. He still panted a little, the fine soft hair on his belly rising and falling. Innis could see her feet, focus on her feet. Saw Fay kneeling, hands flat on the stone floor, blood like a gauntlet covering her forearm. Fay and not Fay: Fay beaked like a hawk, towy fair hair ruffed about her face: Fay emanating a fierce cold rage that Innis could not emulate or even imagine.

'You killed Josh, you pig. You'll hang for that,' Fay hissed. 'Now give me back my kiddie and get out of my mother's house.'

'She ain't your mother. She's my mother,' Gavin said. 'You want her, you can have her. Only you ain't going to have nobody, Fay, not her, not Quigley, not his baby neither. I didn't come all the way from Fream just for you to tell me I ain't no good for anything. You're wrong, girl, I am good, I am good, I'm better good than she ever thought I was.' He drew Vanessa against him and crossed his arms over her. 'Why did you have to come back

to them?' He shook his head. 'Well, I completed my business in
Fream, now I got to complete my business here. Finish it right
here, right now and you ain't the one to stop me, Fay.'

Innis propped herself up and strove to find balance.

Gavin glanced at her. 'What you going to do, Mam, pray for
me to let go? Nah, nah, nah, nah. I aim to finish it right here and
now so you can spend the rest on your days wondering if it was
you or me that done the bad things.'

'Put down the baby,' Innis heard herself say. 'Gavin, put down
the baby before you hurt her.'

'She ain't hurt. I'm the one hurt.'

'Gavin, you pig!' said Fay. 'Give her to me.'

'Where is he? I know he ain't at Biddy's house.'

'Give me my baby,' Fay said, 'and I'll tell you.'

'The kiddie might mean something to you but she mean
nothing to me,' Gavin said. 'Where's Quig?'

'Pennypol,' Fay said. 'He's at Pennypol. Do you remember
where that is?'

'I remember everything,' Gavin said. 'It's all stored inside my
head.'

Fay lunged at him then fell back, hands raised in surrender at
the sight of the knife pressed into the soft white wool of the
shawl.

'Don't,' Fay whispered. 'Don't hurt her.'

'She'll go where she has to,' Gavin said. 'She got no more say
than I have.'

'Where are you taking her?' Fay said.

'Going home, sweetheart, to find Dada,' Gavin said and
moved out into the darkness with Vanessa wrapped in his arms.

'It's nothing,' Biddy said. 'Really, it's nothing.'

She squeezed her fingers into the waist of her skirt and felt a
warm, damp patch hardly bigger than her thumb. There was a
curious lack of pain, only a little scissoring stitch when she

breathed, no worse than a stiff corset string. She sat bolt upright on the fourth step of the staircase, holding her side, breathing as shallowly as possible. She waited for panic to strike, shock, but so far she felt perfectly all right. She watched the carpet lift and shift itself eight or ten inches across the polished floor, saw a flame rise up from the smouldering logs in the hearth as they were fanned by the draught from the open door.

Aileen said, 'Gavin came.'

She was seated two steps below Biddy, head resting against the newel post. She seemed neither dazed nor distressed, merely weary as if the effort of being rational, even for a moment or two, had exhausted her. She did not look round when Maggie knelt to examine Biddy's wound; did not, it seemed, have the strength to retreat into mental oblivion where cause, effect and consequence had no explanation except the one that she chose to impose upon them.

'Oh, my! Oh, my!' Maggie said. 'You're bleeding, Biddy.'

'I know I'm bleeding, damn it,' Biddy snapped. 'For God's sake, pull yourself together.'

'I will be going to the stables, that is the nearest place. If Mr Rattenbury's not there I will send someone into Crove to fetch help.'

'No,' Biddy said. 'We don't need help. We'll deal with this situation ourselves. Did you tell Gavin that his wife was at Pennymain?'

'I had to tell him. He asked where Quig was. It was Quig he really wanted,' said Maggie. 'He would have cut your throat and mine and Aileen's too no doubt if I hadn't told him. He is a mad person, Biddy, do you not see that?'

'Of course he's mad,' Biddy said. 'That's why we're going to keep it to ourselves, if we possibly can.'

'What if he does away with her?'

'It won't come to that,' Biddy said. 'I'm sure it won't come to that.'

'You, though, you need medical attention.'

'It's no more than a flesh wound. I can feel it through the cloth. Please go downstairs and bring me up a bowl of cold water and several clean towels. Scissors too. Take Aileen with you.'

'No, I will be going for help, and that's that.'

'If you do,' Biddy said, 'it's the last thing you will ever do in this house. Now if you aren't going to fetch me water and towels I'll just have to fetch them myself.'

Biddy pushed herself to her feet. She felt a little light-headed. The worst was over, though, the threat had moved on. She had survived her nephew's return. Whatever Gavin did now was none of her business. They had all abandoned her and could look out for themselves.

She pinched her fingers into her side. Pain had started up, true pain not the scalding little pains of imagination. She experienced a sudden solid sense of reality as she listened to the bellowing of the wind and the slashing of the rain. What a fine house this was, she thought, what a fine, solid house Austin had left her to hide in.

'Bolt the doors, Maggie, and make sure that all the ground-floor windows are secure,' Biddy said. 'I doubt if Gavin will come back this way but we mustn't be caught unprepared if he does. Do that first, then fetch the scissors and we'll see just how much damage has been done to me.'

Maggie backed away, horrified at the sight of the bloodstains on Biddy's pretty blouse. 'I will, I will, I will,' she whispered, then turning on her heel rushed down the corridor that led to the kitchens.

'Be quick,' said Biddy, puffing out her cheeks, and shakily sat down again.

She waited impatiently for Maggie to return and then, almost angrily, gripped the collar of her dress with both fists and ripped it downward. She felt the seams resist and knotting her fingers into the material, tugged and tore at the fabric until the hooks and buttons and finally the threads parted. She pulled the dress down to her waist, the bodice too, and exposed her breast and the flesh of her torso.

There was blood, not rich or thick or sticky, just a smear of it like varnish across her belly. Aileen was watching her, the girl's head cocked, a strand of grey hair dangling across her brow, her eyes keen, alert and interested.

'Bad,' Aileen said: it was not a question.

'No, not bad,' Biddy told her.

She bent to examine the wound. As she did so the slash across the top of her hip opened wide and blood pumped out. She was gratified by its colour, a gorgeous scarlet, and by the little pulsation that activated it.

It made her feel alive to see blood again, her own blood, dense and unadulterated. She dabbed at it with her fingertip then wiped her palm across the wound. Nothing serious: just a shallow cut five or six inches in length that went no deeper than the skin and one layer of fat beneath. There was no perforation, no penetration. She would not die from Gavin's knife, would in fact bear the scar rather proudly, proudly and secretly like the memory of a lover's kiss.

She pinched the lips of the wound with forefingers and thumbs and, lifting her head, called out again, 'Maggie, Maggie, be quick,' while Aileen, slumped below her on the stairs, shook her head and, with many a rueful little sigh, repeated, 'Bad, bad, bad. Bad, bad, bad,' until Biddy told her to cease.

Quig had taken refuge in the cottage among the plants and tools. It was dark in the cottage and he could not find the old flint tinderbox on the shelf under the ladder to the loft. He knew it was there because Fay had found it. Fay had even lit a candle with it once when they had been caught out by dusk. The tinderbox had lain on the shelf for twenty years at least, Quig reckoned, and it had given him an odd feeling to see the spark ignite the tiny pile of teasel that Vassie had collected.

He was too wet and exhausted to go hunting for Vassie
Campbell's tinderbox tonight, however. He had managed the
crossing from Foss only by the skin of his teeth, rudder, ropes
and sail barely under control and the boat filling up with
seawater with every break of the waves. He had baled with
his hat and thought back to the time when Ronan had made a
whisky run to Oban in a storm and had lost not just his boat but
his elder son. Then he, Quig, had come round the corner of
Pennypol Bay and had picked up the familiar shape of Olaf's Hill
through the rain and had reefed the sail and taken the oars and
brought it in across the angle of the bay to the jetty. He had even
managed to tie the painter to the ring before he had flopped
ashore and crawled to the cottage a quarter-mile away.

The cottage smelled of dampness and growth. Curious how
the crop released such a dry green smell. Curious too how the
sagging turf roof managed to withstand the seasonal gales and,
apart from drizzling little pockets near the gable, keep out the
rain. Would Evander's house on Foss be as taut as this old
cottage? he wondered, as he huddled against the hearthstone and
stripped off his oilskin and rubbed his chest and aching
shoulders. He felt warmer now and, in his way, secure. Now
that it was over he realised that in making the crossing he had
discovered a kind of emancipation that was very satisfying. He
would rest for ten or fifteen minutes before he trudged back to
Pennymain, though. He rested his head against the wall and
thought of Foss, of the Foss that had been and would be again,
and drowsed and jerked awake and drowsed again, huddled on
old Vassie Campbell's hearthstone with the gale howling like a
banshee overhead.

He had not been asleep for long but when he wakened he was
cold to the bone. He sat up, shivering, and listened for the sound
that had brought him out of sleep: not the brassy notes of the
storm but some tiny sound within it, like the piping of a curlew
or the mewling of a cat.

It had been foolish of him to fall asleep in wet clothing. He scrambled to his feet, shuddering and shivering, and slapped his arms about him. Then stopped, listening again. Then moved into the doorway, peered out in the darkness, and saw the pale shape against the mud at the top of the plots, a milky shape on the wet black earth that he had turned over only a week ago.

At first he mistook it for a tuber that had been washed to the surface, some sort of vegetable, oval and firm; then he heard the mewling again, so faint and weak that it was almost unreal. He stepped from the shelter of the doorway into the teeming rain and, running now, flung himself down upon it and covered the tiny tuberous shape, scooped it up and knelt in the mud of the plots of Pennypol with Fay's child cradled in his arms.

He fell away, sliding, a split second before the blow. He felt the air slice away and rolled on his shoulder, the baby held to his chest, rolled again as the adze buried itself in the earth an inch from his head.

He leaped to his feet and ran blindly down the slope towards the beach with the infant bobbing silently in his arms. He could feel her little limbs slack as seaweed under the shawl.

Stricken with terror, he plunged on until the rabbit fence caught him across the thighs and he fell, rolling instinctively on to his back, into the bracken.

'I can see you, Robert Quigley. I know where you are.'

He burrowed into the bracken, holding the child against him. He could see nothing, touch and sight merging until he knew not which sense was which, or where he was. Crouched on all fours, he stopped. He put out his hand and with the crook of his finger gently lifted away the folds of the shawl and wiped Vanessa's mouth and nose. To his relief she snuffled and gave out a strange little sneeze as if she had just wakened from sleep.

He listened for the boy. No boy now: Gavin Tarrant. Listened for Gavin. Heard only the raging wind and gusts of rain in the withered bracken, the black boom and surge of the sea. Back arched, he waited for the curved iron blade of the adze to strike him. He trembled with fear, not for his own safety but for the safety of the child, with the fear that he might let her down.

He counted under his breath. *Five, eight, ten, twenty.* Sensible thing would be to leave the baby in the bracken, crawl away, stand up and let Gavin see him, the way a mother hare will divert attention from leverets hidden in the grass.

He could not abandon Vanessa, though. Couldn't leave her alone in the rain and the darkness. He dropped to the ground and rowed himself forward with his elbows. Felt a sudden space before him as the bracken thinned at the rim of the beach. He lifted his head, peered out at the waves roaring on the beach and the towering jets of water that sprayed over the jetty. He was reluctant to take to the beach. Would be easily seen on the beach. Could not risk doubling back to the cottage either in case Gavin was still prowling in the vicinity. For all he knew, though, Gavin was close by, stalking him, the adze raised, that implacably boyish snout poking and sniffing him out.

Quig wiped the baby's face again. Felt a puff of breath upon his fingertips: a sign, a sigh of resignation, of life in her still.

Lighter now: at night the sea was always lighter than the land. Waves leaping high over the jetty gave him a point of reference. He glanced behind him. Saw only impenetrable blackness, bracken tossing and shaking like something alive. He looked again towards the jetty. Two tracks led from it. One to the cottage. The other cleaved to the edge of the bracken until it curved towards the dyke at the foot of Olaf's Hill. A neglected track, stony and sparse. If he could find that track he could make his way on to the hill and on to the ridge and would have the lights of Pennymain to guide him. If Gavin did trail him to Pennymain at least he would have the rifle he'd hidden there to even up the score and, if the worst happened, he would make a stand in the garden of the cottage to keep the women safe. He steadied himself, then, holding Vanessa tightly, scuttled in the direction of the jetty.

Out of the shelter of the bracken, knees bent, the baby against his shoulder. He crooned to her, patted and soothed her, walked at a half crouch across the sward towards the butt of the jetty. He could feel dread lift from him. If he were cautious and patient his plan would work. Once he reached the hill Vanessa and he would be safe. Spume from the jetty stung his cheeks and smarted in his eyes. He swung away from the sea to shield the child.

And Gavin said, shouting, 'I see you, Quig. I got you now.'

Quig knelt on one knee and carefully placed the baby on the ground.

Then he stood up and turned around.

Quig had shown her not only where the rifle was hidden but also how to load it. She ran with the gun in one hand, eight bullets tucked into the pocket of her skirt. She had told Innis what she intended to do while she had put on her overcoat and tied on her Sunday-best bonnet. She would have taken a lantern but she didn't want Gavin to see her coming. Resolute rather than calm she headed down the path and through the wicket gate. She ran with the rifle held against her thigh, the bullets safe and dry in her skirt pocket and, in spite of the gale, reached the crest of Olaf's Hill in twenty minutes.

The bay was like a photograph gone wrong. Mr Musson had a camera and had amused himself by taking photographs of flowers and had developed them by the scientific method in the shuttered little closet behind the greenhouse. She had watched once or twice, for he was proud of his hobby, and he had taught Josh how to use the chemicals. Josh was dead now, murdered for no reason other than to appease Gavin's jealousy and the rage that had been his birthright. Fay struggled over the rain-lashed summit and looked down. The bay was sketched out in light that was no light save that of the sea and the rain. She buckled before the ferocity of the wind on the ridge and dropped on all fours while she pondered what to do next. The Campbells' cottage was like a dark stack of peat beyond the dark ocean of bracken and the dark earth of the plots, the moor defined only by rain.

Fay rested for a moment then started down the slope towards the broken dike. She stumbled over it, righted herself and went on, steadily and warily, towards the line of the wall that Innis and Biddy and old Vassie had built to keep sheep off their grazings: old stories of men dead and gone and women withered into dust. She might have been part of that ungentle time, might have preferred it to Fream's strawberry beds and flowers and high, soft summers. She felt water in her eyes. Tears. Tears for Josh. Tears for her lost baby. Then tears were replaced by cold, insinuating hatred.

Sheltered behind the end of the long wall, Fay fished out the bullets, thumbed them into the rifle and slipped the bolt. She crept around the gable and entered the cottage with the rifle held against her hip.

Nothing there: no sign of Gavin or Vanessa.

She stepped on to the plots and stood there with rain pouring down and great gusts of wind slapping her coat against her bare legs. He was here somewhere. She sensed it. She knew that he had to kill Quig to annul his guilt and anneal his rage. Old scores held no interest for her. She cared not whose son he was or what legacy of wickedness had fashioned him, or who was to blame for Gavin.

All she wanted was her baby back.

'Gavin,' she shouted. 'Gavin.'

She hesitated, shouted out again, then, still shouting his name, slithered down the length of the plots, stepped over the rabbit fence and headed for the jetty where Quig, if he had made it back from Foss, would have tied up the boat. She waded knee-deep through the bracken, blinking away salt tears, peering into the darkness, the rifle held up in both hands.

She was guided to the jetty by the oceans of seawater that broke thunderously over it. She thought she could see the boat tossing wildly by the wall of the jetty but she was afraid to go too close to the surge that poured and sucked in the darkness. She had never known fear like it, purpose like it. She advanced without conscious thought, without courage, on to the sward that led to the jetty and felt the spume sting her face. She wiped her sleeve across her eyes and looked again. Saw them. Saw the grotesque shape outlined against the waves. Ran towards it, shouting Quig's name.

They were wrestling with the comical intensity that fully clad men bring to the art of combat. Any sounds they uttered were lost in the shriek of the wind. Even when she reached them Fay could not make out which man was which or which man had the upper hand.

They fought on the flat at the tail of the jetty, skittering and slithering, retreating for an instant then uniting again, fused into a single dark and indistinguishable shape that twisted and sank and rose amid the slick sheets of seawater. The adze in Gavin's fist was swung with a scything motion that forced Quig to side-step or leap over the blade. She watched Quig move in and snatch Gavin's clothing, smother the flailing arm so that the adze pecked aimlessly in the air while Gavin tried to find purchase for a final blow.

She watched them grapple for half a minute before she stepped forward and raised the rifle. She felt the wind tug at it, and gripped it firmly, left hand along the stock, the smooth sensuous shape of the guard sliding beneath her palm until her forefinger found the trigger.

'Gavin,' she yelled.

He glanced up. His pale, peaked face separated itself from the shadowy mass. He seemed – Fay thought – startled to see her but whether or not he saw the rifle she had no way of knowing.

'Gavin,' she shouted again and just as Quig pushed him away, tilted the rifle, snatched at the trigger and fired point-blank into her husband's face.

*　　*　　*

Quig tipped the carrots out with the sand, broke up the boxes with his heel and, using Vassie's tinderbox, managed to induce a spark while Fay stripped the baby. She peeled off her overcoat and skirt, tore her petticoat into swaddling, rubbed her daughter's limbs and pressed her close to her breast to warm her. Quig had found some dry sacking in the side room of the cottage. He folded the musty stuff and laid it over the infant and Fay's bare legs then knelt and blew into the struggling flame until the boxwood caught. He picked up a new hoe, broke the shaft into pieces and fed them one by one on to the fire so that, within minutes, there was a blaze.

He sat back and stared out at the darkness beyond the threshold.

'Is she still breathing?' he asked.

'Can't you hear her squawking?' Fay said.

'Is nothing broken?'

'Nothing that I can see,' Fay said. 'She's bruised but bruises will heal quickly once she is warm.'

Quig nodded. 'We were lucky.'

'I don't think it was luck,' Fay said. 'I think they'll come for me tomorrow and I'll be taken away.'

'Why will they take you away?'

'For killing him with a gun.'

'If you had not killed him he would have killed all of us, the baby too.'

'That's not how the law will look at it,' Fay said.

'How do you know how the law will look at it?'

'Josh told me.'

'Josh? I thought Josh was dead?'

'Oh, he's dead,' said Fay. 'I don't doubt Gavin killed him and my poor Josh is broken up and buried on the high peaks and he won't be found.'

Quig had stopped shaking but a great weariness threatened to overwhelm him: shock at the events of the past half-hour together with the exertions that had preceded them.

'I know what the law will do to me,' Fay said, 'how I'll be marked out afterwards even if a jury or a judge finds me innocent of a crime.'

Quig said, 'How do you know this, Fay?'

'We spoke of it often enough,' Fay said, 'Josh and me. Josh made a point of finding out what the law might do to a wife who kills her husband.'

'Did Gavin know about your conversations with Josh?'

'Not him.' Fay smiled faintly and shifted Vanessa up beneath the sacking so that her head appeared and her pink fists groping for the teat.

Quig marvelled at the resilience of small life forms, the innocence that protected them, and the greed. He said, 'Do you have milk, Fay?'

'Aye, I've milk. When she's warm enough, she'll feed.' She stroked her daughter's dark hair. 'After that, though, we'll wrap her up and carry her to Pennymain to tell Innis what's happened and to notify the proper authorities.'

Quig eased himself forward. His back was racked with rowing, his chest bruised. There was a throbbing in his right arm but no blood, not one drop of blood upon him. 'When did you and Josh discuss your plan?'

'When we were together.'

'After your marriage?'

'Afterwards, yes,' said Fay.

He searched her face for a sign of remorse: found none. She might have been seated by the fire in Innis's house, her baby on her lap, crooning a lullaby while they waited for Daddy to come home from the sea. He experienced a wave of something that was neither pity nor compassion. He waited for it to go away, but it did not. He squatted on his heels in the old way and studied her intently. He had marked her as weak, a cripple, a victim, another lame duck who would adore him for taking her under his wing. He had been wrong this time. Little Fay Ludlow was more of a warrior than any of the Pictish queens who had combed these shores for husbands in days long gone.

He watched her adjust the sacking and nudge the baby's mouth towards her teat then he said, 'How do you know that Gavin is dead?'

Fay winced slightly as the baby tugged on her nipple. 'You saw him, Quig. You saw me shoot him.'

'Shoot at him,' Quig said. 'How do you know that you did not miss?'

'Surely he was dead when the wave caught him and swept him into the sea?'

'He has gone into the sea, that's true,' Quig said, 'and we cannot be sure if the sea will ever give him up again.'

'What do you mean, Quig?'

'Who is to say what happened tonight or who fired the shot that killed your husband or how he really died?' Quig said. 'Is it not my rifle?'

'I thought it was Biddy's rifle.'

He shook his head. 'Well, there is no need to go splitting that particular hair. As far as anyone is concerned it is my rifle.'

'And what?'

'I fired it.'

'Is that what you'll tell the authorities?'

'There is no one to contradict me.'

'I'll contradict you.'

'Will you?' Quig shifted position and drew closer. 'Do you think it is all up with us, Fay? Do you want it to be all up with us?'

'No, that's not what I want.'

'What if we say that Gavin never arrived at Pennypol?'

'But Vanessa, the baby? How did she . . .'

'Only Innis knows that Gavin took Vanessa away with him.'

'Innis won't lie. She ain't on our side, Quig. And Gavin's her son. She must have loved him at one time.'

'Did you love him at one time?'

'Yes. Yes I did.'

'More than you loved Josh?'

'Josh is dead,' Fay said sternly. 'Josh has nothing to do with us now.'

'Will he not be missed?'

'Sir Johnny will think he ran off to find me.'

'Will you not miss him, Fay?'

'I'll not miss Gavin, no,' Fay said.

'Well, there you are.' Quig put out a hand and brushed the baby's brow. He remarked the dew of perspiration on her, the heat that feeding drew out. 'Josh will not be missed. Gavin will not be missed. You are the only one who can tell the procurator what really happened, that I did not pull the trigger or that Gavin was ever here with us at all.'

'Are you saying you'd give yourself up for my sake?'

'If necessary, yes,' Quig said, 'but it may not be necessary.'

'Where's the rifle?'

'I have the rifle.'

'What if Gavin's washed up with a bullet in his head?'

'We will tell them that he must have shot himself.'

'They'll know we're lying.'

'Even if they do,' Quig said, 'I do not think they will care very much or make too much fuss about finding out the truth. We're just islanders and are expected to squabble among ourselves. I think we can get away with telling them that Gavin died of a self-inflicted wound. If that really will not wash with the fiscal's officers then we will tell them that I shot Gavin while defending you.'

'What a schemer you are, Quig,' Fay said. 'Tell me, though, how did Gavin lay hands on your wife's gun?'

'He stole it from me. Biddy will back our story. She hates scandal more than she hates you,' Quig said. 'Look, the fire is going down and I have no more fuel. We had better be making a move soon.'

'Can't we stay here? It's warm enough without a fire.'

'No,' Quig said. 'We cannot stay here.'

'Why not?'

'Because Innis must be told as soon as possible,' Quig said. 'And because I want to be back here on Pennypol before dawn breaks tomorrow.'

'Why?' Fay said. 'What for?'

'To find Gavin's body, if I can.'

'And if you do?' Fay said.

'I will make sure that he is never seen again.'

'God, Quig, but you are worse than I supposed you to be.'

'Worse,' Quig said, 'or better?'

'That remains to be seen,' said Fay.

Innis's relief at having the baby returned safe and sound outweighed her grief. She looked grey and haggard but had steeled herself for tragic news and accepted Quig and Fay's account of the events at Pennypol if not with equanimity at least with fortitude and a degree of understanding that surprised her daughter-in-law.

It was still only mid-evening when the couple trailed in to Pennymain. Quig carried the baby, tucked down under his oilskin. She was quiet now and seemed content, as if the smell of the man and his warmth were comfortingly secure. When Innis unwrapped her and put her down on a blanket near the fire she kicked and laughed and grabbed at the firelight as if all that had happened to her had been no more than one of life's adventures and no ordeal at all.

The kitchen had been cleaned, all trace of blood scrubbed from the floor. Poor little Kilty's body had been stitched into a bolster-case and laid out in the laundry by the tubs. On the table Innis had set out fresh dressings, a basin of clean water and a brown bottle of the herbal lotion that Vassie always used for the healing of wounds. The injury to Fay's arm was clean-lipped and not deep. No tendons or muscles appeared to have been severed.

Innis bathed it carefully, applied lotion and bound it with a strip of linen cloth while Quig, in dry trousers and shirt, held Vanessa on his knee and tried not to nod off.

'Tomorrow,' Innis said, 'we will send for Agnes MacNiven to take a look at Vanessa and made sure that she has not caught a chill or a fever. Agnes will know.'

'What will we tell her?' Fay asked.

'We will tell her that we got caught in the rain, that is all.'

'She won't believe you,' Fay said.

'She will have no reason to doubt us,' Innis said.

'Aren't you going to tell her the truth?' Fay said. 'Aren't you going to tell anyone the truth?'

'I do not know what the truth is,' Innis said.

'Mamma, you do know that Gavin's dead, don't you?'

'I have accepted that fact.'

'He was swept into the sea. He couldn't possibly have survived,' said Fay anxiously. She glanced over her mother-in-law's shoulder and Quig. 'Is that not so, Robert?'

'Aye, that is so,' Quig said.

'What was he doing on the jetty?' Innis said.

'Looking for me,' Quig said.

'Is that how it is to be?' Innis said. 'Is that how we will explain him away?'

'Mamma, Mam, we're not trying to explain Gavin away,' Fay said.

'Tomorrow morning, early,' Quig said, 'I will go down to the bay and look for him. I promise you, Innis, you will have him back if that is what you wish.'

'I do not think I want him back,' Innis said. 'He can do us more harm now that he is dead than he was ever able to do us when he was alive.'

'What do you—' Fay began to protest but Quig cut her short.

'You are right there, Innis,' he said.

She sat down on one of the kitchen chairs and folded her hands together as if she intended to pray for guidance. Her eyes were wide open, however, and she contemplated not heaven but her grandchild. 'An accident, it was,' she said. 'All just an accident.' She looked up at Fay. 'Whatever you tell me I will believe it. Whatever you decide to do I will accept.'

'It's the truth, Mamma, the whole truth.'

'No, nothing is ever the whole truth,' Innis said. 'I learned that long ago.'

'He – he didn't suffer,' Fay said.

'Oh, but he did,' said Innis and then, lifting herself from the chair, went into her bedroom and quietly closed the door.

It was still dark when she wakened him from a troubled sleep. He opened his eyes instantly and saw that she was already dressed in the coat that she wore only in the worst weather or for the dirtiest jobs. She had a shawl about her shoulders and a scarf tied over her head, shawl and scarf pinned down by a narrow leather belt cross-buckled across her chest. She looked, he thought, like a tinker or perhaps like one of the women Evander had scoured up from a horse fair or a cattle market. She had boiled water and made tea, not in a pot but in two canisters, and had buttered bread for him and laid out three or four slices of cold ham.

Quig eased himself forward in the chair. He was stiff, stiff in every limb and his ribs felt as if they had been cracked one by one. He groaned at first movement, groaned and eased himself upright. He tried to stretch but could not, not at first. He locked his fingers together and forced them over his head, easing the ache in his spine and shoulders.

'What time is it, Innis?'

'After four.'

'Has the wind dropped?'

'A little.'

'Is Fay asleep?'

'She is.'

'We will let her sleep, will we not?'

'We will,' Innis said.

He did not have to ask her why she was clad in oilcloth and shawl and great clumsy rubberised boots. He did not have the heart to deny her. He said nothing while he ate a bit of breakfast and drank the hot, sweet tea. He dressed quickly there in the kitchen while Innis moved about like a mole, her hands pale and small on the ends of her bulky arms. She washed the tea-canisters and plates, dried them and put them away in the cupboard under the dresser. She opened the door of the stove and shovelled in a few lumps of coal and one of the wedges of peat from the basket. Then she went out into the washing-room and came back with the bundle in her arms.

'We will bury him too, Quig,' she said. 'Kilty, I mean.'

Quig nodded. He could not find words to speak.

'Come then,' Innis said. 'If you are ready we will go and look for my son.'

He was not hard to find. He lay in the crook of the bay close to the jetty half buried in a dense tangle of kelp that had been thrown up by the storm. In the tangle too were other things that the sea had rejected: bottles and shattered boxes, rope-ends and spongy floats from the nets of the trawler-men, all heaped fresh on the mound of sand and shingle that had been left when the tide ebbed.

The sea was still strong and dark and unrepentant but it seemed distant now, withdrawn from the shore. Under the belly of the cloud light seeped on to the waters, Mull's headlands were becoming visible and the sullen little islands that layered the horizon to the west were rising up again.

There was no sun and no possibility of sun but the rain had stopped and wind had backed and there was a rhythm to the day again, a strange harsh rhythm that Innis and Quig both understood.

He glanced at her and she nodded.

He waded into the slippery weed and hunkered down.

Gavin lay face down, his arms tucked neatly under his head as if he were asleep. There was no sign of battery, of mauling. He was clean and neat and as polished as the kelp stalks around him. Quig turned him over. His eyes were wide open and his mouth too. In an hour or so the gulls would have found him and the crows and there would have been no eyes in the sockets and his tongue would have gone, the flesh picked away here and there from his cheeks and neck.

Quig put out both hands and cradled the head, lifted it cautiously, turned it one way and then the other. There was no wound, no bullet wound, no graze or groove or scar. Gavin's head was unblemished save for a frond of green weed that straggled down from his brow. Quig picked it off, smoothed the white flesh, touched his thumbs to the young man's eyes and closed his eyelids.

Within him he felt a great ache of relief. He would not have to lie now, would not have to lie to Innis or to Fay or even to himself. There *was* no wound, no scar, no blood: Gavin Tarrant, like his uncle before him, had drowned in a storm off Pennypol. He leaned over the body, the wet hair cupped in his hands, and shed tears, soft tears that were part selfish, part sorrow for the boy that Gavin had been.

He looked round at Innis and nodded.

She nodded in return.

He stooped and lifted Gavin from the tangle and carrying him in his arms like a child picked his way carefully back to the beach and, with Innis following, back up to the cottage at Pennypol.

There *was* no aftermath, no enquiry, no repercussions, and in the cold clear days of early November Quig and Fay Ludlow finally left Mull for Foss.

Quig, of course, had been back and forth in the closing weeks of October and had purchased the big boat from the salmon-fishers after all. The bulk of timber and stores had been ferried over to Foss by puffer along with a hefty load of fuel. The island's rat population had been diminished by Quig's unpleasant efforts and he thinned it still further with more baits and by digging a deep pit in front of the verandah. He made a corner of the bungalow habitable, manhandled the tarpaulin on to the roof and battened it down tightly as an extra precaution. He worked alone, three or four days at a stretch, and lost weight and felt better than he had done in years. He no longer doubted that he was doing the right thing and that Fay and little Vanessa would be safe with him on the offshore isle or that, come spring, the past would be put behind them.

There were no enquiries about Gavin. Nobody seemed to care that he had vanished into thin air and the few folk who had noticed him on his crossing from Oban on the *Grenadier* had apparently failed to identify the odd-looking man in the English smock with the Campbells of Pennypol.

Maggie knew the truth, of course, but Maggie had sense enough to keep her mouth shut about Gavin's reappearance, though discretion did not prevent her dispensing gossip about Robert Quigley, his lover and his abandoned wife. She continued to serve her mistress at the big house on the headland, however, to look after and put up with the sisters — one mad and the other melancholy — for Maggie had no interest in finding another husband yet, though Hermann, it seemed, had taken rather a fancy to her and was making the sort of advances that might eventually wind up at the altar, if she could put up with his dog.

Fay stayed out of sight on Pennymain and looked after her baby who, Agnes MacNiven pronounced, had not been harmed by her drenching.

The cottage was quiet with the spaniel dead and buried now and Quig away for much of the time. Innis and Fay had little to say to each other that did not concern the welfare of the baby. There was no hostility in Innis towards her daughter-in-law; she no longer pitied the English girl or felt responsible for her.

Something Quig had let slip in the course of that grey, wind-swept morning when they had hidden Gavin's body in Pennypol had alerted her to the fact that Fay was not helpless or weak or as blameless as she pretended to be. Perhaps that was just as well, Innis told herself, for over the years she had learned how subtle and cunning love can be in its beginnings and endings, and farming on Foss and living with Robert Quigley would be challenge enough for anyone.

She was thankful that she still had Gillies, an honest man, more devoted than she had any right to expect. When Janetta and Patrick Rattenbury married she would see even more of him at Pennymain and their chaste, unperpetuated relationship would surely strengthen and endure and last out the years.

Innis received several outraged letters from Becky and a pompous letter from Rachel in whose composition she suspected that her nephew Donnie had had a hand. There was even a rare letter from her brother Neil enquiring about the rental of the isle and how his quarterly payments would be met. There was something too uncompromising about her mainland family now, too urgent and striving for Innis's liking. She had lost that sense of striving long ago and the sacrifices she had been called upon to make to maintain her faith seemed small by comparison.

On the morning of Fay and Vanessa's departure Innis accompanied them to the jetty at Pennypol. She had not ventured over Olaf's Hill since the morning after the storm and found the place changed in odd, inexplicable ways. It was as if Quig had emptied not just the half-ruined cottage but all the land around it too. The plots, scoured of plants, had been dug over, trenched and dressed for the winter, and the moor, withered now and low, had no sheep upon it, for Barrett had driven the remaining ewes over to the home pasture. Even the headlands looked different, smoothed out and whittled down: clear weather did that, of course, the first cold shining days of another winter beyond which, not so far off, lay another spring.

Approaching fifty now she could count out the strawberry seasons that God had promised her, but twenty or thirty more summers seemed far too few. She wanted to go on for ever, changing yet unchanged, to endure as the land endured.

Her pleasure in those fine November days was therefore tinged with sadness at the realisation that it would end soon and that she could no more predict its ending than she had comprehended its beginning, that one was as unfathomable as the other when you came right down to it.

She held Vanessa in her arms until the last possible moment before she handed her down to Fay in the boat and watched the fair-haired girl settle her in the nest of blankets that Quig had thoughtfully laid out in the stern; cosseting and spoiling her already, Innis thought, as if she were a lady or a lame duck, which was perhaps the best you could expect from a man of character like Robert Quigley.

Barrett came lumbering down from the moor at the last moment. He was shy now, embarrassed at what Quig was doing, what the girl, the stranger, had made him do, but there was too much respect between Quig and him to let the leaving go unremarked. He had brought a sack with him, an entire boll of oatmeal drawn from his own small store. If he was uncertain of Quig's destiny – and of his own – he gave no sign of it but dumped the heavy sack down upon the jetty, wished everyone well and immediately departed, leaving nothing behind but the oatmeal and a pungent whiff of pipe tobacco.

From the jetty Innis watched the boat swing out into the tide.

She saw Quig move confidently to the sail. He was sure of himself again, certain of his skills, the old agile skills that had become so rusted during his years at Fetternish that he had thought them lost for ever. He looked lean and almost boyish, Innis thought, while he worked the boat out into the bay and as pleased with himself as if he had found the answer to a riddle that puzzled everyone else.

She was glad for Quig, glad for the girl too. She knew that she would always be welcome on the little isle with its unimpeded views of the horizon, and that when her time came Quig would make sure that she was buried by Gavin's side in one of the graves on the green sward on the very edge of the Atlantic.

Innis watched until the little boat passed out of sight around Mingary Ard and then, dry-eyed, she turned for home again.